Other books in the Rogue Warrior® series:

Also by Richard Marcinko:

ROGUE WARRIOR®
HOLY TERROR

Richard Marcinko
and Jim DeFelice

POCKET BOOKS
New York London Toronto Sydney

POCKET BOOKS, a division of Simon & Schuster, Inc.
1230 Avenue of the Americas, New York, NY 10020

This book is a work of fiction. Names, characters, places and incidents are products of the author's imagination or are used fictitiously. Any resemblance to actual events or locales or persons living or dead is entirely coincidental.

Originally published in hardcover in 2006 by Atria Books

ISBN-13: 978-0-7434-2278-9
ISBN-10:   0-7434-2278-3

This Pocket Books paperback edition May 2007

10 9 8 7 6 5 4 3 2 1

POCKET and colophon are registered trademarks of Simon & Schuster, Inc.

ROGUE WARRIOR is a registered trademark of Richard Marcinko.

Cover design by Carlos Beltran
Cover photograph of airplane © Indexstock / Peter Schulz

Manufactured in the United States of America

For information regarding special discounts for bulk purchases, please contact Simon & Schuster Special Sales at 1-800-456-6798 or business@simonandschuster.com.

*Dedicated to the many first responders who
left their families and loved ones to aggressively
attack the "War on Terror" in Iraq and Afghanistan
and then had to come home to attack the
demise left by Hurricane Katrina*

Part One

Italian Holiday

If we wish to be free—if we mean to preserve
inviolate those inestimable privileges for which
we have been so long contending—if we mean not
basely to abandon the noble struggle in which we
have been so long engaged, and which we have
pledged ourselves never to abandon until the
glorious object of our contest shall be obtained—we
must fight! I repeat it, sir, we must fight! An appeal
to arms and to the God of hosts is all that is left us!

—PATRICK HENRY

1

A piece of advice in case you ever find yourself on top of the dome of St. Peter's Basilica in Vatican City—watch out for the cross at the very top of the spire. It is a hell of a lot sharper than you'd think.

The roof tiles are pretty slippery, too, particularly the ones with the pigeon shit on them.

On the other hand, the view is to die for. Especially if you're up there with a maniac who's waving a Beretta Model 12S 9mm submachine gun in your face.

Yeah, I know what you're thinking: That Beretta's a great gun, but the frame tends to crack under the weight of too many hot rounds. The maniac would have been much better off with an H&K MP5; a lot less chance of a misfire.

I would have pointed this out myself, but he didn't seem in the mood for constructive criticism. He had a shitass grin on his face, the sort that says, "Eat lead and die, Marcinko."

The tips of my fingers started to sweat. They say the dome over St. Peter's is the biggest in the world, but at that moment it felt extremely small. When he swung the business end of the 12S toward me, it felt absolutely claustrophobic.

My own weapon lay on the roof below, out of ammo. It looked like I had two options—throw myself at him in the vain hope of somehow wrestling the gun from his paws before he managed to kill me, or . . .

I couldn't think of an *or,* actually.

But maybe I should explain how I came to be in such an exalted position in the first place. It's not every day that you get a private tour of the most famous rooftop in Christendom. And what got me out into the Roman sunshine wasn't your typical goatfuck . . . it was a truly *artistic* one, the sort of thing that would have made Michelangelo proud. So let's go back to the beginning. . . .

This particular adventure began with a fax that arrived at Rogue Manor on Christmas Eve a few months before. The sheet was blank except for a Web address in the middle of the page. It was a bit past 10 p.m., and Rogue Manor was empty except for yours truly. With nothing else to do but await the arrival of Ol' St. Nick, I turned on the computer and typed in the address, which mostly consisted of numbers and backslashes. I vaguely recall thinking I'd see a picture of Santa and one of his elves in a compromising position. Instead, I found myself looking at a page filled with type so small I had to hit the magnifier button three times. It turned out to be a turgid dissertation on the coming end of the "Crusader Epoch," the inevitable clash of "a great civilization with a decript [*sic*] one," and the unstoppable rise of the True People of the Book. Clement Moore, or whoever wrote "'Twas the Night Before Christmas," has nothing to worry about.

We get tons of emails, faxes, and letters from whacko crazies at Rogue Manor, and this one probably would have faded into the hazy recesses of my mental round file except for the signature at the bottom of the Web page. The "communiqué of fervor" had been signed with the name "Saladin."

In case obscure, failed world leaders doesn't happen to be your favorite *Jeopardy!* category, here's a quick info dump on Saladin: Also known as Salah al-Din and a half-dozen similar variations, Saladin was a twelfth-century Egyptian warrior who took Jerusalem from the crusaders. He built the wall that surrounds the old city and was the first pan-Arab to try to consolidate all Arab people under the green banner of Muhammad. He failed—not for want of trying or low body count—but has remained a source of inspiration ever since. Many an Arab leader has used him as a role model, reinterpreting history and the legend through his own distorted glasses. Nasser, Saddam Hussein, even the Shah of Iran viewed him as an inspiration. Osama bite-my-butt Laden didn't use the name, but it isn't hard to see parallels between his aims and Saladin's goal of a pan-Arab empire.

Over the years I've had various encounters with would-be Saladins, some of whom were actually credible opponents. Probably the most notable was in Cairo during the 1990s. I won't bore you with more backstory* than necessary here; suffice to say that the name piqued my interest. The Web page was on a site that belonged to an international drug company. Clearly, it had been hacked into. When my computer guy checked with the firm the day after Christmas, they expressed complete surprise.

At least that's how he interpreted the words, "Holy shitfuck—what the hell is this?"

(My self-anointed "computer dude" and all-around tech expert is a tech-head wop dweeb named Paul Guido Falcone, a wiseass known to us as "Shunt." Shunt has shunts in his head. They're some sort of metal inserts placed into his skull because he was born with water in his skull; I think of them as brain gutters. He's loads of fun with metal detectors.)

A few days later, another fax arrived with a new Web address. Here was posted a new dissertation repeating the main points of the first—history was on the side of the schizophrenics, etc. It concluded by making some predictions: A new leader would arise to knit together the worldwide network of murdering assholes, and his name was—guess now—Saladin.

And by the way, as a display of the new leader's power, a small incident would occur the next day as a signal to the brothers of faith and insanity that the time for war would begin.

The time was given as 00:00:01, but no place was specified. Even though it was an open-ended and

---

*The marketing department suggests a plug here for *Rogue Warrior: Green Team*, where some of these adventures unfolded.

nonspecific threat, I reported it anyway, filing the information with both Homeland Security and the CIA (also known as the Christians In Action). I also forwarded a bunch of heads-ups to a number of friends and acquaintances in the terrorist threat business, figuring one more wild-goose chase would just make the holiday season that much more enjoyable.

At roughly the same time I was burning up the phone lines, a fax similar to mine arrived at al-Jazeera, the mouthpiece long favored by crazies and psychos wrapping themselves in the word of Muhammad, blessed be his name. The fax was turned over to the reporter in charge of whacko ramblings, who dutifully plugged the address into his browser and began reading Saladin's communiqué, which in this case was written in Arabic. While most of the rant was familiar—war of civilizations, death to the crusaders, etc.—this one contained more specific predictions relating to mayhem, promising uprisings across the globe, especially in that holy wasteland known as Afghanistan. It also mentioned that a certain liquefied gas ship on its way from Malaysia to a new port in China would be blown up to start the new millennium of Allah's Paradise. Once more the time was given as 00:00:01.

The reporter considered the matter, then decided to report it, only to find that the ship had been blown up. He subsequently determined that the time of the explosion was correct or at least close enough to count—assuming your watch was set to the time in Mecca, Saudi Arabia, arguably the center of the worldly universe if you're Muslim. The reporter wrote a story, and for maybe twenty-four hours the world's intelligence agencies spent considerable resources trying to profile Saladin. I received not one, not two, but three separate calls from analysts at the Christians In Action about Saladin, the Web pages, and the faxes. I told them everything I knew, which wasn't much. The NSA—"No Such Agency," the ultrasecret eavesdropping and electronic snoops over at Fort Meade—did a frantic search through its archives to see what it had snooped out on Saladin without knowing who he was. The Chinese loaded a group of special agents aboard a destroyer and shipped them over to interview the survivors. Forensics specialists from six or seven countries flew out to the wreckage, most of which was at the bottom of the Pacific and out of reach.

The sum total of all this work was a big fat zero. Nothing that the crew members said proved conclusively that a bomb had caused the explosion. The safety record of the company involved was rather lackluster, and while it would have taken extraordinary incompetence to cause an accidental explosion— well, let's just say that extraordinary incompetence was not in short supply.

The experts concluded that the explosion had occurred *before* the faxes were sent. Because of this, they decided, it was possible that Saladin had heard of the disaster and was trying to take credit for it to boost his own standing in the community of crazies. This especially made sense given that they could find no other evidence of his existence before the fax I received. And in fact there was almost no evidence that he did exist, except for the faxes and Web site.

I agreed to let the NSA babysit my fax line for a

few days; nothing came in other than some long-shot predictions on the Super Bowl. Saladin quickly slipped off their radarscope.

And mine. The lack of follow-up over the next few days convinced me that this was just one more Osama wannabe looking to become caliph on the cheap. Any asshole with a computer and some rudimentary knowledge can hack his way into most corporate systems, and visions of grandeur are as common among Muslims as they are in the rest of the world's population.

It wasn't as if I didn't have other things to do. Red Cell International—my security consulting firm, a successor of sorts to SOS Temps—had been awarded several contracts the previous summer and fall. While we continued to do some training for Homeland Insecurity and the Defense Department, more and more of our business was with private industry. Most of these were very straightforward assessment gigs, where yours truly and his various minions earned big bucks telling corporate security types why their procedures weren't worth the paper they weren't written on. The *best* jobs involved simulating terrorist and corporate espionage attacks against the conglomerates. Not only did these pay absurdly well, but they were a *hell* of a lot of fun. One of our favorite ploys involved kidnapping the company CEO the day before our assignment was supposed to officially begin. We'd take him to the fanciest restaurant in town while his head of security frantically searched for him, enjoying a ten-course dinner while keeping tabs on the Keystone Kop response via video and audio bugs we'd planted at corporate HQ. The only downside was that most of these corporate fat cats were embarrassingly small tippers; it got so I had to intercept the bill and add the amount myself before having them sign. Otherwise the waitstaff never would have served my team if we returned.

These domestic assignments led to additional work overseas, training and in a few cases providing choirboy services in foreign pleasure resorts, like beautiful Kandahar and lovely Baghdad. We sang, we hummed, we disposed of the garbage when necessary. Our standard contracts include nondisclosure clauses about as long as this book; the lawyers say they mean I can neither name the companies we work for nor say what we did. The lawyers can suck turds as far as I'm concerned, but since a lot of these assignments are ongoing, in the interests of protecting my people I'd prefer to keep discussion of methods and means to a minimum. Suffice it to say that we did what had to be done, reaping the appropriate rewards but also occasionally suffering the sort of hits that made such rewards a necessary incentive.

As far as this particular yarn is concerned, the most important contracts were in Afghanistan, where three different Western companies required our assistance to varying degrees. Sometime that February—weeks after Saladin's faxes had begun to fade and curl at the edges—we noticed an uptick in operations directed at the companies we were working with. And, eventually, at Red Cell International itself. There wasn't a pattern that we could put our fingers on, but we were interested enough to call a company-wide conference to discuss it. For various reasons, including the quality of the beer, we picked a date in March in Germany.

Which fit in nicely with my own schedule, as I was supposed to be in Italy right around the same time to address an annual NATO meeting on the new realities of terrorism.

For me, Italy will always be a land of romance, tomato sauce, and women with very short tempers. I was stationed in Naples in southern Italy in the late 1950s and early '60s. I blame a lot of my subsequent development on the horrors of working for the fattest, laziest UFO (Ugly Female Officer) in the Navy; the horror of that early assignment propelled me to frogman training, and far exceeded any combat situation I faced in later years. If ever I lack motivation for a PT session, the mental image of her butt cheeks flapping in the breeze never fails to get me in gear.

I returned to the Land of Garlic and Oregano several times in my Navy career, with both the SEALs and Red Cell, running training operations, security drills, and a few things I can't tell you about unless I shoot you first. All in all, I love Italy, especially when someone else is paying for me to be there.

My decision to attend the NATO conference was influenced by the fact that Karen Fairfield had already signed up for the four-day session set for mid-March. Besides being my main squeeze, light of my life, and far-better half, Karen heads Homeland Insecurity's Office of Internal Security Affairs (OISA). Her boss assigned her to go to the conference because he had to be out of town attending his son's wedding; her only role there would be to smile at the receptions and try not get lost while touring the Roman ruins. I'd already toyed with the idea of joining her when the invitation arrived. Making suitable arrangements with the NATO pooh-bahs took all of five minutes; they agreed not only to find a nice hotel outside of Rome but to stock the minibar with Bombay Sapphire. I took care of reserving the Ferrari myself.

A midlevel NATO functionary named Colonel Boffo Buffano met us when we arrived after an overnight flight at Fuminico airport. Flanked by a pair of Italian soldiers, we were whisked through customs, and after battling the morning rush-hour traffic found ourselves relaxing in a Renaissance-era castle cum ultramodern hotel. Karen has an especially good cure for jet lag; after we indulged in it, we headed out for a late lunch with an old friend, Dr. Paolo A. Bolognese. I met him in Rome back when I had SEAL Six and he was surgeon for the Italian army *carabinieri* battalion; we were there to do a takedown on an aircraft and he was standing by to fix any boo-boos. The doc now heads the Department of Neurosurgery at North Shore University Hospital back in *Lung* Island, *Noo Yawk*, and is associate director of the Chiari Institute, *the* place to go if your brain or spinal cord ever gets kinked. He happened to be over in his native land to chat about something called "laser doppler flowmetry applied neurological interoperative ultrasound." In plain English, he can peel a brain like an onion, one layer at a time.

The doc started talking about new techniques over lunch. He had me lost until he compared what he did to taking apart IEDs and booby traps. He may do heads, but I still do kneecaps, and we had a great time talking about our respective specialties.

After lunch, Karen and I headed over to the opening reception at Villa d'Este in Tivoli, a typically over-the-top Italian garden that has impressed visitors with a mortar-range view of Rome since 1572. Festivities began the way every NATO military operation ought to—hors d'oeuvres and cocktails. My idea of an appetizer is Bombay Sapphire straight; our Italian hosts were happy to oblige.

Counterterrorism has become a bit of a growth industry of late, and cocktail hour allowed me to meet some of the new blood in the field. The Poles and Germans are always good for a few laughs, and I was impressed with a few young turks from Romania, of all places. And then there was Baucus Dosdière, a runty dark-skinned Belgian by way of Morocco and France, who had recently been hired by the Vatican to oversee a counterterror squad for the Holy See. You may laugh—I know I did—but if there's an organization that knows a thing or two about terror, it's the Catholic Church; these are the folks who brought the world the Spanish Inquisition, after all.

If you muck with the spelling a bit, Dosdière translates pretty literally as "Backass" in French, and the name fit him. Though he had white European ancestors—it's amazing the things people tell you during cocktail hour—Backass's native African blood predominated. In his estimation, this had helped him win his job from the cardinal overseeing his office, either because Africa was underrepresented in the Church hierarchy or the cardinal misapplied the theory "it takes one to know one." Backass hinted heavily that it was the latter, and he had enough of a sense of humor to enjoy the joke. He had spent his childhood in northern Africa and the Middle East, where one of his grandfathers had been a high-ranking French foreign legion officer and his uncle had worked as a diplomat. He apparently had family connections with old money in the Middle East and Belgium; I guess he was literally the dark sheep of the family. He'd worked for the Moroccan Security Force as a very young man, then gone to work for two different private security firms, including one that had helped reorganize the Gendarmerie of the State of Vatican City, which brought him to his present job.

Tourists are familiar with the Pontifical Swiss Guard, the guys who hold long curtain rods and dress like they stepped out of an opera. Most of their job is to look good, and while they do protect the pope, the heavy-duty police requirements are generally handed over to the Gendarmerie of the State of Vatican City. External security is handled primarily by Italy's Inspectorate of Public Security to the Vatican State. A new organization had been formed to handle terrorist threats both in and outside of Vatican City. Supposedly, the pope had decided to clean house after rumors surfaced of connections between the old security chiefs and a shadowy neofascist group known as Parco dei Principi, or more colloquially as P2, or, in English, "Power Brokers."

(Don't bother going to your Italian-English dictionaries, it doesn't translate exactly. But that's not the only thing that's twisted about P2. Supposedly, the group was formed after World War II and adopted a strategy of continual warfare in hopes that eventually the people would clamor for the return of a Mussolini type. There were connections literally all over the place, even to the U.S. and the beloved Christians In Action, also known as the CIA. The conspiracy is too wild and woolly to lay out here; the important thing is that the pope and some of the clerics around him wanted a fresh face from outside Italy, and that helped Backass get the job.)

Backass answered to a cardinal and a committee of clerics, none of whom knew much about security except that they didn't want to spend any money on it. He had been tasked with improving security at St. Peter's Basilica, but couldn't directly control the security force there or even appoint his own deputies. Not that things in Vatican City should be any different than anywhere else in the world.

Backass took a shine to Karen—can't blame him there—and started talking to her about Rome, asking what she'd seen and was interested in. Somehow the conversation veered toward places to eat. Backass unleashed a string of rapid-fire opinions, offering advice on what dish to order where and how to deal with the notoriously finicky waiters. Finally, he mentioned Gabi di Gabi, a froufrou place Karen had read about in a magazine on the flight over.

Karen winked at me and said she'd just *love* to eat there, figuring that would get him to shut up. Instead he pulled out his cell phone, called the restaurant, and made a reservation; we even ended up eating on the Catholic Church's dime, which is either a joke or a reason to go to confession, I'm not sure which. Afterward, we took a ride through the hills above the capital, putting the vintage Ferrari through its paces as we wended our way back to the hotel. Rome isn't the tropics, but March can be quite nice, and the starlit evening was everything we had imagined. With the top down, there was just enough of a chill to encourage Karen to lean closer for warmth. We arrived back at the hotel in time for a nightcap, then repaired to the battlements for a night of *la dolce vita*.

My speech wasn't scheduled until the next evening. After working up a bit of a sweat in the castle's dungeon the next morning, Karen and I did the tourist thing, heading to the Coliseum to gawk at the place where lions and Christians once held family picnics. We strolled through the ruins of the Forum, the original center of Roman bureaucracy and the judicial system. The paper pushers and stone chiselers may be long gone, but I wouldn't be surprised if some of the cases filed during Caesar's time are still waiting their turn on the docket. I'm not much of a tourist—I like to pillage if not rape when I'm visiting a country, and anything less seems like a waste. But Karen reveled in it, imagining she heard the roar of the Goths approaching as she walked amid the ruins.

That may just have been the lousy Italian drivers, who race through the city faster than half the cars on the NASCAR circuit. We escaped with our lives as we walked to the conference, which was being held in Mussolini's old haunts at the Palazzo Venezia. *Il Duce* is said to haunt the hallways, probably looking for a lost train schedule. We didn't run into the ghost, but we did happen upon the same American Delta Force troopers who had freed Italian hostages from Iraqi captors a few months before. They were here to get a well-deserved pat on the rump from the political types. Meeting the Delta boys was an honor and a privilege. I was lucky enough to call the man who established Delta Force, Colonel Charlie A. Beckwith, a friend, and I'm sure he would have been pleased with these young heroes, who even at the ceremony were insisting they'd done "nothing special, but our jobs."

I also met the ambassador to Italy, Gordon G. White, and his charming wife, Petra. White had been a political appointee—read, big fund-raiser—but I didn't hold that against him, especially after he announced that he was a big fan of my books, beginning with "the first and best, *Rogue Warrior*." You know how modest I am, so of course I immediately began to blush and ask for another drink. I also checked my wallet, because usually when a political type compliments you, it's going to end up costing you big bucks down the line. But White wasn't like that, or at least was damn subtle about it. He introduced me to the resident head spook (a waste case; I won't even go into it) and a Brit MI6 man whom I actually already knew, though we both acted as if it were the first time we'd met. The MI6 agent—I'll call him Shakespeare—nudged me aside a minute or two later and showed me a printout. I glanced at it long enough to realize it was a diatribe about the need for "war with the crusaders." There was no signature, and I didn't make the connection to Saladin until he refreshed my memory about the tanker strike back in December.

Shakespeare had been among the people I'd told about the faxes, and we exchanged info dumps on Saladin. He knew a lot more than I did, connecting him to a loose network of Islamic terror groups. Besides the Malaysian gas tanker explosion, he was supposed to have supplied money to groups involved in an attack in South Africa and the American embassy in Spain. An Egyptian group opposed to the government had posted communiqués similar to his (and exploiting the same security holes in the host computer systems) on Egyptian government computers. Shakespeare believed Saladin was spreading money around in various ways, supplying funds to operations in Europe and Asia. Especially ominous, in Shakespeare's opinion, was his funding of religious schools in Pakistan and Muslim charities in India—activities that had once helped bin Laden climb to the pinnacle of the movement. Saladin was bidding to make himself the indispensable caliph in the coming millennium. And we didn't even know his real name.

Time out for half a second while I address a common misconception regarding money. Most of us tend to think of six- and seven-digit sums when we hear talk about terrorists and their funding networks. We know (or think we know) how much it costs to equip antiterrorist units and naturally assume it costs the same or more for the bad guys. The truth is, terrorism in most cases is a low-budget operation. The help comes cheap and most of the necessary tools of the trade are in good supply, whether you're talking about AK-47s or the chemicals necessary to blow things up. A few thousand dollars represents a good hunk of change for your typical tango. Even the high-profile "actions"—such as the obscene attack on New York and Washington, D.C., on 9/11—cost no more than fifty thousand dollars, all told. (It cost the United States approximately $80 billion and still counting—pretty good return if you're into economics.) That's not chicken scratch to me, and I doubt it is to you, but the point is that a few dollars here and a few thousand there skimmed from a seemingly legitimate charity group—which these bastards have done for years—makes a significant contribution to the cause. And that's not even to mention the "coincidence" of such groups employing people sympathetic to terror networks. One of the ways we *ought* to be fighting terrorism is by clamping down on the supposed charities using American money to bite us in the ass, and worse. We've taken a fitful start over the course of the past year, but we're still *way* too worried about public opinion outside the U.S. to make the dent in the revenue stream that we need to.

Lecture over. I'll put the soapbox away.

Shakespeare produced another Web page. The address had been faxed to al-Jazeera a few hours earlier. (It would turn out that I got one, too, though I didn't know it at the time.) The page was in English. Saladin predicted a "major blow to the heart of the crusader empire" at "a time of their choosing."

"They pick the place and we pick the place?" I asked Shakespeare.

He didn't understand what I meant at first, and I had to show him the words, "a time of *their* choosing."

"Should be 'our' choosing. Obviously, he should spend a little more money on translators," Shakespeare said.

"What do you think the target will be?"

The MI6 operative shrugged. There were too many possibilities.

"Very few people are taking Saladin very seriously," added Shakespeare, walking to the bar for a refill. "Your own CIA thinks he's an egotistical windbag taking credit for others' achievements. Such as they are."

"Sure. Who wouldn't want to take credit for mayhem and murder?"

"I think he's real," said Shakespeare. "And he's somewhere in Europe. I think he's doing more than supplying people with money. I think he'll launch a big attack—a very big attack—very soon."

"Are you saying that on general principles, or because you have hard information?"

Our quiet corner had become considerably less so, and Shakespeare frowned as he looked at some of the people nearby.

"Tomorrow," he suggested. "At a more private location."

We agreed to meet in the afternoon, then went back to mixing with the hoi polloi. A half hour later we were ushered into the ballroom next door, where we were served a seven-course dinner. It wasn't until the waiters were hustling around with espresso that the "business" portion of the evening began with the ceremony honoring the Delta people. Then came what for most was the purpose of the evening: A succession of speeches from various state security chiefs proclaimed what a great job they had done over the past six months following the capture and immediate suicide of Sheikh Abu Abdullah, known to the West as Osama bin Laden. There was so much backslapping going on that I was surprised they didn't have a chiropractor on call.

When my turn came to speak I walked to the front of the room, took my speech out of my pocket, looked at it, then ripped it in half. Somebody had to be the skunk at the party, and it looked like it was me.

"I think I ought to start by saying that the work

capturing Osa-my-butt's Been Eaten was the best SpecWar activity I've seen, bar none," I told the audience. "The American, Italian, and Pakistani units that worked together to pull it off deserve all the recognition they've received. We've seen great work over the last year and a half by countless SpecWar outfits across the world, most of whom can't be mentioned because their operations remain highly classified."

Everyone figured that I was going to extend the orgy of self-congratulation and applauded loudly. I let them enjoy themselves for a bit before continuing.

"But our struggle is far from over. On the contrary, it's more dangerous now. Every whack job in Islam is vying to become raghead in chief."

Some of the people in the room smiled. A lot more grimaced, whether because they couldn't follow my vernacular or they sensed where I was going, I couldn't say.

"We're only in the first stages of battle, the very early beginning. We haven't gotten serious. And we need to. We have a very limited opportunity, while the opposition is still relatively disorganized, to stop the war from getting to the point where the non-Muslim countries of the world—NATO, the U.S., Russia— reach the point that the only way to deal with the opposition effectively is to retaliate in a massive way. I'm not talking about what happened in Afghanistan or Iraq. I'm not talking about taking over Chechnya. I'm thinking about what right now is unthinkable, what's off-limits because we don't want to work out the logic of the situation. I'm talking about the sort of retribution that would take place—that would have to take place—if the people who are employing terrorism for their purposes actually began to threaten Western civilization and large parts of the population in a serious way.

"Let's state the problem directly. If the successor to bin Laden exploded a nuclear weapon here in Rome, how would NATO respond? Would nuking Mecca be out of the question? If Moscow were covered by a nuclear cloud, and the guts of the weapon were shown to have come from Iran, would the retaliation end when Chechnya was turned into dust?"

More than a few people gasped. Even though these were professional soldiers and military leaders, most didn't want to face the implications of the threats the Islamic extremists had made. They didn't think what I was talking about was possible. They saw, or wanted to see, the struggle they were involved in as a series of small, isolated fights that could be dealt with incrementally—a firefight here, a raid there. Even after 9/11 and the Madrid train bombings, they didn't take the extremists' capabilities or their rantings seriously. Of course, Europeans had made that mistake with extremists before, in this very hall.

Not that Americans should pat themselves on the back. We gave half of the bastards who flew the planes into the Pentagon and World Trade Center the right to vote.

I mentioned that, and I admitted that the problem was as serious for the nonextremist majority of the Muslim world as it was for the rest of us. But I wasn't talking to imams, and so I continued with the unpleasantly obvious, telling the Europeans in the hall that it was time to face up to the fact that they had built their economy over the past two decades on cheap labor from northern Africa and the Muslim world. Now the bill was coming due in unexpected ways. There were no easy ways to pay it. Ratcheting up security precautions and striking terrorists where they live—the things I'm an expert in—were the easy part of the problem—and we hadn't even done them very well.

"How hard do you think it would be to slip a weapon in here?" I asked. "There were metal detectors at the door and an X-ray machine—what percentage of weapons did they catch? Fifty? Ten? I'd say, the only things they caught were the weapons that wanted to be caught."

At that I reached into my waistband to pull out the Glock 26 that I had smuggled past the front-door check. That got a gasp—but not nearly the reaction that followed a moment later, when I shot the SOB with the grenade at the back of the hall.

I hadn't planned on the show-and-tell. As much as I like ad-libbing, working without a script can be a bit like batting a live hand grenade around in a crowded ballroom.

Which is exactly what happened as my bullet struck the ersatz waiter dead-on in the forehead. He'd been pulling the pin from the grenade when I shot him, and the now-live weapon flew upward. The man next to him tried grabbing it in midair, a very foolish if natural impulse. He missed, and the grenade bounded upward like a volleyball.

Have I ever mentioned that Karen was a championship volleyball player in high school?

Karen took the tap and smashed it toward the

window twenty feet away. It broke through the glass and exploded a second later, fortunately over an area that had been cordoned off as part of the security against car bombers. Mussolini's ghost on the window balcony nearby may have taken it on the chin, but no living creature was harmed, not even one of the pigeons flocking on the roofline.

The thick walls of the building muffled the explosion. A millisecond of silence followed as disbelief reigned. Then the security people sprang into action and all hell broke loose. The waiter turned out to be the only tango crazie in the place, but it took a good hour and a half to figure that out.

Or three Bombays from the portable bar next door, if you want a more precise measure of the time.

How did the waiter slip the grenade through the security cordon, which included a metal detector and an X-ray machine? Unfortunately, he wasn't around to tell us. My suspicion is that it had been brought inside and hidden a few days before, and that he picked it up with the tiramisu. I'd spotted him out of the corner of my eye as I was winding up my speech. He roused my suspicion by moving two or three times faster than any Italian waiter ever moves unless the kitchen is on fire.

Karen was the hero of the hour. Diplomats and hobnobbers swarmed to her. She handled it with her usual smooth poise, charming all these European men like a movie star. Ever the sensitive supportive male, I threw a few appreciative beams in her general direction while I sipped my gin. Somewhere between the first and second glass, the acting head of NATO, the French general of generals, *Generale* Mustard, waltzed over with his staff of sycophants and gave me the evil eye. Mustard didn't have a mustache, but the ends of it would have been twirling if he did. He just about snarled as he called me "Monsieur Dick" and said that my speech lacked balance.

"That's a relief," I told him.

One of Mustard's lackeys swallowed his tongue— probably fatal, considering where it had been. The *generale* made like all Frenchmen and beat a retreat. I heard a snicker behind me and turned to find Backass, the Papal security legate.

"A grave security blunder," he intoned. "Heads should roll."

"I was thinking of a much lower part of the anatomy," I told him. I was feeling polite, so I didn't mention that I'd seen him cowering under a table on the opposite side of the room.

The Italian detectives charged with investigating the incident eventually required my presence in a room down the hall that had been allocated for debriefing. I knew from my Navy career that the typical Italian police interview is long on circuitous questions and cannolis, short on sweat, but I could tell this one was going to be different as soon as I was led into the room. The detective in charge skittered around, practically bouncing off the walls with uncontrolled adrenaline. He stood all of five-two and had shaved his head; the blood vessels at the top pulsed bright blue and he looked a little like a bocce ball with legs. The detective sputtered in Italian that the country's honor had been spit on by the incident. I didn't disagree; the problem was that he seemed to blame this on me, hectoring me about my uninvited Glock so much I finally asked whether it would have been better to have left it at home. His head pulsed a few seconds, then he snapped his fingers and I was led away, interview over.

Foreigners are not allowed to carry weapons into the country without express permission. I'd skipped the paperwork, not only for the Glock, which as you probably know is a small hideaway-type personal weapon, but for my PK as well. I had to surrender the Glock to the forensics team conducting the investigation, who for some reason wouldn't take my word or that of two hundred eyewitnesses that my bullet had nailed the tango. They'll undoubtedly send it back when they finish their work, which with typical Italian efficiency will be about thirty years from now.

The truth is, I doubt anyone smuggling a gun into the country would be in serious legal danger, at least not if they got a jury trial. Italy is enlightened enough to have passed a law allowing homeowners to shoot any and all intruders, simply on the grounds of being in a bad mood. You have to love a land that puts pain-in-the-ass in-laws on par with robbers.

Karen was still enjoying the fawning attentions of assorted NATO pooh-bahs when I found her. We retreated and once more took the winding road north to our hotel castle, where a complimentary bottle of champagne had been delivered to our suite, courtesy of the American ambassador who'd been in the ballroom. We spent a few hours unwinding, then slept in the next morning, getting up around *mezzogiorno* for Chianti and lunch. Karen wanted to get in more sightseeing before another round of the gratuitous violence that passed for receptions and cocktail parties at the

NATO wingding. I told her I was in the mood for a little sightseeing myself.

"I'd like to see St. Peter's and the Vatican," she
said. "What do you want to see?"

Some questions can only be answered with a
smile.

We compromised: After a half hour upstairs, we
boarded the Ferrari and sped down to Vatican City,
the gallbladder-size Catholic state wedged into the
pancreas of Rome. At one time, the Catholic Church
owned or dominated a good hunk of the Italian
peninsula, including Rome, but during the nineteenth
and early twentieth centuries it lost most of its terri-
tory to Italian nationalists under Garibaldi. People
don't remember him for this, but Mussolini actually
won a great deal of admiration for working out a set-
tlement with the church during the early days of his
regime that created Vatican City and ended decades
of angst and turmoil. If he'd done the honorable thing
and retired after that, his fat ass would never have
ended on a butcher's meat hook a decade later. Then
again if he'd done the honorable thing, he wouldn't
have been Mussolini.

Basilica is Italian for "big fucking church." And St.
Peter's is a *big* big fucking church. The outside looks
more like a monster bank than your typical house of
worship. Two huge semicircles of columns hold the
square before it in place, and the doorways look as if
they were designed for people the size of the Jolly
Green Giant. You will not doubt your position in the
universe when you stand in front of it—you are a
puny little ant.

No, it was *not* the first time Demo Dick had ever

set foot in a church. Yours truly attended St. Ladislaus Hungarian Catholic School, where the nuns taught readin' and writin' the old-fashioned way—they pounded it into us with the help of razor-edged rulers and lead-weighted rosary beads. I still carry some of the scars, but at least when I go into a church I can genuflect in the right places. And my ecclesiastical background makes me understand that Jesus died on the cross for our sins; if I do not sin, he may have died in vain. Hard on my body, but somebody has got to do it.

St. Peter's is bigger than a football stadium, if you can imagine a football stadium with walls made out of marble and enough candles to heat a small town. Every saint worthy of the name and a few who aren't have a relic or a statue inside. Michelangelo designed the dome and contributed the *Pietà*, and just for good measure painted the ceiling next door in his spare time. The side aisles are lined with chapels and altar areas, each of which could be the centerpiece of a church anywhere else in the world.

Karen and I threaded our way through a patchwork of tour groups as we made our way down the center aisle toward the Papal Altar and the Baldacchino, a massive, four-pillared monument beneath the dome. It looks like a holy canopy bed and sits in front of the entrance to St. Peter's tomb. The Baldacchino is the focal point of the basilica, the center of Catholicism's spiritual traffic circle. Behind it sits St. Peter's Chair, another huge altar at the back of the church. Made out of gold and bronze, it looks like the exhaust of a Scud missile taking off in the sun, which I pointed out to Karen.

She rolled her eyes. Some people just don't understand art.

"Do you want to see the grottoes?" she asked, changing the subject. The grottoes are a collection of papal burial crypts and chapels below the main floor of the church. I see enough dead people in my line of work, and had no desire to go underground to see any more. We agreed to meet upstairs on the roof in an hour and a half. (Besides a great view, the roof has a number of religious shops. At one time you could just about buy your way to heaven there, but now the best you can do is a St. Christopher's medal blessed by the pope.) I wandered away, continuing to survey the basilica's art with my keenly developed connoisseur's eye. Some of the most beautiful women in the world graced the church, and gazing at them was nothing less than a religious experience.

You pray your way and I'll pray mine.

Easter was several weeks off, but the church was already being prepared for what amounts to Christendom's Super Bowl extravaganza. Wires, lights, and speakers were scattered around the nave; here and there the skeletons of pew boxes were piled high. They look pretty sturdy once they're put together, but unassembled they're more like the stands you see on the side of the typical jayvee football field, dented and forlorn. Workers armed with architectural drawings and large thermoses of cappuccino gathered at several strategic locations, alternately furling and unfurling their plans. Every so often one of the men would do something constructive, like pick his nose, but for the most part they spent their time shaking their heads and staring at their papers.

A choral group had assembled in the Chapel of St. Sebastian. They began warming up with a few slightly off-key choruses of "Gloria with an Excedrin Headache." The singing brought tears to my eyes—it was that bad—so I turned to head in the opposite direction. As I did I nearly got run over by two workmen rushing across the front of the nearby altar, huffing and puffing as they pushed a large speaker across the floor. Something about the workers struck me as odd, but I had to stare for a few seconds before I realized what it was: They were actually working hard enough to break into a sweat.

That's not only unusual in Italy, there are several laws against it.

Curiosity piqued, I followed. A group of Philippine tourists cut in front of me, and by the time I sorted through them the workers had vanished. They had left their speaker box next to the Altar of St. Thomas—he was the only apostle with the balls enough to say seeing is believing.

I put my hand up against the speaker box and it rolled freely across the floor. Not only that, but the grill was hinged at the side and secured by a magnetic latch similar to what you might use on a kitchen cabinet or closet. The interior was empty; the front speaker was just a cardboard disk.

I was puzzling over that when four nuns in heavy wool habits and thick five-o'clock shadows beelined out of the passage behind the nearby altar, heads bowed beneath their headpieces as they whisked forward like running backs in a wedge formation. My first thought was that they had just come from one of the Vatican's exorcism classes, where they'd gotten some of their prayers mixed up. Then I had a flash of ancient déjà vu, as if I were back in grammar school and needed to find a plausible substitute for the "dog ate my homework" line. I wouldn't have been surprised if one of them had pulled out a yardstick and whacked me across the face with it.

A Beretta submachine gun—now *that* surprised me.

I threw myself over the nearby altar rail and rolled to the ground as one of the nuns teased the trigger on the submachine gun. Someone shouted and the chorus's "hallelujah's" one chapel over turned into a cascade of "holy shit's." Instinctually, I reached for my gun—forgetting that I had surrendered it the night before.

Goatfucked. On vacation no less. See what happens when I go to church?

2

I hope Sister Mary Jo Elephant is reading this, because I owe her a small tip of the nun's habit for the inspiration that hit me next. Mary Jo was one of the nuns in sixth grade who supervised Confirmation class. Her forearms were thicker than my thighs, and if the sixth-grade class had fit on an altar, she could have bench-pressed it, kids and all. But Sister Mary Jo's physical prowess wasn't what inspired me while I was belly and cheek to the cold marble floor. I flashed on the last time I had kissed dust in a church, felled by a hymnal tossed at a hundred paces during one Confirmation practice when I broke operational silence to comment to a friend on the bodacious size of Billie Jean Tarlet's nascent ta-tas. The lesson I had learned then wasn't to keep my appreciation of the female anatomy to myself, but that your typical Catholic Church is stockpiled with weapons.

St. Peter's, being the largest church in captivity, was a veritable armory. The first thing I noticed was a large incense urn dangling above my head, suspended from the ceiling by metal rods linked together. I climbed up on the altar and leapt out, aiming to grab the urn and swing across the chapel, where I planned to sprawl across the back of the nearest nun. The theory was good, but as my fingers grabbed the hanging urn I realized I had neglected to factor in the machinations of my old friend Mr. Murphy, whose rules dictate that anything that can go wrong will go wrong at the worst possible moment.

Despite having an Irish last name, Murph was very comfortable being in Italy. He saw to it that the chain broke before I could get enough of my momentum on it to swing across the chapel. I landed ass-flat on the floor and slid forward on the well-polished marble. I hit the nun like a bowling ball taking out the top pin, sending her tumbling into a nearby reliquary. The glass case containing the mummified remains of a pope knocked the bastard cold.

The phony nun's gun slid in the opposite direction. I dove after it.

By now it should be obvious to all that these weren't Sisters of Charity looking for penance. (I would know since that was the order that nurtured my Slovak pretzel while attending St. Ladislaus in New Brunswick, NJ.) They were terrorists who'd come in hidden inside the fake speakers, helped by comrades disguised as workmen. So I'll stop calling them nuns and damning the good sisters' names.

One of the tangos ran over just as I pulled the weapon into my mitts and began firing. I squeezed off a burst and got him across the knees, dropping him just long enough for me to get a better shot and put him out of his misery. Then I took care of the bastard I'd bowled over earlier—no way I wanted to be blindsided by a scumbag.

* * *

If you had the balls to climb all the way up to the ceiling and hang by your fingernails from the painted panels above the rotunda at the center of the church—assuming you had *really* sharp fingernails and could see through the pillars—you'd see a total of four four-man teams of terrorists, dressed in either nuns' habits or workmen's outfits, moving through the nave or center of the church. I'm with group number one near the first side altar to the right. Two of the four are dead nearby; the other two are heading after a tour group from Germany that has bolted in the direction of the main doors at the front of the church, a considerable distance away. You can tell that the tour group isn't going anywhere, because tango quartet number two is pulling out its instruments for an improvisational number near the entrance. Tango group three has corralled some Japanese tourists near the Tomb of Gregory XIII, which is about halfway down the nave on your left. The last tango bunch has commandeered the area near the *Pietà*, which is an area close to the doors, on the left side of the church if you're looking down from the dome. They have more than three dozen people on the floor near them.

People are running and crawling and diving and screaming throughout the rest of the building—there are about a half-dozen exits easily accessible from the main part of the church, and God only knows how many others lead outside from the labyrinth of rooms and hallways behind the main walls. The four or five hundred tourists inside the building when the firing began are using every one of them.

The security service's emergency response team

has rallied to the portico area, which is up near the doors.* (This is an armed security force present in the basilica while it's open. They're nominally undercover, mixing with the tourists. The people with the blazers who act as if they're security people were actually unarmed; despite their titles they're more like glorified tour guides with flashlights. Most are helping people find the way out; the others have been shot and are in various stages of dying.)

Of course, that view is only available from the ceiling. From Dick's-Eye View, it's chaotic as hell. All I can see are the dead men and the nuns with the machine guns, who have just disappeared around the corner.

I went to the body of the second terrorist. If he had another box of bullets in the nun's outfit, I couldn't find them, so I grabbed his weapon instead. I looked up and saw another nun running toward me. As I leveled the Beretta to fire I realized she had rosary beads on her belt. Why that told me she was legit I have no idea—call it holy inspiration if you want—but I didn't shoot. I waved my arms at her to get down; when she did I saw two tangos in nun drag behind her. I didn't have to look for rosary beads, or the lack thereof—they had their submachine guns up and ready to fire. Two kisses of the trigger brought tears to their eyes—along with 9mm bullet holes, which rapidly

---

*I'm making some of the details of the security arrangements vague and slightly misleading, just in case some arse decides to use my words as a blueprint for destruction. Doom on you, fuckhead!

filled with blood. They folded to the floor in a heap, already on their way to hell.

I went over and grabbed the real nun, telling her in Italian that she was safe but had better take off her headgear.

She looked at me as if I'd asked her to have sex with a donkey.

"*Perché?*" she stuttered. "Why?"

"Because the terrorists are dressed like you are. The more different you can make yourself, the better."

She blinked, mumbled a prayer, and then pulled off her hat. That was as far as she was going, and I wasn't going to ask her to go any further. I pulled her along with me as I ran toward the entrance to the catacombs where I had last seen Karen. The gated entrance had been closed. Before I could debate whether to try shooting through the locks, a chorus of submachine guns started singing a heavenly hosanna on the other side of the church.

We ducked around the thick pillars, watching as tracer rounds flashed on the other side of the basilica. The guns were firing toward the doors at the front of the church.

Two men dressed in workmen's clothes ran out from the side, then began firing from behind the Papal Altar, which was behind me in the middle of the church. I'd have to deal with them before trying to go after Karen; otherwise they'd be in a perfect position to shoot me in the back.

"I want you to stay here and don't move," I told the nun in Italian. "Stay down and be quiet."

"Can I pray?"

"Praying's good," I told her.

She put her hands together and began. "Oh Lord, my Rogue Warrior smote the shit out of the blasphemous bastards, showing no mercy as he reams their unholy asses and sends the sons of bitches to their fiery reward . . ."*

I'd picked up two more submachine guns along the way, so that I now had four weapons. Rather than taking them all with me, I pulled out the mags—basic thirty-shot boxes of 9mm Parabellum—on two of the four guns and stuffed them into my belt for spares. I held one gun in each hand as I moved out. The Beretta measures about sixteen inches from nose to stubby butt end; the metal stock swings up to give you more stability when firing under your arm, but it's not really meant for one-handed shooting. To remind you of this the designers put a grip at the front. But you can get away with it if you have big-enough hands and your adrenaline is pumping.

I retreated toward the back of the church, circling around in a loop while their attention was focused on the security people who were trying to get in on the far end. When I was behind their position, I launched myself sideways onto the floor like a kid tossing a sled down a hill. I aimed to skid on my shoulder across the floor, firing as soon as they came into my sights. But I had miscalculated how fast I would slide, and after only a brief burst slammed against a slab of marble at the far side of the chapel. Fortunately, I hit the wall with the thickest part of my body—my skull. The crack sounded like an explosion, reverberating through the rotunda like a pound of C4 in a sewer pipe. When I

*The translation is rather free.

blinked my eyes open, I saw that I was holding four guns in each hand.

Which was handy, because eight terrorists were jumping up in surprise from behind the rear pillar of the Papal Altar a few feet away.

Eight went into eight three times—a brief, solid burst from my guns took them all down. The rattle cleared my head, and when I blinked again, there were only two guns in my hand, and two men on the floor. My eyes had no sooner focused than a fresh swarm of bullets whizzed over my head—two more tangos had climbed up into St. Peter's Chair behind me and were firing from behind the bronze robes of the first bishop. I rolled to the right just out of their line of fire, protected by the corner and rear pillar of the Papal Altar.

Even if I could have found a firing angle without getting plastered, the bastards were well protected behind the artwork, whose metal was as thick as the walls of a main battle tank. But even an M1A1 is vulnerable to air attack, and so were they. A set of elaborate crystal chandeliers hung on either side of the altar, arranged one atop the other like a ladder of light to heaven.

It took me three tries, but when I finally nailed the chains, the chandeliers rained down on the punks like fire from heaven. One thick piece of glass, about the size of a Ka-Bar knife and twice as sharp, hit one of the tangos at the back of the neck. He dove forward from the altar with his arms outstretched, blood spurting from his neck like a fountain. Tango Two tried to avoid the shower of shrapnel, jumping out and then running in front of the altar.

Bad move. I squeezed off a burst, and his skull exploded like an overripe pumpkin. His blood blended in well with the red marble on the altar behind him.

The tangos had been firing at a pair of plainclothes security men who'd been at the left corner of the basilica, down at the far end behind me. They were crouched near the marble columns about midway down the nave, in front of the Choir Chapel. Both men stood, pistols drawn. I ducked instinctively, but they didn't fire at me. Instead they tossed them on the ground, apparently because the terrorists over by the *Pietà* had demanded they do so or their hostages would be killed.

As if they were really going to let them go if they didn't, right?

I ran back to the entrance to the catacombs. The nun I'd helped earlier was talking to a priest crouched behind the locked gate to the entrance. The priest explained that the tourists, which presumably included Karen, had already escaped to the outside of the church. He'd come up to see if he could help anyone else to safety, only to find the door locked.

Neither the priest nor the nun was familiar enough with the basilica to tell me if there was a passage at the side of the building I could use to get into the chapel behind the terrorists at the *Pietà*. I suspected there were plenty, but without a map or guide this was no time to play Hansel and Gretel. I came up with a much easier way of sneaking up on the scumbags.

"Sister, take off your robe," I said.

The nun's response was immediate—she let fly with a hard slap across the face. Fortunately, I've had a lot of experience with that. Explaining what I had in mind headed off a second blow, but the nun wasn't convinced it was a good idea until the priest offered a plenary indulgence, which is the Catholic equivalent of a good-conduct pass to heaven.

"You will both avert your gaze!" said the nun.

A few minutes later, a hunched-over tango dressed in nun drag came down the center aisle of the church, bent under the weight of the dead comrade on his shoulder. It was yours truly, of course, with one of the Beretta peashooters in my paw, hidden behind the limp leg of the dead tango. I was nearly to the *Pietà* chapel when two security people stepped out from the portico area and zeroed in on me. My short hairs puckered—I didn't want to shoot them, but I wasn't particularly in the mood to get shot myself. Before they could fire, one of the terrorists near the *Pietà* laced the area with gunfire and they jumped back. Luckily for them, the terrorist wasn't much of a shot.

I groaned under the dead man's weight. One of the tangos came out to help, while two others stepped forward to cover us. That made things ridiculously easy: Bang-bang-bang and down went Tango Number One. Bang-bang-bang and down went Tango Two. Bang-bang-bang and down went Tango Three.

At least, he *should've* gone down. He was the easiest shot, the bastard who'd come up to help me with my burden, so I was three feet away from the son of a bitch.

It's not easy to miss from three feet, and I didn't. Unfortunately, whoever had packed the terrorists' ammo had neglected to follow the rudimentary pre-caution of packing a few tracers into the very end of the row to tip off the shooter that his well is running dry. Standards are slipping everywhere these days.

I jerked the dead body over my shoulder, walloping the tango in the head. He fell backwards into Leo XII's tomb. Leo coldcocked the son of a bitch—the tango's lower extremities were impaled by a piece of marble on the monument.

The forces of Satan were taking a beating, but they hadn't been vanquished yet. As I reloaded, the last tango in the *Pietà* chapel grabbed one of his tourist hostages and held a gun near her head. He shouted in very bad Italian that I had better not do anything or he would blow the infidel's head off.

In retrospect, it was kind of funny that someone who had shot up a church called someone else an infidel, but at the time I didn't get the joke.

Three or four hostages, all women, were cowering on the left side of the chapel across from him, in front of the bulletproof barrier that protects the statue. There were two guards lying in pools of blood nearby; the three tangos I had wasted were scattered behind me. Most of the other hostages had managed to scoot up toward the front of the church when the commotion began, or were hiding in the flowers and statuary nearby. Somewhere behind me were three or four members of the Vatican security service, though I didn't know exactly where.

"Maybe we can negotiate," I said, first in Italian, then in English.

The tango grinned. Which gave me an easy target. I put three bullets between his mouth and hairline.

"Negotiate that, motherfucker."*

If you've been keeping score at home, you know that I've had a modestly successful day: twelve tangos to one splitting headache, an acceptable exchange ratio. But you also know, since you had that dome-eye view of things, that there was one group of terrorists unaccounted for.

I did not know this. And so when the Vatican security people came running up from the portico area where the doors are at the front of the church, I put my weapon down and pulled the head gear off to make it clear I was a good guy. They shouted some shit in Italian that I should stand back, not move, that kind of crap. I yelled that they could fuck themselves: Weren't they watching what I'd just done?

They had, but apparently they weren't taking any chances. Now that I'd done their jobs for them, they rewarded me by giving me an up-close look-see at their weapons.

Nine-millimeter Beretta handguns, nothing special. Unless, of course, you're staring up the barrel at the loaded chamber.

Cooler heads and sarcasm finally prevailed: I held out my hands, told them who I was, and asked if they had expected me to gift wrap the dead tangos instead of leaving them where they fell. One of the men's English wasn't quite up to snuff and asked me to

---

*On paper, this looks a lot more dangerous for the hostage than it was in real life. I was holding the gun, remember, in my hand, and had a clear shot. His weapon was alongside her head and he was looking at me; he'd've had to look away and move his hand to actually shoot her. By that time he was dead.

translate, which sent his companions into laughing fits. I laughed, they laughed—the only people not laughing were the slimes with the Berettas up in the dome. They were rather pissed off about the bad turn their enterprise had taken, and expressed their opinion with a fresh clatter of gunfire.

Fortunately, when Michelangelo was designing the dome, firing lines for submachine gun–toting dirtbags were not one of his main considerations. The bullets rattled ferociously, but harmlessly, as they splayed against the marble floor at the center of the church a few yards away.

A gnomelike Italian in a blue suit was in charge of the unit. He introduced himself as Lieutenant Luigi Piccolo. The last name translates as "little" or "short," and the good lieutenant lived fully up to it, his head bobbing to about my chest. Shortstuff had heard all about my exploits at the NATO party the night before, had seen my picture in the paper, and professed to be a big fan, having read every *"l'avventura di Demo Dick."*

"What sort of reinforcements do you have outside?" I asked, taking off the nun's uniform and grabbing back the submachine gun I'd been using.

Shortstuff shook his head sadly, then explained that the Vatican had recently initiated a series of counterterrorist measures that were supposed to keep the basilica safe from attack. These included gates that automatically locked once a "panic button" was pushed. The locks could then be opened only by supplying a twenty-four-digit secure code through a special remote system. Great idea, *I guess*, if you think that someone is going to attack from the *outside* and you'll be able to stop him before he gets inside. Not such a great idea if he's already inside and inside is where you want to be. It's the typical "concentric circle" syndrome: Keep the prime target in the center and build layers of defense so lawyers can document trespassing, intent, malice, etc. The plan has nothing to do with stopping—which is good, because it doesn't. Good for the prosecutors, that is. It sucks for the victims.

A dozen security people had been inside when the attack began. Not surprisingly the tangos had chosen the shift change to strike, knowing that in true Italian style there would be a decent gap between when the force started heading for the showers and the rest came in to take their place. The tangos had killed four of the men and shot up another one pretty badly; that left seven, two of whom had minor wounds but declared themselves fit for battle. All were equipped with radios and 9mm Beretta hand-guns. The radios could not communicate with the outside; the basilica had recently installed a series of jamming devices to prevent the remote detonation of bombs, and an alternative—like line-of-sight infrared or even a wired landline—had not yet been adopted.

It'd be easy to blame these shortcomings on the fact that we were in Italy. But half-assed planning, insufficient training, and equipment issues are par for the course around the world, and the Eye-talians were no better or worse at any of it. As individuals, the men on the security team were all personally brave, and every one of the dead men had died with his gun drawn, trying to return fire. The fact that they didn't have to die just makes the screw-ups in planning and management suck that much more.

Shortstuff explained that by now alarms would have alerted the *carabinieri* or military police, which would be sending the Italian equivalent of a SWAT team to the basilica. He suggested that we stay put until they arrived.

I told him it made far more sense to get upstairs now. If the tangos could smuggle guns inside the church, bringing in a few blocks of Semtex would be child's play.

I had no doubt the Italian *carabinieri* would show up, and having seen them in one or two NATO exercises I even thought they would be rather efficient. But I also realized that the Italian *"gli SWATi"* operated on Italian time. *Mamma mia.* In American English, *pronto* means "do it yesterday." In Italian, *pronto* means "sometime this century." Or next.

"All right. There's a stairway through there," said Shortstuff, pointing to an archway across the nave.

We'd have to run through the terrorists' line of fire to get there. But that was the easy part. The bends in the stairway inside would provide a number of ambush points, and even if the terrorists didn't want to waste manpower on the steps themselves, they could post someone up at the top or along the walkway above. I hate fighting stairwells; I lack the patience, and grenades bounce down with a sickening series of thuds before the big boom.

There was another entrance on our side up closer to the altar, but it was in full view of the terrorists. Shortstuff knew of at least one other way to get up there, through a hallway on the right-hand side of the transept, which is the arm that forms the cross in the basic church layout. The easiest way to get to that hallway was to walk under the dome—clearly not an option here. Alternatively, you could work your way up and around from our side, exposing yourself only briefly to being seen as you crossed near St. Peter's Chair. Even there you might be able to crawl behind the statues and avoid being seen. That, too, would take quite a bit of time; you'd have to watch for an ambush from the side as you went.

My own observation provided a fourth route, somewhat more direct than the others, though it involved thinking outside of the box—or rather, the church. Many of the altars were built with columns, which I could use to climb up to a balcony level filled with floodlights used to light the interior during mass and ceremonies. Above that level were windows, which I could escape through to the roof; from there, I could climb up onto the dome above the balcony where the tangos were.

Shortstuff was impressed by the plan—or at least that's how I chose to translate the string of adjectives that spewed from his mouth when I explained it.

"*Impossibile,*" he repeated over and over, interspersing the word with some choicer terms.

You can't buy encouragement like that.

I had him divide up his men into three groups, with each unit taking a different route through the church. I would provide a temporary diversion for all three to help them get into position, then go up to the windows.

Shortstuff's version of a pep talk ringing in my ears, I gathered some extra ammo from the tangos I'd wasted and stuffed the mags into my pants. The Beretta submachine gun I had didn't come with a strap; I don't mind carrying a cannon in my pants, but I draw the line at a submachine gun. I took off my belt and rigged a bandolier, strapping the submachine gun to my pecks.

Like the ones I'd stumbled on earlier, the group of tangos tasked with hitting the *Pietà* area had used a large fake speaker to help them get into position. The framework of the speakers was sturdy, but the top was flimsy plywood that wouldn't do much to stop a spitball, let alone 9mm bullets. But you work with what you have.

I pushed the speaker to the edge of the chapel, positioning it while the group charged with dashing across to the staircase opening got ready. I had an inspiration while I was waiting, and pulled off my shirt, latching it at the side with the help of two large staples from the kneeler on the side altar. From a distance, it would look like I was cowering behind it—or at least I hoped it would.

Shortstuff whistled. When I looked over, he gave me a thumbs-up. Then in true Rogue Warrior style, he flashed a military-perfect three-finger salute.

Minus two fingers, of course.

I returned the salute, then shoved the speaker forward. A barrage of 9mm bullets splintered it into pieces, the tangos burning their mags on the easy target. The speaker tipped, fell, and crashed under the torrent.

At least I think it did. Checking my handiwork wasn't on the agenda. Instead I raced to St. Sebastian's Altar, looking to shimmy my way up the marble columns. It took about two seconds to realize that wasn't going to work, but I did find a way to wedge my feet against the rectangular side panel and my back against the marble, and in that way pushed up to the first ledge above the altar. From there I stood and just managed to grab the fancy marble scroll things at the top of the column, using them to haul myself up to the ledge that ran around the side of the chapel.

At that point, Mr. Murphy intervened in the person of a corrupt seventeenth-century marble dealer, who had foisted cheap stone off on the pope. The first scroll had held my weight easily; I pulled myself up and scrambled to the side arch. The next move was to get around a large archway and into the upper alcove area, where I could climb up the side of a thick pier at least partly blocked from the gunmen. To get there, I had to hang my ass out over the middle of the church, an easy target for a second or two. As I sized up my approach, I noticed the thick marble and figured I'd use it to swing around into the niche, where I'd be protected by a statue of a saint. It would have worked perfectly, too, except that the marble broke in two as soon as I trusted it with my weight.

I had just enough momentum to grab the bottom of the statue as I fell. I slapped my chin and face against the stone base beneath the niche but hung on, so I didn't complain. Much.

Dangling thirty or forty feet off the ground, I was an easy target for the tangos up in the dome, and they commenced trying to write their names in my backside. Shortstuff distracted them with covering fire long enough for me to scramble up behind the saint's cape. But getting across to the next niche was impossible; they weren't cut symmetrically and there was nothing to grab on to to swing across. So instead I climbed onto the saint's shoulders, grabbed the column top—more fancy scroll stuff—and pulled upward, praying as I did that the contractor's wares had been properly inspected before installation. This time the marble held, and maybe because of Shortstuff and his pistol, the gunmen didn't try getting a good angle to fire at me. Their blasts chipped the hell out of the columns a few feet away, but missed me.

I climbed up over a foot-wide ledge and pulled myself onto one a few feet higher and three or four times as wide. Large spotlights sat in a track at the lip. Twelve feet above that ledge was a wide galley with even larger spotlights mounted on thick stands. I hung my butt out and started to climb. As I got my hands on the top ledge, 9mm slugs began poking at the marble nearby. The bullets missed, but the chips peppered my side as I scrambled upward and over the low wall at the edge of the galley, pulling the Beretta submachine gun from the makeshift bandolier as I rolled onto the floor. I spun over and got to my knee. One of the tangos was running toward me from the direction of the dome. Our eyes met for a second, and I saw his flash with fear, as if he'd finally realized what a world of shit he'd gotten himself into. I yanked up the Beretta to fire, but before I could he threw himself behind one of the nearby light poles.

Chickenshit move, but it saved his ass.

Temporarily. He was between me and the windows I wanted to go through. Gun trained on his hiding place, I ran toward him, waiting until I could get a decent shot. As I closed in, he jumped back out into the walkway. A burst from the Beretta encouraged him to continue off the edge. He flew toward the cathedral floor, landing with a splat so loud I heard it as I broke the glass on one of the windows.

The windows open onto the main part of the roof. It looks more like a strange theme park of spiked fences and miniature buildings than a roof. The dome sits at the center, topped by a cupola that's sometimes called St. Peter's Crown. Imagine the Capitol dome in Washington with one less set of windows and you have a rough idea what the dome on St. Peter's looks like. There are a set of large windows and columns that circle the base. They rise from a stone wall about ten or twelve feet over the roof. There are stairways to the roof, but I simply jumped up onto the bricks covering one of the utility entrances and climbed from there to the base.

If you look up at the dome windows from the floor of St. Peter's, they seem crystal clear. Light flows through them, glittering off the gold-plated artwork below. Up close, though, they're covered with a thick layer of Roman soot. I rubbed enough of the grime away to see a large blur on the balcony across from me, and two less distinct ones to the right. One of the smaller blurs moved to my right; his companion followed.

They left something behind. I couldn't tell what it was, but I suspected it was a bomb.

I leaned closer to the window, pressing my face and hands against it. As I did, the framework holding the pane in place gave way and the entire window assembly crumbled, which sent me flying into the church, sailing toward the floor three hundred something feet below.

3

I can't say my life flashed before my eyes, but the floor of the cathedral certainly did. Then my right foot snagged the lead frame of the window just enough to change my direction. I threw my hand out to grab the rail—instinct and reflexes, no conscious thought involved at all. I missed, slapping my forehead against the metal pipe instead. I took harder shots on dates when I was a teenager; nonetheless this one cleared the fog from my brain. I folded like a deck chair, fortunately on the balcony that surrounds the dome.

My ears were ringing, and the sound had a very familiar rasp to it. If I didn't know any better, I would have sworn it was the voice of Roy Boehm, the creator of the SEALs. Boehm served as my tutor and patron saint, and it's always his eloquent, refined voice I hear in the dark days of my soul.

What he says isn't very profound, but it is direct: *Attack! Attack! ATTACK! You fucking piece of whaleshit! Off the deck and fight like a man.*

Boehm never gave me an order that didn't require immediate compliance. I swung the submachine gun up and began firing at the two tangos immediately in front of me. Both died with something other than smiles on their faces, but I didn't have time to admire my handiwork—Murphy slipped his fingers into the Beretta and jammed the son of a bitch about halfway through the mag.

There's a CIA analyst in the basement of Langley who's cheering as he reads this, not because he hates me but because it means that the boom business in terrorism has caused standards in training and equipment to decline. To him, my borrowed submachine gun is a welcome waypoint on a downward slope plotting the bad guys' inevitable decline and fall.

Personally, I would have felt a hell of a lot better if the trend line ran through a different weapon, namely the one belonging to the tango opposite me on the cupola walkway. I did my best impression of a fish out of water, flipping forward and diving behind the fallen bodies of his comrade as the bastard did some touchup work on the nearby frescoes. One of his bullets creased my pants leg, and another singed my butt.

Which not only hurt, but pissed me off. Shoot me in the head, shoot me in the heart, but don't try to butt-fuck me or there'll be hell to pay.

I flattened my body parts against the floor behind the dead terrorists, their bodies jumping with the 9mm slugs their friend was spitting from across the way. Neither of the slimers had a weapon that I could see, and I wasn't in a position to frisk them.

Shortstuff chose this moment to appear with one of his men at the entrance to the balcony. Never have I felt so glad to see a hairy Italian in my life. The tango on the other side of the dome did not share my enthusiasm and spent the rest of his mag chasing Shortstuff back into the archway. I jumped to my feet, determined to rush him before he could reload. But instead of fishing out a new box of bullets he climbed up on the protective screen around the railing and jumped.

If he had jumped to his death I would have personally paid for his funeral . . . after I stomped on his squished remains. But instead of going downward, he leapt toward the ledge under the nearby window, swung one of his legs up and managed to scramble upright and then through the window. (Give the devil his due—that ledge has to be twelve or more feet over the floor of the balcony, and just to grab the slippery marble and hoist yourself takes enormous finger strength. And frankly it's easier to fall over that security screen than it is to leap over the top. But fear is a powerful motivator.)

"Look for bombs," I shouted to Shortstuff, jumping onto the screen to copy the tango's monkey routine.

"There's a door—that way," yelled the Italian, pointing a short distance.

Well, duh.

I ran through it out into the hallway, ducked right and left. Shortstuff yelled again, but I didn't hear what he said. Most likely it was something along the lines of: *You don't have a weapon with you, asshole.*

Which wasn't the same as being unarmed. The terrorist who'd gone through the window had fallen or jumped from the stone base down to the roof. When I got out, he was just getting himself up, limping as if he'd busted his ankle or trashed his knees. Driven by adrenaline, he began running toward the front of the church.

By now, the Italian military and police response teams called in to back up the Vatican people had finished their coffee breaks and were en route. A pair of gunships, Augusta A129 Mangustas (basically Apaches with garlic breath) whipped down from the north, the spearhead of a larger flock of aircraft, including two Chinook choppers loaded with assault teams.

The roof of the basilica looks like a little city. The roof of the nave or the center aisle of the church looks like a long building in the center. It's flanked by fences and odd-shaped structures. The tango took a turn around one and veered toward the nave, heading in the direction of a workman's ladder. I caught up in time to get a kick in the face. He hauled himself up onto the roof, when I clambered up behind him he was retrieving a pistol from beneath his coveralls.

I had one of two choices—jump back down, or throw myself forward in a wild attempt to knock the gun out of his hands before he got a chance to fire. I chose the latter, which raises the inevitable question: Which is faster? A speeding bullet, or Demo Dick?

That day, at least, it worked out to a draw, as my fist arrived in the tango's midsection just as he began firing. Bullets flew past me, the gun flew to the side, and tango and I tumbled toward the side of the roof.

And kept tumbling. After three or four spins, we went our separate ways. He flew to the left of a small hip roof and sailed off into a fence, striking the top railing hard enough to split his head like a crushed grape.

And *moi*, or *Io* as the Eye-talians would say?

I didn't go anywhere. The bandolier I'd fashioned from my belt snagged me upside down in the gutter as I headed face-first toward the terraced roof. One second I was poised to fly through the air like Super-man. The next second I was still there, waiting for my close-up.

By the time I got myself unhooked, the SWAT team was fast-roping from the Chinook forty or fifty yards away. Shortstuff and his team surrounded the now-dead tango, and then turned their attention to me.

"We're getting a ladder," he yelled. "Don't let go!"

I wasn't planning on it.

When everything was sorted out, it looked like this: Four four-man groups of terrorists had come into the cathedral, posing as workmen and clergy and using the fake speaker boxes to carry their weapons. The idea had apparently been to capture as many tourists as possible, then probably kill them and themselves. They had not brought explosives with them; the shadow I'd seen on the dome balcony turned out to be a backpack with extra mags for their guns. Considering what *could* have happened, things had gone extremely well. Even so, four of Shortstuff's men and eight unarmed security people had been killed, with two others wounded. Six tourists had been killed and fifteen or seventeen* wounded in the attack. Tour guides and unarmed security people had managed to lead most of the civilians to safety, and while the press seemed to forget them in the brouhaha that followed, I won't. In many cases, the guides had not been properly trained on evacuation

---

*In typical Italian fashion, the authorities never could decide on the number injured. I have no idea why there was a discrepancy, except for the obvious: Italians can't count, especially when casualties outnumber their fingers.

procedures and used their common sense to quickly find the nearest exits or secure hiding places. Just as important, they remained calm. I'm sure the families of the people they led to safety realize how much they owe them.

Not one of the tangos had survived. My fault to a large degree, I know. If I had thought about it, I might have tried to save two or three of them for deep-fried interrogation, heating their balls over a vat of boiling olive oil to get some useful information. But you don't get do-overs in this business. And the investigation of the *"terroriste diabolice"* as the media called them wasn't my concern. My own take was that the group had been fairly incompetent; if I went to all that trouble, I would have made damn sure to bring a few explosives inside to make a more permanent comment on the architecture.

Karen and I had a reunion in the Governor's Palace next to the cathedral, where I'd gone with Shortstuff to debrief. Backass arrived a short while later, thanking me profusely for helping avert a catastrophe. He was so excited that his English was a little hard to understand, but I think at one point he may have offered me a cardinal's pointy hat. I turned him down, though I did accept one of his business cards and promised I'd stay in touch. Even God can make use of the devil sometimes. I finished telling the police and military intelligence people what I knew, then left with Karen to find a pair of pants without air-conditioning back at the hotel.

The excitement of the afternoon meant I missed my appointment with Shakespeare, the MI6 officer I'd met the night before. Unfortunately, he couldn't re-schedule: En route to the café where we'd arranged to meet, he was hit by a truck. At the time, the fact that the vehicle ran up onto a curb to strike him and then sped away didn't seem particularly noteworthy to the Rome police; they handled two or three similar cases every week. Shakespeare's official cover made him appear to be just a businessman, and by all appearances he was just an unlucky SOB. The police report called it an accident.

To be honest, it may have been. MI6 later conducted its own investigation and came up with nothing. The typical Roman at the wheel makes the worst Boston cabbie look like a grandmother on her way to a Sunday afternoon tea, and truck drivers are even worse. But considering everything that happened afterward, I'd put even money on his death not being the result of typical Roman indifference to pedestrians.

The information he was going to share about Saladin died with him. If anyone else in MI6 knew anything about it, they didn't come forward to volunteer it, and as it turned out I wasn't in a position to ask around.

It did cross my mind that afternoon that the thwarted takeover of the basilica *might* have been the big event Saladin's communiqué promised. But I doubted it. Like most of the people who knew about him, I thought Saladin was more than likely a blowhard wannabe whose only asset was a computer and some hacking skills.

Backass decided to honor my basilica climbing with an Italian-style reception the next evening, replete with plenty of cheek kissing and Asti. I was starting to OD on Roman hospitality but Karen wore down my resistance during a pleasant lunch at a hilltop trattoria a few miles from the hotel; Backass had hinted that the pope might attend and even I couldn't turn down a chance to meet the pontiff. When we got back to the hotel, we discovered that Backass had sent a Vatican Mercedes to take us into town; the armored sedan was nice, but what won me over was the fully stocked bar in the back. After instructing the driver on how high to fill my glass with Bombay, Karen and I started upstairs to change. We were about halfway to the elevator when someone shouted my name. I turned around, and found myself confronted by six large men with bad buzz cuts, all clearly American. They were well dressed; their dark suits matched and none of their Kevlar was showing.

"What's this? An escort?" I asked.

A squeaky voice answered. "Richard Marcinko, aka Demo Dick, aka Rogue Warrior?"

"AKA, who are you?" I asked. I couldn't spot who was talking behind the wall of flesh, though I did notice a flurry of movement behind me. Several men stepped out from the statues on either side of the elevator.

"Richard Marcinko, you are under arrest," continued the squeaky voice. The wall parted and a man in an Air Force uniform stepped through. He stood about six-three and weighed, oh, maybe a hundred and ten pounds counting the uniform and the briefcase he had in his right hand.

"Who the hell are you?"

He introduced himself as Major Squeakynuts,* and declared that I would come with him.

"Why the fuck would I do that?" I asked.

"Because there's twelve of us and one of you," said Squeakynuts. "And you wouldn't want resisting arrest to be added to the charges against you."

Squeakynuts turned out to be a U.S. Air Farcer from the Office of Special Investigations and Thumb Sucking. After a fruitful exchange of obscenities, I discovered that I was suspected—suspected, not *charged*—with violating security at the Air Fart's rest stop for nukes at Sigonella in Sicily.

Don't bother breaking out a map. I'd been nowhere near Sicily in the past few days. In fact, I hadn't been there in roughly a decade. The "suspicions" were either very old or ridiculous, most likely both.

A little bit of background for those of you unfamiliar with my history. After starting and commanding SEAL Team Six, I moved on to other challenges, eventually forming a counterterrorist training/covert action unit known as Red Cell. Our primary task, at least on the books, was to run exercises designed to discover and demonstrate flaws in security procedures at U.S. installations. Most of my victims wore the crisp whites beloved by the U.S. Navy, but occasionally I got a chance to spread my ill will to our brethren services. Among my early assignments was a directive to "visit and test" the Air Force's nuclear babysitting arrangements at Sigonella.

*I didn't get the exact spelling.

Sigonella is located on the eastern side of Sicily, about where a soccer player would kick the island if it were really the football it looks like on a map. The bulk of the base is actually a U.S. Navy installation "shared" with the Italian air force. Our Air Farts use it as a transshipment point, moving "items" down the road to supposedly secure magazine areas, separate from the Navy base. (These "items" were weapons that caused mushroom clouds to appear when used. Some of the details—heck, *all* of the details—about their storage and existence here remains classified.) Red Cell pulled the pants down on the Air Force operation, demonstrating that it would be child's play to grab a couple of gadgets from under their noses. The general overseeing the radiation counters went fairly apeshit—that's a medical term—when he got my report. He swore that he would have my head delivered on a silver platter at his earliest opportunity.

That had been somewhere in the vicinity of two decades ago; he'd've retired by now, which meant the statute of limitations on my head ought to have expired. Joking aside, Sigonella was barely a footnote in my Red Cell career, a few days of frolic and fun in the sun before getting down to more serious business, and I hadn't given our escapades there much thought until my arrest. (*Red Cell* details some of our exploits in greater detail. Just remember it's all fiction, whatever the government claims.)

Time out for a quick info dump on Sigonella for those of you who haven't read the earlier books or have never had the pleasure of traveling to Sicily. Besides being the birthplace of the Italian Mafia, a lot of Sicily is owned by Libyans. This includes the olive groves surrounding the airfield at Sigonella. (Qaddafi is our friend now, right? *Ha!*)

Most of the airfield's perimeter security is provided by Italian conscripts. (No offense, but there is a reason the shortest book in the world is titled *Italian War Heroes*.) The deterrent is a low barbed-wire fence that I can go under just as easy as I can get over.

As you'd expect in any joint venture, command and control is an issue. Think of the old Abbott and Costello routine, "Who's on First." Now put half of the conversation in Italian and the other half in English, and you'll see how confusion can run up and down the chain of command. The Italians have a commanding officer and we have a commanding officer (CO). Our guy can make decisions pretty freely or get guidance from CINCUSNAVEUR (the in term for Commander in Chief U.S. Navy Europe). But the Italian CO *must*— and I do mean *must*—coordinate most major decisions with Rome. And anything other than whether to use marinara or a meat sauce on the spaghetti is considered a major decision. (That may be one, too, now.)

Our people live in housing outside the base. Most take a bus or car to get to work. Ambushing them and holding them hostage is a piece of cake. When I was running Red Cell, quite a number of our guys were hitchhiking back and forth, which is even worse.

One thing I will say: The locals are friendly. Hell, they ought to be—they make money off us. There is a "communist" party within the government, but it's more like the Italian version of the Kiwanis Club than the party we saw during the Cold War era. On the other hand, in today's Italy, even the right-wingers are concerned about being considered a "pawn" of the

U.S. What this means is that there's little pressure on the Italians at Sigonella to work with our guys. And since Sicily in not within a war zone—and let's face it, it can be a *damn nice* place to hang out when it's not raining—there's a lack of concern for what is going on in the real world.

Squeakynuts insisted that my apprehension had nothing to do with the past. He also insisted that there was no way I was being released from custody. To emphasize his point, his men flashed M4s, complete with grenade launchers. Discretion dictated that I send Karen to the ceremony to sip champagne and collect my medal while I went with Squeakynuts to find out which old friend in the Pentagon I was going to have to call to get my ass unhooked from the donkey cart. I thought he would take me to the embassy to get it straightened out, which would mean the ambassador would be in a position to help me out. Stupid me— going to the nearby embassy would have been the logical thing to do, which of course meant it was the last thing I should have expected. Within a half hour, I found myself in the rear of a C-130 Hercules on my way to Sicily.

This was a *real* C-130—an ancient "slick" with nothing but tie-downs in the back. I don't mind sitting on aluminum for a few hours, but the Herky Birds are *loud.* Take ten of your average motorbikes, multiply the sound by a factor of ten, and put them and your head in a garbage pail for three hours and you get the idea.

Things went from ridiculous to sublime when we reached Sigonella. Major Squeakynuts introduced me to his boss, Colonel Crapinpants, who took me in to see *his* boss, General Kohut. Kohut told me that there had been two or three probes of security over the past few days by "actors unknown." Apparently Red Cell's exploits had been engraved in the local lore to such an extent that when Crapinpants learned I was in Italy, I became Suspect *Numero Uno*. I was flattered, naturally, but I did wonder what my motive would be. Few people tempt a stretch in a federal hotel just to relive some of their glory days.

"You wanted us to look bad," suggested Crapinpants.

"Why would I go to that much trouble? You guys make yourselves look bad every time you shave."

That got a yuk from one of the enlisted Air Force security people, whom I've found to be generally decent sorts when their officers aren't around to lead them astray. Kohut gave him a sour look, and I have no doubt that the man will be old and gray before his next authorized leave.

It didn't take much more discussion or sarcastic remarks for me to figure out what was really going on here. The flyboys wanted my help figuring out who was probing the base, and had gotten the bright idea of using invented charges as a way of persuading me. The charges were laughable, but there were a lot of them, ranging from unauthorized presence on a military installation to contemplated destruction of U.S. property. They couldn't make even one of them stick, but they could tangle me in enough red tape and spaghetti sauce to keep me in Italy for the next six months if I didn't help out. So I decided to play along, at least for a while.

The probes were varied; a fence cutting here, a

few firecrackers there. Locals had been seen, always at a distance, watching when patrols responded to alerts. Crapinpants thought someone was trying to test and evaluate his defenses, and he was absolutely right. The question was who, and why.

The why seemed obvious—someone wanted the gadgets the Air Force had there. The who, though, was more difficult to answer. The smallest of the nuclear chestnuts the Air Force stored here were many times more powerful than the weapons dropped on Hiroshima and Nagasaki. Terrorists were obvious suspects, but any of two or three dozen nations would pay millions, perhaps billions, for one. And not just countries in the Middle East like Syria, which would view a stolen weapon as an equalizer in a war with Israel. Taiwan could easily view a nuclear device as an equalizer in its perennial conflict with China. South Korea might think one prudent to protect it from North Korea. Even if such nations weren't directly involved in the snatch, they would certainly be in the market to buy it if an independent party pulled it off.

Two things worried me about what Kohut and his people said. One, the probes had been well organized, spaced out over several days, and very low key—generally signs of a professional. And two, I doubted the Air Force people had picked up on all of the probes. It was the ones they missed that would present the biggest problem.

I took a tour of the facility and pointed out a few problems. I won't get into specifics for obvious reasons, but in general the facility was vulnerable to hostage-taking, unauthorized entry by (fake or stolen) supply and emergency vehicles, fence-line penetrations, and all manner of diversionary incidents.

Say, Dick, aren't those the same things it was vulnerable to back in your Red Cell days?

Um, yes.

Oh. Carry on.

Besides general complacency and rigid thinking, one of the biggest problems for security organizations these days is the overreliance on gee-whiz doodads to do the work of mark-one eyeballs. Don't get me wrong: motion sensors, miniature bugs, infrared video, night glasses, UAVs—these are all useful tools. But they're just tools, only as useful as the people putting them to use. And if you don't have enough people, and if you're rotating people in and out so fast that they hardly have time to find the bathroom before leaving, you're asking for trouble.

But give credit where credit is due: The high-tech gear had come away with what police call a "partial plate"—several digits from a license plate belonging to a truck parked along the road to the facility. The truck turned out to have been stolen—a true shocker, no?

Kohut had been concerned enough about the case to call for help, and besides the Air Force security people and the DIA slugs, and a misplaced FBI agent, the State Department had assigned an expert on international terrorism named Francis Delano to help with the case. Delano's real asset was the fact that he spoke Sicilian as well as Italian. (Don't let the textbooks fool you. They're two different languages, each with its own set of curse words.) Delano had been tasked to liaise with the local yokels largely because of his language skills, and when I found out about the license plate and truck, it was Delano I went to see. By now it was fairly late—or early, depending on your point of view—but I called over to his hotel anyway and even managed to get him to pick up the phone after twenty or thirty rings. I explained that I was looking into the situation at Sigonella, had only a few hours or so to spare, and wanted to pick his brain as soon as I could.

Now, if possible.

Delano groaned. I took that as a yes, hung up quickly, and had one of the Air Farce security people drive me over.

Delano greeted me at his hotel room with a bottle of wine in his hand—and a loaded Colt.

"I'll take the drink," I told him. "You can keep the gun."

"You're Marcinko?"

"Dick."

"You know it's 4 a.m.?"

"Yeah, but it's never too early to have a drink in Italy."

Delano loosened up inside. Contrary to all expectation, he turned out to be an almost competent investigator, possibly because he had come to the State Department after a career in the Army's Criminal Investigation Division. My experience with State Department employees is that they usually don't know whom they're working for, us or the countries they're assigned to. Generally they side with the latter. Frankie not only knew who paid for the butter on his bread but was sparing with it, the first government worker I've met in my life who declined to put personal items like his morning coffee on the expense account. If all government workers were as honest as he was, we'd have paid off the federal debt ten years ago.

Frankie poured us some wine and gave me an info dump on the situation from his perspective. He began indirectly, talking not about the probes or the truck, but Sicily itself. He knew a bit about the island, he said, because his grandparents on his father's side had come from here, although they had left from Palermo, the major port on the west.

Sicily had a long tradition of being at odds with the central government. The craggy coasts made it an easy place to sneak in and out of and the rugged terrain made it easy to hide. On the other hand, Sicilians tended to be clannish and distrustful of outsiders. It wasn't impossible for foreign terrorists to operate here, Delano said, but they would have a number of handicaps. Physically, Arabs and northern Africans could easily pass as residents, but once they started to speak, their accents and lack of fluency in the difficult Sicilian tongue would give them away. In short, he didn't think an outside group was responsible for the probes; the police would have heard about them long ago—not necessarily from complaints, but from gossip at the local bars and cafés.

"What about a homegrown group, like the old Red Brigades?" I asked. The Red Brigades were communist cells that operated throughout the country in the 1960s and '70s.

"They're old men now, the few who have survived. Besides, they weren't very active in Sicily," said Delano.

"Who then?"

Delano shrugged. "I don't think we're at the point where we can rule anything out. Or in."

He had set up a meeting with the local authorities to discuss the matter first thing in the morning, and invited me along. I told him I'd be glad to, then took his yawns as a hint that it was time to let him catch some beauty rest.

Karen shared no anxiety when I caught up with her by phone a few hours later. On the contrary, she was excited—she wanted to hop right down and spend our last two days in Italy basking in the Sicilian sun.

Who was I to stand in her way? Especially since the Air Farce was going to spring for her tickets.

"Dosdière was disappointed that you weren't at the ceremony," she told me.

"I'll bet."

"He gave me the card of someone who needs help on an open-ended project. It has his cell and business numbers."

Open-ended projects being my stock-in-trade, I gave the someone a call while waiting for Karen's plane to arrive that night. His name was Jean Capon, and he was an executive vice president for a company called BetaGo, which provided computer and electronic services in Asia and Europe. He was coy about what the services actually entailed, but his hints made it obvious that they were largely financial transactions involving decent-sized transfers between bank and brokerage accounts in a dozen or more countries. While the bulk of the work was electronic, the firm had to move paperwork and some hard currency around as well. There were regular transport routes in Asia, and this was the part of the operation they wanted checked by someone "impartial and competent."

Transporting currency and paperwork—the latter being information stored on computer media like disks and tapes, rather than actual paper—is unglamorous but potentially well-paying grunt work. A lot of international concerns need to move records and money around for various reasons, most of which are never revealed to the movers. Watching the shipments is not exactly sweat-breaking work, though it can become bloodletting if things go wrong. The fees take that into consideration. I've done it myself in Asia and Europe; one of these days I'll write about helping provide security when one old-money firm shipped U.S. dollars from Japan to Brussels. They had a way of fiddling with the international dateline to make big bucks off the interest—quite a gig.

The fact that BetaGo needed someone to observe the operation implied that there were questions about what was happening there. Answers to questions yield fees based on recovery commissions: big bucks as well as big risks to go with them. That's a combination I couldn't turn down. We firmed up a basic fee structure, then set up a meeting for the following week in Tokyo, immediately after our company conference in Germany. I love Japan, and not just because I enjoy sushi. One of my favorite people in the world, Toshiro Okinaga, makes his living as a policeman in Tokyo. Calling Tosho a policeman is like calling me a sailor—he supervises his own team of *Kunika* warriors. *Kunika* is a special unit of the Japanese police that handles counterterrorism tasks; the group is so secret that if you plug the name into a search engine on the Internet you won't find out anything about them. They shut down the Japanese Red Army in the 1980s, and have played an important role in fighting a variety of terrorists, foreign and homegrown, in the years since. They're every bit as efficient and relentless as you would expect the descendants of samurai warriors to be.

I'd first met Tosho and friends back in my SEAL days, when Red Cell ran some exercises at a U.S-Japanese base at Yokosuka. Tosho is a hell of a shot and a seventh-degree black belt; he can also put away the Kirin like there's no tomorrow, a truly important quality for a SpecWarrior. A chance to spend some time and wet the whistle with an old friend would be a definite fringe benefit of the gig.

I checked my watch and called Rogue Manor, where my business affairs were being managed in absentia by Danny Barrett. I've known Danny since he was a Marine Corps captain a billion years ago in Vietnam. There he worked the CORDS program as an advisor, helping the Christians In Action gather intelligence from gooks. After graduating from the Marines, he went into police work and became a detective. We hooked up again a few years ago, and since then Danny's been a vital part of the operation, in effect an executive vice president. He has a good head for numbers and a detective's knack for ferreting out facts; he can be a little gruff at times, but who am I to complain about that? Most important, he understands that you lead from the front; that's a prerequisite of being a Marine, and it's one of my golden commandments of SpecWar.

Even though it was around midnight back home,

Danny was up and working, scanning reports from Red Cell International's far-flung empire. The big meeting in Germany was only three days away, and he was working hard to make sure everything was squared away before heading overseas. He brought me up to date. There had been another attack on one of our convoys in Afghanistan, but otherwise things were quiet. I told him about BetaGo, handing off the job of preparing the contract work and doing the background checks, which are routine before we begin an assignment with a company we haven't worked with before. Updates finished, he turned me over to Trace Dahlgren, who was burning the midnight oil overseeing the six Red Cell wannabes, fresh-faced recruits for our international security division.

Trace is a good example of the "new" military and what I mean when I say the young turks wearing U.S. togs are better than ever. The new breed is very different than the class I graduated Frog School with back in the day. Not better necessarily, just different. And very good.

Trace worked for Delta's female squadron* and is an expert in Jeet Kune Do, the martial art that Bruce Lee made famous. She's as good a shot with a pistol as I am; hell, she'll tell you she's better. At five-eight and one hundred and thirty pounds, she has assets male shooters don't, which makes her deadly undercover. Trace's green eyes sparkle like jewels in the light, but they are guaranteed to burn through your skull if you cross her.

---

*Officially, Delta's "funny squadron" doesn't exist, and hasn't since it was created in 1993. Then again, neither does Delta.

Then again, if you do that you won't have to worry about her stare—she'll kick your ass sooner than look at you.

Trace is a vicious trainer, which is why she oversees the program. Her workouts have been known to bring tears to the eyes of male recruits, and if anything, she's tougher on the women.

There's only one problem with having Trace in charge of the training programs—she hates the job. Not the duties, but the fact that she's missing out on the action in the field. To get her to take the post, I had to promise to rotate in regular replacements—a promise she reminds me of at every opportunity. Her present stint was due to end with the meeting in Germany, and I could hear the anticipation in her voice when she came on the line.

Trace's replacement was Sean Mako, who was due back from some personal time any moment. Sean is a former SEAL who served with Teams Two and Six before freelancing for the CIA in Iraq and someplace in Central America so secret that even Sean isn't sure where it was. Past affiliations are no testament to character, fortunately, because Sean has done yeoman's service and then some with yours truly.

After squaring away some details about the newbies, Trace shared some of her latest research into her Chihuahua Apache forbears. Saying that her ancestors were hardy people doesn't cover the half of it. According to some legends, they survived in the Mexican desert by drinking coyote urine. True or not, the Chihuahua feel they have a special relationship with the animal and the spirits they believe can inhabit the beast.

As a young girl, Trace had what we white folk would call a "vision," and for years the rituals and practices of her tribe were important to her. By the time she joined the Army, however, her beliefs had begun to waver. Gradually, she left many of the "old ways" behind. In the last year, a relative's request that she act as a spiritual guide for a young girl, becoming a kind of "godmother," had brought her back to her roots. She told me now that over the past several nights she had had dreams of a jungle.

"Coyote ran with me," she said. "We were looking for Child-of-the-Water, but he could not be found."

"Weird dream."

"Child-of-the-Water made the white man from fish," said Trace. She said this in the same tone someone might use to describe the weather.

"In your dream?"

"No. After the beginning of time."

"What does the dream mean?"

"It means what it means," she said. And that was the end of the conversation.

I met Karen at the airport around 10 a.m. Since "first thing in the morning" in Italian translates into "sometime after lunch" in English, we had time for a quick nap at the hotel before I hooked up with Delano to visit the local investigators. With a few hours beauty rest and an ample lunch, Delano was in a much better mood, even telling me to call him Frankie. He'd spoken to Crapinpants and Kohut. They had nothing new to report; the security teams had not detected any probes or evidence of same over the past twenty-four hours.

"A good sign?" asked Frankie as we drove.

"Maybe a very bad one," I told him. "You only probe until you find a weakness."

He nodded, concentrating on the traffic for a while. Then he said, "You know a General Gill?"

"I don't know. Air Force?"

"I'm not sure. He's a two-star, and he has some sort of fancy title at the Pentagon. Apparently he was stationed down here when he was a captain, and because of that or his job, or maybe both, he's taking a special interest in the situation. He's in Germany right now, but he's flying down to meet with Kohut this afternoon. Kohut's rather upset about it."

The name tickled something in the dark recesses of my brain. "How long ago was he stationed here?"

"Has to be close to twenty years, I'd say, if not more. I didn't get into details. He had something to do with security, which is one reason he's upset, I guess."

There *had* been a Captain Gill here around the time of our Red Cell activities. I remembered him vaguely as a hostage victim we'd used to get access to the base during one of the exercises. He'd given my men such a hard time that as punishment we had him take us out to several local bars and pay for drinks all night. Of course, given that he was a real jerk, sharing drinks with him would have been more torture than fun, so we left him home and just took his credit card. My memory was hazy, but it was likely that we had neglected to inform him that we'd borrowed it.

"I think I remember a Captain Gill, very vaguely," I said. "But I doubt he's same guy. We called him Pus Face—he had a huge zit on his nose."

"Well he's apparently heard of you. Kohut wants you to meet him in his office around three."

"I doubt I'll be free."

Frankie glanced over at me, then smiled.

Mangia is Eye-talian for "eat until your brains explode," and Detective Maria Mangia was a feast. She had raven black hair and a smile that would have sent Mona Lisa into hiding. At five-three, I doubt she weighed much more than ninety pounds, but every ounce had been perfectly placed. (I would have volunteered to weigh her, but she was armed.)

"Signor Marcinko, welcome to Sicily," she said, extending her hand as Frankie and I were shown into her office. The sleeve of her jacket hiked up just enough to expose well-muscled forearms. Sicilian women have evolved these over time to keep their men in line; one slap is generally good for a week to ten days of good behavior.

"I have heard very much about you," said Mangia, grabbing my hand like grip pliers. "We're very honored to have a real dog-breath asshole among us."

Being called a dog-breath asshole by a beautiful woman can be an unnerving experience, but I remembered my manners. "Well, fuck you very much."

"You wish," she said, waving us in.

Ms. Mangia's father was an American seaman who had remained in Italy after duty there in the late 1970s. Our paths had never crossed, but he was an avid reader of the Rogue Warrior books and she had absorbed the Demo Dick legend at a young age. I took out a pad and made a note of her address, promising to sign a few for her old man as soon as I got home.

Preliminaries out of the way, Ms. Mangia told us

that the locals had connected the stolen truck with several others in the area. They had also connected it to a low-level lowlife who specialized in things like car thefts—not locally but in Naples on the mainland.

The lead had come from local car thieves, which made it somewhat suspicious. However, one of the vehicles had been recovered, and—because the Americans had filed the complaint—a forensics team had been put to work scouring it. They had obtained fingerprints that matched the suspect's.

The suspect was someone named Sanmarco Biondi, and he was wanted by the police for auto thefts not just in Naples but in much of Sicily. The crimes were believed to be initiated by the Mafia, which ran a tidy operation finding late-model luxury sedans and shipping them to Africa and the Middle East, where they were sold as new vehicles.

I tried not to show any surprise, but I was floored. Tenuous as it was, the Mafia connection put the probes at Sigonella in a new light.

Assuming, of course, that it was related.

Ms. Mangia began pressing us for information about the crime the truck might be connected to. I had an easy excuse; I just shrugged, saying I'd only gotten involved recently as a favor for my friends at the base. Frankie bobbed and weaved in a friendly way, becoming vaguer and vaguer as the detective tried to find out which part of the facility the truck had been spotted near. She wasn't dumb, though—the Air Force's nuclear operation is an open secret locally, and the fact that I had shown up probably confirmed what she suspected when the information had been passed along. The detective was properly worried about security operations at the base, since their failure could have dire consequences on the citizens she was sworn to protect. Frankie tried to address her concerns with a few words about a black market cigarette operation, but she wasn't buying. She turned to me and said softly, "If there is something that concerns us, we expect to know immediately."

I nodded. I agreed we owed her that. But it wouldn't be up to me; I was at best an unpaid consultant.

"You've done a lot as it is," said Frankie. "There's no danger. This is merely routine."

Ms. Mangia's frown said she didn't believe us, and she was still wearing it when we left.

Frankie and I discussed the Mafia angle as we drove away. Southern Italy was in one of its periodic economic troughs—you and I would call it a depression—and even the mob was having a hard time. Turf wars in Naples as well as Sicily had taken their toll on all the local bad guys. Murder, extortion, and robbery just didn't pay what they used to, and many of the local "Men of Honor" were looking for new ways to make a dishonest living. Grabbing a nuke might be the ultimate get-rich-quick scheme; anyone who snatched it would be able to purchase the small country they'd need to hide in when the operation was over.

"Most likely it's a coincidence of some kind," Frankie concluded finally. "But just to be sure, maybe we should try finding this car thief Biondi in Naples. The FBI agent who's been helping our task force has some contacts with the unit there that watches the Mafia."

I grunted. The idea wasn't terrible, but I had a better one. Rather than increasing security at the base, the thing to do was make it even sloppier. With a little strategic incompetence, we could direct the probe to a prepared target, then follow them after the snatch. This way we'd do a lot more than simply stop the theft of a nuclear device—we'd know who wanted to steal it, and who had put up the money for them to do so.

"If the Mafia really is involved, it's potentially a bombshell development," I told Kohut when I presented my idea back at his office. "If they have a buyer already—this is very bad news. Stopping them here may not stop the next operation. It certainly won't discourage the buyer."

Kohut was too fond of his pension to give the green light. Fortunately for him, he had a superior officer to pass the buck to—Pus Face, who, an aide reported, was even now touching down on the other side of the field, beyond the roaming flocks of goats and sheep.

In my excitement about finding that the Mafia might be involved, I'd forgotten about the general. Now I was trapped.

Pus Face and I had our tearless reunion in Kohut's office twenty minutes later. He'd gained fifty pounds at least, but his face remained as blotchy as ever.

"*Commander* Marcinko," he said when he saw me. He didn't take my hand—a good thing, since it saved me from having to hunt down some antibacterial soap later on. "How are you, Dick?"

"Fine, General, yourself?"

"Pissed off," said Pus Face. "Mad. Angry." He

turned his glare toward Crapinpants, who just about did. The colonel briefed the two-star on the probes and their implication. Pus Face's nose began glowing about halfway through, and by the time the security officer was done, his entire face was as red as his pimples. He'd been put in charge of a special Pentagon security task force a few days before, and was still in the process of pulling together a staff. A successful operation to steal a nuke was the last thing he wanted to deal with. Even if the fallout on his career was likely to be light, he'd still be expected to devote considerable resources to the situation. At a minimum, that would cut into his golf time.

As of this writing, Pus Face is considered a candidate for the head of the Joint Chiefs of Staff. Pus Face earned his exalted position the old-fashioned way: He licked a thousand butts to get it. There's a long tradition in the Air Force of promoting combat pilots to leadership positions, basically on the theory that having flak explode in your face qualifies you to make the hard decisions at the top of the chain of command. The theory may be flawed, but it does contain a certain nugget of logic. Pus Face is proof of what happens when you try to "open things up" to a "variety of experiences," as a PR specialist would spin the fact that he's never served in harm's way. True, he's pushed paper around the globe: Hawaii, Germany, and even Riyadh, where he was assigned *after* the first Gulf War for a grand total of two weeks. After acting as a security flunky at Sigonella—far down on the bloated chain of command at the time—his most important job ever was to make sure a squadron of cargo planes had enough jet fuel to fulfill their mission. Not that that's not important, but it should give you some idea of the level of his "engagement" in weighty defense matters.

But I will give him this: He knows how to cover his ass. And he was definitely in that mode right now. There were a dozen* devices at the base; Pus Face wanted them moved to a safer facility immediately.

Kohut objected vehemently. Authorization to move the weapons had to come directly from his boss and would present a number of problems, not the least of which was the inherent danger involved in transporting such cargo at a moment's notice. There were a host of reasons, practical and strategic, why such a move made no sense at all. What if these probes had been designed to get the U.S. to move the devices out? What if some protest group found out? Would we start shuffling bombs and missiles around the world anytime some joker lobbed a warm can of soda over a perimeter fence?

I'm not sure how much of an impact these arguments actually had on Pus Face. The bottom line was that he didn't have the authority to order that the bombs be transported. Rather than say that, however, he turned to me and asked what I thought.

"I agree with General Kohut," I said. This was an historic occasion, the first time ever I had agreed with anything an Air Force officer had said. I celebrated by changing the subject—and pushing my own plan. "We should do everything we can to protect the weapons. But we can't stop there. These people may turn out to be quite relentless. We have to catch them in the act, and hang them up by their nuts."

---

*Again, forgive me for not being too specific.

Kohut winced as I continued. He didn't want any intrusion onto the base, and he made that clear. Pus Face, however, seemed interested. It might have been simply a reaction to Kohut's discomfort. More likely, he suddenly saw an opportunity to take a lemon and turn it into lemonade. Capturing a nuclear thief red-handed would shine even the dullest star on his collar.

Still, it wasn't the sort of idea that could be signed off on without testing the political waters back home.

"Let me take it under advisement, Dick," he said, his voice oily. He hesitated for a moment, and I got the feeling he was going to ask me if I knew what had happened to his credit card. Then he frowned and told me I was free to go.

Generous of him, really, given that my presence in Sicily was purely voluntary. I didn't bother to point that out. I went back to the hotel. When I got there, Karen told me that Danny had forwarded a Web address; Saladin had sent another fax.

The rant was familiar; a war of civilizations was coming, and devout Muslims must prepare themselves for battle. Again, the cataclysm would begin "at a time of their choosing and a place of great significance." Saladin continued on for three thousand or so words, proclaiming that the days of the crusaders were numbered. He ended by saying, "Yesterday was nothing. Look to the future."

The page had been dated yesterday. Which meant the reference *might* have been to St. Peter's. At least in Karen's eyes.

"It was more general than that," I told her. "It's like saying the past. This is why people think Nostradamus predicted the future," I added. "If you say something generic enough, it can be interpreted in many ways."

"You still think he's just a crazy?"

"He's definitely a crazy."

"You know what I mean, Dick." She frowned, and I felt a little uneasy, as if I'd let her down.

"I don't think he's a serious contender for bin Laden's spot at the top of the food chain. Even if he had something to do with that tanker, there are too many other legitimate candidates."

"If he's responsible for the murders in St. Peter's, that would add to his reputation."

"To an extent. But it wasn't spectacular enough."

"Because of you."

There was only one way to meet that argument— I kissed her, and suggested a little downtime before dinner.

Though pleasurable, that may have been a mistake, since it meant I was in the hotel when Frankie called forty-five minutes later.

"Do you want to meet at the airport in the morning, or can you find your own transportation?"

"Excuse me?" I said.

"Naples. Do you need a ride, or do you have your own transportation?"

"What's in Naples?"

"Our car thief, remember? The Italians have a good lead on him and are setting up an operation to arrest him," said Frankie. "I figured you'd want to be in on it."

"Not even tempted. I can't stand Naples."

"Naples?" said Karen, lying on the bed next to me.

"I've always wanted to see an opera there. When are we going?"

Naples is a crowded, dirty little city on the western coast of Italy below Rome, about where the shin would be if the peninsula really were a leg. It's belonged to just about everyone during its checkered history. It will always hold a special place in my heart: Some of the best bar fights of my life took place there.

Whether it was body memory or just the humidity, my knuckles swelled as I pulled the bright blue *polizia* windbreaker over the top of my black BDUs and stepped out of the car. Frankie, the FBI liaison, and I had driven about fifteen minutes north of the city, where we rendezvoused with a hastily assembled Italian strike force in the parking lot of an abandoned fish restaurant. State policemen and members of the GIS or *Gruppo Intervento Speciale*, one of Italy's counterterrorist squads, were getting ready for the show, adjusting the straps on their body armor and double-checking their ammo. It had been quite some time since I'd worked with the GIS boys, and I didn't know any of the kids around me. Two of them checked me out, making sure I had a bulletproof vest underneath the windbreaker, and offering me a helmet, which I declined. Their concern for my safety was touching, but what really impressed me was that someone had gone to the trouble of finding an H&K P7 pistol for me, just like the model Italy's gun importation rules had forced me to keep home. The German handguns are not entirely rare in Italy, and maybe it was just a coincidence, but it would be just like an Italian to take the trouble to find out what sort of weapon I preferred to pack. They're awesome hosts.

The Mafia bosses our suspect worked for had a nice little complex up the road, a kind of auto service mall and detail shop for stolen vehicles. Once delivered, cars were inspected, then altered in a state-of-the-art shop that exchanged some of the manufacturer's parts for less-expensive replacements. These could be sold elsewhere, often used to make shipments of fakes appear authentic. A body shop in the complex could change a vehicle's appearance if desired. There was even a railroad siding where the vehicles were loaded onto cars and shipped out, usually to Bari on the other side of the peninsula. There they would be taken aboard ship and transported to Africa, Asia, or the Middle East. Interestingly, the docks at Naples were never used, at least according to the inspector with the anti-Mafia unit of the national police who'd briefed us on the way over. He suspected this was because of a disagreement between different members of the local criminal hierarchy, but it may just have been an effort to keep prices down. Mafia control of the port made using it very expensive, and even the mob avoided it if possible.

You can't put together an operation like that without a great deal of cooperation or at least strategic inattention from the authorities. There's crime and then there's crime, but this was more like a business enterprise. The local Mafia expert, a police lieutenant named Carlo di Giovanni, estimated that the auto ring handled between fifty and a hundred cars a week, every week. Both supply and demand were considerably higher, he claimed; the ring kept a lid on the number of vehicles transported to ensure fat profits and steady work.

Frankie and the FBI liaison had been very careful when explaining why Biondi had to be apprehended. Sigonella had not been mentioned at all. Biondi, they said, was wanted for crimes against Americans on Sicily. Frankie had hinted that a general's car had been stolen and that the general demanded a scalp; *la vendetta* was a concept the Italians not only understood but wouldn't question too deeply.

Three dozen members of the national police anti-Mafia unit, along with two dozen GIS people, would raid the complex, moving in after the suspect arrived. Another dozen policemen were already ringing the place. Sanmarco Biondi was being trailed in the city by an eight-member team using six cars; they'd watched him steal a Mercedes ten minutes earlier and were on their way north now. Our helicopters were in the air and would be arriving any second.

The plan looked great on paper; whether it would work or not depended on a number of factors impossible to predict.

Not the least of which was Biondi, who managed to slip the trail team shortly after we took off.

Situation normal: all fucked up.

The Italians in charge of the operation immediately began debating what to do—move in now, or wait until he showed. The national police captain said wait; the GIS people said go.

Situation normal, stage two, otherwise known as TARFU: Things Are Really Fucked Up.

The argument continued for a good twenty minutes. During that time, Biondi had not only failed to show up, but the units posted near the complex reported that the lights that had been seen earlier had been extinguished.

Situation normal, third and final stage: FUBAR—Fucked Up Beyond All Repair.

Everyone now agreed it was time to drop in. It took maybe five minutes for the choppers to land, and another sixty seconds for the teams to secure the facility. Things went so quickly Mr. Murphy didn't even get a chance to pop his head in.

Maybe because he was too busy laughing it off nearby. There were exactly two people in the complex; both looked old enough to have helped kick the Germans off the island in World War II. Instead of the dozen or so Mercedes, Jaguars, and other premium autos we'd been briefed to expect, the building at the center of the complex contained a beat-up Fiat and a bicycle that had seen its best days before Mussolini had been born.

Clearly, the Mafia had been tipped off.

The anti-Mafia policemen were used to this sort of thing, and took it in stride. The GIS people wanted to vent their frustrations by using the auto repair sheds to brush up on their demolition skills, but the commanders overruled them. Blowing up buildings without a court order is frowned on in Italy. And here I thought they were an enlightened society.

Frankie rode with me back to the opera to pick up Karen. When we were a few blocks away, he thanked me for my help. I'd told him I could only stay for a few days and he figured that with this fiasco I'd be gone.

"What are you going to do next?" I asked.

"That's up to the Air Force. But I think our best bet is probably looking for Biondi."

"Biondi's not going to turn up," I told him. "More than likely he's dead."

Frankie thought about it for a moment, then nodded. "Do you need a flight back to Sicily?"

"I was thinking of hanging around Naples for a few days," I told him. "Karen's never been here. I thought I'd show her the sights. You can always call me if something comes up, but I don't think there's much for me to do back at Sigonella."

Frankie shrugged. Given that I was a volunteer— and a forced one at that—neither he nor anyone else was in a position to tell me what to do.

The Mafia operation had impressed the hell out of me. It also scared me, in a way. If those guys were trying to steal a nuclear bomb, sooner or later they'd succeed. Not necessarily at Sigonella—Crapinpants had made enough changes and brought in enough people that even Red Cell would have a difficult time snatching the family jewels. But there were dozens of other installations around Europe. The scary thing was that the American ones were the best protected.

I'd decided to stay in Naples to do some sightseeing, all right, but what I wanted to see wasn't in any of the tour books.

Eighteen hours later, after a day on the beach with Karen, a drive on the local highway in a rented Testarossa, and a brief nap, I took Karen to the airport and bid her a fond *arrivederci*. Then I made my way back to the city's narrowest streets, looking for a café frequented by career pickpockets and other low-level thieves. (I'd say that it was in a seedy part of town, but *seedy* describes ninety-five percent of the city.) I gave the room a preemptory scowl as I entered, a non-verbal warning not to fuck with the newcomer. Then I walked over to the corner where the two meanest-looking dirtbags were sharing a table and straight vermouths.

"What the fucking hell is this bullshit all about anyway?" snapped the short one as I sat down.

"And it's a pleasure to see you as well, Trace," I told Trace Dahlgren, pulling out a chair. She may not have a drop of Italian blood in her, but she had the Neapolitan death stare down.

"Hey, Dick," said Sean Mako. He pointed to the vermouth, which I'd told them to order. "I don't have to drink this stuff, do I? It's kind of sweet."

"It was just to let the owner know you were okay," I told him. "He's the son of an old friend." I doubted anyone else had ever ordered vermouth since the place had opened.

I called over a waiter and got us a bottle of Pelle-grino, which is Italian for overpriced water. Then I filled them in on the situation. Sean reacted the way Sean reacts to everything. He grunted once or twice, nodded a few times more, and basically recorded everything I said without saying a word. Trace, on the other hand, obviously hadn't had much sleep on the plane. Even bitchier than normal, she cursed up an unladylike storm about the incompetence of everyone from the U.S. Air Farce to the Italian GIS. This was a very good sign—several weeks of training tadpoles had made her more ornery than ever. Woe be to anyone tonight who got in our way.

We were going back to the auto mall. I wasn't interested in Biondi—as I'd told Frankie I thought he was probably dead. It was the headman I wanted. To save myself the trouble of hunting him down, I planned on leaving my calling card and then making it easy for him to find me. As an incentive, I'd borrow the shop foreman and make it worth his while to call for help.

The briefing for last night's operation stated that the mechanics typically arrived just after 9 p.m., about a half hour ahead of the first stolen car. They'd fire up the espresso maker, make sure their equipment was ready to go, then wait. The vehicles crossed the threshold every twenty to thirty minutes once things got going. That suggested one of two approaches to getting into the facility—arrive an hour or so ahead of time and surprise the workers when they arrived, or drive up in a stolen vehicle and take them during the operation.

Taking them beforehand not only seemed easier but had the extra benefit of conserving time, and so we took that option. Unfortunately, our intelligence proved to be inadequate. Biking over around seven-thirty to do the pre-strike recce, I discovered that guards in pickup trucks had already taken up positions blocking the two winding dirt-and-gravel roads that led into the complex. I could hear the sound of an air-drive ratchet in the distance; our friends were already at work. I went down the road a bit, then circled back to Sean and Trace, waiting in a van I'd rented earlier in the day. There's a little car thief in all of us, and so it wasn't surprising that Trace wanted to fall back to plan B: steal some vehicles and get in through the front door. But di Giovanni hadn't mentioned the guards, and I wondered what else he'd left out or simply didn't know. It was not inconceivable that the people guarding the roads had lists of the expected thieves or the vehicles that would appear that night. While we could blast our way past the pickups, any gunfire would alert the people inside the complex.

Smarter and safer, I thought, to simply sneak around the perimeter, grab what we wanted, and leave. A hypo of Demerol would keep him quiet on the way out. We were armed, of course—it's easy to get weapons in Naples, even the MP5Ns I prefer, and we'd also stocked up on flashbangs, radio gear, and other goodies—but my preference was to complete the operation without inflicting casualties if possible. The *Mafiosi* were going to be pissed enough as it was.

The railroad tracks provided an easy route into the complex, and a fresh recce showed they were unguarded. That's often the case. No one expects a locomotive to sneak up on them.

We stashed the van and made our way up the siding, moving to within about thirty yards of the main building. The *Mafiosi* had moved two railroad cars into the complex earlier in the day, and we'd have no trouble getting right up to the cars without being seen. But there were two roustabout types taking turns breaking bottles near the rails, in between loading the cars. They weren't paying enough attention to be a direct threat. Even so, we couldn't count on walking right by them to the building without being seen. Skirting them meant backtracking fifty yards to a rock-strewn slope, descending about fifty feet, and then circling through a grassy field to come around on the other side of the building. I told Trace it was her turn to stay behind as tail gunner; by the time her kvetching ended, Sean and I had gone through the field. We crawled ten feet behind a low wall and had a clear view into the main building where the cars were worked on. The lights inside the warehouse threw a large rectangle of white out into the macadam in front, making it easy for us to see if anyone came out of the building. The light succumbed to shadows within ten yards or so; everything beyond that was pitch black. As long as we stayed outside that box of light, we would be invisible.

I could see two cars inside the warehouse, a Ford on a lift, and a Mercedes sitting near the door with its hood up. Two other Mercedes were parked in front, waiting their turn. As I watched, a mechanic closed the hood on the Mercedes inside. He started it up, snapped on the lights, and drove it out of the garage down to the railroad car, where the roustabouts guided him across the metal planks as he loaded up. Meanwhile, another worker came out and took one of the other Mercedes inside. Within four or five minutes, another car came up the road to take its place. The driver behind the wheel of the car, an Audi A8, bore more than a passing resemblance to a former U.S. president. To this day I'm convinced it *was* him, seeking a more honorable profession than politics in his retirement. He closed the door on the vehicle and walked back down the hill. The workers inside the garage went about their business without acknowledging the arrival of the car or even seeming to notice.

So far, I hadn't seen a foreman or anyone who looked like he was in charge. We could just grab one of the mechanics, of course, but I wanted someone more valuable to the operation; I had to leave for Germany the day after tomorrow, and wanted this taken care of before then. I told Sean I was going to go over to the side of the building where there were windows and see what the layout was, but before I could hop over the wall a dark blue Fiat sedan pulled up the road.

It was obvious right away that this wasn't a stolen car. The vehicle was several years old, and had slight but noticeable damage to the grille. It also pulled right up near the door.

Can you guess who got out of the car? No, not Biondi. Police Lieutenant di Giovanni. I guess he was *very* qualified to be a Mafia expert. The workers couldn't genuflect fast enough or low enough as he walked into the warehouse: *He* was the capo of the operation.

All right, then, I thought. This was going to be dirt easy. The *paesani* in the warehouse were unarmed. Sean and I would trot over and wait by the door for di Giovanni to come out. I'd grab him, Sean would toss a few flashbangs on the ground, and we'd drive away happily ever after.

And that's *exactly* what happened.

Almost.

4

Sean and I had just trotted to the shadows at the side of the building when two pairs of headlights started up the road. We took a few steps back and hunkered close to the building. I sensed something was wrong as one set of headlights arced to the left, the vehicle pulling up behind di Giovanni's. But it wasn't until I saw that the vehicle was a van that I knew what was happening.

"Shit!" I yelled.

The van's side door flew open and two men jumped out, machine guns blazing.

"Dick?" said Trace over the radio as the warehouse lit up.

"It's some sort of ambush—get di Giovanni into the car," I yelled to Sean. "Trace—we'll meet you in front of the warehouse. Take the second van."

Sean kicked a flashbang under the van while I leveled my MP5 at the jokers with the machine guns. They'd been decked out in style—Belgium Minimis and bulletproof vests complete with ceramic inserts; their employer didn't skimp. The plates are excellent protection even at close range against anything smaller than a howitzer. Problem is, they don't do jack for bullets in the head.

Rather than pulling up behind the other vehicle, the second van accelerated and swooped to the left, flanking the first. Realizing that this would take it too far from Trace to easily deal with, I yelled for her to help Sean and then put two shots into the windshield, taking out the driver. The vehicle lurched against the wall, stopping with a crash; the door flew open and five or six men emerged, all firing Minimis in my general direction. I ate dirt, pushing the earthworms away as I crawled to the wall and hopped over. Sean was already inside the warehouse—I could hear him in my earbud—but I couldn't tell where Trace was.

Somewhere around about here, a voice in my head pointed out that my presence in the Naples area was voluntary and unpaid, the point being that if I was going to do something utterly stupid like get my anatomy remodeled, I ought to at least be on someone else's workman's comp policy.

The voice didn't belong to my conscience; it was far too practical and sober for that. It was Karen, who was sitting in the observer/copilot's seat of a Bell JetRanger, coming in hot and heavy from the south. She was watching the escapade with the help of a long-range starlight video camera secured to the nose.

(*Arrivederci* means see you soon, and this was more than soon enough. She didn't have to go home until tomorrow night. Her role in the operation had been to secure the helicopter, which in typical Italian fashion was a good half hour behind schedule. But I wasn't in a position to complain.)

"Buzz these bastards while I flank them," I told her. "I'll get south of them when you pass. Don't come back a second time—I don't want you getting hurt."

"You'll never hear the end of it if we do," she said. "This damn helicopter costs a fortune."

By the time the people with the machine guns hit the dirt, I had managed to get almost all the way behind them. As dust sprayed everywhere, I hopped back over the wall and ran forward so I could see what I was shooting at. Unfortunately, I ran into an obstacle along the way—a guard from the other road who'd double-timed up to find out what all the commotion was. We rebounded off each other maybe six feet, both stunned by the collision.

Stunned is a condition I'm familiar with. I hopped up and gave him a kick to the head to keep him on the ground. I would certainly have shot him, except that I'd dropped my MP5 in the collision.

By the time I found it, the people from the van were emptying their Minimis at the chopper, which had the pedal to the metal and was disappearing beyond the hill. Their gunfire made it easy to see where they were, and I emptied the MP5 at them.

Inside the warehouse, Sean found di Giovanni cowering behind one of the vehicles, a 9mm Beretta shaking in his hands. Sean batted it out of his hands, gave di Giovanni a swat, and then poked him with the Demerol. He threw him over his shoulder and hustled outside just after the helicopter passed, streaking to my right as I fired at the Minimi *amici*.

The men in the van had killed the guards on the road they took up to the site. But they'd left the other set intact, figuring to get away before they could respond or call in reinforcements. Those reinforcements were now en route, or so it looked to Karen, who saw four pickups tearing up the highway from a farm two miles away. Worried that the helicopter would be an easy target if it landed nearby, I told her we'd meet her at the parking lot we'd used the night before.

"The last Mercedes," I yelled to Sean, stuffing a fresh magazine in my MP5 and backing toward it. I stopped at the car in front of it, pried open the gas cover, then took a handkerchief out of my pocket. Two or three of the bozos back by the van began firing in my direction as I lit and pushed the burning rag into the gas opening. The vapor system on the vehicle was in good repair, preventing the car from exploding . . .

. . . for about five seconds. Then a thick arm of fire shot out from the vehicle, and the luxury sedan lit up the night.

I barely got our car backed away in time, whipping around only a dozen yards from the flames. As I started down the road I saw the pickup truck that had been guarding the turnoff barreling straight for us from below. Probably unsure whether we were on his side or not, he veered to the left, trying to block the roadway. I veered to the left as well, which got me around him more or less intact, minus a little scraped paint and lost chrome as I glanced off a nearby tree. I continued a little farther, hoping to make it to the Y where the two roads met before the cavalry arrived. I didn't quite make it, as the quartet of high beams announced.

Quartet, as in four across. The trucks were driving side by side, trying to block the road.

When a certain strategy succeeds, my motto is to keep using it until you beat it to death. So I waited until the last possible moment again, then veered hard left. Not having my headlights on, I didn't know how close I was to the wall at the side of the road.

The answer was: very.

We rebounded back, smacking the front fender of the first pickup and twisting into a mangled pretzel of a car wreck. The front end of the Mercedes crumpled down like an accordion and the airbags deployed; I found myself sucking formaldehyde-treated plastic, or whatever the hell it is that they make those damn things with.

Airbags fetch a good price on the black market, and the markup was too tempting for the local *Mafiosi* to resist. As bad as swallowing airbag dust may be, it's better than going through the windshield, which is what happened to at least two of the people in the pickups. Another four or five of the men who'd been traveling in the rear beds went airborne, splashing on the road behind us.

We weren't making a commercial for the Traffic Safety Department, so we didn't bother to count the victims. I helped Sean pull di Giovanni from the car as Trace did a *Crouching Tiger/Slashing Mafia* routine, demonstrating her martial arts skills on two thugs who had the misfortune to come through the car accident intact. We left them reeling as we retreated down the hill, through the woods and to the van. Ten minutes later, we were in the JetRanger, heading back to the airport. Di Giovanni snored loudly in the backseat. I borrowed the chopper pilot's phone to call Frankie after we touched down to refuel.

"We'll have a deposit for you in about two hours," I told him. "The capo of the car operation."

"Who?"

"Di Giovanni. The Mafia expert. I don't know how much he knows about Biondi and what he was up to. I can't ask him until he wakes up." I glanced at my watch. If past experience was any guide, he'd be out for three more hours. "After that, we can figure out what to do next."

"Di Giovanni?"

"Yeah, the Mafia expert. Hopefully he's important enough to get the big boss involved, whoever that is. I doubt we'll get any straight answers from di Giovanni, at least not that we can trust."

"There's more to this than we thought," said Frankie. "A lot more."

Oh, if I'd only known how right he was.

Part Two

Old Friends

Our reliance is in the love of liberty which God has planted in our bosoms. Our defense is in the preservation of the spirit which prizes liberty as the heritage of all men, in all lands, everywhere.

—ABRAHAM LINCOLN

5

The gunfire at the warehouse site did not attract the local police—surprise, surprise—but within an hour, calls were being made to locate di Giovanni. By the time we arrived in Sicily, Kohut had taken calls from several Italian officials, including what in America would be the attorney general's office. Our presence as observers on the raid the night before was just a little too coincidental. Apparently di Giovanni's associates decided they would do better with him in the government's custody than in ours. This surely meant that they had decided to terminate the association, something I pointed out to di Giovanni when he came to in the hangar we appropriated at Sigonella after landing. We could help him, I said, but only if he helped us.

Still groggy from the drugs, di Giovanni blinked at me but said nothing. I asked a few questions about Biondi, which he answered with more blinks and then a shrug and shake of his head. When I asked about *terroriste* on the island, he responded with a genuinely puzzled stare.

Trace offered to give him a personal Jeet Kune Do

demonstration, but I vetoed it. Frankie was already on his way over with some marines to take charge of the prisoner. Denting his fenders wasn't going to get us anywhere. There are definitely situations where the application of acute force can yield timely results. In this case, though, it seemed unlikely. The Mafia code of silence, or *omertà*, may be overrated, but it still takes more than a few dinks and dunks to get someone at di Giovanni's level to speak freely. The pressure has to build over time, psychologically as well as physically. Besides, he was still fairly doped up; I doubt he would have felt half of the pain Trace inflicted.

Frankie arrived a few minutes later. Kohut was spitting bullets over at his office, convinced that I had created an international incident for the sole purpose of screwing up his retirement. Di Giovanni was to be turned over to the Italian authorities immediately, if not sooner.

"If you do that, you'll never get anything from him about Biondi or anyone else," I told him. "I doubt he'll live twenty-four hours."

"Agreed," said Frankie. "But Crapinpants won't say boo, and I'm low man on the totem pole here. It's Kohut's ballgame."

"Did you point out that the *terroriste* are still around?" I asked.

"The Italian government apparently worries him more. I checked with the ambassador," Frankie added. "I thought I ought to give him a heads-up. He said it's a military matter, and he'll back whatever the Pentagon wants."

There was an opening, I thought. Kohut wasn't the Pentagon; he was just the local Air Farce commander, who could be overruled if the circumstances warranted. The trick was finding the person with balls enough to overrule him.

Pus Face?

It was worth a try.

The aide who answered the general's phone must have thought I was a bill collector. The general had left orders that he not be disturbed, and it took the words *nuclear catastrophe* to get the general to the phone. His first words were, "What blew up?"

"General, this is Dick Marcinko. I have the *Mafioso* responsible for trying to break into Sigonella, but Kohut wants to give him back to the Italians. We need to hold on to him long enough to flesh out the terrorist network, find out what the connections are, that sort of thing. Forty-eight hours—"

"Marcinko?" He pronounced my name as if he'd never heard it before.

"Yes?"

"Marcinko?"

This time, the tone implied that he had heard my name once too often. I turned the phone over to Frankie, figuring that as a State Department employee he would be better at diplomacy. Frankie spent about ten minutes explaining the situation. His last words were, "but—but—but"—never a good sign.

"He said he'd have to sleep on it," said Frankie, handing the phone back.

Actually, Pus Face wasn't going to be sleeping on anything. He was exhibiting typical C^2CO behavior. Translation: "Can't Cunt Commanding Officer," a species which must test the water, get ducks in a row, run the flag up the pole, etc., etc., before making a controversial decision. For all his vim and vigor a few days before, Pus Face wouldn't get off the pot or take a shit without making sure the air freshener was in place.

Ah well. It was worth a shot. Besides, I was due in Germany.

I gave di Giovanni another chance to punk out and come over to our side, but he only scowled. Frankie reluctantly turned him over to the two policemen who showed up a little past 11 a.m. the next day—the crack of dawn for an Italian government worker. By that time, I was on my way up to Rome to catch my flight to Germany.

Pretty much my whole life, I've gotten in trouble for sticking my nose where other people didn't want it. I'm so used to people telling me to fuck off that most days I figure it's part of my name. In this case, I had already gone above and beyond the call of duty. I'd done what I could to head off a theft at the base. We hadn't apprehended the tangos, but I did think that their operation had been derailed, at least temporarily. And my involvement had not cost the U.S. taxpayers a dime.

"Call me if the government wants to hire me to help flesh this out, check security procedures further, or what have you," I told Frankie when he made a pitch for me to stay—pro bono, of course. "In the meantime, I have honest work to do."

"Yeah, all right."

Maybe I'm a softy, or maybe I'm just a glutton for punishment—I felt bad when I punched the end button on the sat phone, I really did. But I still punched it.

* * *

No, I didn't abandon them *completely*. I left Trace behind, and on my dime, too. If Pus Face came to his senses or Kohut lost his, she'd be in position to help interrogate di Giovanni. In the meantime, she would work with the Air Farcers to make sure their security was up to snuff in case the tangos returned. She even volunteered to help out with morning physical training. It was a proposition the numb-nut Air Farcers promptly agreed to, no doubt relishing the idea of her in workout togs.

The poor fucks never knew what hit them.

I would not have made a good German: wiener schnitzel and oompah bands have never been my strong points. But I do love the beer. And German society has a certain precision, a kind of correctness to it that makes it easy for a visitor. You can count on the train schedules, and the bartenders always give the correct change.

Our big meeting took place in a city on the Rhine we'll call Rhineville, just on the off chance that we use it for a meeting again . . . and to help avoid possible civil suits. The people I employ work hard, and it's not unusual for them to blow off a little steam during downtime. I'd be a hypocrite if I said I couldn't understand bar fights or other team-building activities. (It's not true that we schedule them, however; the best bar fights are always spontaneous, and at Red Cell International, we always strive for the best.) As for the rumor that one of my people rode a motorcycle through the hall of a local hotel, I can categorically deny that the rumor is true.

To the best of my knowledge, at least two motor-cycles were involved.

Just kidding. We didn't stay at any of the local inns. For one thing, security would have been a bitch and a half. Even if we managed to rent the rooms incognito—and I assure you we would have—my friend Mr. Murphy would have undoubtedly had a reservation there as well. Sooner or later the word would have gotten out, tempting all sorts of crazies to try and make their bones by frying ours. I imagine we'd also be a tempting target for some of the European intelligence services. One of these days I'll kill a few trees talking about how the spying operations are directed at the U.S. by our allies. I'm not exactly a high-priority target for them, but the krauts would have been interested, if only to trade some of the information with Mossad, which likes to keep as up to date as possible on American interests in Iraq, Afghanistan, etc.

So instead of hunting down the local Holiday Inn, we went whole hog and rented a castle for our confab. I can't take the credit for finding the place. Al "Doc" Tremblay, one of the original plank holders of Red Cell and a close friend and business associate, was in charge of making the arrangements. He selected it largely on the basis that it was easy to isolate and available at a reasonable cost; the fourteenth-century battlements were just a bonus. Towers with huge helmetlike domes stood at each corner. (Imagine the Kaiser helmets used by the German army in WWI and you get the picture.) The main building was a six-sided monstrosity that rose from the battlement walls on the river side. It had apparently had its own helmet at one time, though by the time the twenty-first century arrived only a few splinters of the support timbers and the shadow of a razed stairway remained. If you didn't mind the risk of falling—in other words, if you'd had enough beer to cloud your judgment but not enough to make you lose your sense of balance— you could climb all the way to the top by wedging your fingers against the stones. From there you could see all the way to Austria and France, or at least claim that you could.

At some point in the past fifty or sixty years, the family that owned the castle had tried to operate a small hotel there. They'd built a one-story building against one of the outer walls, setting it up like a no-tell motel with rooms opening directly onto a macadam walkway. The rooms all leaked, but were otherwise serviceable as temporary dorms, with electricity and running water; we spread tarps on the roofs and prayed for clear weather. We brought in two oversized rec vehicles to use primarily as kitchens, but the best cooking by far was done on the large portable grill Doc set up in the courtyard. (I do mean large. It could handle three medium-sized pigs, though Doc preferred to roast those in a homemade pit.) We held our company meetings in a stone chapel built against the northern wall. The relics and artwork had been stripped centuries ago, but the stone altar remained. Before long I was being called Cardinal Dick by one and sundry, to whom I of course returned the favor, sprinkling a few off-color religious epithets into my usual terms of endearment.

Security-wise, the place *was* a castle. Doc and the four men he chose for the reception committee (he called it the Asshole Patrol) came in a week early and went over the place with a variety of electronic doo-dads, making sure it was clean and would stay that way. Doc must have bought or borrowed toys from every "skunk works" we know in Europe, along with the goodies my friends at Law Enforcement Technologies in Colorado Springs lend us to field-test. Besides checking for bugs and guarding against intruders, they turned the chapel into a secure conferencing facility. It may not have been as secure as No Such Agency's "black" operations center in Maryland (they don't exist; you can't get any more secure than that), but by the time they were done, eavesdropping was out of the question.

There were only three ways in and out, each easily closed off and guarded. Small video cameras, as well as posted watchmen, surveyed the countryside and nearby river. We could have withstood a company-sized assault for three or four days, at least.

Our presence was explained in the nearby town with rumors that a secretive American pop band had rented the castle for rehearsals. According to the rumors, the band itself wasn't supposed to arrive for another month—Doc had taken a three-month lease—so there was no reason for the curious to come out and sneak a peak.

My "vacation" in Italy had left me out of the loop for a few days, and I had a lot of catching up to do on our various projects. Afghanistan was at the top of the list, of course, but our accounts in Iraq, Turkey, and Romania required hand-holding as well. Not that I mean to be so flip: My people had their nuts on the line in each and every instance, and they deserved and got my undivided attention. My name is the one at the top of the letterhead, but let me give credit where credit is due: Red Cell International kicks butt because every single employee is first-rate. Honestly, the men and women who work with me make *me* better, and there's not a day that goes by that I don't realize that.

Not that they don't point it out constantly . . .

Some of what we talked about had to do with commonsense security precautions and where to draw the line when taking risks. You can't get too risk adverse in this field, but on the other hand you have to be able to keep everything in balance. It's one thing when a country's survival is on the line; I have no problem fighting for my country or ordering others to do so, even if it means close friends are likely to go home in a plastic baggie. It sucks big time. Believe me when I say I know exactly how *much* it sucks, but it's a necessary part of the struggle to remain free.

Getting killed so some corporate suit can report a five percent increase in annual profits is another matter entirely. I see absolutely no reason someone like Doc Tremblay should endanger his personal retirement plans to fatten Ken Lay's 401k.

The first three days of our five-day conference were a blast. Day One began before the sun rose with group PT in the castle yard, under Tiffany Alexander's grueling, sadistic leadership. Tiffany learned from the best—Trace Dahlgren—and she was every bit as evil as the master that first morning, jacking the bp of every male in the courtyard simply by rolling up the sleeves on her tight-fitting Lycra sweats and warming the group up with a few bends and stretches. By the time she moved onto fart-jacks, groans were echoing off the stones. Workouts with Trace are always motivational. She knows how to goose the male ego and make you feel like an absolute wimp-shit if you can't keep up. And you *can't* keep up, unless she wants you to. Tiffany is slightly more subtle. You look at her and you just *know* you can't let her down by failing to give her that one, last, impossible repetition . . . and the next and the next and the next. Because if you didn't, you would break her heart. And you'd never want to do that.

Meanwhile, she's hopping up and down like the Energizer Bunny, not even breaking a sweat. ("Women don't sweat, Dick. They perspire. But they don't even do that. Now, can I have ten more push-ups, please? Just your left arm this time.")

My butt hung close to the ground by the time PT ended after ninety minutes. If we'd been back at Rogue Manor, I would have been able to escape by claiming there was paperwork to catch up on, but there was no rest for the wicked in Germany. Sean had organized a five-mile predawn run. In theory, it was a strictly voluntary affair, but of course it was mandatory, especially for yours truly. Being older than everyone else, or nearly everyone else, on my team brings with it a certain responsibility to keep up with the Joneses. If I can't quite beat their asses like I used to—I have to try harder.

I don't mind running, and even at my allegedly advanced age, eight-minute miles aren't too taxing. But good old Sean decided that things would be much more interesting if we ran with full packs. He loaded the packs with metal barbell weights and paper to keep them from shifting while we were running. Supposedly the packs were simulating combat kits. A "normal" (if there is such a thing) rucksack load for a special operator might weigh forty pounds or so, with as much of that as possible being ammunition. (You'd also carry as much as you could in a tactical vest, as well as in your pockets, on your belt, your head, clipped to your nose—you *cannot* have too many bullets.) But these packs were definitely heavier than forty pounds. One or two of my shooters questioned him about that. Sean just shrugged and said Danny had loaded them, and to take up the matter with him.

I've noticed that Marine officers have a little bit of the sadist in them, and even though he's retired from the Corps, Danny's no exception. Maybe it's learned behavior from basic, where Marine drill instructors are reputed to remain the most seriously ill fuckers in the business. Maybe that camo they apply to their faces does something to their brains. All I know is, complaining is the very worst thing you can do; it only encourages them. So I took my pack and carried it without a word.

Whatever the pack weighed when I started, it felt five times heavier by the end of the first mile. My chest heaved and I was having the damnedest time keeping up. I'm built more like a linebacker than a receiver, and I accept that I can't keep up with the rabbits on my team, but ordinarily I can keep them relatively close, especially on a five-mile course where endurance is a little more important than sheer speed. But that morning it seemed like everyone was kicking my butt, even young Shit-in-Ass. (If he has a name other than that, no one has used it at Red Cell International since he came aboard. It's printed on all his paychecks.)

Now first let me say that Shit-in-Ass is a very fine shooter and an excellent all-around SpecWarrior. Allegedly, one of the youngest soldiers to get Ranger-qualified—he enlisted with the help of some bogus documents, a fact the Army did not particularly appreciate when they found out several years later—Shit-in-Ass found his real calling as a demolitions expert. I'm not talking about garden-variety demolition either. Shit-in-Ass is a true artist, creative and knowledgeable. The young man can blow up a bridge with the stuff you have under your kitchen sink. He's the only person I know who can open a door with C4 and not only leave the door intact but leave it standing on its hinges. (I, by contrast, would turn it into a toothpick. But then no one has ever accused me of being cheap with explosives.)

But Shit-in-Ass got his nickname on his very first day of boot camp because of the way he ran, and the name stuck. A big Louisiana lad, his butt hangs down so far, the seat of his sweats are in danger of scraping the ground. Plop-plop-plop he runs, and with every step his backend gets lower and lower. He always manages to finish somehow; it must have something to do with the law of gravity. But he is always at the end of the line. Back home, I'm sure he's a "card carrying" coon-ass!

Except for that morning. When we hit the mile mark that morning, I was staring at his low-riding butt, not a pretty sight. I'm not ashamed to say that this pissed me off, and I sprinted to catch up, cursing at myself for missing several days of road work and obviously falling out of shape. This was the wrong thing to do—I caught and passed him about two hundred yards later, but we had a long way to go, and the sprint drained my reserves. By the end of the second mile, Shit-in-Ass was huffin' and puffin' in my ear. I held on through the third mile, telling myself that I wasn't getting old. Even if I was getting old, I wasn't letting these young bastards kick my ass in public. By the fourth mile, I was conceding that I *was* getting old, but that I was not going to be the last one back at the castle. The pack had started to bunch up a bit and I was able to draw within ten yards or so, husbanding my strength for the last half-mile.

Anyone can run a half-mile. A half-mile is nothing. Eight hundred and eighty measly stinking yards. I've pissed farther than that.

I had about ten yards on Shit-in-Ass and was about twenty behind everyone else when the castle ramparts came into view. The sun was just coming up over the horizon and one of the vans we'd taken out to keep an eye on the runners had pulled across the road ahead. Eighteen huffing and puffing shooters spread out in front of me, each runner a marker on my way to respectability. If I passed nine, I'd have a respectable, middle-of-the pack showing.

I leaned forward and humped into high gear. My side stitched up and I got a cramp the size of Colorado in my left calf. Now I've been through a hell of a lot worse on runs like this. I had diarrhea during UDT Hell Week (Underwater Demolition Training, roughly the equivalent of today's BUDS school for SEALs). I ran just fast enough to escape the stench of the shit dripping down my leg and complete the required laps. This was nothing compared to that.

But it wasn't kicking back on the couch with a beer and a bowl of chips, either. The people I was running with were every bit as competitive as I was. They might not have been used to beating my furry little ass into the ground on a morning run, but now that they had me in their rearview mirrors they wanted to keep me there. I could hear the growls and curses as I picked up speed and passed runner number seventeen. (I forget who was where in the line.) Sixteen started to sprint a half-second before I caught her. Fifteen was already fading but fourteen matched my pace and started to pull ahead. He didn't wear down until we hit the entrance to the castle; by then, we had pulled into the lead of our little section, finishing exactly at the midpoint of the group.

I shed my pack, flopped to the ground, then rolled back up to my feet, sensing that if I didn't wind my muscles down gradually I'd seize up into a statue and end up a lawn ornament. A big cooler of Gatorade had been set up near the north wall; I figured I'd hydrate and then hit the showers before breakfast. I was just about at the cooler when I realized that Sean, Danny, and Tiffany were laughing their asses off a few yards away. It was only then that I realized I had been seriously had. My pack had been weighed down to simulate a combat load, but everyone else ran with paper packed into their rucks. The whining had been a ruse to make me think everyone was being treated the same: like shit.

Slimebags.

Of course, the fact that even so I had managed a decent finish meant the joke was on them, even if they were laughing.

I didn't mention it, and neither did they. They still don't know that I know what they did—or at least they didn't, until they read this.

The run earned everybody a hearty breakfast, postshower. Then we moved on to the entertainment portion of the program. We'd imported a Krav Maga specialist for an early-morning self-defense demonstration. For most of my people, this was just a brushup; the Israeli martial arts have been integrated into special-ops training over the past few years. But others were learning about the skill for the first time, and were impressed by the ability of the instructor to take down two armed assailants before they had a chance to shoot him.

The assailants *were* armed, and not with blanks. As part of the show, the instructor fired their weapons after the men were subdued. Theatrical, but effective.

The afternoon consisted of two weapons seminars, with a demonstration of new nonlethal grenades and a Taser that could shock a bear at one hundred yards, a good distance farther than standard weapons. One of the grenades carried a net and tear gas combination to snare and disable a subject. We had some fun with a few of the grenades that lacked the tear gas. Tiffany found that the key to dealing with the net was to take a Zen-like approach, calmly slipping it off rather than going at the sticky material willy-nilly. This would be harder with tear gas in your eyes, of course, but still possible. Nonlethal weapons are very much in vogue these days, both with police departments and military units tasked to dealing with civilian populations in urban environments, either as occupation troops or peacekeepers. But they've got a way to go before they're going to be a reliable answer to old-fashioned lead. Frankly, if somebody pulls a gun on me, I want my answer to be as lethal as possible. Let somebody else take a chance on fancy nets or sonic-wave machines, another crowd-control device being tested by the Army.

Cocktail hour, dinner, and then civilian-style entertainment capped the night. Nothing's too good for my employees, and while I bust their buns in the field, I do try to find ways to make it all worthwhile. Toward this end I had arranged to deploy several big-name entertainers to Europe, including a rap star and a comedian so funny and so foul-mouthed that he had us all in stitches before he even opened his mouth. For security reasons, the entertainers weren't told in advance exactly where they were going, and the rap star was a little touchy because the ground rules called for no "bling bling." But I'd had personal dealings with each person before, and they welcomed the chance to do the shows, provided their regular fees were paid. We met them at a nearby airport, blindfolded 'em, choppered them in and choppered them out.

During the day, Danny, Doc, and I went through a regular series of debriefings, pulling guys out from sessions and basically getting them to brain dump on their situations. I asked as few questions as possible, trying not to get in the way as they regurgitated what they'd been through over the past ten to twelve months. Nearly as important for getting a true snap of the world situation were the evening "mixers," a genteel term for keg parties, itself a euphemism for the open-ended festivities following the entertainment portion of the program. Alcohol may not improve the memory, but it certainly loosens the tongue.

Before heading over to Europe, I'd studied the after-action reports, incident briefings, and situationers, so I had a context to fit the gossip into. We don't do much paperwork at Red Cell Inc. but we do pay attention to the institutional memory that can help other members and future operations. For the last two or three years, we've used digital camcorders for more reports, dumping everything into a computer system that uses a language translator to form an index. (It's good, but not perfect; I'd say there's a fifty-fifty chance that "cock breath" will show up as "cocktail bread," a whole other thing.) The reports were pretty good, but the face-to-face sessions and lubricated debriefs gave me details that didn't seem important to the people in the field. Afghan tribesmen wearing boots instead of sneakers cut from tires, for example. M16s with grenade launchers replacing AK-47s in the field. Modern line-of-sight and satellite radios instead of tin cans for communications—all developments of the past three to four months in Afghanistan, and all signs that an outside source was shoveling funds to the local yokels.

This coincided with the noticeable uptick in attacks on our company personnel. Coincidence? I think not.

The main actor in these attacks was a mujahideen group under the leadership of Ali Goatfuck, a doctor who'd failed his licensing exam in Libya (which tells you how smart he was) before finding his true calling as a butcher for Allah in the borderland southwest of Islamabad, Pakistan. Our various sources said Goat-fuck called the shots from the safety of Pakistan, leaving his mostly teenage followers to take the risks in Afghanistan. After two days and nights of gathering information, Doc, Danny, and I had a board meeting to discuss what we had found. We took all of five seconds to a reach a consensus: Ali Goatfuck had to be caught and strung up by the short hairs, assuming he had any, the sooner the better. It would have to be done on the company dime—the U.S. wouldn't be interested because it was in Pakistan, and asking the Pakis to do anything would be about as useful and rewarding as pissing into the wind.

I tasked Danny to come up with a plan by the end of the week.

"Slicing Goatfuck's neck will take care of half the problem," I told the boys. "Next we have to find out who's got the bankroll and hang *him* up by the short hairs."

"Follow the money," said Danny. He spent a good number of years living off the taxpayers as a detective with the D.C. police department, picking up investigative skills as well as an affection for doughnuts. The cash that was funding the guerillas would be a direct line back to the real slimebags we wanted—and very likely one of the people angling for Osama's spot as top raghead.

Saladin, perhaps?

The idea certainly occurred to me. Saladin had singled me out obviously; that's why I was getting the faxes. It wasn't unreasonable that he had given money to Ali Goatfuck (and presumably others) with the expectation that my people would be targeted, quid pro quo. From what I could see, the idea wasn't necessarily to get me, or at least that wasn't a main goal. Saladin wanted attention: publicity, fame, anything that would lift him in the eyes of the maniacs he wanted to follow him in the Great War of Civilizations, as he called it. Taking on Demo Dick was a means to that larger end.

Of course, it could be someone with a grudge; there were plenty of those. The one thing I knew for sure was that this wasn't going to end with us taking out Goatfuck; we had to terminate his sugar daddy as well.

First we had to find him. Danny suggested that the trail of bank transfers would lay out the framework of the organization, showing where all of its nooks and crannies were. That sounded good in theory, but in real life it was going to be harder to do than finding a speck of flour in a snowstorm. We might be able to do it when we got Ali Goatfuck—but only if he got his money from a bank, and only then if he kept some sort of paper record of his transactions that we could use to find the account. Call me cynical, but I'm guessing Goatfuck would be a cash-and-carry kind of guy.

"I say, follow the shoes," suggested Doc. "These guys are all wearing new boots. A lot of people have mentioned them. Made by Bota, or something like that. Mountain boots, not combat boots and certainly not the rubber tires they were wearing a few months back." He dug into his pocket for the small memo pad he'd used to take notes. The boots were high quality, light, with a rigid sole. One of our guys who did technical climbs said they were on par with mountaineering boots made by Scarpa or Kayland, shoes used by professionals that would go for more than $300 a pair. "They're not Nikes," added Doc. "Who paid for them? Where did they come from? There's where the money is."

"Probably stole them," said Danny. "Or smuggled them over the border."

"Maybe," said Doc. "But maybe not. They're not banned for importation or anything, and they're not obviously dangerous. Why go through the hassle of hiding them?"

"Couple of pair of shoes, shit, who's going to notice or remember, one way or another," said Danny.

"There've been more than a couple," said Doc. "Everybody has mentioned the shoes. They had to come in the same shipment at the same time—you figure Ali Goatfuck has a couple of hundred guys? Unless he gives out these boots as a door prize for going after our guys, I'll bet he outfitted his whole army with them. Two hundred boots—that's enough to remember. Serious dough, too."

Danny didn't concede exactly, but he grunted in a way that made it clear he thought it was worth checking. We decided to zero in on the shoes, asking our guys specific questions about them to try and nail down as many details as we could. Then we'd feed the information to a private investigator I knew back home who specialized in tracking down overseas assets. His most lucrative work was for divorce lawyers and plaintiffs' attorneys suing the pants off foreign companies.

I went to bed feeling as if we'd made some good progress on the problem. Even more important, I was looking forward to hurting Ali Goatfuck where it would hurt for generations.

Yes, I intended on doing more than just looking over the plan. You lead from the front, remember? Besides, I hadn't been to Pakistan since the days of the Afghanistan operations against the Russians.* I was anxious to go back. The part of the country where the mujahideen were operating is so wickedly rugged that just walking through reminds you how awesomely adaptable the human species is. I fell asleep with visions of ass-kicking dancing in my head, and my stomach fluttering from an adrenaline rush.

Alas, dreams don't always come true, and they didn't in this case. And for once, I couldn't blame Mr. Murphy.

Somewhere around 3 a.m. local time the next morning, an hour and a half before reveille (and an hour and a half after I had hit the sack), my satellite phone rang. I answered and found myself talking to a duty officer at the U.S. embassy in Rome. Before I could tell him to get bent, he told me there had been an "incident" in Sicily, and Trace needed my help right away.

"Why didn't she call me herself?" I asked.

Never ask questions you don't want to know the answer to.

Among the things that I realized after our adventure at the auto mall was that the attack we interrupted had not been engineered by another Mafia

*Can't talk about it. Sorry.

group. It wasn't because I thought a Mafia hit would have been better planned and executed. A rival would never have wasted the skilled workers inside the warehouse, preferring instead to eliminate the leadership and then appropriate the business. Di Giovanni must have realized it as well; otherwise, he would have tried to cut some sort of deal to keep himself out of Italian custody where presumably his rivals could get him.

So if the mob didn't go after him, who did?

To me, the only possible suspects were Biondi and the tangos who had been working with him. Biondi might want to take out di Giovanni if he thought he had crossed him or otherwise ratted on him, which of course I knew wasn't the case; whether Biondi knew it or not was another question. But if he wanted revenge, Biondi would presumably have found an easier place to extract it.

The tangos, on the other hand, would have a limited knowledge of di Giovanni or his enterprise. Their interest would be entirely in erasing any link to them. Which was something they would only bother to do if their operation was ongoing.

So I left Trace behind, not just to make sure the Air Farcers followed my directions about increasing security, but to help them set up a decoy in case the tangos went ahead with their operation. Kohut had told *me* I couldn't set up anything along those lines, but he hadn't told her that. And Crapinpants was too busy sticking his nose up Kohut's butt to notice what his captains and noncoms, with help from Frankie and Trace, were doing.

Which was basically gift wrapping an AGM-129 Advanced Cruise Missile and leaving it for the tangos to steal.

Background: The Advanced Cruise Missile carries a W80 nuclear bomb, and looks like your typical long slender pointy thing—in other words, a middle finger with wings. (Just so you draw the proper mental picture, these wings face backward. Either that's to give the bomb more maneuverability once launched, or the contractor made a mistake and the Air Farce was too dumb to realize it.) Under ordinary circumstances, the bomb carried by the missile is a very serious piece of meat, many times more powerful than the atomic weapons dropped on the Japs during WWII. Let me put it to you this way: if it were dropped on Moscow, everybody within a ten-mile radius would get more than a bad case of sunburn.

In this case, the weapon's nuclear payload had been replaced with metal and concrete, approximating the weight of the real deal. Tracking devices had been inserted, and the complicated innards had been removed or disabled. Surveillance teams were set up and rotated clandestinely. (Measures were taken to safeguard the actual weapons at the base. I'm not stupid enough to say what they were.)

A little past midnight, the tangos got into the compound with an eight-wheel commercial truck, the sort of thing an appliance store might use to deliver washing machines and refrigerators with. They grabbed the missile and took off. Six different teams began following the truck with the weapon across the Sicilian countryside. A tracking aircraft aloft picked up the signals from the fake bomb.* With all these people involved, it would have been truly fucked up if the thieves managed to give them the slip.

And they didn't. The truck rendezvoused with a second vehicle that had taken part in the operation; a short time later they were met by a third car, which possibly was running surveillance or had simply been held in reserve. They did a Chinese fire drill, with everyone changing places while the "gadget" remained in place. They then set off in three different directions. The Air Farcers and Christians running the surveillance operation stayed with the program, breaking teams to trail the two other cars but keeping most of their resources on the truck.

If anyone had asked me—and they had—I would have predicted that the bomb would be transported to the coast, transferred to a large boat, and brought out to a cargo vessel just offshore, which would transport it to its final destination. Sicily is an island, after all, with a long history of smuggling and maybe a million hidden landings, harbors, caves, and beaches per square mile. The American and Italian navies had been alerted for just such a contingency, and immedi-

---

*There were supposed to be two aircraft on duty. The one that didn't show up was a U-2, which was to have been tasked from Cyprus. That sortie got scrubbed because of more pressing needs in the Middle East. Instead of relying on the transponder, the spy plane would have had a pod beneath its wings that followed the truck with high-tech cameras and computers. The gear can track specific objects on the ground through all sorts of terrain and condition, and there's no need for other tracking devices. The failure of the U-2 to show is a sore point, especially with Trace; if it had been aloft, what follows never would have happened.

ately after the snatch an Italian destroyer a few miles offshore closed in, training its surface radar and searchlight on every twig and piece of flotsam nearby.

Both of the cars, after some switchbacks and feints, headed in the direction of Brucoli, a small fishing village on the coast. The truck, though, went north, roughly in the direction of Mount Etna. (That's the big volcano smoldering in the background of the postcards.) The route was along one of the better roads in that part of Sicily, roughly the equivalent of a county highway in America, assuming that county highway curved every twenty yards to miss old buildings and had last been paved during World War II. The approaching dawn meant traffic would soon be increasing, and the planners began debating whether to move in immediately or wait to see how things shook out, taking the risk of complicating the apprehension.

When the intrusion was detected, the Air Farce captain in charge of the detail on duty had alerted Crapinpants to what was going on. The colonel reacted well enough, demonstrating considerable fortitude by not only stifling whatever anger he had at having been left out of the loop but actually joining the operation, which made it impossible for him to duck responsibility if it went to shit. (It also positioned him to get some of the credit for its success, which was probably what he was thinking.) Unfortunately, this meant he had to be consulted on what to do as the operation continued. In and of itself that might not have been fatal—Frankie seems to have a way of talking people into doing what was right—but when the time came for a decision on what to do about the truck,

Crapinpants decided it was time to get input from General Kohut.

Big mistake.

Let me back up half a step and explain something. While I would have voted for hanging back, there were decent arguments for moving in right away. Two assault teams, one composed of SEALs and one Italian paratroopers, were airborne and ready to pounce. The helicopters could not stay up indefinitely. Taking the van on the highway would be relatively easy at night when the road was deserted; there would be next to no chance of innocent bystanders being injured or blowing the operation. Plus, they knew where the truck was; there was always the possibility that Murphy might show up and hide it somehow.

Worse than making the wrong decision, however, was making no decision. The assault teams were told to stand by as Crapinpants tried to get his boss. Since they didn't know if they were attacking or not, they had to assume they were and couldn't refuel, etc. The trail teams had to back off. Uncertainty began to creep in. The infamous question, "Are we going or not?" began to run through people's heads. Its brother, "Well, what the hell *are* we doing?" soon followed. Questions and debate are great during the planning stages. They help focus an operation and eliminate the unknown, or at least reduce it to a manageable level. But once the bell rings, they become devastating. They introduce hesitation, and he who hesitates gets lost.

Literally, in this case.

The truck continued on its merry way, passing east of Etna and then up an unmarked road into the foothills of Monte Pizzillo. The road wasn't on the

maps, but satellite photos of the area had been prepared ahead of time and it was quickly located. The
photos showed that the road was steep and narrow;
switchback followed switchback. It ran up the mountainside and then down the other, connecting with the
highway again. It couldn't really be called a shortcut
because of the terrain. Which told Frankie and the
others that something was up. The thinking was this:
*The road was crappy and the terrain was for shit. The only
reason the truck would go up here was to stop somewhere
along the way, either to transfer the weapon or perhaps hide
it for someone else's pickup.*

Or, to see if they were being followed.

Which was it? If the former, following them up the
road wasn't that big a deal, even if the trail team was
spotted; it'd be academic in two minutes, which was
how long it would take the helos to arrive. If the latter,
however, following them was the worst possible thing
to do.

The trail team closest to the vehicle was running
about a quarter-mile behind when the truck turned
off. Worried that they would end up too close and be
spotted, they stopped at the turnoff and radioed for
instructions. The pooh-bahs had them continue
down the highway to the other end of the dirt road
and wait. A second team was directed to stop a short
distance from the turnoff in case the truck pulled a
U-turn.

The debate on what to do hit high gear. Now there
were additional factors to consider—the local terrain
and vegetation made a helicopter landing problem-
atic. The ground teams might have trouble here as
well. A pair of Marine Corps Cobra gunships were

available at Sigonella. Should they be scrambled? Their firepower might be welcome, but their distinctive engines might tip off the people in the truck that someone was coming for them.

Trace—remember her?—was part of the trail operation. She had rented an MV Augusta F4 "Viper" motorcycle, a stylish Italian bike as pretty to look at as it was sweet to ride. When she caught up to the team at the turnoff, she decided to ride up the road as a scout. With the help of a local motorcycle shop, Trace had made one further alteration to the customized kit, adding extra-large mufflers to quiet its throaty roar. Sacrilege, I know, but it made it possible for her to get close without being heard.

Meanwhile, the truck kept going, though very slowly. The switchbacks and steep, rutted road made its progress gradual to say the least, and at least once or twice it stopped for a few seconds, only to start moving again. Three minutes, five minutes, ten minutes—the truck ambled slowly on its way. Finally, it started on the downhill side and the teams scrambled to resume the surveillance. Unsure whether the truck would go north or south, they took up a variety of posts.

Assuming a decision had been made to stop it sooner rather than later, the intersection with the highway would have been the place to grab it. But no decision had been made. Crapinpants still hadn't been able to reach Kohut.

The truck made it onto the highway and started north. Trace, who'd been about a half-mile behind, gunned the macaroni machine and closed the distance, keeping the brake lights in view as it danced down the macadam. Within about two minutes, they neared a small village called Casa di Nero.

You can't find Casa di Nero on most maps, at least not those published in the U.S. If you're interested in seeing where it is, get the best map you can find and spread it flat on the table. Put your right thumb on Monte Etna, and spread out your hand. About where your forefinger is, you should see a little burp of a place called Mareneva. Casa di Nero is half a fingernail to the north, in the rugged mountainside. The village consists of one small church, one slightly smaller barn, and six or seven broken-down houses. There are one and a half roads in the village, the half being a rock-strewn rut that would be considered a drainage ditch in any other town.

The truck pulled up the main street and then around the rut, heading past the church to the barn.

"Move!" said Frankie in the command post. There was no sense waiting for Kohut to wake up now, and Crapinpants agreed, or at least didn't object.

One of the assault team helicopters had run low on fuel and had started back to tank up. After a few seconds of confusion, the pilot figured he had enough gas to join the party anyway, and the full assault team was able to make it to the dance more or less the way they had planned. The Cobras showed up as well. The teams were down within five minutes or so of getting the order to go.

The tangos were about to hide the vehicle in the barn when the helicopters appeared. Both of the terrorists ran as the choppers and ground vehicles came in; one made the mistake of pulling out a pistol. The only thing that was left of him and his companion

when the gunfire stopped were bones, and half of
those had been shot away. Even the Marines in the
Cobra gunships fired at the suckers. I saw the pictures
later on. They're not pretty.

I know what you're expecting—the ground ops
open up the back of the truck, and it's empty. Somehow, the slimers have managed to pull a voodoo move
and outfox the Americans and Italians following them.

Not quite, though. The truck wasn't empty—it
had the wings, nose, and, most important, the tail section of the device, which was where the numb-nut
technical expert had put both tracking devices.

Where was the warhead? At roughly twenty feet
long, it's small for a nuke but won't fit in the average
backpack. It ought to have been easy to find.

But only if you knew where to look.*

The two carloads of tangos who had been part of
the operation were stopped immediately, even though
they were too small to hold the weapon's guts. One
car was stopped in Foce di Simeto on the Golfo di
Catania. The team there also apprehended a helmsman and a small speedboat that landed a few minutes
later, obviously for the next leg of their journey.

The men in the second car proved more dedicated
to their task—they blew themselves up rather than allowing themselves to be taken in a small town farther
south along the coast. It was considerate of them,
really: It saved the Italians the expense of a trial. Then

*Which was the point about the U-2. Had the truck, et al.,
been under optical (or synthetic radar, or infrared) surveillance
instead of relying on a locator signal, the warhead could have
been spotted. Even if the handoff was somehow missed,
the file from the mission could be quickly reviewed.

again, maybe like me they were annoyed that Italy doesn't have the death penalty, so they knew they'd never get what they deserved unless they took matters into their own hands.

But back to the bomb. Where was it?

If you said the tangos who struck first left it back at the base, go to the head of the class. . . . Then suck an egg. Because the only way that would make sense would be if the thieves knew where the locator devices had been placed. Under that scenario, the theft would be a diversion, taking our attention away from the base while a second team infiltrated and grabbed the real one. Brilliant theory—but probably a bit too brilliant, at least in this case.

But Crapinpants got it into his head that that was what had to be going on and went apeshit. He contacted the security people and gave them orders to shoot anyone they saw on sight—I'm not exaggerating, either. Though he was told that there had been no further intrusions and that the family jewels were intact, he didn't believe that and began screaming that the stolen weapons had better be found. In layman's terms, he'd cracked under the pressure (such as it was) of the situation. It happens, but when it happens to someone who's wearing a birdie on his collar and is attached to a phone, the consequences can spin out of control.

Within ten minutes, someone at the base told Crapinpants that a suspicious truck had been spotted on a road just outside the perimeter of the Air Force area of Sigonella. Whatever the person actually said, by the time Crapinpants reached Frankie he was convinced that the truck held not the dummy warhead but a real bomb. Recognizing a runaway train when he saw one, Frankie stepped back and let the Air Farce take care of the vehicle, which of course was soon surrounded by every available airman, sailor, soldier, and marine within a fifty-mile radius of the base.

In fairness, the Air Farce security people on the scene insisted that the truck couldn't have been involved; the van that the terrorists used had not come down the road in question. But the fact that none of the men held a rank higher than tech sergeant meant their opinions counted for nil. Acting on the possibility that the truck and bomb might be booby-trapped— hey, why not?—a robot and dogs were brought out to check the damn thing out.

All of this would have been shit-ass hilarious if it didn't divert attention and resources from the effort to look for the dummy bomb itself. Clearly it had been off-loaded somewhere on the hill. The team that had landed got ready to do so, but had to wait while the helicopters went off to refuel. Trace, never one to twiddle her thumbs when she could be sticking them in someone's eye, gunned her bike back toward the mountain. She went up the steep road, taking the switchbacks as slowly as she could. It was about five in the morning; the night was clear and there was plenty of light to see by on the highway. But here the trees and terrain threw everything into a dark shadow. Finally she decided to stop and put on the night optical glasses tucked in her tactical vest. As she was pulling it on, someone grabbed her from behind.

Trace's reflexes took over; the bike flew one way, her assailant flew another, and she spun in the air, feet kicking out at another assailant, or at least his shadow.

Her foot didn't hit anything—it's possible nothing was there—and she landed slightly off-kilter on her haunches. She coiled her five-foot-eight-inch frame like a cobra, looking to strike something. The man she had thrown lay moaning on the ground a few feet away. When nothing else moved, Trace reached for her Kimber Compact .45, pulling the pistol from its pocket inside her vest.

Her night goggles had fallen to the ground near the bike. As she sidled toward them, something moved about ten yards away. She brought her gun up, poised on her haunches, trying to make out what it was.

The next thing Trace heard was a very loud buzzing in her ears. A half-second later, she felt as if her breath had been snatched from her. Then her body tingled, and not in a good way. It was as if she had put her hands onto the wires coming from a nuclear reactor.

A Taser dart had hit her at the back of the neck. The thin wires that stretched back from the dart to the gun had transmitted upward of fifty thousand volts of electricity, a bit more than you'd need to light your average Christmas tree . . . and run your refrigerator and the rest of your house while you're at it. Her body went apocalyptic; she felt as if she were frozen and on fire at the same time.

Tasers work by paralyzing the body; they fry the body's natural electric system like an E-bomb would, temporarily frying the circuitry. Most normal human beings would have shut down completely at that point, kind of humming to themselves and glowing for a few minutes. But not Trace Dahlgren. She whirled around, grabbed the wires that had spiked her, and tried feeding them to the bastard with the Taser weapon who was only about twenty feet away.

Of course, the fact that her nervous system had been jolted out of kilter meant she was about as successful as a rag doll. As she lunged at the bastard, two other men came up behind her and put out her lights the old-fashioned way—with a rifle butt to the head.

See what happens when you don't wear a motorcycle helmet?

Frankie and the others back at the command post heard some of this through Trace's radio. In short order they had the two available cars blocking off the road. Then they sat tight, waiting for the helicopters to finish refueling and get back in the air. They were doing things by the book, which said the first order of business was to contain the situation, then go in and get their guy (or gal).

If I'd been there, I would have given the book a good heave—in that sort of situation, time is critical, and the more aggressive you are, the better your chances are of grabbing your person alive. You don't learn that in books, mostly because the majority of the books are written by guys who weren't there.

The whack sent Trace into an odd state of semiconsciousness. She saw things moving around her, real things and fake things.

For a few moments, the fake things seemed more real. Two reddish-gold coyotes stood over her, speaking in a Chihuahua Apache dialect. Gradually, Trace came to understand that they were debating whether they should intervene. One wanted to, arguing that White Shell Woman would be angry if her children were harmed. The other said that the battle was not their affair and they should stay away.

As I understand it—and being a "white man" Trace says I *can't*—Apache legend claims that White Shell Woman is the mother of Europeans. Trace says that her vision represented an argument in the spirit world about whether the powers that protect the Apache should get involved in the fight against terrorism: a war that she, like Saladin, interprets as a war of civilizations. If the coyotes made up their minds, they didn't hang around to share the decision with her. They slowly faded into the background as the four tangos around her became more distinct.

Trace interpreted this as an important if puzzling message. To her, the fact that she had it means she's worthy of an important role in her tribe, something she's questioned. Me, I think she was just whacked on the head. But then again, that can be as religious an experience as anything else.

The tangos were also having a debate. Trace couldn't tell what language they were speaking, except that it wasn't English; even so, she somehow understood every word, or at least thinks she did. The men had been in the process of covering their tracks when she stopped nearby. Their attack had been a mistake, as they had been instructed to remain unseen if at all possible. From what they were saying, it seems likely that they mistook her for one of the farmers who lived nearby. For some reason they didn't explain, they weren't supposed to hurt the locals.

The fact that they had gone against their orders, argued one of the men, meant that they better dispose of the evidence. Another argued that this would eventually be discovered, and the consequences would be even more severe. At this point, Trace groaned. They trussed her hands with a pair of old handcuffs and put a set of leg irons on her feet. Trace saw that the links were old and corroded, and she thought—knew, she insists today—that she could pull them apart if she had to. But she remained still, deciding to wait until she was sure how many others were around and her head was a bit clearer.

After the chains were on her hands, two of the men took shovels and trudged off a few yards away, where they started to dig. It's possible that they were going to bury her alive, which technically wouldn't have violated their orders. ("Hey, she was alive when we threw that last spadeful of dirt on her face. It wasn't our fault she couldn't breathe . . .") At about that point, one of the helicopters got close enough to be heard. The tangos began to panic and decided to make a run for it. They took a long pole and slung it between the chains holding her limbs.

At that moment, Trace would have struggled to free herself, except that one of the coyotes returned. He stood on two legs. She felt his breath, and watched as he lifted his head to howl. And then he was gone.

In retrospect, the vision probably saved her life. She realized two of the tangos had been covering her from a short distance away, guns trained on her. If she'd put up any resistance, they could have easily shot her.

Trace's head continued to clear as they moved into the brush and down the mountain's west side. She couldn't see all that much, but soon realized that she and her porters were at the tail end of the formation, with the two other men scrambling ahead down the rocks. She decided the handcuffs would make a decent enough weapon if wrapped around someone's neck; this gave her the outlines of a general plan— she'd rock herself to the side, pulling the stick out of the hands of the man closest to her, roll up, and grab him by the throat.

Before she could implement the plan, the helicopter they'd heard earlier buzzed that side of the slope. The crew was using infrared glasses to look for her. As it happened, they missed her on that pass, but the tangos didn't know that—they dropped their prize and began running down the hill.

Trace found herself sliding in the dirt. She levered her body with her elbow, trying to get up; instead she ended up flailing face-first into a pile of rocks. She bounced up and saw one of her captors five or six feet from her. Forgetting that her legs were chained together, she lunged for him. She tripped, falling well short.

Somewhere during this tumble, the helicopter made a second pass and the crew spotted what was going on. Two flares shot out from the helo, and the night sky turned fluorescent white. The guys on the ground must have finally realized they were truly fucked, because they stopped running and tried to hide. (The assault team later found a Volkswagen parked at the base of the mountain, their apparent destination.)

Trace heard gunfire—and, she claims, the howl of a coyote. She saw three tangos running to her left, and pushed herself up to follow them. As she did, someone grabbed her by the back of her tac vest and held a gun to her neck.

Big mistake. She had her elbow in his gut and his body flying over her down the hill in less than a heartbeat.

Trace saw two or three Italian paratroopers running up the hill, and the tangos running toward them.

The coyote stood between them, shaking his head.

"Hit the deck!" Trace yelled, intuitively understanding what the vision meant. "Down! Down!"

She followed her own advice without waiting to see if the paratroopers did—good thing, because just as her lips kissed the dirt, the three terrorists blew themselves up.

6

By the time I got to Sicily, Trace had been shipped to the hospital and released, the latter in response to threats by her to inflict bodily damage on the medical staff if they didn't let her go. She'd had a series of head X rays, all negative—but what did you expect?

All told, only two terrorists had been taken alive. One was the man who had held the gun on Trace; he'd been hit by shrapnel from his friends and wasn't expected to make it. The other had gotten into one of the cars after the heist. Unfortunately, the Italian paratroopers had grabbed him. I'll spare you the jurisdictional bullshit; the long and short of it was that he was handed over to the Italian authorities before Frankie or anyone else competent had a chance to "interview" him.

The Italians are great talkers, but their techniques with prisoners leave a lot to be desired. They seem to think that making someone eat their nightly pasta without sauce is the moral equivalent of hanging them upside down by their toenails for thirty-six hours and zapping their gonads with a cattle prod. Not that they would do that either.

The dummy bomb had been hidden just off the road, about thirty yards from where Trace had dropped her bike. Frankie realized that they had hidden it there with the idea that a second team would come and pick it up; hoping against hope that the operation would proceed, he had holes drilled into the device and two tracking devices installed. Then he set up an extensive surveillance net. It was a wasted gesture, but it did give the Eye-talians something to do.

Both our navy and the Italians' began reviewing data from radar and other sources on shipping, the theory being that the bomb was to have been taken out that day. As Trace pointed out when she picked me up at the airport, that made no sense—if the tangos were planning to get the device off the island immediately, the truck would have gone straight to the rendezvous. More likely, the people who had designed the plot believed that the immediate response would be to seal off the island, and that it would be safer and easier to get the bomb out when the "heat" died down.

I suspected that the people who actually took the weapon from the base were to have killed themselves if caught there, as the three with Trace had done; they had probably been chosen for that part of the mission because they could be counted on to follow through. That suggested to me that the ringleader of the mission was around somewhere, maybe not directly observing—if he was, we should have been able to see him—but still close enough to make sure things went right.

At the risk of being called a racist or, *gasp*, a "racial

profiler," let me point out that all of the individuals involved were of apparent Middle Eastern extraction. The dead men were in too many pieces to be identified by photographs, and their DNA didn't match any of the very small amount on file for known terrorists. Neither prisoner was carrying ID and neither identified himself, but by the time I met with Frankie, the one from the car had been fingered as an asshole named Ali al-Hazmi—not coincidentally related to one of the 9/11 hijackers. That actually hurt rather than helped our operation. For one thing, everybody and his uncle wanted to grab the scumbag and beat the shit out of him . . . er, engage in meaningful dialogue over a nice cup of tea. For another, it got Pus Face's attention.

"9/11. On that magnitude. Big. Huge. That's what we have here, Dick. Catastrophe. Major. Immense." Pus Face's sentences shriveled to single words whenever he was excited or under pressure, and he was both when I met with him, Kohut, and the rest of the usual suspects that afternoon. He prowled Kohut's small office like an elephant looking to gore a tiger. As I was the only tiger present—Trace had feigned a headache—I stayed on my guard.

"This is huge, Dick. Huge. A coup." Pus Face turned to Kohut and nodded solemnly. He had decided that he had approved the decoy-and-surveillance setup; I suspect that he was well on his way to believing it was his idea.

Kohut kept glancing toward me from the safety of his desk. The arrest of al-Hazmi had set off a hosanna of congratulations from Washington, and I think he was worried that I would derail the accolade train by pointing out he had originally vetoed it. His secret is safe with me, however.

Oh. I guess it's not. Ooooops.

"Now that we have the ringleader, what's next?" asked Pus Face.

I explained that we didn't have the ringleader, the big boss or anything close. The mastermind would probably not have exposed himself on the mission. Al-Hazmi might have been the operational commander—he seemed to be the only one smart enough not to wear an explosive vest—but he was probably no higher than that.

"Which is why you have to pry him from the Italians and let me talk to him," I said. "He's our connection to the next rung on the ladder."

"Yes," said Pus Face. But it was one of those yeses that clearly means no.

"Why not?"

"I'll work on it."

"Working on it's not good enough," I told him.

Pus Face started hemming and hawing about jurisdictions, diplomatic and otherwise.

"I'm sorry. I thought those stars meant something," I said finally.

Ordinarily, questioning a general's pull leads to immediate results. In this case, though, Pus Face simply continued making excuses, blaming al-Hazmi's isolation on the Christians In Action. What I didn't realize at the time was that Pus Face had already been sidelined by the Pentagon and the intelligence agencies. The title he'd been given had no real power; he could bark at people like Kohut all day, but in the end they were outside his chain of command and he could do little more than pee on their rugs if they didn't cooperate.

Had Pus Face been competent, this would have seriously endangered America's efforts to make its overseas bases secure and protect various interests from terrorism. Since he wasn't competent, it mainly kept him from doing more harm than most career generals do. In any event, I soon ended our little tête-à-tête, saying I had to go check my messages.

"You may have new leads?" he asked.

"One can only hope."

"Great."

"I'll keep you in the loop," I told him. The last part of the sentence—"when hell freezes over"—may have been inaudible; I was out in the hall by then.

I tried pulling some of my own strings with Christians In Action, but there were too few IOUs in my favor jar to swing any concessions from Langley, and I didn't know any of the local people. I even gave the ambassador to Italy a call, but he was out doing whatever it is ambassadors to Italy do. I fell back to regroup with Trace over an early dinner at her hotel.

With the terrorist angle temporarily shut down, it made sense to pursue the Mafia side of the equation. Damn good sense—but even so, I didn't think of it. When I got to the hotel room to freshen up before dinner, the light was blinking with a message. ("Freshen up" is Marcinko-speak for grabbing a cold one from the minibar.) When I figured out the phone system, a gravely voice greeted me with a phone number.

Someone picked up on the second ring. "Is this Dick Marcinko?" he said.

"It is. Who are you?"

"That's unimportant. Welcome to our island."

"It's a nice place," I said. "Why am I talking to you?"

I guessed the man was Italian because of the way he pronounced my name—with a hard Italian "c," as if it were spelled "ch." But he was speaking English— *Noo Yawk* English, like maybe the kind of *Noo Yawk* you would hear around Bensonhurst. For those of you who don't know, that's serious Guido country. And I say it with the greatest affection—and a loaded machine gun in my hands.

"Don Alberti wants to meet you," said the man. "Be at 'U Cafone in Catania at 11 p.m. You know it?"

"I can find it."

"One thing, Mr. Marcinko. Don Alberti respects you, because he has heard of your reputation. So you will be treated with respect. But you must remember, respect is a two-way street."

"Sure." I had no fucking idea what he was talking about. "Can I bring a date?"

"A date? Yes. One date. I would advise against bringing anyone who would have difficulty understanding the situation." He hung up.

The name Alberti means nothing to most Americans, and I'd bet next month's allowance that few Italians north of Palermo know it either. But in Sicily, the name would be instantly recognized, especially by the police. Gerlando Alberti set up and ran a network of heroin factories for the Sicilian Mafia as a young man. What Henry Ford was to the automobile, Alberti was to smack. Gerlando eventually got caught by the government and put on trial, but his family remained important in the Mafia hierarchy. Don Alberti—*don* being a term of honor for an important Mafia member, kind of like saying *Duke*—was a grandson of the man who had set up the factories. (An illegitimate one, actually, whom other family members claimed shouldn't even have the name. But we'll let them sort out their private squabbles.)

Forget what you've seen on *The Sopranos* and all the other TV shows and movies. Most *Mafiosi,* especially in Sicily, are brutal, ruthless killers; they tend not to play well with others, and a good portion are so stupid they can't count past ten. A few are pretty decent businessmen; most couldn't make money at a bank if they had to play by the rules.

So why go to the meeting?

That was Trace's question, though she added a few colorful adjectives when she asked it.

"The food in the hotel sucks," I told her. "At least I'll get a good meal. Besides, maybe the Don wants some books signed."

"It's probably a fucking ambush."

"No. They're too lazy to bother calling me first. If they wanted to kill me, they'd already have taken a shot."

Trace pretended that she didn't agree. Still, she insisted that she was coming with me. Her face and legs were scraped and bruised from her adventure with the nuke thieves, but the deft application of makeup camouflaged her wounds. Not that anyone would have looked at them given the miniskirt and blouse she wore. When we showed up at the restaurant, the maitre d' nodded at me, glanced at Trace—glanced again at Trace—and then led her across the room to a table at the rear. I followed.

A man about sixty years old sat at the large round table. His thick black hair was combed straight back on his head; he wore a cream-colored suit with no tie, his blue shirt buttoned at the neck. The expression on his thin face seemed relaxed, confident, and friendly. Only two other places were set, both of them opposite him. He rose as we approached, smiling. I knew from the backgrounder I'd studied before coming over that this was Don Alberti.

"Demo Dick. A great honor." Alberti's English was very good, with only the barest trace of an accent. He nodded at me. I nodded back. "And Trace Dahlgren. You are even more beautiful than he has described in his books, Ms. Dahlgren. I can only assume you are twice as intelligent, and three times as dangerous."

Trace gave him a look that meant "fuck yourself," but didn't bother translating.

A pair of waiters had shadowed us to the table. They pulled out our chairs and even unfolded our napkins and placed them in our laps. The man helping Trace started to drool and had to retreat quickly to the men's room.

Don Alberti launched into a brief critique of each of my books, starting with the first, which of course he thought was the best. I did what I usually do in such situations: I pasted a diplomatic smile on my face and sipped the Bombay Sapphire that he had thoughtfully ordered for me. My eyes, meanwhile, vacuumed the place for useful information. The don's bodyguards were sitting several tables away; there were only four of them, split at two tables. This told me that he felt extremely secure here, and not simply because this was home turf. Another two dozen or so people were eating dinner, older couples mostly; from their clothes I guessed they were members of the local business and social elite, not a very difficult guess given the moneyed look of the restaurant itself. In America, even the most successful Mafia kingpin would be considered brash and uncultured—part of the attraction, I'd say. But in Sicily, a successful don had an entirely different aura. They were connections to a long and honorable heritage of resistance to foreigners, a group that included any Italian who didn't live on the island.

Alberti had ordered for us, and a parade of local delicacies began marching across the table. I had a few nibbles—the poached baby octopus was damn good—and waited for him to get to the point of the meeting.

"And so, how do you like Sicily?" Alberti asked, about the time a waiter was plopping down a bottle of Sambuca for the espresso.

"Very lovely island." I turned to Trace. "My associate tells me it's a great place to ride a motorcycle."

Don Alberti smiled and looked across the restaurant to a table near the front of the room. A man in his thirties rose and strode toward us, taking a seat at Alberti's right hand. He looked like a younger, even thinner version of the don. I assumed this was Alberti's son, who the backgrounder said acted as his chief of staff. The skin under his eyes sagged from fatigue; the sockets seemed to have been bored into his skull. His voice was instantly familiar: He was the man who'd left the message and answered the phone when I called.

"The events at the American base were very unfortunate," he said. "They show how grave a threat the world faces."

"That's just *too* rich," said Trace.

The two locked stares for maybe thirty seconds. Her glare wasn't just vicious; I could tell she was trying to decide whether it would be better to cut Junior's heart out and feed it to him, or simply drop-kick it into the next time zone.

"You think that men of honor would threaten the national defense?" said Junior, ending the staredown.

"Which men of honor?" said Trace.

Junior leaned forward. Before he could say anything, Don Alberti raised his hand.

"Signore Biondi's involvement in the affair was a grave violation of trust, even though it would never have been authorized by his employer, let alone the *cupola*," he said. He wasn't talking about architecture; *cupola* referred to the mob's ruling commission. Though he was ostensibly talking to his son, his eyes were pinned on me. "*Signore* Marcinko is right to worry that we are connected with this. It is a matter of great shame."

I picked up my espresso and took a sip.

"I believe some background on the individual would be useful," Alberti added.

Junior frowned ever so slightly—maybe for our benefit, trying to play a reluctant source to make what he said seem more believable—and then began talking about Biondi. According to him, Biondi was a low-level handyman, more freelancer than soldier. Though he did a lot of work in Naples, he was actually a Sicilian native, and came back at least one a month, ostensibly to see his mother. During one of those visits a few months back, he had been approached by a Libyan looking to acquire American goods.

"You make it sound like he was boosting toilet paper," interrupted Trace.

"Originally, it was supposed to be cigarettes," said Junior. "Of course, if he had been a local, he would have known that Sigonella should have been off-limits," added gravel voice. "The American base has always been off-limits. When his interest became known, he was told not to get involved. Unfortunately, he was not an intelligent man."

Junior continued Biondi's tale of woe. After he had scouted the cigarette delivery schedule but not stolen them, the Libyan changed his assignment. He proposed a robbery of the Air Farce facility, where according to the Libyan the Americans kept considerable cash for payroll. Biondi objected on the grounds that it was too dangerous, regardless of the payoff. But the Libyan explained that he didn't need Biondi to participate; he only wanted to know what the base defenses were. Hence the probes that were detected, which had helped the Libyan set up the theft.

Di Giovanni—an associate of *another* family, Junior assured me solemnly—was an innocent if stupid bystander whose main concerns were in Naples: a proper place for them to be. Unfortunately, it appeared that the *signore* would perhaps be retiring from the car business permanently, now that his factory had suffered so much damage. In fact, his health was rumored to be very poor. Extremely bad. Terminal, even.

Pity.

Junior's version had a good number of holes—no one could be quite as stupid as Biondi was being made out to be, and it seemed highly unlikely that the *Mafiosi* had *no* idea what he was up to—but the rough outlines of what Junior said were probably true.

Not that we were about to admit that.

"This is bullshit," said Trace when Junior concluded. "Total bullshit."

I tapped her arm. We'd planned this, of course, but the flash of anger in her eyes seemed as real as any I've ever seen. If Trace ever went into movies, she'd win an Academy Award her first time out.

"We tend to be a little skeptical in America," I told Don Alberti soothingly. He nodded, and Junior reached into his pocket for an envelope. For a second I thought they were going to try to pay me off—there's a first for everything.

"This will show where the money to pay Biondi came from," said Junior. "Of course it was in cash, so there's no proof that he got it."

"Where is he?" Trace asked, taking the envelope.

"I would like to speak to him," I added, addressing Alberti.

"Regrettably, Signore Biondi will not be in a position for a conversation in the near future. Or anytime after that."

"Shame."

"Yes. Stupidity has its consequences."

I nodded. I was curious whether the tangos had gotten Biondi or whether the Mafia had, but it was clear I wasn't going to get an answer I could trust if I asked.

"There's a location you will be interested in," added Junior, gesturing at the envelope.

"One thing that will interest you a great deal, Dick," interrupted Don Alberti, "is the name *Saladin*. The Libyan mentioned it in a conversation with Signore Biondi."

"Who's the Libyan?" asked Trace.

Don Alberti gestured as if he neither knew nor cared.

"Ali al-Hazmi," I said. "Was he involved?"

Alberti shrugged again. Junior's face was also blank; it seemed possible they didn't know.

Al-Hazmi was Saudi, not Libyan. The implication that someone else had met with Biondi didn't contradict my theory that al-Hazmi was the operation's chief. He might have used him as a cutout, or he might even be the Libyan.

"What about Saladin?" asked Trace. "Who's he?"

"A character in your boss's books," answered Don Alberti. "Beyond that, I don't know." He raised his hand to one of the waiters, gesturing for more wine.

Frankie wasn't entirely convinced that Don Alberti was telling the truth, the whole truth, and nothing but the truth regarding Biondi. The bank account data checked out, showing transfers that had come from Libya and were apparently untraceable beyond that, the deposits having been made in cash. That wasn't exactly a whopper of a surprise and on its own meant nothing: The Mafia essentially owned the bank in question and could have easily planted the money.

Still, the information would give Crapinpants and the Italians something to spin their wheels on for a few days. It would also impress Pus Face, though I didn't particularly care if he was impressed or not.

What about the address we'd been given, you ask?

For some reason, I forgot to share it. Can't remember my own phone number some days. . . .

The address belonged to a cozy little set of battlements high on the hills above the sea, about ten miles south of Taormina.* It looked fairly rustic from the air, which was how I first saw it the next morning, courtesy of an overflight by an old buddy of mine named Spaghetti Sam. Sam is somewhere on the other side of seventy, but he puts in a sixty-hour work week and spends his nights kicking back with Chianti and fancy Cuban cigars at his compound near Capo Rizzuto on the Ionian Sea. (That's about where the Achilles' heel would be if Italy was a real foot.)

Spaghetti once flew Bell UH-1H Iroquoises, better known as "Hueys," for Air America during the little disagreement in Southeast Asia sometimes referred to as the Vietnam War. Air America was an outfit put together by the Christians In Action to run missions either too dangerous or too dirty for the Air Farts to get involved in, which is not to say that the USAF kept its wings clean in the war. Spaghetti had been trained by the Army but left that service under circumstances he never bothered to explain. He racked up an incredible

---

*The chickenshit lawyers don't want me to use the actual address, since the property is owned by people who had nothing to do with what went on there. Like I believe that.

record with Air America, claiming to have been shot down between five and thirteen times. (The number varies depending on how much he'd had to drink.) Whatever the truth of his tales, he made enough money to bum around Italy for a few years after the war. Eventually, he decided to come out of retirement and got work flying helicopters for a power company. Some jobs on the side eventually enabled him to buy a fleet of helicopters and set up a tourist taxi business near Rizzuto. The exact financial details of the operation are a mystery to me; I have a feeling it's better for all concerned if they stay that way.

Spaghetti agreed to come over to Sicily and help out as soon as I called, but I think he was still a bit pissed that I had woken him around 3 a.m., immediately after my meeting with Alberti. Either that, or he was trying to demonstrate why his Dauphin AS 365N was such a popular model when dressed in military drag. We took off calmly enough, but once he pulled up his landing gear he pushed the nose down toward the sea and juiced the throttle, clearing the carbon out of the fuel injectors. If we didn't break the sound barrier, we were damn close, and I swear we were low enough to look up at some of the waves. Trace's face settled into the rock mask she uses when faced with imminent nausea. It was a good thing Spaghetti didn't have a mirror to see her in the back; I'm sure it would only have encouraged him.

After a good ten minutes of hotdogging, Spaghetti brought the helicopter up to a safer altitude and began flying more like the tour operator he was supposed to be. We arced around toward the tango castle, moving lackadaisically as if we were hunting for topless sunbathers on the rocky coast. Trace worked a telephoto-equipped Nikon while I looked over the area with a pair of binoculars. The castle's stone walls rose straight up from the cliffs. I never got around to checking the history of the place, but a number of similar buildings and their ruins dot the Sicilian shores. Many were built during the Middle Ages as strongholds for the local lords. A good portion were eventually used by smugglers. In most cases, the sea long ago battered the nearest stones into submission, the walls surrendering in a tumble. But a few not only remain intact but have been renovated by their owners, who use them as hideaways or, in a few cases, expensive bed-and-breakfasts.

This one seemed a few steps from ruin, but far from opening its doors to rich tourists. The walls bowed in two or three places but were otherwise intact. There were two openings on the water side. One was a gated archway, the sort of thing you would find at the end of a bridge over a moat, except that it was at sea level. I estimated the entrance would be about twelve feet wide, big enough for a whaleboat to squeeze through if it were open.

A large metal door stood about thirty feet to the south of this. Located higher on the wall, it looked as if it were intended for boarding ships. A stone walkway ran across the top of the wall, connecting a pair of five-sided towers on either end. The towers were missing their roofs and interior timbers, but otherwise looked sturdy. The walls that extended landward from these towers ended in sheer rock, which formed the fourth side of the squarish building. The walls were thick enough to have rooms in them, and on the first pass, the area between the walls looked like an open courtyard; it wasn't until the second pass that I realized it was actually a flat roof.

A road skirted the southwestern wall, ending under a stone arch about as wide as the one on the ocean. The approach was guarded by the tower; there didn't appear to be a walkway on that side of the structure. To the west, what looked like a W cut into the rocky precipice turned out to be additional battlements. They would be difficult to attack but did not have a full view of the area below, especially since the vegetation was quite thick. I couldn't see any connection to the castle itself. We didn't spot any guards.

On our third pass, this time from the land side heading northeastward, Spaghetti began to curse. He rammed his throttle full-bore for power and the Dauphin surged ahead.

"Radar," he announced. "J band. Gun dish. *Assholes.*"

Let me translate: Someone nearby had turned on a radar that operated on the J band. Typically, this type of radar would be used to guide antiaircraft artillery (hence, "gun dish"). A radar's characteristics are typically used to diagnose what sort of antiaircraft weapon you're up against. In this case, the radar was rather old, a type made by the Ruskies way back when I was tossing spears in Vietnam, and usually used to sight weapons like the ZSU-23, a four-barreled antiaircraft gun that remains in service around the world. It had also been used in other short-range systems, including the SA-9.

"I didn't see any guns," said Trace.

"Doesn't mean they weren't there," said Spaghetti.

"Why does a tourist helicopter have a radar-warning receiver?" asked Trace.

"How come you're so nosy?" snapped Spaghetti.

I let him cool for a minute or so, then asked if his device was sophisticated enough to get an exact location on the radar. Spaghetti grunted ambiguously. He banked to the west, taking the chopper farther out to sea.

"I didn't see any sort of radar dish or antennas. Could they mount the radar inside the building somehow?" I asked.

Spaghetti grunted again, but then said, "Probably on the rocks. Under a net. A dish. Fucking assholes."

I suggested that Trace could load her camera with infrared film before the next pass. The sun would warm the metal surface of the radar dish and make it easier to see.

"I don't know, Dick," he answered. "I don't like some people's attitude. You know what I mean?"

There's nothing worse than a temperamental helicopter pilot. Before I could say anything else, Trace chimed in with what I take was a misguided attempt to use psychology on him.

"He's just a chickenshit."

"I was dodging bullets before your grandfather realized he couldn't hold his liquor," Spaghetti told her. "Where'd you pick her up, Dick? Kindergarten?"

"If she gets out of hand, I'll just throw her over my knee and spank her."

"We can make a run over and drop her into the volcano," said Spaghetti.

I turned and gave Trace a quick shake of the head. Whatever witty comeback she was contemplating died on her lips.

"The question, little girl, is not whether we're going back. We're not pansy-asses. The question is whether we bother to break their signal or not. Or do I have to explain everything to you?"

"I'd rather we didn't make it any more obvious than necessary," I told Spaghetti. Using the jammer would make it impossible for the radar to track us. On the other hand, it would tell the people working the radar that we knew they were watching us.

And yes, it *is* unusual that a civilian aircraft had a jammer. Why Spaghetti needed one . . . let's just assume that he had a good reason for it and leave it at that.

We flew northward a bit, pretending to do more sightseeing, then headed south. Trace got the camera ready as Spaghetti lined up the flight path. He took the helicopter up to five thousand feet, which we figured was about the maximum range we could use for the camera setup and still end up with something usable. As we passed over, Spaghetti would broadcast a request to a nonexistent air controller, making it sound as if he was on a tourist hop. The idea was that the helo would appear to be heading back to the spot it had come from, rather than zeroing in on the castle.

There was only one problem: Five thousand feet was pretty much dead-meat range for the gun or missile systems that were normally attached to the radar.

"That lights, you hang on tight," Spaghetti said,

pointing to a dull yellow panel at the center of the dash. "You too, little girl. And don't mind the flares. I wouldn't care so much," he added. "But I just finished paying the bank off on this son of a bitch, and I'm underinsured to boot."

The light was attached to an infrared detection system that would warn of a missile launch. It didn't go off, though the radar detector did. Spaghetti motioned to the rock at the side of the castle, but the direction finder on his detection unit wasn't precise enough for a pinpoint location; we had to wait for Trace to develop the film.

"Maybe it's a dish, maybe it's bullshit," she said a few hours later, showing me the image. "If that old fart had gone a little slower, I might have gotten something useful."

One thing about Apaches—if they take a dislike to you, there's no way in the world you can get back into their good graces, and it's not worth even trying.

"Useful or not, I think we ought to go take a look around," I told her. "You in the mood for a midnight swim?"

If this had been a SEAL operation, we would have made our way up to the ocean portal via our own special taxi—an Improved SEAL Delivery Vehicle. The ISDV is basically a minisubmarine that gets you close enough to a target so that you spend your real energy on the mission, not swimming there. They're a step up from the older SEAL Delivery Vehicle, which was more like an upside down canoe that went underwater than a real submarine. In the SDV, you sat on a wet bench and froze your nuts off, trudging ever so slowly toward your target. The new improved versions keep a swimmer warm, toasty, and dry until the dance.

I can just hear one of my ol' sea daddy chiefs snorting about that: What da *fuck*, Marcinko? You afraid your tootsies gonna fall off if they get wet, you lameshit numb-nut *lazy* sumbitch?*

"Lazy" being the worst four-letter word in a master chief's vocabulary.

We did it the old-fashioned way, swimming from a boat landing about a half-mile away. Believe me, if you were part of the old UDT program, where the Little Creek waters rarely got much over forty degrees and the tide could approach two knots, the Mediterranean seems like an ocean of milk. Then again, if you *were* in the UDT program, you probably had a chief screaming words to the effect of: "You sorry little pukeshit, Marcinko—you think this is *easy*? Easy is *exactly* when it hits you in balls, you good-for-diarrhea shit asshole."

About two hundred yards south of the castle I came across a mine anchored just under the surface of the water. It wasn't a WWII souvenir, either—there were several more nearby, a regular picket fence guarding the gated entrance. We ducked around them easily enough, and made our way to the arch. The spikes that guarded the entrance were placed about a meter apart, more than sufficient to keep a boat out, but not much defense against a swimmer. Even better, they extended only a foot below the water.

---

*I'm not dumping on the minisubs. They make insertions possible in conditions that would be impossible in the old days. I'm just jealous.

By now it's probably occurred to you that this might be an elaborate trap. Any number of people might be honestly said to hate ol' lovable Dickie's arse and the rest of him. They would pay dearly to see his head smacked against the rocks. The fact that the Mafia was involved doesn't exactly increase your confidence level either, I'll bet. Nothing is more honorable for a "man of honor" than murder and double-cross.

So what would you have me do? Send a little robot in there ahead of me to take a beating if it was a trap?

Good idea. Call me collect when you get one perfected. Just make sure it works under all sorts of conditions, needs no downtime, and can be counted on to save your ass when the shit starts flying. In the meantime, I'll keep putting my neck on the line, just like the other poor grunts in our Army, Navy, Marine Corps, and Air Force. If you want to kick ass, you have to take the risks that come with it.

I eased my way under the gate and slipped upward to the surface. It was too dark to see the roof, and not much was visible in front of me either. I found the wall and worked my way along it. It was man-made, and the stones were tight together. After about thirty feet I found a wooden platform poking out of the side about thirty feet from the gate. I went around it slowly, deciding it was a docking area. Ten feet beyond its back edge I found another stone wall. I worked my way around the wall to the other side and back to the gate. As far as I could tell, there were no openings at or near water level.

It was so dark that I could barely see the hand in front of my face—which, fortunately, belonged to

Trace. We stowed our gear by tying it to the bottom of the platform. Then we took out our goodies from the waterproof bags we'd tugged along with us. MP5N in hand, I turned on my LED wristlight and slowly played it around the space. A wooden door sat above the docking area. The wood looked ancient, yet intact. Three thick bands of rusted iron held the panels together. I took my diving knife and tried using it as a lock pick. That was useless. The latch was inaccessible, secured behind a thick iron plate. The hinges—assuming there were any—were either on the other side or recessed into the wood and stone.

Time to regroup and rethink. We found two openings above us, small squares that were probably once part of the castle's plumbing system. Or maybe still were. All I knew was that they were too damn small to wiggle through.

"What now?" asked Trace.

"We look underwater for an opening."

"And if we can't find any?"

"Unless you packed some WD-40, we swim back out and climb up the wall," I told her.

"That sucks."

"Pretty much."

The walls gave way to solid rock about eight feet from the surface; the bottom of the little inlet was another eight or so feet below that. A thick layer of muck covered the floor; just about anything might have been in it, including several skeletons. The stones themselves were covered with a blackish growth, but there weren't any fish, and certainly no octopuses patrolling the depths. So when I felt a tug on my leg as I surfaced I knew Trace had found something.

The passage was about midway down the wall just to the right of the dock. It was stone on all sides, about as wide and high as the slot for a coffin in a crypt. The comparison seemed particularly appropriate as we came to an elbow that led straight upward. Trace had no problem sliding through; I scraped the side, knocked my knee, and nearly broke my arm—not a problem, really, as long as I could get to the surface soon and get some air into my shrieking lungs. I pushed through the ooze all around me and managed to move upward, squeezing next to Trace as we surfaced.

We came up at the top of what looked like a chimney in the middle of a stone room. A dim blue light filtered in from high above. I stared at it for a minute, then realized that I was looking at the sky. We had gone through a passage to the southeastern tower, surfacing in what must have been a guardroom, back in the days when wood beams filled the large key-holes in the side walls.

A narrow ledge rimmed the tower's circular walls about six feet from the surface of the water. We climbed to it, our fingernails scraping up bacteria for everything from lockjaw to tuberculosis. The ledge was a bit wider than my butt, but offered nothing more than a rest stop. A bricked-over doorway sat about a third of the way up; another was about four-teen or fifteen feet above it.

"To the top?" asked Trace.

"Sounds good to me." I pulled out my MP5N and slung the strap around my neck; I wanted the gun handy in case we encountered lookouts at the top.

There was just enough light for us to get by without

using our flashlights. The stones were tightly spaced together, but their irregular shape made handholds plentiful, if you had the patience to find them.

Unless you were Trace. In which case you had incredibly sticky fingers and could scoot up the wall twice as fast as a spider. She disappeared over the ledge, going in the direction of the walkway on the wall and the other tower opposite this one.

While my objective was to capture at least one tango and have a heart-to-heart talk about what was going on. I was, however, prepared to be realistic. If the odds turned out to be overwhelming—say, if we found that those ZSU-23 guns were accompanied by three or four main battle tanks—then we could always back off and call Frankie or the Italians.

What I was not prepared to do was come away empty-handed. So when I heard an outboard motor in the distance as I reached the top of the tower, my first reaction was, "son of a bitch."

My second reaction was to grab tightly at the wall, because I had almost slipped. Reminding myself that I didn't want to have to start over, I reached up and pulled myself onto the ledge. I stood, and found myself staring at the horizon.

A light flashed off in the distance on the surface of the water. It was a small needle, thin and off in an instant. But it was too far to have been the boat.

I leaned over the stone wall and saw what I was looking for. While we were climbing through the tower, a rigid hulled boat had come up close to one of the doors that opened from the castle. Something dangled from the door now—a rope ladder.

The motor went from a low, quiet idle to an ass-kicking high rev. The boat jerked in the direction of the pinprick of light I'd seen.

Clearly, the people in the boat were going to get away. I didn't want that to happen. There was only one way to stop them. So I did the stupidest thing possible:

I jumped.

7

Maybe jumping wasn't the stupidest thing possible. Maybe firing the MP5N as I fell was.

But what the heck. It was going to get wet anyway.

How many bullets I got off before I hit the water is anybody's guess. At least some hit the three figures in the boat, including whoever was steering, because the last thing I saw as I hit the water was it lurching back toward me.

I had about a half of a half of a second to wish that it would go the other way. The bow *may* have missed my head by two inches; I was too busy pretending to be a concrete anchor to get a good estimate.

Two strong strokes to the left and I surfaced about twenty feet from the boat. It was moving toward me, but not on purpose. The helmsman had fallen dead against the wheel.

Getting aboard a runaway boat from the water is more difficult than stopping a runaway train by a factor of only ten or so. You take your best shot and you have a fifty-fifty chance of getting clipped by the propeller. And that's if no one on board the boat tries to help.

I got a hand on the rubber hull but couldn't hang on. The boat turned again, its circle wider. It seemed to be slowing, not trying to run me over, but I didn't trust it. Something leaned off the side. Sensing I was about to be shot, I ducked under the water, stroking in the other direction. When I surfaced, the boat had begun to drift sideways toward the castle.

If I'd been a giraffe, maybe I'd've been able to see into the damn thing and understand what the hell was going. But as low in the water as the boat was, I was still lower, and between that and the dim light, all I could see were a few shadows. I pulled out my diving knife and began stroking warily toward the boat. As I got closer, I saw that the shadow at the side had an arm off toward the water. Still not trusting that I wasn't being suckered into a trap, I dove, resurfaced, then came over to the side and pulled down on the arm. As the body flopped into the water I shoved myself under the hull and came up on the other side. When I pulled myself up into the boat, it was empty.

While all of this was going on, Trace had been standing up on the wall watching. I looked up at her and waved; she waved back. Then she disappeared.

There are a million reasons for a person suddenly not being where they were. At that moment, I couldn't think of any but one: She'd been ambushed by someone in the castle.

As I turned to find the wheel and controls of the boat, I saw the light flash again on the sea. It was about a mile away.

I'd have to get back to it; Trace was more important. I started the engine and turned the boat around, heading for the door on the castle wall. Similar to the one we'd seen inside, there was no handle or anything else to grab to open it with. I was just about to get out and scale the wall when Trace shouted down to me.

"Dick, what are you doing?"

"Looking for you," I yelled back. "What's going on?"

"Nothing! The place is deserted."

"All right. Jump."

"Jump? Fuck you."

"Later—right now there's someone offshore that was supposed to meet these jokers. Let's go see who it is. Come on, before they leave!"

A fresh string of expletives ended with a loud splash in the water.

After I fished her out, we headed for the light. When we got within a half-mile, we saw a shadow looming low on the water, the sort of inky smudge the conning tower of a submarine makes against a very dim background before it sinks into the water. (Yes, I have seen it, many times. A very lonely sight, especially if you were supposed to be on the fucker.)

I could describe an interesting chase scene here, with us arriving just as the submarine dives. I could say how I leapt from the boat, grabbed hold of the periscope, and stuck my tongue out at the captain before it disappeared beneath the waves.

But none of that happened. We crisscrossed the area where I'd seen the light a dozen, two dozen times without finding anything. There definitely had been *something* there, but it was gone now.

"Fireflies," suggested Trace sarcastically.

"Then where was the boat going?"

"Only a million other places up and down the shore."

We went back to the castle to search the place more thoroughly. Besides the boat garage and door on the sea, there was only one entrance that connected to the building's interior rooms. This was near the northern tower, and was down a stairway so narrow only one person could fit at a time, and even then if you had decent-size shoulders like mine you'd have to turn a bit sideways. The stairway opened into a corridor only a few inches wider. Ten rooms sat on the left of the hall. Only one had a door, and that seemed to have been a combination lookout post and control room. Roughly twenty feet wide but only six deep, it had a slit that looked out toward the sea. A control panel of toggle switches had been mounted in the stone beneath the opening, with a thick metal-sheathed cable running out into the corridor and then downstairs. The switches worked an electronic lock in the watery garage below, as well as lights there and on the parapet.

Three very thick cables ran across the floor from the corridor and stopped under the slit window, their ends curving upward as if they were snakes.

"They had cable," sneered Trace.

"My bet is that there was a panel from the radar here. We'll trace the wires back later."

There was no bedding in any of the upstairs rooms, and except for some plain white bags and a dozen empty plastic bottles, there was no sign that anyone had stayed in the place for any length of time. The bags were long and narrow, the sort we'd use in the States for a loaf of Italian bread or a French baguette. The bottles were unlabeled and all but one were empty; that one held water, and I guessed that the others had as well.

"They weren't here long," said Trace. "And they were neat."

More than that. If they'd been here more than a few hours, they'd slept on a stone floor; we didn't find any bedding, not even a blanket, in the rooms downstairs. Nor was there any furniture; no chairs, no tables, nothing but ancient dust.

The section of the castle between the walls had once been a large central hall. The timbers had collapsed long ago and much of the floor and whatever else had been inside lay in a large pile of rubble. The beams that held the roof above didn't look as if they were in the greatest shape either. Perhaps a quarter of them had been braced, but these repairs looked pretty old themselves. Whoever had been holed up here had used the area for target practice; we found a few shell casings scattered on the stone walkway.

We tracked the cables back up to the tower and then the wall on the land side of the castle, onto the hill where it was covered by camouflage netting to look like a cluster of rocks. There was no antiaircraft gun or missile battery for that matter. My guess is that the unit was used as an early-warning system to track aircraft that showed too much interest in the place. Someone standing on the tower and armed with a Stinger or similar shoulder-launched

antiaircraft weapon would have been a more than
adequate defense, especially if cued to the general
direction by the radar operator.

Just a theory.

I found a type number stamped inside the radar
unit, along with a sequence of letters that turned
out to indicate when it had been modified and re-
furbished. But if there had ever been a serial number or an ID plate, it was long gone.

So was the boat when we went down to leave.

The first thing I did was make sure I had a full
load of ammo in the MP5N. The second thing I did
was drop to my belly and crawl out farther through
the doorway over the sea, staring into the dim twi-
light.

We'd left the boat tied to the gate below. Trace
had tied the knot, and she swore now that she *had*
tied the knot, and damn tight, too.

"I'm not questioning it." It was about a half
hour before sunrise and the area directly below the
castle lay in deep shadow. I had to stare to make
anything out.

"Fuck. I tied it tight. They were all dead. Weren't
they all dead?"

"Don't panic."

"Screw yourself, panic. I'm not panicking. They
were dead. I saw them die."

One was dead, definitely. The other two men
Trace had seen in the boat had disappeared before I
got there, falling off into the water and *presumably*
dead.

Presume? Is that the same as *assume?* The word

old-style Navy chiefs define as: *assume—to make an ass of U and ME?*

Which one of my old chiefs said that?

Every last one of them.

We spent the next hour searching, first for possible ambushers, then for the boat, and finally for the bodies of the men who'd been in it. But we found *niente:* nothing. I considered smashing my fist against the stone wall in frustration, but decided against it. You never know how long you're going to have to wait to see a competent doctor in an Italian hospital.

Crapinpants and Kohut didn't appreciate the fact that I hadn't invited them and ten thousand troops to my private sneak and peak at the castle. Frankie resented my holding back the information as well. But I wasn't in the mood to apologize. Nor was an apology warranted; by the time they would have been able to mount an operation the tangos would have been long gone anyway. It took until late that afternoon to get a helicopter up to search the coastline and nearby waters. Call it Murphy or incompetence, but five minutes into its search the helo developed engine trouble and had to return to its base. A full-scale search wasn't launched until the next day, and the boat was never found. Nor were the bodies of the men who'd been in it.

I concentrated on the road less traveled. I called an analyst friend of mine at Langley (where the Christians In Action hang their hats) to see if the radar unit could be tracked down using the model and modification numbers I'd recorded. He passed me off to a clerk at the NSA—aka No Such Agency—who found a dusty file drawer (metaphorically speaking, since the databases the secret spy agency keeps are all on computer) that indicated the unit was *probably* part of a shipment to Egypt replacing units destroyed by Israel in the Six-Day War back in the sixties. I took that information to a friend of mine at the Defense Intelligence Agency. Several hours of hold-Muzak later, I determined that the radar had been on a ZSU-23 (Zeus) gun vehicle that was still allegedly active in Egypt, even though it was older than the hills and several pyramids.

"Officially, it belongs to a unit near the Sudan border," said my friend. "My guess is that it was actually surplused ten years ago and they lost the paperwork. I'm looking at a satellite photo of the unit and there are zero Zeus guns."

The lousy records meant I'd hit a dead end, though even if the unit had been officially recorded as surplus it would have been hard to trace further. Its most likely disposition would have been "destroyed," which in Egyptian is another way of saying "sold on the black market."

On the other hand, the fact that the radar had been in Egypt at one time made the next little tidbit I picked up that much more interesting. After a check with the official sources showed that there were no vessels anywhere near the shore that night, I found a few unofficial sources to talk to. A conversation with a friend in the radar (not sonar) department of a never-to-be-named U.S. Navy ship revealed that there was a submarine in that area of the Mediterranean that night, albeit a decent distance away. And guess whose navy owned the sub?

Egypt's would be correct.

Granted, the submarine, a Chinese-built Romeo-class diesel boat, was reported to be about thirty miles away at the time. The sub—which by the way had been updated with the assistance of *American* companies and equipped with goodies like U.S. Harpoon missiles—could make about fifteen knots on the surface, and went a good bit slower underwater. It wasn't inconceivable that it had been near the castle when I saw the light.

I dug into my little black book and made some more calls, easing my time on hold with a tall glass of Dr. Bombay's boredom cure. The submarine had sailed from Alexandria—HQ for the Egyptian navy—about a week before and was due back in another week. It had traveled so far from home to prove to NATO that the Egyptians are real swell guys and can be counted on in a crisis, and therefore deserve a few billion more in military aid to beat the piss out of their citizens and build air-conditioned villas for relatives of the ruling class.

In other words, they were taking part in a NATO training exercise, just concluded. The submarine was now on its way home to Alexandria, a fact that I was able to confirm. My inquiries eventually brought me to the American naval attaché assigned to Egypt, a Captain Green. Naval attachés are basically spies in uniform. I know because I was one in Cambodia during the Vietnam War, and among my duties was dispensing advice on how to run the war against Pol Pot and taking a few pleasure cruises to see if my advice made any sense. These cruises were aboard varied combat riverine craft that I needed to keep

the Mekong River open to resupply Phnom Penh
with beans, bullets, oil and luxury items. They were
so much fun I broke four ribs and punctured my
lung. But the experience was worthwhile in the end,
for it introduced me to the wonderful medicinal
powers of Dr. Bombay, whose elixir has proved to be
a cure-all for me.

Green knew about the submarine and the NATO
exercise, but wasn't particularly helpful when I
asked what he knew about the commander. He kept
asking why I wanted to know. I told him that I
thought the submarine had been much closer to
Sicily than was believed, and he quite rightly asked
what the big deal was. I told him that I believed the
submarine had been trying to rendezvous with
someone onshore but didn't get into the nuclear
weapons angle. I didn't know Green and I wasn't
sure exactly how far I could trust him. And besides,
there wasn't much sense accusing the Egyptian navy
of being involved in a plot to steal nuclear weapons
from the U.S. unless I had real proof.

Pus Face told me this himself, shouting so loudly
over the phone I probably could have heard him
without it, even though he'd flown up to Berlin to
continue doing whatever it was he pretended to be
doing. Pus Face's attitude toward the situation
bounced back and forth like a pinball because he
was constantly calculating the benefit-loss equation.
Unlike Kohut, who now simply wanted everything
to go away so he could retire in peace, Pus Face had
ambitions for another two stars and then a career
beyond the uniform. This had him twisting in several different directions at once. Catching a deadly

terrorist leader would be a *good* thing—but causing Egypt to break off diplomatic relations with the U.S. would be a *bad* thing. Foiling a plot to steal a nuke from Sigonella was a *good* thing—but losing a chance to grab the thieves was *bad*. The more angles to the situation, the tighter the knots Pus Face tied himself in. Apparently, Pus Face was trying to take the lion's share of the credit for stopping the theft, and telling anyone that some of the thieves may have gotten away wasn't going to make him look good.

(Why would Pus Face take credit for that? Why would anyone believe that he deserved credit? Oh, dear reader, you have a lot to learn about the world.)

Late in the day I got an update from Doc about our company party and the planned operation to visit Ali Goatfuck in Pakistan. One of our sources in Afghanistan had reported that Goatfuck was on his way to Islamabad, the capital of Pakistan, to meet with other resistance figures.

"May be a good place to grab him," I told Doc.

"That's what Danny thought. He's on his way. He should be on the ground by now."

I felt a twinge of regret. It wasn't that I didn't trust Danny and the three shooters he brought with him to do the job. I wanted to be there. But I couldn't tell him to wait for me to hop on a plane and meet him. Parachuting into the middle of an ongoing operation has any number of drawbacks, beginning with the not-so-subtle message it sends that you don't trust your men to do the job.

Doc sensed my disappointment and changed the subject. He was about to head from Germany to Afghanistan, to inspect our operation there personally.

"This will cheer you up. Apparently Goatfuck has spread the word that anyone who kills one of our guys will get ten thousand dollars American. Unless they manage to kill Marcinko. You're worth a hundred grand. They have pictures of you on a little leaflet."

"Is it a good likeness?"

"Not bad. Must've gotten it out of a magazine somewhere."

Ah, it's nice to be wanted. I've learned to take these things in stride as I've matured. The news even made me a bit nostalgic, reminding me of the Vietcong wanted poster that appeared in the tourist Mecca known as the Republic of Vietnam. The photo there came from an article on the SEALs and *moi* which appeared in a male magazine . . . available in our PXs in country (duh!). And you thought the commies only read those things for the articles.

"You better watch your ass around me," Doc added. "I could use a hundred thousand. Donna has her eyes on a nice little speedboat."

Donna is his wife, which is why she's known as "St. Donna" to anyone who knows Doc.

"You're just jealous because your head's worth less than mine," I told him.

"Ragheads never were much good judging character," he retorted.

Our project to track the shoes had not gotten very far. The manufacturer contracted with several companies that acted as distributors. There were only a dozen, but simply getting them to answer calls or email was proving to be a problem. There was a considerable language barrier, even when using email.

Nine of the twelve were located in Eastern Europe and Asia, where we would have little way of pressuring them to cooperate.

And then there was the tenth, M.E. Boots & Gear, which was located in Cairo.

Definitely worth a visit, if I were planning on being in Egypt anytime soon.

Which, I thought that evening, might not be a bad idea. I wanted to know who the hell Saladin was, and while Danny might pick up something in Pakistan, tracing the shoes was our next best bet. At the same time, the possibility that the Egyptian submarine had been involved in the terrorists' operation bothered the hell out of me. Egypt may not be our most dependable ally in the world, but it's important strategically—and it has received a hell of a lot of my tax dollars over the years. Involvement by the military in an operation against America? Almost unthinkable.

The key word in that sentence is "almost."

By the time I went down to find Trace and go out to dinner, I'd decided I'd go over to Egypt to poke around. Besides visiting the shoe distributor, I'd knock on a few office doors belonging to friends of mine to see if they knew anything about Saladin. And then I'd hop up to Alexandria and see what I could determine about the submarine.

"I was just thinking of something," said Trace as we waited for our drinks to arrive. "Weren't the scumbags in Rome using the same guns?"

"A couple. The others had Beretta 12Ss." Our drinks arrived.

"So were these guys. Two Minimis were found in

the car, and they were firing some in the castle." She reached into her jeans and pulled out a pair of shells. One was from a 5.58 x 45mm NATO round—Minimi ammunition—and the other was or at least appeared to be 9 x 19mm Parabellum of the type used in the submachine gun.

"Those size bullets can fit in all sorts of weapons," I reminded her.

"We can have some ballistics tests done," she said. "It's like fingerprinting a gun."

"I doubt the same guns were used."

"But we would know they were the same type."

"It doesn't prove anything, Trace."

"Boy, you're negative." She took a sip of her wine, eyes flashing. "It would be *interesting* to know, wouldn't it?"

"Interesting, yes. But we need bullets, not shells."

"Ought to be easy to get. I would definitely check with the Rome police to see if there's a connection."

"The investigation is actually in the Vatican's jurisdiction." I pulled out my sat phone. Dinner in Italy is a leisurely affair; it could be hours before anything actually arrived. Figuring that I might just as well put the time to good use, I dialed Backass to make sure ballistics tests were done on the gun.

Backass was traveling, and the two assistants I talked to knew jack and said less about what was going on with the investigation. I left my number and forgot about him—until ten minutes later, when the phone rang and his truly came on the line.

"Trouble seems to follow you around the world," said Backass, who'd heard of our Sicilian adventures. He claimed to have been wondering about a connection with the Vatican thugs on his own and would be in the area to consult with the local *carabinieri* in the next few days. "Maybe we can meet for dinner," he said. "I know a very good seafood restaurant. The *calamari* is a dream."

Backass may not have been much of a security chief, but he would have made a hell of a restaurant critic. I told him I'd need a rain check, then asked what else he knew about the terrorists who'd struck at the Vatican. The answer was not much. Two of the dead tangos had been in Spain before the attack—they'd gotten there from Morocco. The others had been more careful about erasing their paths. The attempts to trace the weapons and other items they had hadn't turned up much either. The Minimis were part of a batch of fifty-six guns shipped to Indonesia a year before. They were purchased under a military aid contract (three guesses whose tax dollars ultimately paid for the weapons) and then subsequently "misplaced." Not all of the weapons, incidentally, had ended up in terrorists' hands; two had been used in a bank robbery in Singapore a month earlier. The authorities there had already done a great deal of legwork trying to track them back to the source, but had come up empty.

The incident at the church had helped Backass get some of the money he needed and allowed him to finally overhaul the security structure at the basilica, bringing in his own people and taking direct control of security there. But he was also feeling serious pressure from above to discover who was responsible for the attack. While the pope had issued a "prayer of forgiveness" for the slimers, the prelates around him wanted justice. I suspected that they also wanted

Backass's head for failing to protect the world's most important Catholic Church.

He mentioned Saladin—the Web page implying that he was behind the attack was now common knowledge—but then dismissed him as a crank.

He wasn't too confident about that, though, because he asked if I agreed.

"He's definitely a crank," I told him. "The question is, what else is he?"

"Yes." Backass thought it over. "Others have taken credit as well. But there don't seem to be any real leads."

I mentioned the neofascists who were hoping for a new Mussolini, more to see his reaction than from any evidence they were involved.

"You believe P2 exists, then," said Backass.

"I keep an open mind on all conspiracy theories."

"You should on them. Definitely."

"Would they shoot up St. Peter's?"

He gave me a mealy-mouthed answer to the effect that it couldn't be ruled out. Personally, I wasn't sure that any such animal existed. But if it did, all of the theories I had heard had it being virulently anti-Communist and pro–Catholic Church, to the point of including at least one bishop. Even a dyed-in-the-wool conspiracy theorist would have trouble believing that the people behind P2 would shoot up St. Peter's.

"The investigation is not in my hands," admitted Backass. "I must concentrate on what I can control. I'm taking steps to strengthen security in the future."

Good idea. Make sure you get that barn door good and secure now that the horses are out.

* * *

Doc woke me up the next morning with a phone call from Kabul, the garden spot of exotic Afghanistan. He'd been in the city all of two hours, but he'd already done a month's worth of work.

"We got one," he said. "Dead, though."

"Real shame."

"Yeah. Everybody here is broken up about it."

The dead man had been trying to plant a Claymore mine rigged with a remote triggering device in a road near one of the installations outside the city where Red Cell trainers were doing their thing. Maybe he thought the fact that it was past 1 a.m. made him invisible, or he thought that too many government contracts have made my people start acting like actual government employees, punching the clock at four. In any event, one of the skeleton crew we'd left behind had seen the asshole through a night optical device, got the idjit on tape—don't want to be accused of hurting scumbags without a legal reason to do so—and then led two of the people we were training out to try and capture him. He wanted him alive for the information value, a sound decision.

The team started to sweep around, looking to see if the man with the mine had friends watching his back. He did—and being good friends, they hit the plunger as they took off, killing their comrade. Our guy got a few slugs into the back of their vehicle, but they were too far away to be caught.

Claymore mines are an old but solid weapon that date to a discovery during World War II by a hun and a Hungarian, namely Schardin and Misznay, who figured out how to do a lot of damage with metal when it goes boom. When hordes of Chinese came pouring over the North Korean border in that little brush-up over there, the U.S. Army took their ideas and used them to narrow the odds. The weapon sprays metal balls in an arc, as opposed to a circle, allowing the people on the right side of it not to get any boo-boos. The "classic" Claymore or M18A1 was used in Vietnam; packed with seven hundred steel ball bearings it could make mincemeat of a patrol trying to sneak up on an American position or infiltrating down a trail. It's simple to set up, as long as you know what the words "Front Toward Enemy" mean. (Or, the special West Virginia version: "If the contour of the mine fits the curve of your forehead— it's facing the 'bad guys.' If the contour faces away from you—you're going to eat it!")

Our dead tango had the bad fortune of being on the wrong side of the weapon when it went off. Claymore wounds are not very pretty, and comparing his body to Swiss cheese would not be inappropriate. However, he was so close to the weapon that, while the ball bearings literally took his head off, they left his face almost unscathed. This made it easier for our guy to identify him as one of the employees he'd been assigned to train.

Nice, huh? But not shocking. Nor was it all that surprising that the man's background had not been checked by the people who hired him, who would have found with very little effort that it was entirely fictional, right down to the address he gave as his home. But by the time Doc landed in Kabul, our man had tracked down the place in Kabul where Ali Goatfuck had lived with two roommates—undoubtedly the ones who had pulled the trigger on him.

In America, these sorts of leads would, presumably, get an army of FBI agents checking through records and trying to trace Ali Goatfuck back three generations to a shepherd in Istanbul. In Afghanistan, Doc couldn't get even a yawn out of the local police chief, who admittedly had better things to do than worry about who a dead raghead really was.

On the other hand, Afghanistan not being America, there was no problem with pulling apart Goatfuck's crib. Among the things that Doc discovered were some folded Egyptian pound notes and a Cairo phone number. The number belonged to a rug merchant. Doc hadn't had any time to check further, but was ready to hop a plane to Cairo to do so.

"That's all right," I told him. "I'll pay him a visit myself. I'm leaving for Cairo in a few hours."

I gave him a quick brain fart to bring him up-to-date. Doc served in Cairo as command master chief of the Navy medical lab, which means not only does he know where all the bodies are buried but he put a few of them there himself. He suggested that he come over to back me up just in case things got interesting, and I agreed on the condition that our Afghanistan operations were squared away before he left. I knew they would be; Doc has that sort of effect on people. We arranged to meet in Cairo in two days UNODIR—*unless otherwise directed.*

He gave me a quick—for Doc—rundown of possible sources and a heads-up on where to stay, eat, and find good Western booze at a decent price. If Doc ever gets tired of working for me, he could make a good living as a tour guide. He knows more about most places around the world than the natives.

Trace wanted to play tail gunner on the Cairo jaunt as well, but there were too many loose ends to be tied up in Sicily. For one thing, there was a good possibility the tangos might try another run at Sigonella. Psychologically, the base security people might let their guard down after thwarting the theft—not intentionally, of course, but some things are just human nature. I wanted Trace to kick butt and keep that from happening.

I also suggested that talking to Don Alberti again might be worthwhile, if done under the right circumstances.

"You think I can just put on a short skirt, waltz in there and sit on his lap, and he'll tell me everything he knows?" she asked.

"I wouldn't sit on his lap. His son's lap, maybe."

Trace gave me one of her sarcastic smiles. A woman as smart and tough as she is doesn't *have* to use sex as a weapon, but when she does the effect is devastating.

I suggested that she borrow a pair of plainclothes *carabinieri* as escorts, but she just scowled.

"I don't need eye candy," she told me. "You go on to Cairo. I can handle the Mafia on my own."

I did an MTT exercise (mobile training team) with the Egyptian army in the early 1980s when I was commanding officer of SEAL Team Six. We worked with elite members of the military, bringing them up to speed in a number of areas. We did our maritime work at the Suez Canal, and I vividly remember diving over the tanks at the bottom of the canal, a strange and, in its way, beautiful sight. We did weapons training in the outskirts of Cairo, out past the "City of the Dead." Our sightseeing included walking along the grandstands where the crazies shot Sadat for trying to do the right thing for his countrymen and make peace with Israel.

"City of the Dead" probably sounds like a tourist attraction, and in a way it is—if you're a terrorist pilgrim looking to pick up pointers or maybe recruit some fresh blood. Calling it a slum for the living doesn't quite do it justice. Calling it a six-square-mile gaping hole to hell is more accurate. Houses built of mud lean against mausoleums, and the stench of shit, piss, and sweat hangs over the place like a thick swarm of mosquitoes. I highly recommend visiting the place if you're ever in Egypt: it'll tell you exactly why you're damn glad to be an American.

The City of the Dead is not high on the list of tourist attractions, however, and it wasn't on the bus tour I signed up for immediately after checking in at my Cairo hotel. Then again, I only got as far as the second stop. Having made sure that I wasn't being followed, I left the group and walked over a few blocks to the office of Mouhadmam Jamal, an Egyptian whom I first met on the MTT assignment. At the time, Jamal was an enlisted aide to a well-connected colonel; he left the military and joined the Egyptian intelligence service or Mukhabarat El-Aam shortly afterward. He and I have kept in touch over the years, mainly through I-scratch-your-back/you-scratch-mine arrangements.

"Dickhead!" yelled Jamal when he spotted me in the hall. "You're two hours early!"

"My camel had the wind at its back, goat breath."

We exchanged a few more terms of endearment on our way to his office. Nothing makes me feel at home like a few curse words from an old friend. I gave him the name and address we'd connected to the phone number Doc had found in Afghanistan.

"Doesn't strike me," said Jamal. Like most well-educated Egyptians, he speaks English very well but occasionally produces odd phrases, mixing American and Egyptian colloquialisms together. "Why is it important?"

"Someone's been giving my people a hard time and I'm trying to find out why." I explained a bit more of the background, though I didn't mention the possible connection with Saladin.

Jamal told me it would take him a few hours to look into things, and offered to meet later at a café where we could share a traditional hookah—the communal pipe so popular with Egyptians. I don't smoke—except after sex, and then I don't look—but I told him I'd meet him anyway. In the meantime, I thought I'd look into buying a new pair of boots.

M.E. Boots & Gear was located in a cramped suite of offices a few blocks from the boat landing on the Giza side of the Nile River. From their Web site, I'd gotten the impression that they had a massive warehouse, but in reality the business held on to very little stock, functioning more as a middleman processing orders than as a reseller. Or at least that was the impression I received from the vice president of sales, who took one look at the Rolex peeking out from the sleeve of my finely tailored business suit and immediately decided he was my best friend. His enthusiasm dimmed slightly when he heard my cover story. I was playing the role of an overseas rep for a high-end boot manufacturer in the States who found himself in Cairo unexpectedly and decided to see if I couldn't drum up a little business. It wasn't the product that bothered him but the location where it had been made; American goods, he explained, were difficult to sell without being relabeled locally.

"And how would that work?" I asked innocently. His enthusiasm returned—relabeling could bring a hefty profit—and within a few minutes we were chatting about the market. One thing led to another . . . but what it didn't lead to was information on who had bought the Bota shoes.

"I do not believe I'm familiar with that line," he said.

"They're one of our main competitors," I said. "I understand the shoes have become popular in different parts of Asia and Africa. If I could show my boss definite sales they had made—"

"We have handled very excellent boots by Scarpa," he said.

"Do you have hard numbers?"

He shrugged apologetically, saying that "my girl" who keeps the files was out. I got the impression she was out indefinitely; the place looked like Rogue Manor after a hurricane or staff party, take your pick. I let him deflect the conversation, looking for a way to circle back. Before I could find one, two men walked into the outer office, jabbering loudly in Arabic about a deal for some Nike knockoffs.

"Could you excuse me for a moment?" he asked. "I have to consult with these gentlemen."

I got up to leave but he insisted that I stay put; it would only take him a few minutes. He closed the door behind him as he went out.

It took me about thirty seconds to find a bank statement I could use to check into his accounts—one sat two sheets down in the "out" basket on his desk. Unfortunately, the files in the cabinet nearby were not only in Arabic but were very haphazard and disorganized: nothing under "s" for scumbags or the Arabic equivalent. Nor was there a file for Bota that I could find before he returned.

I took his card, promising to send a few samples of our wares in a few days when I returned home. With some time to kill before I was due to check with Jamal, I crossed back to central Cairo and went over to what is known as Downtown, an enclave of dusty gyp joints and high-class, overpriced shops. I was supposed to meet Jamal up by the American University in an hour and a half; with that much time to kill I figured I could wander into the rug merchant's shop and get a quick recce in. Along the way I practiced some of my gutter Arabic, refining the Egyptian accent on a café waiter and a man selling beads at a street corner. My Middle Eastern language skills are self-taught; I won't fool anyone into thinking that I'm a native, but I can make myself understood well enough to get a good deal on a camel. More important, I can understand the lingo sufficiently to avoid being stuck with a three-legged one.

For some reason I'd had the notion that the rug shop would be a small stall, a typical mom-and-pop outfit catering to tourists. But the place turned out to be a large warehouse which, according to the Arabic sign, dealt only wholesale. I adapted my earlier cover story accordingly, strolling in as an importer-exporter who dealt with furniture stores in North America and Europe. I started out in French, claiming to be Belgian, and then worked over to English as the international language. The conversations got me to a friendly, chubby man who claimed to be the brother of the owner, who was off on a buying expedition. I'll spare you the gab; the bottom line was that I didn't find out anything a subpoena could be hung on back in the States.

Fortunately, I wasn't operating back in the States. My real purpose was to examine the security arrangements. These consisted of metal locks and an extremely primitive wire-and-magnetic contact system, the sort of thing I learned how to get around when I was nine or ten years old. I poked through a few dozen silk rugs making sure there were no video cameras hidden in the ceiling or covert motion detectors on the overhead beams. Then I bid Amir's brother adieu and headed over to my rendezvous with Jamal.

Many Egyptians like to smoke a flavored tobacco called "shisha." The stuff is extremely powerful, along the lines of hashish (not that I would know). To make it more palatable—I guess—they put it in a special water pipe called a hookah. The tobacco is actually roasted on charcoal instead of being lit, and the water filters and cools the smoke. If you're into that sort of thing—and I'm not—it's supposed to be a great experience.

Jamal offered me a smoke but I politely declined. The coffee in Cairo's more than enough to give you a buzz; it's stronger than hell and filled with sugar. A few sips will cure all that ails you.

Jamal had not been able to find anything of worth about the business or its owner, Amir Husni Bakr. The business did not have a file, and neither did Amir. But perhaps there was a reason: Amir's cousin was an up-and-coming Egyptian deputy navy minister named Abu Bakr.

Whose responsibilities, as it happened, included overseeing Egypt's submarines.

I tried not to jump to any conclusions as I shook the information tree for background on Bakr. You didn't become a deputy minister in the Egyptian government without being well connected, and Bakr had links in every direction: business, military, government. He was either distantly related to half the government or had gone to school with them, or both. He liked to throw lavish parties and was known to steer big contracts to friends. He wasn't married, and had a reputation as a ladies' man.

The one thing he didn't seem well known for was his religious beliefs. Not one of the people I spoke to, from an Egyptian general to a nurse Doc had recommended as the queen of Cairo gossip, remembered him expressing any sort of spiritual sentiment.

Which put only a slight dent in the theory that he might be Saladin. I decided that I ought to go over to his cousin's rug shop and ask a few penetrating questions. Unfortunately, by the time I got there the place was locked up tight and everyone had gone home.

Shame, really. Though that is often the case at 1 a.m., even in Cairo. But seeing as how I was already there, I saw no reason not to proceed on my own.

Defeating wired burglar alarms on windows is as easy as cutting glass; it took all of thirteen seconds to hot-wire a connection that made it easy for me to push inside. Once inside, I secured the window and set up my own burglar-alarm system—a motion detector with wireless alert connected to an earbud to let me know if my back was exposed. Then I went to work.

My first stop was in the back office. The company had only one computer, which made my first job relatively easy. I slipped a disk into the 3.5 drive and booted it up, watching as a program written by Red Cell's resident computer geek examined the machine's capabilities. The machine had a CD-RW drive, meaning that it could write on CDs, which was what made the next step very easy. (Better would have been a DVD-RW drive, which would have made the operation faster, but you can't have everything.) I tapped a few keys and the CD drawer opened. Within thirty seconds, the computer was recording the contents of its hard drive onto a set of disks I'd brought along.

Shunt compares the program to a standard backup routine like Norton Ghost. It scans the drive, compresses the contents, then spits it onto the blank CDs. The program is entirely automated; the hardest part is standing there feeding it CDs every few minutes. Unfortunately, it's limited by the speed of the drive and the capacity of the CDs; even though it's sophisticated enough to not to copy standard things like Microsoft Windows or Office, rifling through ten gigabytes of data or so and spitting it onto a bagful of CDs takes time.

Rather than putting my thumbs up my nose while I waited, I rifled the desk drawers, looking for something useful. I found a checkbook and removed the last page of checks for reference. Then I went over to the file cabinets and started scouting through them. Boring stuff, except for the vintage *Playboys* in the bottom left-hand drawer.

It took nearly an hour for the program to lap up everything potentially interesting. When it was finally done, I backed out of the program, took my disk out, and turned the computer off. Then I pulled out the computer and turned it around, trying to figure out which one of the wires at the back went to the keyboard.

No, I wasn't overcome by geek lust or a perverted desire to view electronic couplings. I needed to install the hardware key logger I'd brought along. Key loggers keep a log of every stroke on a keyboard, recording everything a user types. Key loggers were invented by spy agencies years ago to steal computer secrets. Businesses use them now to spy on workers. You can buy fairly effective models over the Internet if you're so inclined. They come in both hardware and software versions. The one in my pocket was a bit of a hybrid, a hardware model that could dump its captured keystrokes over the Internet. This avoided detection by the common software scanners. A command program was stored in the Windows program file area, replacing legitimate but seldom-used files in the Tour folder—and yes, if I were you, I'd look into deleting some of those files on *your* computer first thing in the morning.

In order to work, the logger had to sit between the keyboard and the computer. Installing it was a snap—or would have been if I could have gotten the plug from the keyboard to release from the computer.

Getting things out of holes is usually not my problem. Obviously, Mr. Murphy had secured this one with a daub of Krazy Glue—the connection just would not come off. Finally, I took out my knife and helped it along, trying to find just the right amount of pressure to get it out of the machine. This involved tremendous willpower—I was sorely tempted to teach the computer the proper meaning of "reboot" with the heel of my shoe. It snapped out at last. I worked the hardware logger into the computer first, then went through another finger dance to get the keyboard cord in place. Just as I finally got it back together, the buzzer in my ear attached to the motion detector went off—I had company.

One of these days, Mr. Murphy and I are going to have a very serious discussion.

I put the computer back and tiptoed to the door. I still had to install the software portion of the logger, but even if I'd wanted to make a run for it, that wouldn't be a good idea—two flashlight beams slashed across the open space, zeroing in on the office.

Employees looking to get a jump on the next day tend to turn the lights on. Same with security guards.

Flashlights *are* used by thieves . . . and intelligence agents sent to plant bugs.

Sap in one hand, pistol in the other, I stepped back behind the door and waited. Whoever they were, I didn't intend to introduce myself. The world would certainly be better off with two less thieves, and the same could probably be said for two members of the Egyptian internal security apparatus. But shooting them here would add all sorts of unnecessary complications. There was a narrow space next to the row of filing cabinets to my right; it wouldn't completely hide me, but it would make me less likely to be spotted if they closed the door. On the other hand, I couldn't pop them over the head from there; if they saw me I'd have to shoot them.

Call it a consolation prize. I made it to the corner as the first beam of light entered the room. I took a diver-sized gulp of air and held it, watching as another beam of light entered and found the phone on the desk. A moment later, two men entered the room. They were black-baggers from the Egyptian secret service, here to plant a bug in the office to capture conversations. (The phone lines would have been tapped outside or at the central phone office.) They entered the room together; one moved toward the desk and the other—

The other took a few steps inside and turned around, his back about three inches from my nose.

He didn't believe in deodorant. Which was unfortunate.

I held the sap up, ready to strike. I honestly thought I'd be using it any second, and two or three times raised my hand ever so slightly, building up the momentum to give it just the right body English. But he didn't turn around, and his partner concentrated on planting his bug at the bottom of the phone. When he was done, he grabbed the flashlight, made a quick pass at the files on the wall opposite me, then left. His partner never turned around.

I rebooted the computer and installed the software, once again using a script Shunt had devised to automate the procedure. When the computer beeped to show that it was working, I retrieved my CD and shut it down. By 4 a.m. I was back at the hotel, enjoying a nightcap before turning in for a few winks before sunrise. But there is no rest for the wicked— my satellite phone began ringing before I could even slip between the sheets. (I'd say "jammies" but you all know I sleep in the raw just in case I get lucky.)

It was Danny with an update. They had a lead on Goatfuck and had worked out a plan to get him.

"He's with a woman," said Danny. "It's not his wife."

"Isn't adultery punishable by death under Islamic law?"

Danny either didn't see the humor or wasn't in much of a joking mood. "We can take him tonight. It may be crowded."

"Minimize the damage if you can, but we want the prize."

"Agreed."

If this had been a SEAL operation, I'd probably have to have consulted with a team of Department of Defense lawyers and babysitters to proceed with the mission. God help you if you cause "unnecessary" collateral damage in the course of an operation. Or if you do something without asking "Mommie, may I?" beforehand. At Red Cell International, we don't believe in letting lawyers and babysitters make the final call. Nor do we concern ourselves with environmental impact studies imposed by the likes of the U.S. Army Corps of Engineers, a mandatory step for any military maneuver lasting long enough to take a whiz these days.

Heartbroken that the girlfriend of a murderer might get accidentally shot when we thumped her boyfriend? Tell it to the three-year-old daughter of my Afghan op Goatfuck had nearly killed. Or the relatives of all the people he *had* succeeded in killing. All but two or three were civilians going about their daily business, trying only to survive in a country wracked by decades of war. Who deserves more sympathy?

Rhetorical question. You don't have to answer.

8

Snagging the bank accounts proved to be something less than the coup I'd thought. Shunt, working with the detective to track Saladin's money trail, had hit a brick wall. Not because the bank's computer systems were protected by state-of-the-art security, but because they didn't have computers that accessed the outside world. In fact, examining the statement I had taken showed that it had probably been prepared on a typewriter.

It seems almost incomprehensible that a bank wouldn't have a computer system, but many in Egypt don't. Quaint—and also a very effective way of guarding against high-tech snoops.

The detective was now researching the boot distributor and its principals, trying to trace possible connections to known terror organizations. My CDs from the rug merchant were now on their way back to Shunt. The key logger had already checked in earlier; aside from learning about a few porn sites he'd never visited, Shunt had yet to get anything useful.

The appearance of the spies in the warehouse raised the question of how far I could trust Jamal. The answer depended on what his motives were—if he'd been doing it because, as an Egyptian who remembered Anwar Sadat, he was opposed to international terrorism, that was good and he could be trusted. If he was doing it to gather dirt on a well-connected political figure, that was less good and he couldn't. Not that his intentions had to be completely honorable or that even dishonorable ones wouldn't be useful. But it was a reminder that our agendas didn't necessarily coincide.

I spent most of the morning catching up with old friends I thought might know something about the deputy naval minister, Bakr. A bit after lunchtime I checked with Trace. There had been no new attempts on the base. She reported that the Air Farcers were "tense but cute." I'm not exactly sure how she would have translated that for a fitness report. Her meeting with Don Alberti had produced no new information, but had led to two marriage proposals. Neither had been from the Don, or she might have considered them. The boat that had disappeared out from under our noses remained MIA, but one of the terrorists' bodies had washed up on the shore. So far, he hadn't been identified. Trace had some leads of her own to check into about the supposed Libyan who had rented the castle; she hoped to have more information about him within a day or so.

Doc arrived at the airport on schedule that evening. Two of our shooters were trailing him: a former Army Ranger we called Grape because of a large purple blotch on his black cheek, and Big Foot, a SEAL veteran who despite his nickname comes up to my chest. These two guys are a real Mutt & Jeff combination physically—Grape goes six-four and looks like he could eat a truck for breakfast—and they're a mismatch personality-wise as well. Big Foot is ornery by nature and will cut your balls off as say hello. Grape is cut more from Doc's mold, a talker and wheeler-dealer whom people trust even when they have no clue what the hell it is he's saying. I don't think the two men would have been friends if it weren't for the fact that they were members of Red Cell International, and had me as the common enemy, so to speak. But they were friends, and more important, they worked together extremely well. Their basic skill sets complemented each other's. Despite the fact that he has Native American blood in him, Big Foot looks like an A-raab and can speak the language well enough to get himself thrown out of a brothel. He's very, very good with explosives and the things that make them go boom. Grape took two years of electrical engineering before wandering into the Army. One of his specialties is rewiring kids' toys for grown-up uses, like detonators and spycams. As you'd expect, both are excellent weapons handlers and versatile thinkers, adaptable to any situation.

I briefed them on the way to a restaurant Doc claimed was the best in the city. While it was tempting to think that Abu Bakr *might* be Saladin, we needed to gather more information about him before jumping to that conclusion. I wanted especially to find out about the submarine—where exactly had it been that night, who was aboard, that sort of thing. The best place to get answers to some of our questions was Alexandria, the sub's homeport and the location of Bakr's office.

Cairo is easily the most famous city in Egypt, the

country's capital and business center, as well as one of the world's great tourist attractions. But Alexandria has a charm all of its own, and not just if you're a navy man. Just ask the man for whom it's named, Alexander the Great. Or Caesar, or Napoleon. All of the great figures of world conquest and a lot of the minor ones have lusted over the place. Ignore the traffic, the car horns, the pollution, the bugs, the smell of sweat rising from pavement in the shimmering heat. Alexandria is an exotic place, where East and West mingle and anything is possible.

Doc and I exchanged glances as we drove around Midan Tahrir near the center of town the next morning. Traffic was fierce, but it was nowhere near as difficult as the last time we'd been here, four or five years before. Then, the city had looked like a parking lot, and we were sweating the transport of a terrorist who was due for his own private interview back in the States. Coincidentally, a rug had been involved then, too—though it happened to be around the terrorist at the time.*

We headed over to Egyptian Naval HQ, Doc to chat up the uniforms there about submarines, and *moi* to gather information on Abu Bakr via a few backgrounders with acquaintances and acquaintances of acquaintances. Big Foot and his grumpy frown went with me as I made the rounds, starting in a trailer that served as temporary intelligence headquarters for the Egyptian fleet. (I've always thought of intel types as trailer trash, and this proved it.) From there I worked my way over to the operational center for

*For more details, see *Green Team*.

the navy's special operations group, where I looked up a few men I'd met as an observer and consultant during the original Bright Star joint exercises during the 1990s. Then I moved on to the *real* onshore home of the navy—the coffeehouses and smoking bars in the city.

I looked up a number of officers I'd met years ago as lieutenants who were now ... still lieutenants. Despite the fact that the navy had been expanded and modernized under President Mubarak, there was a logjam in the upper ranks. That meant that promotions took eons for anyone without family connections, even if a man had proven his ability and worth. No one I met complained, but I could see how a junior officer could easily become discouraged, and worse.

None of the men I spoke to knew Bakr very well. Their take was that he was a typical politician, intent on using the post as a stepping stone to bigger and better things. He wasn't seen around Alexandria much, nor was he particularly identified with the submarine fleet. My informants didn't think he was on the fast track to higher office, however. Traditionally the smallest (and least prestigious) service in the Egyptian military, the navy had lately fallen in esteem because of a scandal over the procurement of new destroyers. That fallout hadn't touched Bakr, but it hadn't helped him either.

Doc's information was more promising. The submarine that had been on maneuvers the night I went for a swim off Sicily was commanded by a man considered close to Bakr, and a bit of rebel by the rest of the navy. He was devout, and clearly so; he had gotten rid of a housekeeper because her son was rumored to be dating a Christian. Still, he would not have been entrusted with the command if he was considered a religious extremist.

The boat was not due back in Alexandria for several more days. Using his silver tongue, Doc obtained a list of the crew members who'd boarded the submarine when it left port; if one or more turned up missing, then we'd have pretty good proof that there was a connection with the Sicilian operation.

We needed more, though. And so, just after 7 p.m., we piled into our rented car and headed south for a visit to Bakr's palatial estate thirty miles south of Cairo on the Nile. (Take the road to al-Lisht and hang a left. Drive until a large cement wall blocks your view of the muddy blue water beyond. It's on the other side of the wall.)

Stymied by the traffic out of Alexandria, we didn't arrive until after four. Under other circumstances I might have considered our timing exquisite, but from the moment I saw the compound from a sand dune a mile away I knew we'd need a little more prep time before going in. Even at two in the morning in the middle of nowhere, twelve guards were watching the grounds. Video cameras covered every inch of the surrounding terrain as well as the nearby river. There were two ways in—a long, narrow road from the highway, and a small dock on a man-made lagoon from the Nile. Both were patrolled as well as studded with cameras. There was no way to sneak in without being seen.

So we'd have to be obvious about it.

While Grape and I scouted the surrounding area for a convenient base of operations, Doc and Big Foot hung around long enough to follow some of the guards as they went off duty just before dawn. One of the men headed to the mosque for morning prayers; they followed. Big Foot looks like an Arab, but it was Doc who did most of the talking in the nearby café after prayers. Before you could say the words *caffeine buzz*, he had learned that Bakr was having a party of assorted foreign navy types the next night. From there, coming up with a plan was as easy as haggling at the market. (Say *"La'a, da ghaali awy"*—No, that's very expensive—over and over until the price drops.)

Danny called in the next morning and left a one-word message on my voice mail: "Done."

It was a few days before I was able to get the entire story about the operation. Ali Goatfuck had come to town to meet with several Pakistanis who were supportive of his cause—and a conduit for his funds. Danny and his boys followed Goatfuck to the meeting but couldn't get close enough to listen in. After the session, Goatfuck went to a safe house on the outskirts of Islamabad—not the hotel where he had stayed the two previous nights. Our guys got past the two guards outside the building, slitting their throats with the sharp snap that's become so popular of late among jihad wannabes. But Goatfuck apparently had some sort of premonition that his time was up; when Danny got inside he found the bastard kneeling in prayer at the foot of his bed.

"Up, motherfucker," Danny told him, extending his gun toward his head.

Goatfuck flinched just enough for Danny to realize that he had a grenade in his hand. He pressed the trigger on his MP5 and simultaneously dove out of the room, yelling to the others to take cover. When the grenade exploded a second or two later, Goatfuck's midsection took most of the blow.

Real pity, that. I'm crying just thinking about it.

None of our guys were hurt, but even though the explosion had been muffled, it was loud enough to raise alarms in the neighboring hovels. Danny and team exfiltrated from the area. He turned his attention to the Paks whom Goatfuck had met with, figuring that they might lead us back to Saladin.

I didn't have these details at the time, but I knew that Danny had accomplished his mission without taking casualties. The message had been sent: If you screw with Dick Marcinko's people, they're coming back at you three times as hard. But we were only just beginning.

Back in Egypt, Bakr's party was in full swing by ten o'clock that night. Music blared over the walls, wafting on the breeze as a captain from the Brazilian navy drove up to the gate and was waved inside.

The captain wasn't me; it was Doc. We'd decided that my face might be just a little too familiar right now, given all of the adventures in Italy. Besides, I wanted to do the fun stuff myself.

Grape was chauffeur and lookout. He dropped Doc and his sidekick, Ensign Big Foot, near the door, then pulled the car to the far side of the compound, nudging between the other Mercedes. As soon as he cleared his throat, I slipped out the back door in my dress black BDUs. Crawling on my hands and knees, I proceeded to the other side of the lot, avoiding the surveillance cameras. From there I ran like hell to a set of French doors on the wing of the house that housed Bakr's office. I had a little trouble with the lock, but within a few minutes I was inside in a hallway, heading for the room at the far end. I was just about to reach for the doorknob when I heard a sound inside.

It was a sound I've heard before, many times: the sort a woman makes when she is in a very, *very* good mood.

I did the only polite thing: I knocked.

Then I scrambled back to the nearest doorway, sliding back into the shadows to see what happened. About sixty seconds later, a good-looking European woman in a black cocktail dress hurried down the hallway, working on her makeup as she went.

Abu Bakr followed a half minute behind. Unlike the woman, his steps were confident, measured; I didn't get a good look, of course, but I imagine he was smiling the smile of a man who'd just grabbed a good piece of ass. I raised my estimate of the Egyptian navy and proceeded into the room, where I unpacked my gear and began draining the hard drive of information. Bakr had spent decent bucks on a top-of-the-line Dell PC; the unit came with a DVD-RW drive, which made my job even easier than it had been at the rug joint.

Brazil, God bless them, doesn't have much of a navy, and what they do have stays miles and miles from the Mediterranean. This suited Doc's purpose pretty well, since it made it unlikely anyone else at the party had met someone who might be able to contradict his cover story. To explain his presence in Egypt, Doc constructed a cock-and-bull tale about a

worldwide tour to see how other navies handled
shallow-water tactics. His appearance on the guest
list was legit: he'd called up the assistant minister's
office to arrange a tour, and one thing led to another
(with some prodding on his part). His Portuguese
consisted of two phrases he'd memorized from the
Internet, along with an array of mispronounced
Spanish; he wouldn't need more than a grunt or two
before turning to heavily accented English. Ensign
Big Foot had only to stand nearby and nod. Hell, one
look at the frown on his mug and everyone would
run the other way.

The cover would have been perfect, had not one,
not two, but four Portuguese officers, ranging from
captain to admiral, been invited to the party. All had
recently returned from a trip to Brazil where they had
advised the navy. And they all spoke pretty good
Portuguese.

Silver-tongued Al Tremblay had finally met his
match. But like any good master chief, he did not
panic.

He fainted instead.

It was a perfect two-point landing in the hors
d'oeuvres. Doc had spotted trouble as the officers approached. Thinking quickly, he whispered a warning
to Big Foot and then initiated his diversion. Big Foot
fell right into the act, yelling for a doctor in a pidgin
patois that included every known language but Portuguese.

All I knew about this was the screams at the far
end of the hall. I checked the computer; only about
half of the hard drive's contents had been copied onto
the first of two double-layer DVDs Shunt's program

said were needed. It would take eight more minutes at least to get the rest of the data, and then I had to install the key logger system.

The screams faded a bit, and I decided they weren't worth worrying about. I turned my attention to planting a pair of eavesdropping devices—aka "bugs." These were custom-designed "Rogue bugs," engineered with a little help from my friends after a recent foray behind what used to be the Iron Curtain.

Remember the old Polaroid camera? Remember the film? It turns out that the old film had a material in it that has an eight-year battery life. Cut into small strips, it's just the thing to run a bug for an extended period. (They also use it commercially as a cell phone booster. A three-dollar strip buys you two hours of transmit time.)

Back at the party, the Portuguese naval officers were extremely helpful when they saw that their comrade in arms and tongue had gone down. One ran outside to find the Brazilian's car and driver. (Snow is more likely to arrive in Egypt than an ambulance.) Grape nodded meaningfully, started the car, and made his way around to the front—looking out the rearview mirror all the time, wondering where the hell I was and what the asshole screaming at him was saying. Big Foot and one of the security people appeared at the front door with Doc slumped between them; there were two or three guests and two security people as well. Grape got out of the car, opened the door, and nodded as the Portuguese officer explained what had happened and began translating the directions to the nearest hospital from Arabic to Portuguese. The security men volunteered to go with them—it's likely that Abu Bakr told them to—but Big Foot told him it wasn't necessary. Doc was faced with a difficult decision: if he didn't leave right then, he'd blow the mission. And if he did leave right then, he'd be leaving me up shit's creek without a paddle.

He grunted "go" as they closed the doors. It was the right decision. I've been up that creek many times before.

While I was waiting for the computer to do its thing, I set up my wireless bug in the telephone. We'd taken the precaution of using units very similar to those used by the Egyptian intelligence service, based on the theory that when they were found—when, not if—Abu Bakr would put two and two together and start looking for enemies in the wrong direction. We didn't figure it would last a week, but you never knew; it transmitted to a collection unit (a fancy name for small hard drive attached to a radio receiver) about 1,500 meters away.

Installing the bug took all of thirty seconds, which left me with another seven and a half minutes to kill. I put them to use inspecting the L-shaped office. The desk and computer were in the smaller leg, which measured about twenty by thirty feet. The other half was dominated by a large sofa and bookcase; I assume that had been the setting of the tryst I'd interrupted earlier. Thick curtains covered the windows behind the area where the desk was. I slid them back and found that one of the windows wasn't locked. The window opened from the side. I pushed it out gently, deciding that I'd go out here rather than down the hall.

The desk drawers were locked, but the locks were the sort that could be opened with a letter opener or paperclip, and they presented no problem to my pick. But as I started to ease the first one open, I heard a set of confident footsteps approaching down the hall.

I glanced over at the computer. A timer in the program showed how much longer the operation would need. Of course, since Shunt had written it, this wasn't a simple set of figures blinking at me in the middle of a dark screen. It was a chaotic barrage of numbers flying across space, something Dalí might have painted if he ever tried acid.

TWO MINUTES, 42 SECONDS, AND COUNTING . . .

TWO MINUTES, 41 SECONDS, STILL COUNTING . . .

WORKING ON IT, DUDE.

TWO MINUTES, 40 SECONDS, AND COUNTING . . .

You get the idea. Rather than killing the computer and risking losing some of the data (and making it obvious someone had stolen it), I thought I would turn the monitor off. I reached to the bottom corner, figuring I'd find the on-off switch there. But this wasn't a standard Dell screen. Its designer was an independent type who believed in style over usability: He'd hidden the switch somewhere else on the unit. I spent about five seconds looking for it, then dropped to my knee and looked for the power cord instead. The doorknob turned as I pulled the plug. I rose and stepped back to the edge of the bookcase, hidden in the corner as the light came on and Abu Bakr entered.

Was I tempted to hit him over the head, hoist him

over my shoulder, and carry him back to the States for an interview?

Is the pope Catholic?

But I have to confess that my doubts that he was Saladin had grown exponentially. Between the opulent house and the loose woman on the couch earlier, he didn't impress me as the religious type. Maybe this was all a well-maintained cover, or maybe Saladin was some sort of bizarre psychological alter ego. But I don't put much stock in psychology, bizarre or otherwise. And if I'm going to kidnap a member of a foreign government, I want to be reasonably sure I'm getting the right one. For the moment, whacking him over the head was only the backup plan.

Still, when he took a few steps toward the desk, I thought I might have to implement it. But he was only grabbing a cigarette—yet another Western temptation rare among fanatics. As he lit up, I heard another set of footsteps coming from down the hallway: another woman, a different one from the sound of her shoes, though I couldn't see from where I was.

The light went off just as the door was opened. The woman stepped in, they kissed, and then drifted to the couch. Give Bakr credit—he learned from his earlier experience, putting on a stereo to dampen some of the ambient sounds emerging from the room. Or maybe this "date" just preferred music.

Whatever. It made it easier for me to crawl out and pop the DVD from the drive.

Damn, the gears that worked the drawer in that computer were loud! I swear I've heard quieter tanks. Twenty-five feet away, Ramona or whatever her name was on the couch started moaning in French that she wanted to be taken. I pulled the disk out of the drive, waited for the volume on the couch to increase, then hit the button to close the drawer. In a nod to discretion I didn't bother with the key logger. I turned the machine off, reconnected the power switch at the back, then backed toward the window. The corner of the room blocked my view of the couch, but the audio portion of the program came in loud and clear and left little to the imagination. Sliding behind the curtains, I started out the window just as a set of headlights swept in my direction.

I jumped back against the inside wall. Mr. Murphy had persuaded the car valets to use the area nearby to queue up vehicles; there were far too many people nearby to risk going out this way.

I was stuck in my own private peep show. Just think: If I'd been thirteen years old, I'd've been in heaven.

Doc and the others had left the compound by now, escorted by the security people in two other cars. The safest and smartest thing at that point was to simply follow them to the hospital. There he would stage a miraculous recovery, throw a credit card at whoever was assigned to seek payment, and race back to pick me up. Doc didn't always do the safest thing in life; you might even make an argument that that tended to be his last choice most days. But he nearly always did the *smartest* thing, and he knew that in this case, doing nothing to arouse suspicions further than they had been aroused was the wisest course of action. He'd trust me to find a way out of the compound by my-self; it made more sense than going back and blasting me out.

Though he was prepared to do that if necessary.

Back in Bakr's office, things were reaching their climax. This was definitely a different woman—much quieter, but with a deeper voice. They finished up and headed out. Bakr left but came right back, nearly catching me as I made sure I had gotten the monitor reattached. He only wanted another cigarette, how-ever, and didn't even bother turning on the light. I waited for him to leave, then retraced my steps down the hall to the other room and back outside.

I didn't know about Doc's swoon into the hors d'oeuvres or the other complications until I saw that the car wasn't where I had left it. I crawled around a row of other Mercedes, thinking it had moved or that maybe I'd forgotten where we had parked. About a third of the guests had already left, and maybe an-other third or so had called for their cars. Most of the rest of the drivers were gathered in two clumps across from the parked cars, chattering away.

Obviously, if my Mercedes wasn't available, any one would do. I slipped into a car at the far end of the row, got it started, and then when one of the security men appeared to call for a vehicle, put it in gear and started forward.

The driver must have been standing nearby, but must not have recognized his vehicle; there were so many that were similar it's not surprising. As I ap-proached the front of the house, one of the security peo-ple appeared and waved me down the semi-circular drive that ran toward the door of the house instead of the stacking area the other cars were using. I drove up, wondering how far I could take this before I'd have to stomp on the gas pedal and barrel through the front gate a good thirty yards away. To my surprise, a butler came out, opened the rear door, and in stepped a well-dressed man and woman. They spoke to each other in French, so loudly it was clear that they didn't think I knew the language.

Très bien.

We cleared the gate and I maneuvered toward the highway, which is a mile or two from the river. I decided that it was now time to find out where the hell Doc was, so I pulled my phone from my pocket and hit his preset.

Tremblay's voice exploded in my ear. I told him in Arabic that I was on my way.

"You can't talk, is that it?" he said.

I gave him a clipped "no." I really felt like saying something else, a lot else, most of it consisting of four-letter words.

"We're on our way to the hospital in Cairo," he said. "It's a long story. You need backup?"

I glanced in the mirror. The couple were in their late fifties. The man's head hung back against the seat cushion; if he wasn't sleeping, he would be soon. The woman sat in the other corner, staring at the floor.

"No," I said, and hit the end-transmit button.

A few miles later, the man had begun to snore. I told the woman in French that it was a beautiful evening.

"Oui," she said in a tone that wasn't particularly encouraging, but Doc's gift of the gab had inspired

me. Besides, one thing I've never had problems with was talking to a beautiful woman. Women sometimes think they lose their attractiveness to men as they grow older, but take it from a Rogue who knows— wine isn't the only thing that grows finer with the passing of time.

I told her that I was a replacement driver because the other man's wife was having a baby, and then apologized because I wasn't sure of their hotel. Fortunately, it was the Hilton on Tahrir Square; I not only knew where it was but had stayed there enough to describe how nice the lobby was. She was more interested in the other driver's pregnant wife, and we took the conversation from there. I asked her about Abu Bakr and eventually got what I think was a pretty accurate assessment of him—a charming, well-connected, and very rich man who couldn't be trusted on any level. The woman's husband was a salesman with a French electronics firm, and by the time we reached Cairo she had practically told me the terms of the bribe Abu Bakr had demanded for a contract.

A pair of policemen were waiting for the car when we arrived at the hotel. I greeted them like long-lost friends; they scowled and began reaching for their holsters. I produced Jamal's card and told them that I was under his "direction"; they didn't stop scowling but their firearms remained at their sides. In the meantime, the Frenchwoman woke her husband. Not understanding what was going on, they disappeared upstairs while the two policemen debated between themselves which one was going to wake up the intelligence service captain.

I settled the debate by calling him myself.

"I'll explain the whole thing to you in the morning," I told him. "But for now you have to get me off the hook."

Jamal grunted, saying that he wanted to speak to me as well.

"Talk to your friends first," I said.

"Yes, but remember the words you once told me, Dick, and I have never forgotten: Payback is a bitch."

I'll go further than that: Payback is a yellow cur of a dog scurrying through a slimy alley full of garbage and excrement. I reached this conclusion the next night, in exactly that kind of alley, as I was being hauled there by two thugs who'd ID'd me as a flakey American tourist ripe for the picking. I wasn't, but then they weren't thugs, at least not by profession—they were two of Jamal's men, and we were providing a diversion for a raid on a bomb factory on the outskirts of the City of the Dead . . .

(Was that too much of a jump for you? I'm just following Elmore Leonard's advice and leaving out the boring parts. Here's the executive summary: I spent the day catching up with my team and Jamal. Jamal began by volunteering that he had tapped the rug warehouse, an admission that convinced me I could trust him, at least as far as I could throw him. We traded *some* information—he was now very interested in Bakr, and while I didn't tell him I'd bugged the place, he knew from the circumstances that I had been there and could easily guess. The rest of the day involved a lot of tail chasing and a tiny bit of hand-holding; suffice to say we were no closer coming up with anything linking Bakr to Saladin, or getting more information on who Saladin might be if not him. We now join our regularly scheduled mayhem, already in progress . . .)

Jamal's two agents played thieves while I went against type and pretended to be a helpless and befuddled tourist. We hammed it up for a bit, then, as rehearsed, one of the "thugs" began running with my wallet while the other kicked over some garbage cans. I yelled and went after him, catching him ever so coincidentally at the front door of a mud-hut hovel.

Just at that moment, the assault team poised near the rear of the hovel made its move. One second there was a lot of yelling and screaming at the front; the next second there were flashbangs and a crack special operations squad going in the back. A second wave of policemen clad in protective gear came across the street from a pair of nearby vans as I rolled out of the way.

Taking down a bomb factory is not for the fainthearted; those things can go boom even under the best circumstances. I'd touched on the highlights of the tricky dance during my training visit years before. Jamal proved that he had not only retained what he learned but had taught it to his men. They swarmed inside so efficiently that even Mr. Murphy didn't have time to react. I dusted myself off, admiring the precision of the Egyptian team, feeling a little like a proud papa at his kid's graduation.

The feeling was a bit premature.

A crowd started to gather. This had been foreseen and though outnumbered, the half-dozen policemen assigned to control onlookers had the initial advantage, wielding large plastic batons and very loud warnings to stay back. Two vans, lights and sirens blaring, were headed down the street with uniformed reinforcements, and a contingent of riot police was less than a half-mile away. A helicopter pulled overhead, the beams of its floodlights playing across the ramshackle buildings.

But Mr. Murphy was clearly p.o.'d that he had missed his chance inside. In revenge, he urged one of the members of the crowd near where I was standing to pick up a stick about the size of a baseball bat. The man waited until the policeman nearest him had turned his back, then grabbed the piece of wood and aimed it at the officer's unprotected head.

I jumped to intervene, catching the bat with my left hand mid-swing. He'd put so much weight into it that he flew to the pavement without me even getting a chance to pop him with my right hand. I took a half-step to balance myself, my eyes hunting the crowd in front of me for a second threat.

I should have looked behind me. A hard plastic baton smashed into the left side of my head and neck. I whirled, fought back, and fell, all in the same motion. My fist connected with someone's jaw, but the satisfaction was dulled by a second hard wallop of a baton, this one to the top of my head. Pepper spray exploded in my eyes. I snapped into bar-fight mode, determined to take as many jarheads down with me until my sailor buddies came to my aid.

Problem was, I wasn't in a bar fight. Knocked to the ground, I was dragged down the street even as I flailed. I started yelling that I was with the police, my curses alternating between English and Egyptian Arabic. My eyes felt like the inferno chicken wings at the local barbecue shack. I grabbed one of the sticks that was hitting me and waved it against something that gave way. The next thing I knew, I was thrown into the back of a van. I rolled over and got to my knees. I had to grab my pants legs to keep myself from rubbing my eyes, which would only have irritated them more.

The van bolted forward, throwing me down to the floor. I rocked back onto my butt, clawing for the side of the truck to get back up. Tears were streaming from eyes, washing the cayenne away. I blinked a few times, then managed to get my right eye open. The interior of the van was nearly pitch-black, the only light a thin filter of gray from the top of the door. I got out the small LED flashlight attached to my keychain. There was no one else in the truck. Still struggling to get my left eye open, I crawled to the back door. A large metal plate had been welded in front of the lock mechanism; the only way to remove it was with a blowtorch. I didn't have one handy, so I went to work with my never-fails door opener: my size extra-Rogue right boot.

The van careened around a corner as I aimed my first kick. Rather than hitting the door near the lock I put a good-sized welt in its bottom panel. Cursing, I propped myself against the corner and swirled to the left, combining martial arts with soccer as I pirouetted my foot toward the target. The door didn't budge.

I had one of my small Glock pistols strapped to my calf, but the metal guarding the door lock looked to be nearly an inch thick. The body of the truck was

much more pliable, as my first kick had demon-
strated, and that same thin metal separated me from
the driver.

It took four shots before the van veered onto its
side. I went with it, rolling and twisting as the truck
tumbled out of control.

On my fifth rebound off the roof I thought to myself: *time to reload*. I pulled the magazine out, leaving a
round chambered, and fed one of my spares in before
the van stopped moving. Yea, verily, did my pistol
overflow as the tumult ended. I pointed it at the back
of the van a few seconds later when I heard pounding
on the back.

Pounding followed by a most glorious sound—
not of angels, but the next best thing: Doc's voice.

"Hey shit for brains, are you in there?" he yelled.

"Where the fuck do you think I would be, asshole?"

"Stand back. We're blowing the lock."

Had my brain not been jumbled, I would have
told him not to blow the lock. Doc has a tendency to
use just a *tad* too much C4 when he constructs an IED.
Fortunately, he left the job to Big Foot, who is a stingy
bastard, and he managed to pop the hinges off without wasting yours truly. Big Foot tossed me over his
shoulder and double-timed back to the car.

If you've ever been in the back of a van that's had
its doors blown off, you know one thing: that is a
LOUD explosion. My ears were ringing. But around
the time we reached our car, I started to pick out a
few familiar sounds from the background: Big Foot's
grunts, Doc's curses, and a rat-tat-rata-bam-bam I'd
heard a little too much of lately—the sound of two or

three Minimis running through their ammunition boxes.

Grape and Doc were right behind us, returning fire with their MP5Ns. I tried to stop Big Foot, but once he gets up momentum not even a bulldozer can change his direction, and it wasn't until he tried wedging me into the car that I got his attention.

"We have to get those guys," I said, pulling myself upright.

"No shit, Sir," said Big Foot. "Get in the fuckin' car."

"In the car! In the car!" Doc yelled, adding a few of his choicest terms of endearment. He was about a yard behind us, and had just slapped a new set of bullets into his MP5N. "Drive, Big Foot, drive! Get the hell out of here!"

Had I stopped to think about it, I would have known that Doc and Big Foot were right—we should have gotten the hell out of Dodge. But I wasn't in any mood to stop and think. As Big Foot dove behind the wheel, I ran back up the road, just about colliding with Grape as he leveled his 12-gauge Pancor Jack-hammer in the direction of the gunmen.

Someday I'll quote Grape on the beauty of a bullpup automatic shotgun. For now, I'll just say he covered the road with a spray of lead, four rounds spitting from the angled nozzle of the gun in the space of a second. The shotgun was his preferred weapon; his backup, an MP5, hung off his shoulder.

"This way!" I yelled at him. "Give me your other gun. Come on—we attack, we don't retreat."

Grape blinked at me for a second, and then something lit in his brain. And I swear to God, the next words out of his mouth were, "Rangers lead the way!"

Somewhere up in heaven, William O. Darby* smiled. Me, I nearly busted a gut trying to keep up with Grape as he burst down the road toward the ragheads, who made the mistake of trying to fire at us. Grape ran through the rest of the rounds in his Jackhammer; by the time he dumped the round cylinder at the back of the gun to reload, the three men had more metal in them than a new car. I kept running, scooping up one of the guns that had fallen. Meanwhile, tires were squealing and people were yelling. All of a sudden, everything went quiet. Then Doc's voice boomed out behind me.

"Dick, have you lost your *fucking* mind?"

You can't lose what you don't have. I led an orderly retreat back to the car, which Big Foot had already pointed back in the other direction.

"On some kind of economy kick?" asked Doc as we sped away. "I thought you liked to buy new."

"Minimis are very popular with tangos these days. Some of the terrorists at the Vatican and the people in Sicily had them."

"Saladin?"

"Maybe."

"AK-47s not good enough for him, huh?" Doc's a bit of a traditionalist.

Grape explained how they had seen me being hauled into the van and managed to follow, though

---

*Darby was one of the fathers of the modern Army Rangers, tasked with training and leading the first unit into combat during World War II.

the truck was moving so fast that they had trouble keeping up through the streets. Two other vehicles were with them and it looked like another two were approaching.

"I thought we were going to lose you," he said. "Then, it was like a miracle—the van just flew off the road."

I enlightened them as to the cause of the miracle.

"Question is," said Doc, "were the cops in on it or not?"

"How did it look?"

"I don't know," said Grape. "People were flooding in from the buildings nearby. I couldn't tell."

"There's only one way to find out, that's to ask."

"When?"

"Now's as good a time as any."

Doc grunted. "I'm getting too old for this. Too damn old."

I laughed. He's been singing that tune for years.

Jamal lived in one of the nicer suburbs of Cairo. Though small for the States, the house was a good-sized place for Egypt, complete with a wall to keep the riffraff out.

The better-behaved riffraff, obviously, because we had no trouble with it or with the dogs, who unfortunately for them had not been trained to never take food from strangers. We left them snoozing on several pounds of sedated horsemeat and located Jamal in his bed where he had collapsed barely an hour before, exhausted from the long night. I clamped my hand over his mouth—Big Foot was holding his arms—and put my finger up, pointing to his wife. It would have been a shame to wake her.

Out in his den, Jamal wondered why I had come.

"I thought we oughta talk."

"It couldn't wait for morning?"

"I don't think so."

"Where did you go after the operation?" said Jamal. "I was looking for you."

I picked him up by the collar and put him against the wall. Generally I don't like to treat friends this way, but it was late and I was starting to feel a little tired. And bruised.

"You really don't know what happened to me?"

Jamal shook his head. I studied his face. Some people are very convincing liars—I've worked for a pack of them—but the Egyptian security service captain didn't fall into that category. Still, it was hard to believe him at that moment, because it sure looked like I had been set up.

"Tell me what you found in the bomb factory."

The house had explosives—about a hundred pounds of Semtex. A set of fuses engineered from radio-controlled toys were lined up on a table in one of the two rooms when they entered. Jamal believed the house was the final assembly point, but they had found no completely assembled bombs in the raid. It was possible that the devices were only put together at the last minute, or that the factory was new and they had hit its first production line.

"The cousin of this man is against the government," Jamal said. "I believe they are part of a cell seeking to overthrow the regime."

Was there a self-respecting terrorist cell in Cairo that wasn't? For that matter, was there a self-respecting Egyptian who wouldn't have silently cheered if the corrupt, autocratic, and paranoid leaders were disposed of?

"How did you know to go there?" I asked.

"A tip, as I told you during the day."

"Where did it come from?"

"The phone, Dick. I swear on my son's head—"

"Leave your kids out of this. This is between you and me."

Jamal's eyes opened a little wider. I think he finally understood exactly how much trouble he was in.

"We tried, we tried to trace it of course, but came away with nothing."

"Have you talked to the bomb maker?" I asked.

"He died when we went in. He was wearing a bomb vest and as soon as the men saw that they shot him. If he had detonated it they would have been killed. It was self-defense."

Or maybe a setup from the word go.

"Did the caller who tipped you off mention me at all?"

"No."

"Why did you think of using me?"

"The caller mentioned that tourists were often on the block and suggested that as a diversion."

That sounded bogus to me—but maybe just bogus enough to be real. Still, if it had been a setup, whoever had arranged it had taken a hell of a chance that I'd be involved.

Or else they knew me very well, and knew I couldn't resist going to a dance.

* * *

Jamal looked like he was telling the truth that night, and eventually I left without expressing my displeasure in a physical way. He promised to do what he could to find my would-be abductors, and to look carefully at his own organization, to see if he had a traitor in his ranks. I don't suppose I could have asked for more, but I had a few too many bruises to completely trust him—or anyone else in Cairo.

As a precaution on an overseas mission, we often reserve several rooms in different hotels as backups; we made use of one that night. When we were sure we were secure, I called Rogue Manor, and found that Shunt had been waiting several hours to talk to me. He'd given the disks from the rug warehouse a preliminary scan and found literally hundreds of possible contacts in Afghanistan, Iraq, and Iran to check into. There was a complication, however—if the emails on the system were to be believed, the owner of the rug business had been in jail in India for the past three months. Apparently, he had forgotten to bribe the right official there when trying to take rugs out of the country. His fifteen-year-old son had taken over the business temporarily.

"He's been writing a lot of letters to try and get him out and gathering money for a trip there," said Shunt. "Doesn't look like a good candidate to be Saladin."

"What did you find from Bakr's computer?"

"The disks got here a few hours ago, so I still have to work on them. But from what I see so far, he's broke. Real broke," Shunt told me. "And he can't balance a checkbook to save his life. He has a program like Quicken to do his finances. Bad."

"Maybe it's a ruse or a cover in case someone like me breaks in."

"It's pretty convincing. Disk drive is littered with old files, half-written over. A lot of red ink. He likes women with big chests, too."

That's not a crime—*thank God!*—but it doesn't help make you top raghead either, and anyone who was setting up his computer to throw off an intruder wouldn't leave the sort of soft porn files Shunt described to be found.

"He might still be involved," suggested Doc. "Helping in some way we don't understand yet."

It couldn't be ruled out, but it looked more and more like a dead end. A backgrounder on the submarine captain provided by one of Doc's gabbing buddies also made him seem less likely; the captain had disowned several close relatives for belonging to a radical mosque two years before.

We weren't officially at a dead end. I wanted to check the submarine out and make sure no one was missing. And there was always a chance the key loggers or bugs I'd planted might give us something useful. But for the moment the winds propelling us forward had stalled.

So when I got the message that afternoon that the BetaGo people wanted to push up the timing on my consulting gig, I told them I'd be there as soon as I could. It made more sense for me to hop over there and get that out of the way than hang around in Alexandria, or continue poking my nose under tents in Cairo. Doc and his shadows could do that as easily as I could. Trace had Sicily under control, and Danny was effectively mopping up in Pakistan. Better for me to earn some more beer money than look over their shoulder. *The Rogue Warrior's Strategy for Success* dictates that you hire the best people you can and then get the hell out of their way. It was time for me to follow that advice.

Besides, after all the bumps and bruises I'd taken over the past few days, I figured my body could use a bit of a change of pace. The assignment seemed routine. With luck, I might get a chance to take a day off, see some exotic sights, and maybe even have a new experience or two.

As things turned out, I should have remembered another piece of advice from *The Rogue Warrior's Strategy for Success:* Be careful what you wish for.

9

There's nothing like a Bombay Sapphire at 35,000 feet to clear your head. It helps to have room to stretch your legs, which you do in first class. First class also offers a strategic position to launch a counterattack on any terrorist scumbags who decide dying for Allah is such a good deal that they want to take a few hundred or thousand people with them.

Whatever else you want to say about 9/11—and you can say a lot—the Americans who died aboard United Airlines Flight 93 in Pennsylvania when they rushed the cockpit were true heroes, role models for us all. They stood up and said "We're not going to take it." These were regular, everyday people—not specially trained SpecWarfare operators. Facing certain death, they stood up for their country and their fellow Americans. If you want inspiration, look no further than that hallowed field where they came to earth.

Getting from Cairo to Tokyo involved three different flights. I caught up on some of my phone messages during the downtime between connections. Among the people I spoke to was Pus Face, whose requests for updates monopolized my voice mail's available memory.

My relationship with Uncle Sugar and his various vassals is a complicated one. Red Cell International is a business, and like every other business, we can't afford to work for free. But on the other hand, I can't bill for every single second either. There's also the fact in our line of work you can't always be concerned about the dollar signs. Stockholders may not like to hear this, but there's more to the bottom line than profits.

All of which is my way of justifying why I was torturing myself by talking to Pus Face when I was under no contractual obligation to do so. I also hoped to pull a favor or two out of him, if not now, then in the near future.

Being a general, he was under the mistaken impression that not only did his shit not stink, but that I admired the heaps of it he left in the latrine. Disabusing him of this misperception would have taken more time than the battery in my satellite phone would allow. So I loosened up a few vocal cords I hadn't called on since my old Navy days and made my voice sound almost worshipful.

I didn't pucker my lips. Some things are just biologically impossible.

"General, Marcinko here," I said when he picked up the phone.

"Dick—good man."

Oh yeah. Those of you in the military who have had the pleasure of dealing with superior officers realize what that means: duck!

"Did you get Saladin?" He sounded like a kid at Christmas who'd been expecting a shiny new bike.

"No. Did you?"

He didn't know how to answer that. I took advantage of the pause.

"I have some people in the Middle East who might find it useful to have the cooperation of some Egyptian authorities," I told him. "We might need an official cover for something we're going to obtain off the record. They also might need some transport and that sort of thing. If we could use your name when—"

I got no further than that.

"Under whose authority are you using my name?" Pus Face's voice had risen two octaves.

"I haven't. I wanted to get a contingency plan ready."

"Under whose authority? Whose? For what purpose? Why? Where?"

He undoubtedly sputtered on for a few minutes, but I didn't waste my time or sat phone battery listening. Ultimately, I got a DIA friend to volunteer to help Doc with any arrangements he'd need.

My concerns about Saladin faded exponentially as I approached Tokyo. Some of my fondest memories with Red Cell involve busting chops at Narita, Tokyo's airport and one of the biggest and busiest in the world. Talk about memory lane: I froze my balls off in a culvert near the runway we landed on, and sprinkled a knapsack's worth of IEDs—simulated, of course—around the hangar area. And that doesn't even count the *real* action later on.

I cleared customs and was on my way to grab a ridiculously overpriced taxi when a familiar voice stopped me mid-stride.

"*Marcinko-san! Ohayo gozaimasu*, you round-eyed, dogbreath jackass!"

Ah. Music to my ears. I whirled and with a grin returned the compliments.

"*Ohayo gozaimasu*, and fuck you too, you little monkeybrain cockbreath squirt."

Toshiro Okinaga gave a characteristic chortle. I realized I was lucky to have cleared customs before he caught up with me. Otherwise Tosho would have suggested that the officials give me a hard time. I would have heard the chortle for hours as I answered their questions.

"Come, my car is this way. I have two *Grocks* for you," he added, changing the "l" in Glock to an "r" as if he were an actor in a forties B movie. Toshu's English is as good as mine—he probably knows just as many curses—but he loves to ham up his accent. "But it will cost you, *Marcinko-san*."

Payment was several Kirins at the hotel bar. Even though the beers cost the equivalent of twenty-four dollars American—*ouch!*—I got the better end of the deal by far. The taxi to the airport would have cost twice that much. When I had last seen him he was a lieutenant inspector; he had now been promoted to captain and now commanded his own *Kunika* section.

I'd already given Tosho a bit of background when I called to say that I'd be on my way. After we caught up a bit, he gave me a quick rundown on what he knew of BetaGo. Though owned by Europeans, the company did a good deal of business in Asia and had recently formed a subsidiary to handle it. Part of the subsidiary was to be owned by Chinese stockholders—specifically, members of the Communist

Party leadership and two high-ranking army generals. This wasn't necessarily unusual—the Commies in China have proven remarkably good at capitalism, and having their backing greases the skids inside the country. An old-line Japanese banking firm that used BetaGo's services had also been approached as a possible partner but had declined, probably not because of the Chinese involvement but because they preferred to have their choice of courier services.

"You think someone's stealing from them?" Tosho asked as we punctuated our Kirins with a round of sake.

"They claim they just want someone to look over their operations. It's possible they're just paranoid about being robbed. But I doubt they'd be willing to spring for my services if they didn't suspect something along those lines."

"Money?"

"They move records around mostly. Currency and securities aren't a big part of their business, and there are so many ways of keeping track of them that I doubt that's where the problem is. But data's another story."

Shunt had suggested the industrial espionage angle, pointing out that copying disk backups of data could be easily done. Depending on what the data was, a rival company might pay dearly for a look. But there was no sense in speculating; I'd find out soon enough.

"I'll help any way I can," offered Tosho. "If you need anything, just pick up the phone."

"I intend to."

* * *

There is an old Oriental saying that, translated into English, goes something like this: *Always watch a nation that uses two sticks to pick up one grain of rice, and one stick to carry two buckets of shit.* So I was on my guard as well as my best behavior the next day when I reported to BetaGo's Asian headquarters on the umpteenth floor of a sleek glass-and-metal tower in Tokyo's business district. The receptionist sat at a polished wooden table at the far end of an otherwise empty hall. Over the years I have come to understand that Japanese corporations furnish their offices in inverse proportion to their wealth; if you enter a bank with a lot of furniture, go quickly to the teller and withdraw whatever you've got there. In this case, the bare room convinced me I should have asked for ten times my usual fee, instead of the mere three times we had settled on.

The receptionist waited for me to say who I was, then bowed her head and told me it was a great honor for the Japanese office of BetaGo to host me. Within seconds, the vice president in charge of Asian operations, Yosiro Fuki, appeared, followed by a phalanx of assistants dressed in identical dark blue suits. Fuki, a short, thin man whose English had a good amount of Texas in it, thanked me for coming so promptly and insisted that we would now have lunch. Having done business in Japan before, I knew it was senseless to resist, and I soon found myself neck-deep in eel sushi. This was just the first course of a day and a half of meetings, none of which actually included any mention of business, let alone any specific problems the company might be encountering. Eventually—in a karaoke bar, if memory serves—we got down to the matter at hand. Fuki said that the decision to hire me had been made in Europe and, while he didn't agree with it, he didn't disagree with it either. This was polite Japanese speak for "My bosses foisted you on me and I hate your guts, because you're nothing but a round-eyed spy trying to screw me out of my cushy setup here."

I told him I had no problem with making a copy of my report available to him unofficially before supplying it to Europe.

Fuki blinked, smiled, and ordered another round of drinks—"Bombay in honor of *Marcinko-san*." From that point on we were best buddies. We even shared the microphone on "My Way" later in the evening.

Skipping some of the wrinkles and off-key drunken singing, BetaGo had a number of systems in place to make sure they weren't robbed. Money and securities traveled under heavy guard, usually with help from the local police and military units. The bags and other containers were booby-trapped, and the currency was generally marked. There were several other checks in place. Someone might get away with a theft, but the BetaGo people would know they were robbed. Frankly, I could offer suggestions to boost security on this half of the operation simply from what I heard in the bar that night.

Protecting the backup data that they moved around, however, was in many ways much trickier. Aware that the information might be targeted for industrial or commercial espionage, BetaGo had already taken a number of steps to protect it. The most basic of these were tamper-proof bags and around-the-clock surveillance. A layer of ultrasensitive rice paper covered certain envelopes, making it impossible to disturb them without leaving evidence behind. Small radio tags were placed on packages so they could be tracked via satellite 24/7.

Typically, a pair of two-man teams would be used for a mission, with the teams subject to random supervisor checks. Mostly the couriers were low-key; they didn't pull up in armored cars, for example, and dressed like tourists or businessmen, depending on the situation. (They were all native to the region and fluent in the local language, though not necessarily residents of the country or even Asian.)

Fuki believed that these steps were more than enough. He was not, in fact, convinced that the data—mostly backup files that were being taken to company headquarters for safekeeping—would be useful to all but the most cutthroat competitor. But he acknowledged that he might be wrong, especially since "Europe" had not shown a willingness to spend money on consultants in the past. He was looking over his shoulder, and wondering why.

So was I. The setup sounded secure, which meant there were probably dozens of problems with it. But generally if you have a reason to investigate something, you lay out your suspicions to the investigator, or at least push him in the direction of the problem. I came away from my karaoke session with a sore throat and the impression that my report was going to be used to reassure potential investors or insurers who might have to pay for a screwup.

Like I said, I should have charged ten times my normal fee.

Couriers moved from Japan to China, then to Thailand, Indonesia, Malaysia, Korea, and back to Japan. Pickup times varied, but the days didn't.

Why, you ask? I know I did. Apparently the company spent a lot of money on airplane tickets for the couriers and backup teams. Trying to save some money, the comptroller had negotiated a bulk discount. You guessed it: The terms of the contract called for certain flights to be used. Well, *duh*. And I bet the comptroller got a raise that month.

I spent the next two days following couriers around Japan, noting problems in their security structure that were only slightly more subtle. BetaGo's operations were far from the worst I've ever seen. The people who worked there had gone through background checks. They were required to demonstrate their proficiency on the gun range every few months. (Shooting paper, but at least they knew where the trigger of the weapon was.) They were also decently paid, with regular bonuses and time off. If I were grading security on an A–F scale, I'd give them a C-minus.

While I was honing my karaoke, the other members of Red Cell International were having fun in Europe, Asia, and the Middle East. After he disposed of Ali Goatfuck, Danny and his shooters checked around in Pakistan for potential links back to Saladin and his organization. The slim leads they had withered quickly. By the time someone in Pakistani military intelligence sent a warning that Goatfuck's demise had been linked to "unknown Americans visiting Islamabad within the past five days," Danny and team had left the country. The shooters got two weeks paid vacation. Danny flew to Afghanistan to take Doc's place lending a helping hand to our operations there.

Speaking of Doc: He was within twenty yards of the Egyptian submarine when it pulled into its slip at Alexandria. He could have been closer, but the spot gave him a better vantage point to film the crew. It took him, Grape, and Big Foot about thirty-six hours, but they were able to confirm that no crew members were missing. The submarine's log put it where it was supposed to be on the night of my adventure on the Sicilian coast. (How did they get a look at the log? Let's just say there's an interesting entry in Doc's expense vouchers for that month entitled "research" and leave it at that.)

This wasn't definitive proof that the submarine hadn't been there—I wouldn't record illegal activity in a log book either. But it wasn't promising. Doc wanted to spend a few more days investigating the captain and other members of the crew. He had to stay in Egypt anyway, in case Shunt turned up anything from the key loggers I'd planted, and to "service" the bugs I'd planted at Bakr's. I told him to give it a few more days, but to be ready to pack it up if he were needed elsewhere.

I was willing to admit that I'd made a mistake about the submarine. But I'd seen *something*. What was it?

"Maybe you just need to get your eyes examined," snapped Trace when I spoke to her. "Face it, Dick, it could have been any small boat on the water with a flashlight."

"I saw a conning tower. I've seen them often enough to know what I was looking at."

She grumbled something I couldn't understand—probably an Apache word for "stubborn," though I wasn't going to give her the satisfaction by asking. The boat the dead tangos had used had still not been found, nor had any real progress been made on the investigation into the attempted takeover at St. Peter's.

"How did these people invent spaghetti?" said Trace, venting her frustration with the Italian authorities.

"They did it the old-fashioned way," I told her. "They stole it from the Chinese."

China happened to be the next stop in my review of the BetaGo operation. I decided to take two runs through. One would be announced—the couriers' supervisor would know I was there, though the couriers themselves wouldn't be informed. I'd also talk to the local subsidiary and some of the people who used the service. Ordinarily, I'd've done none of this, but BetaGo's Japanese executives had already decided to help me out by informing the Chinese what was going on. When I found that out, I made sure everyone knew my exact schedule. Then I arranged to be in China two days ahead, so I could pick up the couriers on the run just before the one I was supposed to watch.

The route ran from Shanghai to Nanjing to Wuhan, down to Nanning and then into Thailand, where the main stop was Bangkok, the capital. The couriers used commercial airlines to get from Japan to Shanghai; from there leased aircraft were used. Again, cost consciousness at headquarters—and maybe an inside deal with the Chinese—had conspired to make this a very weak link in the operation. The airplanes were always leased from the same company, which was owned by two retired Chinese army generals. Its entire fleet consisted of two Xian Y-7-100s (Chinese versions of Russian military transports) surplussed by the Chinese military a few years before. Watch the airplanes, and you knew the couriers' schedule. Infiltrate the ground crew at the airports—admittedly not as easy as in the U.S., since in most cases the military ran things—and you had complete access to the couriers' cargo until the plane left for Bangkok. From that point, a number of carriers were used on a seemingly random basis for transport to Korea and back to Japan.

I picked up my Chinese visa—multiple entries, just to be safe—and arranged to see Tosho to hand over the guns I'd borrowed. We ended up at a police gun range, shooting for our dinner—loser paid. It took nearly three hundred rounds before Tosho finally faltered and missed the bull's-eye. I knew better than to accept an offer of double or nothing. He paid off handsomely, with dinner and cocktails at STB 139, one of the classiest (and most expensive) restaurants in the city. We hit the bars after that, progressing from Kirin to sake to Bombay and back again. I skipped sleep— why sleep when you can hoist a few with an old friend? Besides, if you're not sleeping or fucking, why be in bed?

I ended up at Tokyo airport about an hour before

the first flight to Shanghai. I'm sure I looked like a madman and smelt like one, too: perfect dirtbag cover. (SEAL Team Six and the original Red Cell always traveled out of uniform—*way* out of uniform, with beards and long hair to match the civilian outfits. This was one of the keys to our success. Rumor has it that after I left, Red Cell members got new T-shirts and grooming standards. The brass never could figure out why the unit's effectiveness plummeted. Then again, the admirals were probably happy, since making the unit members stand out decreased the number of embarrassing reports on security deficiencies.)

When I booked my flight to China from Japan, I knew only the day that the couriers were leaving, not who they were or which flight they would take. But there were only three flights to Shanghai from Tokyo that day, and I guessed that a company scrimping on airfare wouldn't bother to route the couriers through a third country and pay for the extra stop. I booked seats on all three flights, using slightly different variations of my name to confuse the computers tracking suspicious activity. ("Mar Cinko" may be instantly recognizable to a person as "Marcinko," and thus easy to explain to the clerk at the desk as an operator error made by one of the coworkers. But to the computer, the names are very different and don't set off any alarms.) Fifteen minutes after I got to the airport and checked in, four young men with very bad haircuts and loose-fitting jackets entered the gate area. I'd been expecting just two couriers, but I noticed that one of the men had a carry-on bag tagged with a brown ribbon similar to one I'd seen a courier in Japan use. I discovered a "problem" with my ticket that took me to the desk area just behind them. There were ribbons on all of their bags, even though they were using passports from different countries (three from Korea, one from Thailand). I gathered that I was behind the main team and its backup, which turned out to be correct. Ordinarily they stayed far apart, but in their minds the job didn't begin until they touched down in China, and so there was no harm showing up at the airport together.

I took photos of each with my new Japanese cell phone. I emailed them to an address I could access later, but it would have been just as easy to send them to an accomplice in China.

What if I'd been wrong? What if the men were a third of an international basketball team, traveling together?

Then I would have been in Shanghai early enough to watch the other two flights. But I wasn't wrong. After we reached Shanghai and had our visas sniffed, the men split into two groups. I followed the trail team as they headed toward the new subway line that runs from the airport to the city. That meant leaving my driver outside to catch up with me in the city. It wouldn't matter to him. I'd worked with Lo Po in the past, and not only did he know what to do, he knew he'd be paid no matter what happened.

My Chinese was not the best, even though I'd spent a few hours brushing up on the plane ride with a "long-hair dictionary" and a handy book on idioms. I did, however, have a secret weapon—a prototype of a new Phraselator handheld translation machine leant to me by a friendly ex-SEAL named Ace J. Sarich.

Sarich's company, VoxTec, is based in Annapolis.

The original Phraselator saw service in Afghanistan in 2002. About the size of a Palm Pilot personal digital assistant, the unit has also been supplied to police, hospital workers, and EMTs. (Hold on, tourists—there's a slimmer model in the works.) The standard version uses memory cards that contain nearly sixty languages and 15,000 phrases in a library that can be customized depending on a client's needs. Chinese is easy—try Arabic, Urdu, Pashto, and Dari, which are all offered. You can either say the word you want and get the translation, or scroll to what you want and let the machine do the talking. There are a couple of other nifty features—it's modular, which means you can take off the speaker and microphone and mount a GPS. And while it normally runs on lithium recharge-ables, in a pinch you can slot in two AAs. My proto-type allowed for two-way conversation in real time without having to hit a lot of different switches or swap cards around. Ace says it will be about ten years before the two-way version hits the market; if it's as good as the beta I was playing with, I'd advise putting your order in now.

The hotel was near the World Financial Center and the first team wandered around the area before checking in. Either they were lost, sightseeing, or checking to see if they were being trailed. They eventually made it to the hotel. When I was sure they had checked in I called Lo Po on his mobile and told him where to meet me.

Calling Lo Po my driver may give you the wrong impression about his abilities. His father was an American citizen who moved to Hong Kong to do business soon after Nixon visited the mainland in the seventies. From Hong Kong he set up shop in Shanghai, where he eventually married a local woman; Lo Po is the product of that marriage.

Lo runs a "research bureau" that aids overseas business people. The company is a cross between a detective agency and a security firm. I met him a while back when I was giving a terrorism seminar in D.C.; Lo Po asked so many damn questions during the Q&A that I had to invite him for drinks afterward to get him to shut up. I introduced him to Bombay Sapphire, and in return he straightened out my pronunciation of Mandarin curse words. Lo will never be a better-than-average shot as long as he insists on using his piece-of-shit Chinese Type 59 pistol, but otherwise his skills are above average. He can fly helicopters and is rated as a parachute instructor. His English is good, his German better. And he's inherited his father's ability to deal with Chinese bureaucracy.

We didn't need too many of his skills that afternoon as the couriers made their run. The heavy traffic in the city made it easy to follow their car, a Toyota they had leased ahead of time. Lo Po had rented us motor scooters, but we could have done just as well walking. They had two pickups in the city, and I was able to get close enough to take pictures with the camera-equipped cell phone both times. They were picking up backup files and some papers, physically transporting them out of the country. The files were stored on tape cartridges and DVD disks; everything fit neatly into two medium-sized suitcases.

After their second stop, they headed toward Hongqiao, an airport near Shanghai used mainly for domestic flights. I suppose I could have contented myself with the photos, pointing out that I had spotted the couriers and gotten by their trail team without being stopped. But somehow that seemed too easy.

The couriers' airplane met them at a terminal used for charter flights, rather than at the hangar; they had to pass through a common lobby and a security area. Just as the couriers approached the security checkpoint, an angry policeman pulled them aside.

"*Mai yuk!*" said the officer. "Don't move."

The two men stopped quickly, asking politely what was going on. The police officer demanded to see the bags. Standing next to him was a taxi driver—Lo Po—who said two identical bags had been stolen from a passenger. The policeman might have been doubtful, but in a difficult situation he would trust the word of a countryman over a foreigner, which the couriers' passports showed them to be.

Lo could have pressed his case and probably come away with the bags. The trail team was still outside the building, parking the cars; we could have had the two couriers locked behind bars before they realized anything was up.

The couriers and trail team reunited in the waiting area assigned to their charter. Lo, wearing a new cap and shirt, watched from the tarmac as they walked out from the building to the plane, waved at the pilot, and got on board, folding up the small ladder from the rear hatchway after them. Security at the airport was provided by the Chinese military, but as Lo observed, once you were past the gate, the privates on duty to a man assumed you were where you were supposed to be, as long as you looked certain about it.

And like soldiers anywhere, the few who might question a civilian would undoubtedly shy from stopping an officer.

While Lo was playing *courier interruptus* and then seeing the BetaGo people off, I caught a flight to Nanjing. This got me on the ground a few minutes ahead of the couriers—a good thing, because I had trouble getting the rental car Lo had reserved for me and just barely managed to pick up the trail team. Nanjing was all business, with three quick stops and then a return run to the airport. This caused me some problems since I'd thought they'd be taking off in the morning, and buying a last-minute plane ticket wasn't easy. My interest in doing so aroused the suspicions of airport security, and I had to spin a cock-and-bull story about a nonexistent business partner who'd gotten ill. Fortunately, my handheld translator fascinated the two men who came over to check me out; I told them a few off-color jokes and left them laughing.

I made it to Wuhan about an hour after my targets did. I couldn't follow them into the city, but with the airplane waiting I didn't have to. I made sure I had plane reservations for Nanning on the only flight out the next morning, then took a stroll around the grounds.

The couriers were staying in the city for the night, and a local security firm had been hired to provide security at the airport where the plane waited while they made their pickup. The security firm was actually a local army unit—or maybe I have that backward. Six young Chinese recruits stood around the airplane as it sat in front of a hangar waiting for passengers and crew to return. The soldiers had been well trained—as infantry fodder. Guarding empty-looking airplanes was a bit above their skill level.

I don't look particularly Chinese, but it's amazing how far a pair of greasy coveralls and a few curse words in the local patois can get you. I found a mechanic's toolbox in a hangar nearby, then strolled over to the plane. I nodded and went right to work, checking the air pressure in the tires. (Never know when one of those suckers is going to go flat.) That done, I pulled myself up on the wheel and had a good look at the engine. After I confirmed to my satisfaction that it *was* an engine, I walked around to the other side, where the crew had conveniently left the hatch open and its fold-down stairway deployed. The hardest thing about my entire adventure was remembering which button to push so the flash on the cell phone wouldn't go off when I took a picture of the suitcases stacked neatly in the back.

As the pickups were made, the couriers attached and activated radio tags so they could be tracked by satellite. Similar technology is used in the U.S. to track truck shipments. It's fairly reliable, but it can give you a false sense of security. A radio gadget that fits in the palm of your hand is no substitute for a pair of standard-issue eyeballs.

Actually, the gadget they were using didn't quite fit in my hand, as I discovered after I searched the plane and went to return my toolbox. BetaGo rented the hangar to keep spare equipment. (There was even a little sign declaring that it was theirs and that visitors weren't allowed. Too bad I'm not very good at reading Chinese.) Toward the back I found two of the large boxes used for shipping the materials, along with a complete set of bags, tamper-evident paper, and transponders. I found these entirely by accident, my curiosity aroused by the set of locks on the only cabinet in the building. Having spent nearly a whole minute picking the locks, it seemed like I was due something for my trouble and so I took a transponder.

A *real* mechanic met me as I left the hangar, but with the help of some strategic bowing and a mumbled *"lao jia"* ("excuse me," though if you cross your legs right it's clear you're looking for the restroom), I managed to get past. A few moments later I had changed back into Western clothes and entered the passenger terminal, where I spent the next few hours dozing until my plane to Nanning boarded at six the next morning.

I got to Nanning in time to see the couriers' plane land. Rather than follow them on their rounds, I moseyed over to their plane, which was guarded by another contingent of soldiers from the People's Army. When something works, you stick with it, and so I put on my coveralls and looked for a toolbox. The best I could do was a crescent wrench. Patting it meaningfully, I walked toward the airplane. I got only a few yards before someone yelled out in Chinese for me to halt. I turned around nonchalantly, and found myself staring down at a lieutenant who proceeded to quiz me on everything from world events to my shoe size.

At its best, my Chinese is shaky, and while I had the handheld translator with me I decided it was best not to pull the gadget out. Instead, I explained in English-punctuated Chinese that I was a contract worker for UK Airline Maintenance, and that I was supposed to install a new radar altimeter in a certain airplane, which thus far I had been unable to find. I had no papers, but I *did* have a radar altimeter—or rather a smallish electronic doodad that looked just like a radar altimeter, assuming you had no clue what a radar altimeter looked like. In short order I was being led by the lieutenant to the plane. I fumbled around in the cockpit for a while, then activated the radio tag and left it in plain sight on a shelf behind the copilot's seat. A half hour later I was back in the terminal, standing next to a window at the north side and seemingly gazing idly at the runway.

What sort of reaction would the appearance of an extra radio tag set off? An all-hands alert, isolating the cargo and sending in a response team to check everyone and everything out? An immediate call to the couriers to return and recheck their cases? An alert to the security forces to report any suspicious activity?

Answer: none of the above. In fact, there was no reaction that I could see. The team didn't return for another four hours, and when they did arrive, they gave no indication that they had been alerted to trouble. The plane took off a short time afterward.

The radio tag was equipped with an LED indicator that lit when it was on; even so, it was possible that it was malfunctioning. It was also possible that the aircraft would be locked down when it arrived at its next stop in Thailand. While I doubted this, it was a possibility, and so I decided to check on it by having an associate in Thailand meet the plane. (I was due in Shanghai the next morning so I couldn't do it myself, even if there had been a flight out that night.)

Si Bi Phiung lived in Thailand, but he had been born in Vietnam, the son of an army captain who fled about sixty seconds ahead of the Commie takeover. I'd met the father during my days trying to get a tan in Southeast Asia. He was a tough, no-nonsense soldier who could not be corrupted. His integrity nearly cost him his wife and child—the Viet Cong blew up his home while he was out on patrol, and it was only by luck that they were away with relatives that night. A few months later, he shipped his family over to Bangkok; I had a very minor role helping them get there, and his gratitude has embarrassed me ever since. Now retired, the elder Mr. Phiung worked for Thai Danu Bank in their corporate loss prevention department, a fancy way of saying he kept employees from putting their fingers in the till. Si had his own firm specializing in customs and security arrangements for multinationals based at Don Muang Airport in Bangkok, so he wouldn't have to go far to help out.

They say the apple doesn't fall far from the tree, but in this case it rolled a half-mile after it dropped. Unlike his dad, whom I've never seen without a smile on his face, Si frowns ninety-five percent of the time. But there's no doubt he's his father's son. His eyes pin you like railroad spikes, and if he takes out his pistol, you better say your prayers: He can clip the head off a matchstick at a hundred yards.

I called Si and asked if he could send someone over to check on the BetaGo flight when it landed. No way, he told me—any request from me was important enough for him to do it himself. I thanked him, then gave him a quick rundown of what I was looking for. It helped that he had heard of the company and knew where the aircraft would head after landing. When I insisted he bill me for the time, he gave a little snort that told me this was out of the question. I appreciate the sentiment—but I made a note to myself to send a check anyway.

Lo Po was waiting in Shanghai when I returned later that evening, a big smile on his face. He grabbed my bag and started out. "Mr. Dick, your plane late. You owe me two drinks."

He had already decided on a place for me to pay off: a chi-chi Western club in the Waitan (or in English, "Bund") area of the city where the drinks were as tall as they were expensive, and the waitresses wore skirts so high the customers got nose bleeds just looking at them. China has thrown big-time *yuan* at Shanghai in an effort to make it an international financial center, and if the city is not quite on par with New York, it isn't all that far behind. Among the amenities are luxury hotels, ridiculously fancy restaurants, and exotic clubs. Lo Po seemed determined to show me all of them, and who was I to refuse?

All this partying meant I had only time to shower and shave in the morning when I showed up for my meeting with the executives of Shanghai Century, BetaGo's Chinese partner. I brought Lo Po with me as an assistant and human translator, but like many Chinese executives, the company officials spoke competent English. It was clear within three seconds that while I would be treated with typical Asian courtesy, I might just as well have a big stamp across my forehead that read "Address at your own risk." They provided only the vaguest outline of their operations, cited no problems, and insisted showing me a video presentation on their company. With typical Chinese aplomb, they referred my questions about their operations to the vice president in charge of security, who of course was on the other side of the country and would not return for several weeks. My visit ended with a tour of the hangar where the aircraft used to transport the couriers was kept. Naturally, the second aircraft was out for maintenance and unavailable for inspection. (I spotted it in a parking area on the other side of the airport later. It had been left unattended, and anyone could get aboard with minimal effort. Yes, I have the pictures to prove it.) They were very interested in showing me how the radio tags were activated, but claimed to have no information on the tracking, which was done in Japan. My questions about contingency plans, emergency response units, substitute routes and couriers—all were referred to the absent vice president. My afternoon was rounded out with testimony from some customers about the great service they received, and then I was whisked away to a fancy restaurant for a meal that consisted primarily of toasts to my health, punctuated by dishes of noodles and fried fish. When it was over I collapsed back in my hotel bedroom, as much from overeating as fatigue. I remained dead to the world until roughly 2 a.m. local time, when I was woken by a loud crashing noise.

The noise was me, falling out of the bed. I was shivering and sweat was pouring from every pore in my body. I crawled on my hands and knees to the porcelain god, and assumed the position. I stayed there for thirty minutes, during which I removed a good portion of bodily liquids and part of my stomach, without relieving any of the pain. My heart pounded so loudly it echoed against the walls of the little bathroom, and I was so weak I had to struggle to pull myself up to the sink so I could wash my face. A glance at the mirror sent me back to the toilet—my face was covered with large purplish welts, as if I'd been pummeled during my sleep.

I can tell you this about the Shanghai Medical Center—it's very white. That's about all I saw of it: one continuous blur of light from the ambulance to the emergency room. By the time I managed to blink I'd been seen by five different specialists. The consensus—I'm translating loosely from the Chinese here—was that I was suffering from a mysterious ailment.

And here I thought I was just barfing my brains out.

They hooked me up to an IV at some point to replace some of the fluids I'd lost. They pumped my stomach even though I'd done the job myself. They gave me a number of shots, hitting me with everything from penicillin to eye of newt. After several hours of prodding, blood sampling, and head-to-toe X-rays (I can report that I do indeed have a brain), they arrived at a fresh diagnosis. I was not suffering from a mysterious ailment. What I had was a *very* mysterious ailment.

Glad we got that straightened out.

I soon found myself being wheeled down the hall toward one of the few rooms in the place that had a sign in English as well as Chinese. The Chinese characters looked long enough to be a novel. The English contained one word, in bright red capital letters: WARNING.

Apparently the Chinese words said something along the lines of "American dogs radiated here," because a doctor soon appeared and explained that he wanted me to take some sort of test that involved drinking radioactive barium. I told him I had no intention of becoming a dirty bomb. I was leaving, even if I had to crawl out on what was left of my belly.

My effort to get off the gurney was less than dignified; my head swam and legs wobbled, and if the wall hadn't been handy, I would have gone naked buttfirst onto the floor. I took a deep breath, and with one hand on my hospital gown and another on the wall, made my way back to the room where my clothes were. Two or three staff members tried to stop me after I got dressed, but by then I had enough momentum to find the door and escape. A taxi was just pulling up with another potential victim; I took it as a good sign and returned to my hotel.

Lo Po was waiting for me. I told him I'd had some bad duck or something the night before; he snorted, putting my distress down to alcohol. He drove me straight away to an old section of the city; I waited in the car, still drained of energy, while he went into a small shop down a back alley. He returned with a small envelope containing some sort of powder, which I had to mix with warm water. Lo Po claimed it was a hangover cure. By this point I was up for anything that would make me feel better, and so I tried it. Within thirty minutes the rumbling in my stomach stopped and I could walk without swaying. A short nap restored a bit of my energy, but it wasn't until a prescription from Dr. Bombay at the hotel bar that I felt close to normal.

I'd planned on trailing a courier team through China today, but by now it was too late. Besides, I already knew the holes in the operation well enough for a scathing report; anything else would be just piling on. I decided to skip straight to Thailand.

A light workout in the hotel gym after I arrived restored some of my appetite. There's nothing like the strain of the last rep on the bench press to get the blood flowing. I managed to score a fruit drink at the hotel bar after a good shower, and so I was in good shape by the time I met Si at his airport office around seven that evening.

Si had seen no sign that the transponder that I had left on the flight two days before had been detected. There was no question that it was still aboard the plane: he presented me with a photo of it sitting exactly where I had left it in the cockpit.

We took a ride over to the building that BetaGo used, observing it from another building across the wide parking area. The building was guarded around the clock by at least two employees. Security was boosted about an hour before the aircraft's arrival, and the people providing it weren't fooling around—M16s were issued and obvious. A van with the courier team arrived a half hour before the plane from China. The men appeared to be known by the guards and didn't have to present any identification. Customs officials arrived shortly afterward, and were there to meet the plane. Documents were checked inside the building; if they had opened the suitcases Si hadn't seen.

Once unloaded, the plane from China went to a different part of the airport to be refueled. It flew back north a few hours later after taking on some light cargo.

In the meantime, another set of BetaGo couriers was completing a run in the city. On the night Si had watched, they had arrived several hours after the plane from China. They brought their load to the hangar and *then* contacted a small freight line to complete the next leg. They made the contact in person, with two employees going over and making sure the plane was secure before allowing it to proceed. On the flight the other night, the aircraft had carried several other loads; Si guessed this was not uncommon.

The operation here was arguably more secure and certainly more complicated than in China. Si had decided that there were three or four different ways to penetrate it. He favored impersonating a Customs official—and had found an ID in case I wanted to try it when the plane landed in a few hours.

"Why not?" I said. "But I don't look particularly Asian."

"Not so much problem, Mr. Dick. You Australian, investigate smuggling. Move quickly, act strong, no one question. Inspect nearby plane first, then go there."

The real Customs official was not a problem. Si knew the officer and explained what he was doing, promising not to interfere with his job. Had we been up to more nefarious purposes, we could have either paid him off or disposed of him with little trouble; the Customs officials worked alone during most of their inspections.

We were inspecting a 707 parked near the BetaGo building when the BetaGo plane rolled up. Acting displeased by the failure to find any smuggled wombats, I had just handed back the manifest when the Chinese aircraft powered down. The truck that had come to meet them was maybe fifty feet from me as it backed toward the plane and the rear doors opened.

Which meant I had a front-row seat as six armed men came out of the back, machine guns blazing.

10

There's nothing like the sound of gunfire to cure what ails you. A few minutes before the van rolled up, my stomach had begun rumbling, hinting that maybe the ailment I had survived in Shanghai had not been completely vanquished. Once the bullets started flying, gastric distress became a distant memory.

Si had lent me a Smith & Wesson. I unholstered as I hit the cement. By that time, grenades were going off and men were swarming over the BetaGo plane.

My contract with BetaGo did not call for armed intervention with bandits, but some reactions are genetic. I fired at the nearest gunmen, putting down two before their friends realized I was a threat and peppered the area around me with lead. Most of their ammo went into the airplane above me, but enough splashed around the pavement and the landing gear to keep me down until the vehicle sped off.

Si reached my rental car two steps ahead of me and jumped behind the wheel. He barely waited for me to get in the passenger's side before slapping it in gear. The van was already out of sight, but there was only one way out from this end of the airport so it

wasn't much of a guess which way they had gone. I
pulled my phone out while headed toward the exit and
called BetaGo's Tokyo office, figuring they'd appreciate
a heads-up. But my satellite phone had no service—the
company's satellites didn't cover Thailand or Malaysia.
Doom on me: I hadn't bothered to check earlier, assuming that worldwide meant worldwide.

("When we *ass-ume*, Dickhead," grumbles the griz-
zled old chief I keep hearing in my head, "we make an
ass of you and me.")

I grabbed Si's cell phone from his belt and dialed
BetaGo's main number. Instead of a person I got an
automated phone system. There was no option for re-
porting armed robberies, so I tried the operator. She
either didn't understand me or thought I was some
sort of prankster and hung up. I redialed and
punched in the extension of the vice president who'd
been my contact, Yosiro Fuki. All I got was his voice
mail.

"Hey, *Fuki-san*. This is Dick Marcinko. Five or six
crazy fucks with automatic rifles and submachine
guns just held up your plane when it landed in
Bangkok and stole your truck. Thought you'd like to
know."

By now Si had the little Toyota knocking on the
door of the sound barrier. We careened in the direction of the city, through the expressway traffic. As I
clicked off the phone I heard him curse, and looked
up just in time to see the back end of a large tractor
trailer looming in front of us. We didn't hit it—a Mercedes limo jerked in front of us at the last minute, and
we hit that. For the second time in a week, I tasted
airbag; it's not something that grows on you.

By the time I got myself disentangled and out of the car, two or three other vehicles had jammed into what was now a good-sized pileup at the rear of a log-jam that stretched at least a mile ahead. I started running, hoping the van was stuck somewhere ahead.

March is the beginning of the hot season in Thailand. The day would have been considered downright "balmy" by local standards, but believe me, the heat coming off the roadway would have fried an egg in about three seconds flat. I've swum in oceans with less humidity.

In just about every other traffic jam I've ever been stuck in, a joker or two will blow by on a motorbike, gunning through narrow holes in the traffic. Usually I curse the SOBs—out of jealousy. This time though I prayed for one: I'd've traded my American Express card for it on the spot.

But no motorcycle materialized. I must have run, or maybe swam, a mile and a half before I finally saw the gray van ahead. When I got about twenty yards from it, I realized it was blocking nearly two full lanes of traffic, and the other vehicles were squeezing past—it was what had jammed up the traffic.

Si caught up with me a few seconds later. Ordinarily you have to work with someone for quite a while before you can start reading his mind; it usually takes a couple of firefights or maybe just one slugfest in a bar before you begin working as a true team. But Si picked up what was going on right away. We warily approached the vehicle from opposite sides, though it was pretty obvious what we would find.

The driver was still in the van, slumped back against the seat and staring toward the windshield.

The back of his head and neck were covered with blood, which oozed from a large hole at the side of his skull. Flies were already buzzing in the cab.

The gunmen were gone. The boxes they'd stolen weren't.

Some of them, anyway. I'd been too busy ducking bullets to count how many they'd gotten. I took my phone camera out and took pictures. Then I suggested to Si that it was time to find alternate transportation.

"Mr. Dick—what is going on?" he asked.

"Damned if I know. But telling the police that is going to take a hell of a long time."

Si didn't hang around to argue, leading the way off the expressway toward the local roads nearby.

As I was kissing the ground beneath the airplane back at the airport, I'd realized that this was the shipment that the people who had hired me thought I would be following. So it had occurred to me, as it's probably occurred to you, that this might be some sort of elaborate setup for an inside job.

Call me paranoid. But as a working theory it had a lot more to recommend itself than spending the next forty or fifty years in a Thai prison, or even a few weeks in an interrogation center repeating the words "*mâi ròo*"—roughly: "I don't have a fucking clue what you're talking about."

A few hours later, we reached an office Si kept in Bangkok's Chinatown. After getting something to eat, Si headed back out to work some police contacts. I sat at an antique eighteenth-century English desk going through every number on my mental Rolodex to see what other information I could get about the robbery.

I called friends and friends of friends connected with the embassy and the military mission, hitting up the favor bank for any information they could come up with. At the moment, I knew a hell of a lot more than they did.

After spreading my number around town, I checked in with Danny in Afghanistan. There had been no attacks on our people since Ali Goatfuck's demise. There were rumors in the south that big money would be available for anyone who took up the crusade against "the imperialist Red Cell foreigners," and equally strong rumors that several jihadists had heard of what happened to Ali Goatfuck and realized there were easier ways to get money. He planned on spending a few more days in Afghanistan before heading back to the States.

Doc and Trace were available only via voice mail; I left messages telling them I was in Thailand and would check in later. Three p.m. in Bangkok is too-damn-early in Virginia (three a.m.), so although I could have used a long-distance kiss from Karen, I decided to put off calling for a few hours. Instead, I went out for a breath of what passes for fresh air in Bangkok, walking toward Sanchao Dtai Hong Kong. This is a temple where the locals believe you can "buy" good luck from the dead by making an offering. In my experience, luck is the one thing that can't be bought; Mr. Murphy is the single most incorruptible person on the planet. I kicked in a few *baht* anyway, considering it a cheap investment.

On the way back, I stopped at a street vendor and bought a *kluay ping*—a charcoal grilled banana, a local specialty. I took a wrong turn and had a little trouble finding the office, which proved to be a good thing: two police cars, lights flashing, pulled up in front of the building when I was a half-block away.

Crossing the street quickly, I developed a sudden interest in steel pans, mixing with the locals and tourists at the small street-side stall while watching the police. After a while they emerged empty-handed from the building. All but one drove away; the plain-clothesman who stayed behind sat in a car about half a block away, strategically placed so he could see the entrance to the building.

I found a phone down the street and called Si. He didn't answer; instead of leaving a voice message, I punched in the number of the booth. Five minutes later, Si called back. We were now officially "people of interest" in the BetaGo case. The officials at the company had already spoken to the police, telling them that I had called in.

Fuck you very much. Or should I say, fuck *me* very much.

"Do they think I robbed them, or am I just a witness?" I asked Si.

"The police are thinking *witness*. They found the rental car, too. At the moment, anything goes."

"What's the theory on the fact that the boxes were all left in the truck?"

"One's missing."

"Did they mention that it had a radio tag?"

"I don't believe so. I take it you haven't changed your mind."

"No."

"So you're still driving to Chiang Mai?"

"Probably." Chiang Mai is in northwest Thailand,

and I was even less likely to go there than to turn my-self in. Si was obviously calling from the police station, tipping me off under the guise of trying to convince me to come in and speak to them. "What's your situation?"

"Complicated."

"You think someone's trying to frame me?"

"Hard to know. Could be."

"I guess I'll see you around, then."

"I guess."

In the event of just this sort of contingency, Si and I had arranged to meet outside the National Museum in Bangkok's Old City, figuring it would be easy for me to blend with the tourists there. I left right away, casing the place carefully to make sure it wasn't being staked out. He arrived about an hour later and went straight to the ticket booth. I waited long enough to make sure he wasn't being followed, then bought a ticket and met him inside.

"Interesting art," he muttered, staring at a sculpture that looked like a mangled bronze bagel. "A statement on the futility of modern life."

"I got that myself."

We went out a side entrance and found a place nearby where we could rent a pair of motorbikes. Threading through some of the world's worst traffic, we headed in the direction of Min Buri, where he had some friends I could stay with. By the time we got there it was dark, and I remembered that I had meant to call Karen. After we parked the bikes in the alley, I told him I'd be in as soon as I used the phone booth I'd spotted down the street.

"Not a good time for the phone, Dickie," said Si.

I looked up. He was holding his pistol on me. Two men came out of the house with AK-47s.

"Si? What the fuck?"

I shifted my weight subtly so I could spring at him. I thought I had a fifty-fifty shot if I sprang—a fifty percent chance of getting shot in the head, and a fifty percent chance of getting it in the heart. But I never tested the odds—someone slammed a rifle butt into my head from behind, and the world went dark.

Some kinds of unconscious are good. The unconscious that comes from drinking a bottle of Bombay at the end of a long day for example. Some are bad. This was one of them.

I have a vague memory of being bundled up in ropes and chains, tossed in the back of a truck, and driven for several hours. How long we drove for, and which direction, I had no idea. I do know what woke me up, though: the purring of a kitten. Three of them, in fact. I've never considered myself much of a cat person, but these certainly got my attention.

Then again, four-hundred-pound pussies have a way of doing that.

I'd been deposited in a clearing that sat like a bowl at the foot of a steep rocky gorge. It was now early morning, and enough sun poked through the clouds overhead for me to see two Indochinese tigers sitting on boulders about thirty feet apart across from me, watching as another tiger sniffed the air maybe ten feet from my face. Indochinese tigers once roamed all through Thailand and the surrounding areas. Estimates of how many are left vary, but official counts have found less than six hundred. So just think: I had a good portion of the population all to myself. I can't tell you how *honored* I felt.

I got up to my haunches, moving slowly. One of the very few things you *don't* learn in SEAL school is how to deal with tigers. As a matter of fact, the only ones I'd seen until now had been in zoos or circuses. None were anywhere near as close as this one. If I'd turned and tried to run, he'd've been on my back for a piggyback ride in a flash.

Whoever had put me here had made sure I couldn't do anything foolish: An eight-foot chain held my leg to a nearby pin, embedded in a cement anchor. I got up slowly, sidling toward the eyebolt that held me in place.

The tiger coiled its head back, rocking ever so slightly as I moved. I hoped this meant that it was considering how to retreat without losing face in front of its friends. If so, his buddies weren't buying it. One gave a guttural growl. The other stood up, opened his mouth wide, and roared.

I'm no expert, but I'd guess the roar meant something along the lines of, "Kill the motherfucker now." Because just then the tiger in front of me sprung forward, mouth wide. I pushed to my left, trying to duck him. That didn't work all that well, though at least I managed to avoid his teeth. In my reaction I'd forgotten the chain; my leg caught and I snapped to the ground.

The tiger flew over my body, claws ripping my shirt. I flailed with my arms and free leg, basically trying to convince him that I was not going to be an inexpensive meal. The big cat twisted back and growled, then retreated a few steps, haunch up and shoulders down, looking to spring again.

I moved back to the pin. This time when he jumped at me I was ready—I grabbed the chain with two hands and jerked it up across his chin and neck, smacking him as hard as I could. I wanted to get the damn thing into his mouth, and use it to break his jaw or teeth, but he didn't cooperate, snarling and snapping and finally ducking under, swiping at my side with his left paw. I slammed a short length of the chain onto the side of his head, stabbing his eye; he let out a god-awful yelp and spun away, hulking on the ground a few feet from my reach.

Let me say this about tigers—they have really bad breath.

When I turned my head to check where his companions were, he sprang again. He got me off guard this time, and all I was able to do was poke him with my elbow as I went down. He snapped at me, and I launched my fingers at the eye I had hit earlier, trying to gouge it out. He yelped, twisted, and started to roll away over my feet. I scrambled back, just steady enough to plant my boot in his underbelly. He gave out a loud yelp, and clawed me with his back paw so hard I fell. The pain felt like a bullet had pierced the skin; I struggled to ignore it, grabbing desperately for the chain.

Fortunately for me, the tiger had had enough. It limped sideways, growling menacingly, but clearly defeated. His left eye hung down by goo and sinews across the side of its snout.

His two friends were on their feet. According to the reference books, tigers aren't cooperative hunters, but they apparently can't read either. The pair pranced down together with the precision of a synchronized swim team. I gripped the chain in my hands, trying to catch as much breath as I could. I was in pure reaction mode, waiting for whatever was going to happen to happen. Suddenly they sprung—but not at me. Apparently they believed in doing their bit for the survival of the fittest, and since their companion had proven he was the weakest one in the clearing, he had to go. The cats pounced on him from opposite ends; he growled weakly, ducking his head as if expecting the inevitable. A brawl ensued, with the two healthy cats nosing against each other and then squaring off over the prize. The cat on the left was bigger, with longer paws, but the one on the right fought more aggressively, pushing his face forward like a bulldozer studded with Ka-Bar knife blades. Their prize lay on the ground nearby as they locked jaws and rolled in the dirt. He rolled his good eye toward me but you'll have to excuse me for not feeling much sympathy.

The scrum ended with the cat that had been on the left backing off, growling but submitting. The smaller one—small being a relative term—stuck his nose in the air and shook his head, probably telling him to fuck himself. Then he went over to the fallen tiger, clamped his jaws on its neck, and put it out of its misery. With a last glare at the other tiger, he began dragging it backward.

To the victor go the spoils. And to the loser—me. The other tiger growled at his former companion, then turned and squared his head between his shoulders.

"Come on, you son of a bitch," I told him, swinging the chain between my hands. "Come get what your friend got."

Just a note in case you find yourself in a similar situation: Trash talk doesn't impress tigers.

My heart started pounding in my chest like an out-of-control drum box as the tiger began stalking me. Blood had been draining from my wounds and I was starting to feel a little lightheaded. My right knee creaked; I shifted a little more of my weight to the left.

Then I had one of those inspirations that spring from pure desperation—I growled like the tiger that had won the battle.

This got immediate results: The damn thing roared back and sprung, teeth first.

My roar morphed into a wild man's screech as I swung the chain up between my hands, aiming for the beast's mouth. I got only air—the tiger flew off to the side, rolling in the dirt and yelping.

Something cracked behind me—the smooth, clean whistle of a Remington rifle—and the tiger stopped struggling.

"Don't you know tigers are an endangered species?" yelled Trace Dahlgren, scrambling down the rocks behind me. Toshiro Okinaga, rifle in hand, was right behind her.

Friends have heaved my butt out of the frying pan so many times I probably shouldn't have been surprised that Trace and Tosho showed up when they did. Despite her Native American ancestry, Trace has a special affection for playing the cavalry, and Tosho has a knack for being where the shit hits the fan that's almost Zen-like. Still, I was shocked to see them in Thailand.

Happy, glad as hell, but shocked.

"The BetaGo vice president who hired you to check the operation was found dead in his summer house on the Italian Riviera two days ago," said Trace. She'd brought a medic bag with her and began cleaning some of my wounds. The antiseptic she used hurt like hell. Sadistic girl that she is, Trace used an ointment instead of gin. "He was stuffed in a duffel bag in the crawl space under the house. The police think he'd been dead for a month."

"A month? Who hired me then? A ghost?"

"You tell us."

I had called the executive vice president, Jean Capon, at home and left a message before reaching him on the cell phone. The police knew who I was because of the publicity following my tour of St. Peter's, and managed to get in touch with Trace in Sicily.

Capon had been murdered, and the police were looking for theories about why. Maybe, they told Trace, whatever I was investigating had caused his death.

"A good theory, if he was alive when you were hired," she said.

Actually, I thought it was an excellent theory. I also thought that whatever he suspected was going on had been cleaned up between the time he was killed and I was hired. And I had been retained to present the corporation with a clean bill of health so it could be sold.

Or to be killed. That was the part that didn't make sense—why send me halfway across the world and feed me to tigers, when tossing me to the sharks would do just as well?

And how had Si gotten involved? I'd called him, not the other way around.

Even if I hadn't had tiger slobber all over me, I'm not sure I could have sorted it out then. There were too many pieces to the puzzle—I couldn't even figure out how Trace and Tosho knew where I was.

"Not hard to figure, tiger-breath," said my Japanese friend. "You left your phone number on Ms. Dahlgren's voice mail."

Sensing something was up and worried that she would tip off someone who was with me if she called the sat phone, Trace flew to Japan and met Tosho, who helped her retrace my steps. By the time they got to Bangkok, I'd left my message on Trace's voice mail; they tracked the number to Si's Chinatown office. They used that to hunt down Si, first at the airport and then at places where the Bangkok police believed he would be. (For the record, I had never been a "person of interest" in the BetaGo heist; Si had concocted that. The policemen who'd been sent for me turned out not to be policemen at all, but Si's men dressed up to get me away.)

Trace and Tosho found a young man eager to help—once Trace persuaded him that his life depended on it. The kid was maybe fifteen and did a variety of jobs for Si, who I was discovering was not as much like his father as I had thought.

I recognized the kid in the truck as one of the

assholes who'd appeared with an AK-47 before I got clunked on the head. He didn't speak English and his Thai was unintelligible, but he spoke Chinese well enough for Tosho to say that he was calling on every ancestor in his family to testify that he did not know where Si was.

"He prays that you won't hit him, and will spare his miserable life as promised," added Tosho.

"He used the word *miserable*?"

"My Chinese is rusty, but it was something along those lines."

"Let me talk to him," said Trace. "I know his language."

I held her back. The kid stared at me, his mouth open. He'd tell us anything we wanted to know, as long as he knew it. If we leaned on him, he'd make up whatever he thought we wanted to hear. Gratifying as that might be, it wouldn't help us much.

"Ask him how he got involved with Si," I told Tosho, staring at the kid the whole time. "Why is he a terrorist?"

Tosho didn't know the word for terrorist in Chinese and called him a criminal instead. The kid winced, then began telling his story. He'd been born in Pattani, a province in the south of Thailand about seventy-five percent Muslim; when he was twelve he cut loose from his family and went north to Bangkok to seek his fortune. Things hadn't worked out all that well. For a short while he worked as a male prostitute catering to foreign tourists, but he was a bit too old to be a favorite, and the act disgusted him. He had been drifting along until he ran into Si.

Si apparently wasn't interested in using the kid as a prostitute. He found former members of the profession could be pliable soldiers in one of the businesses he ran on the side. Si made a good sum—probably in the tens of thousands of dollars a month, we later learned—selling tiger bones to Chinamen, in China, Malaysia, and Indonesia, as well as throughout Thailand. The kid was one of the runners, charged with delivering carcasses to a shop in Bangkok's Chinatown, where the items were processed and then shipped out, eventually to be sold as aphrodisiacs and cures for all kinds of diseases.* The kid didn't know where Si was, but he agreed to show us where the shop was. I figured we could take it from there.

It took us a little more than eight hours to drive back to the city, and by the time we got there it was close to 7 p.m. Tosho went to deposit our informer with some friends for safekeeping. Trace and I did a reconnoiter.

My wardrobe was too cut up to play tourist without a change of clothes. Our shopping trip in Chinatown suggested a better disguise. With the help of a long, tattered cloak, an old, wide-brimmed straw

---

*An interesting question occurred to me later on: Given that ground tiger bones and blood was so expensive, how did the Chinese know that counterfeits weren't used? Apparently it's a big problem, and Si's wares were much prized because they were authentic. There isn't space here to go into the different methods he used to ensure this, but besides having Chinese Taoist "doctors" who could vouch for him, he apparently paid for mitochondrial DNA sequencing of random shipments. That's a very expensive test, and it shows how much money was at stake.

hat, a bit of makeup and some wax applied to my beard and mustache, I became a Chinese ancient, prowling the streets in search of ingredients for my Taoist medicine practices. I don't look particularly Chinese, but by keeping my head bowed and mouth shut, I figured I could get away with it. At worst, I'd look like a burned-out Western hippie guru looking for my mojo—not an uncommon sight in the Far East.

Whether because of my disguise or the fading light, no one stopped me as I made my way to the shop. It was a small, two-story affair, pretty typical for Bangkok's Chinatown—the first floor would be used as a shop and the second as living quarters for the family who ran the store.

Our plan had been to do a recon only; we'd come back with Tosho and more weapons than the single Glock pistol he'd lent us. But as I looked over some of the concoctions—and got a feel for the layout of the place—the man who owned the shop gave me a funny look, and I decided that now was as good a time as ever. I put my hands together and bowed my head in the traditional *wai* greeting, then reached out and gave him a traditional greeting of my own: an ancient Slovak headlock, handed down from generation to generation in the Marcinko clan.

"I'm looking for Si," I told him, using English and then pidgin Mandarin. He blinked up from the headlock I'd put him into but didn't answer.

"Dick?" said Trace, running into the shop from the back.

"Go close up the shop," I told her, taking the Glock from her.

She had to go outside to lash down the bamboo panels at the front of the store. Despite her blond hair, Trace's Apache heritage can make her look Asian, and it's possible that with the long blue Thai dress and the straw hat she wore that the passersby thought she was a native. Thais are nonconfrontational by nature anyway, and no one stopped or asked any questions.

The shop owner remained silent, though I'm not sure whether he was trying to be a hero or simply couldn't understand what I was saying. Large, extended families often crowded into the living quarters of Thai homes, especially in Chinatown; it wouldn't be all that unusual to find grandparents and cousins and the like. But the room upstairs was empty except for a desk and a small cot in the corner. In the bottom drawer of the desk was a laptop. I booted it, and when the screen came up asking for the password, I put the pistol to the Chinaman's head and told him it wasn't a good day to die.

He agreed. But he didn't know the password.

"Who does?" I asked.

A torrent of Thai-accented Chinese followed. He might have laid out Saladin's entire network; he might have given me a kickass recipe for fried dumplings. I have no idea.

I took him back downstairs and hunted for the bottles of the powdered tiger bones. Fortunately, you didn't have to read Chinese characters to find them—they had pictures of the beast on them.

"The man you buy this from," I told him. "Take me to him."

More Chinese, this time faster and even less intelligible. I tried to get him to slow down, but my gestures only made him chatter faster.

There was a knock on the front panel.

"Closed," I said in Chinese. "Come back tomorrow."

"Dick, you really have to work on your pronunciation," said Tosho outside. "You're messing up your pitches something awful. Let me in."

Tosho's Chinese is considerably better than mine, but the store owner's accent made it hard for him to understand as well. Eventually, we pieced together this: It appeared that Si was the actual owner of the building; the man we had captured owned and ran the store itself. The tiger parts were butchered in the downstairs room, then shipped to locations throughout Southeast Asia, the operation coordinated from the room upstairs. The storeowner claimed never to have seen the laptop, much less know what the password was.

I grabbed the old man's phone and called Shunt to see if he could help figure out a way around the password. After he finished complaining about being woken up in the middle of the night, he told me there were plenty, but none that would guarantee the hard drive wouldn't erase itself. He suggested I ship it to him overnight.

"We don't have time. What's the next best thing?"

Shunt began spewing about getting around the flash memory and ROM and Martians.

Well maybe not Martians. It was hard to tell.

"Do you have a hacker friend in Bangkok you trust with your life?" I asked.

"Yeah, but he's kind of weird."

Shunt's idea of weird turned out to be someone who held a nine-to-five job in a bank and regularly wore shoes to work. His English was impeccable— better than Shunt's, and without any *likes* and *dudes*. He pulled the disk from the laptop and installed it into another machine, where he used an Assembler debugging program to examine the drive before using Windows. ("Overkill," he said later, but better safe than sorry.)

There were no cannibal programs, and the data on the disk drive wasn't encrypted. But the drive didn't have much information on it either—a single spreadsheet of numbers and anonymous email addresses at large email services. Tosho sent a copy of the list to his experts back in Tokyo; I forwarded one to Shunt. Besides comparing it to a list we kept ourselves, he would pass it over to our friends at the DIA, et al., to see if any of the addresses were on any terrorist watch lists. Trace, her Apache blood up, insisted that we send a list to the groups fighting the exploitation of tigers.

"As soon as we're done, you're welcome to," I told her.

The list we were looking at was a tiny window into the complex world of international terrorism and smuggling, hinting at the intricate connections not only between them but legitimate business as well. The network Si used to transport tiger bones and blood could be used to move anything from flowers to missiles; it was just like UPS, except it delivered illegal goods. Did he transport arms or drugs or anything else illegal? Our source only knew about the tigers, but it was a good guess that he did.

What about BetaGo? Was there a connection?

My guess at the moment was yes, though on the ground where I was standing, nothing was particularly clear. If this were a movie, the villains would have been identified within the first five or ten minutes and we'd be off to the car chase scenes and romantic interludes. But life isn't a movie, and the people who are busting their asses trying to untangle the different networks threatening the modern world aren't working with a script that tells them what happens next. More intelligence sharing between different agencies such as the CIA, DIA, Customs, Immigration, Drug Enforcement, et al., would definitely be useful and *must* happen, but we shouldn't kid ourselves. At the end of the day, the intelligence experts are still going to be looking at a list of email addresses that tell only a tiny bit of the story.

In our case, I thought I could find out a lot more about what was going on by finding Si. But with no fresh leads, I decided to do the next best thing: talk to his father.

Bi Son Phiung lived about fifty miles west of the city, a little beyond Nakhon Pathom. Nakhon Pathom was the center of the Dvaravati kingdom, which dominated central Thailand from the sixth to eleventh century. It's an important spot for Buddhist pilgrims, who consider the shrine in the Phra Pathom Chedi a sacred place.

An unmarked police car watched the entrance to Bi Son Phiung's property. I pulled up next to it and Tosho showed the officer his credentials; the man showed no sign that he knew who we were, but made no move to stop us either.

The house was a large, two-story building that dated from the nineteenth century. It had probably been built by a Chinese or European merchant; the roof wasn't sloped nearly as sharply as the nearby native structures and the balcony and veranda could have come from Italy. A servant met us at the door. He seemed to be expecting us, and led us immediately through the large, high-ceilinged hall to a room at the back of the house. The walls of the hall were covered with large painted panels with Buddhist religious scenes. The smaller rooms were covered with wood veneer. I felt as if I were walking through a museum or even a quiet chapel.

Bi Son sat on an upholstered chair in an otherwise empty room at the back of the house. I had last seen him five years before, in Bangkok; at the time he looked like a slightly older version of the young lieutenant I knew in Vietnam. His face was still smooth, his belly was still tight. Except for the gray at his temples, a casual observer might have thought he was in his thirties, not his early sixties.

The Bi Son who rose slowly from the chair to greet me was an old man. His body was still fit; its athleticism was evident in his graceful bow and the firm handshake as he greeted me. But his face was white and hollow. Deep rows lined his forehead, and the skin around his eyes was black, as if he'd been punched.

In a way he had been, I guess.

"My family owes you everything," he told me. He stared at the floor as he spoke.

For once in my life, I didn't know what to say.

"We're looking for your son, Si," said Trace.

Bi Son didn't bother to look at her. As far as he was concerned, he and I were the only people in the room.

"It is a terrible duty to uphold one's honor," he said, still staring at the ground. "I seek the solace of the Buddha, but my peace is a barren land. Come."

He led us to a door at the side of the room. This opened into a small office. On the desk was a ledger book, the sort used to keep accounts back in the days before computer programs. A green ribbon marked a page in the back. There were several pages of addresses and phone numbers in Thai. I glanced through it, then slipped it under my arm.

Trace started to say something but I put up my hand.

"If I can help you in any way, Bi Son, please let me know."

Bi Son lowered his head but said nothing. We showed ourselves out.

"I don't get it," said Trace as we walked to the car. "Aren't we going to ask where his son is? Is he hiding him?"

"He's not hiding him," I told her. "This book has a list of foreign contacts in it. It'll lay out the network Si was part of. Let's go to the American embassy. The CIA station chief is about to earn himself a very big commendation."

"You're turning that over to the CIA?" said Trace.

"I already know the important thing."

"Which is what?"

"Si was working with the network that supplied Saladin, if not with Saladin himself. He was tipped off that I was on to him or the operation or both, and was either convinced to kill me or blackmailed to do so. I think he was reluctant—the gunmen who struck the plane were probably supposed to take me out along with the couriers. But they weren't given enough information, or maybe Si arranged it so I'd be spared. In any event, something happened after that to convince him that I ought to be fed to the tigers after all."

"I don't see how Saladin is involved at all," said Trace.

"He's been pulling the strings all along. He sent me here," I told her. "The question is why."

Time out for half a second. It's been bruited about lately that I think the Christians In Action, aka the CIA, is rotten to the core. That's not accurate. Incompetent maybe, but that's a criticism of the bureaucracy not the people. There are definitely a few scumbags, but on the whole the officers are decent. Bright kids, a lot of them. The one rap on them I have is that many weren't brought up understanding cultures other than their own. Very few have a *listen* mode . . . just *broadcast/transmit!* But that's as much the fault of their elders as theirs.

The CIA started to sour when the intel pooh-bahs opted to play with satellites rather than putting eyes and ears on the ground where we could *really* see what was going on, and feel the heartbeat of the world. Today, we're paying the price . . . no agents with experience.

Now I will say this: There is definitely a "what's in it for me" mentality inbred in the organization—but you see that in the country as well. JFK said, "Ask not what your country can do for you, but what you can do for your country." Today that historical note is considered hysterical. We design corporations and governmental structures so that "responsibility" and "accountability" are spread across a lateral plane so that there is no definitive trail of accountability. It nurtures and stimulates the "book of excuses" and selfish greed.

Here endeth the lecture. . . . Thanks for your attention.

I was wrong on one count—the head of the Christians In Action, Thailand department, was a woman. Otherwise my guesses had been on the mark. The addresses and phone numbers belonged to smugglers in Malaysia, China, Japan, Italy, Spain, Morocco, Saudi Arabia, Pakistan, and Iran. Only the ones in Malaysia and Morocco had direct connections to terrorist networks; the others dealt with anyone who was willing to pay a fee.

It took a few weeks for the CIA to line up the contact information with the smugglers, who tend not to buy ads in the Yellow Pages. But I found the connection with Saladin on my own within a few hours of returning to Bangkok, playing a hunch. I called the Singapore detective who'd been investigating the bank robbery where the stolen Minimis were used and offered an exchange of information about the possible source of the weapons. It turned out he already had one of the phone numbers in my book.

Have I lost you somewhere? My head was swimming at the time as I tried to play connect the dots, so I wouldn't be surprised if I managed to confuse you, too. Here's what I knew or suspected at the

time: BetaGo was a legitimate company used by terrorists to smuggle money or information on the side;
someone had discovered what was going on and the
terrorists had decided to pull the plug, but not before
using the company to get over to Asia for reasons
that were still unclear. Si had not been connected directly with BetaGo, but he was familiar enough with
the terrorists either to have an interest in killing me
or to be persuaded to do so for them. Saladin was
somehow directing the terrorist network, and had
used it to get money to people in Pakistan and
Afghanistan in exchange for actions against my people there. Saladin aimed to take bin Laden's place,
but exactly what sort of power and reach he had was
unclear. It was possible he was just a joker with a fax
machine and Web access, though I believed he had
considerable money and connections across the
globe.

And Egypt? Had the submarine been a mirage
and Egyptian deputy navy minister Abu Bakr a
wrong turn?

Not exactly, as I found out when I checked in
with Doc after I made it back to our Bangkok hotel.
My silver-tongued friend had discovered from several
of the crew members that there had been an emergency drill on the evening of my Sicilian adventure.
The submarine had surfaced, then practiced its man-
overboard routines for about forty minutes. Interestingly, the event had not been recorded in the log.

"I'm no submariner," said Doc, "but even I know
that sort of exercise is out of place. I'll bet it wasn't entered into the log because anyone authorized to in-

spect it would realize it didn't make sense. I say the ship captain needs to be watched—he would have had to order the drill, or at least signed off on it."

"They didn't drop anyone off on their way to the exercises?"

"No. All the crew was accounted for," said Doc. "I think they were supposed to get the nuclear warhead and return to Egypt with it."

"No, I don't think so. If that were the case, they would have hidden the warhead closer to the water."

"I don't know, Dick. Imagine Egypt with a nuke?"

What Doc was saying did make sense; the Egyptian government had a lot to gain. Still, I didn't think the bomb would have gone to Cairo if it had been stolen. Assuming Saladin was involved—and admittedly I had only the Minimis to link him—he would have taken the bomb off the island as soon as he could and used it to cement his position. If he exploded a nuclear bomb, he'd be even more revered than bin Laden. He'd live up to his namesake.

"We should have the submarine captain investigated," said Doc. "But by who? We can't trust the Egyptians. I can tell the Christians In Action down in Cairo, but they're only going to look at me cross-eyed."

"How many conversations from Bakr have you taped?" I asked Doc.

"Must be a lot. We've been picking up the disk drives every night."

"When were you planning on picking up the key logger?"

"I wasn't."

"I think it might be a good idea if you did. And while you were there, you might replace his hard drive. I hear Dell has an emergency recall out . . ."

Here's what we did: I called Shunt and had him prepare a new disk drive for Bakr's machine. On that drive were encrypted emails mentioning the submarine captain in a plot against the government. When he was finished with that, he took bits and pieces of the conversations our bugs had recorded to make a tape referring to the conspiracy. Both the hard drive and the tape were transported by one of our newbies to Cairo. Doc arranged a service call with Bakr's housekeeper that afternoon. At about the time he was closing the unit up, Big Foot delivered the tape to Jamal. I'm assuming that Jamal wasn't in league with the terrorists; I don't like to think ill of people. But whether he was or not, the tape was the sort of evidence that he couldn't afford to sit on. If there was one, there might be a hundred, and failing to act on a direct threat to the government was itself an act of treason. Besides, this was exactly the sort of case that would make Jamal look like a hero, assuming there was more evidence to go with it.

Evidence soon found on the hard drive at Bakr's residence.

Do I hear a few tsk-tsk's from the peanut gallery? Save your sympathy for someone who deserves it—like maybe some of the innocent people who'd been shot while touring St. Peter's a few weeks before, or the BetaGo couriers who thought they were working for a legitimate company, or the ten school kids killed the next day by a suicide bomber in Indonesia. Papers in the bomber's home indicated that he had planned to kill more people at a church in a few weeks, but had moved up his schedule because the police were moving in.

I know about that incident because it was the information from Si's book that put the police onto him. I feel sorry for the kids. As for their murderer and the bastards who made it possible for him to kill them, may they all rot in hell until the end of time.

Trace, Tosho, and I got rooms at the Oriental Hotel in Bangkok, which is a *serious* hotel. The Thais know how to do hotels—even in your basic roadside joint, you're treated like royalty. The Oriental Hotel is not a basic roadside joint. It has eight restaurants and more bars than I can keep track of. Pretty much everything you'd ever want from a hotel.

My phone calls finished, I caught a forty-five-minute nap on a bed the size of a tennis court. When I woke up, I went to the window and stared out at the river Chao Phraya. From here, it looked quiet and even majestic. The riot of small boats and their constant chaos were far away.

I wished my cares were. Saladin was still out there somewhere, maybe on the other side of the world, maybe down the hall. And he was planning something, something a hell of a lot of bigger than ridding the world of Demo Dick.

After a few strong pulls of the humid night air, I put my clothes back on and went to check out the bars. I found my way to one overrun with palm trees, said to be haunted by the ghost of Somerset Maugham, a Brit who wrote and drank—not in that order—at the Oriental in the days when the sun never set on the British Empire. I didn't see Somerset's ghost, but Trace turned up a few minutes later. She, too, had been thinking of Saladin.

"How does it feel to be the middle of a jigsaw puzzle?" Trace asked.

"How's that?"

"Saladin—you're the missing link that ties everything together. He sent you here to have you killed."

"No, he sent me here to keep me out of the way. The question is from what."

"You don't think he tried to kill you?"

"Probably he did. But I think he also was worried I wouldn't just lay down and die. So he didn't want me running around where he was."

"Where would you have been if this didn't happen?"

"Back at Rogue Manor, firing up the grill and taking the dogs for a run."

"You wouldn't still be in Sicily, looking for the missile thieves?"

Probably not; I'd grown tired of Kohut and Pus Face, and we'd already thwarted the attempt to steal the warhead. But Saladin would have had no way of knowing that. If he were behind the missile theft, he might have been trying to get rid of me before he stole it.

Or after he stole it.

"You're a really lucky bastard, you know," added Trace.

"How do you figure that?"

"If Si had followed the KISS principle, he would have shot you at that house and killed you right away. That would have made the most sense."

•

"Then he would have had to lie to his father about murdering me, and he couldn't bring himself to do that," I told her. "This way, he wasn't the murderer."

"Right." Trace raised her glass as the waiter came over, asking for a refill.

"You're drinking seltzer?" I asked.

"I have to keep my body pure. A concept you wouldn't understand."

I laughed. She didn't. Trace wasn't drinking alcohol because she was helping a niece complete an Apache coming-of-age ritual and had to keep her body pure until the ceremony was completed. Her work complicated things for her; she would have to follow a special ritual to appease the spirits for killing fellow warriors when she returned, or she would jeopardize her niece's standing with the spirits that had to accept her. I admire her dedication, both to her extended family and to her ancestors' ways.

As for myself, I stuck to the Bombay Sapphire.

"You are right, but not about Si," I told her as we sipped our drinks. "It's Saladin who's not a Keep It Simple kind of guy. He can't imagine a plot that's not as twisted and complicated as a piece of spaghetti wrapped around a cat's paw. Sicily was a good example. He took too long to launch his plan, used too many people, and then got too tricky about what he was doing with the bomb."

"All right. Why'd he get the mob involved?"

"I assume to transport the bomb," I told her. "The stolen car network would take it to North Africa."

"Alberti said Carlo di Giovanni wasn't involved," said Trace. "How would the network have transported the bomb if he didn't authorize it? Besides, you told Doc that it would make more sense for Saladin to use the bomb as soon he got it. The longer he held on to it, the more chance someone would find it."

Trace was doing a pretty good imitation of an old chief in the teams, reminding me I hadn't checked all of my *ass*umptions.

"Did they find the bodies of the people who were hiding in the castle on Sicily that night?" I asked Trace.

"No. It's not unusual for someone who drowns to be washed out farther to sea there. Not that too many people drown every year." Trace shrugged. "They didn't find the boat, either. Best theory is that it was sunk or stolen."

"If he was planning to use the warhead in an attack soon after he stole it, what would he attack?"

"I'd stick it on a ship bound for New York."

"If you were trying to start a war with Christianity? Saladin said he's looking for a war of civilizations and religions."

"New York's the biggest, most obvious symbol of the U.S.," said Trace.

"Yeah."

"Where would you attack?"

"Jerusalem, maybe. That's more the center of Christianity than New York."

"You'd kill mostly Muslims and Jews. He already tried to attack St. Peter's," added Trace. "You beat him. If that was him."

I had, entirely by chance. But even if I hadn't blundered into it, how much could the motley collection of terrorists have accomplished? A handful of scumbags with submachine guns could chip a lot of stones, put holes in a lot of valuable glass, and rip the hell out of dozens of famous paintings. They could have killed a hundred people. But the damage would hardly be enough to start a war, even by Saladin's screwed-up logic. Someone who was stealing a nuclear device had grandiose dreams of destruction.

But he'd tried to steal it *after* the attack. All the tangos had done was make things harder there. Backass had used the attack to justify beefing up security, moving more people and equipment in. The same was going on throughout Italy, and in other parts of Europe as well. It might not last, but still—why poke the hornet's nest if you don't have the torch in your hand?

Unless Saladin *wanted* security increased.

We will strike at a time of their choosing.

"What if it wasn't just bad English," I said.

"What are you talking about?" asked Trace.

"'Time of their choosing.' We've always thought 'their' was supposed to be 'our': Saladin meant he would pick the time. But what if he didn't? What if he meant, we'll do it when they want us to do it."

"We *don't* want them to do it," said Trace. "We want them to leave us the fuck alone."

"That's the problem with you, Dahlgren. You don't think like a fucking psycho."

"That sounds like a serious character flaw," said Tosho.

"Fuck yourself, Samurai," said Trace.

"Careful, there are ladies present."

"Eat me."

"He doesn't mean you, Trace," I told her, pointing. The local CIA station chief had tagged along behind Tosho. She pulled a chair over from a nearby table.

"Your information has been extremely helpful," she said. "We've found at least two cells in Indonesia no one knew about. We're going to assist the authorities there in a raid."

"Great."

"The Thai police and military are looking for Si Bi Phiung. So far, no luck."

They weren't going to find him, I was pretty sure, but I didn't tell them that. Si's father had undoubtedly killed him himself because of the dishonor he had brought onto the family. But there was no sense adding to his misery.

"They also have several leads on terror cells in Thailand, among the Muslims here," she added. "The Thai authorities have planned a number of raids. They think the biggest cell is in Ko Phuket. I'm going down there in the morning, and you're welcome to come."

Ko Phuket, a large island province on the Upper Andaman Coast, has some of the most beautiful beaches and tiniest bikinis in the world. Unfortunately, it was right in the path of the tsunami that struck Thailand and the rest of Asia at the end of 2004. It made a decent recovery, though the beaches are a little less crowded than they once were. Even so, between the tourists and day workers, the province was exactly the sort of place an overly clever terrorist might pick to hide in plain sight.

The one time in my life that I actually had a

chance to join in a mission called Operation Fuck-it, and I had to decline.

"I'm afraid we have to catch a plane in the morning," I told her. "Maybe another time."

Tosho volunteered to go along; he thought there might be connections to BetaGo and the Japanese company there. Maybe he was right, but part of me suspects he just wanted a look at the action on the beach.

"We're catching a plane in the morning?" said Trace after the others left. "To where?"

"Rome. I know who Saladin is. The thing I can't figure out is why I didn't realize it two weeks ago."

11

It's hard to have a Hallmark moment in the middle of Don Muang Airport, especially over the phone. Ten million people buzz around you, the connection is terrible, and two or three munchkins stare up at you from the nearby candy kiosk hoping you'll toss them a few *baht* for gum.

But you take what you can get.

"I love you, too," I told Karen. "I promise I'll get home as soon as I can."

"When?"

"Soon."

When you're a sailor, long separations are just another part of Navy life; I wouldn't say that you ever get used to them, but you accept them as part of the landscape, like the gales that churn up the sea. But I wasn't in the Navy anymore, and Karen had never been in the military. We missed each other and swore we'd work on fixing that as soon as we could.

"And when will soon be?" she asked.

"Soon. Very soon."

I was getting sentimental in my old age—and for once I didn't mind admitting it. But I had to finish this.

"We had a good time in Italy," she said.

"We'll have another good time soon."

"I'm beginning to hate that word *soon*."

"Love you."

"Me, too."

The convoluted flying arrangements Trace made had us going to Tokyo via a nonstop flight, so we headed through the departure hall to All Nippon Airlines, where we took our places in a line that snaked halfway back to downtown Bangkok. The misadventures of Si, Saladin, and BetaGo had shaken the airport security apparatus into a high state of alert, which meant that instead of genuflecting before the weapons detector and then proceeding, passengers now had to remove their shoes, twirl twice, and then go through. It made most people *feel* more secure—but did it increase security?

You be the judge.

Once we cleared the checkpoint, I left Trace and went in search of a Western-style coffee kiosk to satisfy my daily caffeine quotient. As I queued up, I noticed an unshaven, dirty-turbaned man standing near the newsstand a few yards away watching me. He turned quickly as I glanced over. At first, I didn't think much of it, but after I paid for my coffee I noticed him staring again. The newsstand had a display of books for sale, and for a second I thought, hey, maybe he saw my picture on a book there and wants my autograph.

If you believe that, I have a long-range, superaccurate Scud missile I'd like to sell you.

I took a long sip of the coffee—weak, a common problem in Asia. Turbanhead was still watching me. I walked a few yards to a stall displaying ladies' scarves. I examined a few, taking careful note of the intricate silk designs . . . and getting a much better view of Turbanhead. A view good enough, in fact, to confirm that I had seen his grimy rags and worried face before.

I pulled one of the scarves up and asked the lady how much.

One hundred *baht*—two and half bucks.

I pulled out ten 1,000-*baht* notes and pointed to the cell phone she had clipped to her belt.

"Let me use your phone? It's a local call."

Her eyes just about left her head as she looked at the money. She couldn't grab the phone quickly enough.

The exceedingly polite airport operator not only answered on the first ring, but agreed to page Trace right away. Turbanhead had just begun to move as she came up on the line.

"Hello?"

"One of Si's scumbags is over here near the coffee kiosk," I told her. "He's one of the slimes I saw before they batted me on the head and dragged me off to be tiger meat."

"Shit. I'm over here near the gate. Hang on."

"No. Get airport security over here first. I'm going to follow him."

I tossed the phone back to the woman and trotted down the hall. Turbanhead went into the men's room twenty yards ahead of me. Following him wasn't an easy call—it was an easy place for an ambush—but I didn't know whether there might be a window or another way out, and I didn't want to lose him.

I slammed open the door hard enough to have it bounce off the wall. No one was standing behind it.

The door opened on a short hall, which led into the room. There was another corner he could hide behind.

I sprung around it, feet set, poised for an ambush.

A man doing his business at the Western-style urinal looked up over his shoulder. I don't know what his nationality was, but the expression on his face was damn easy to translate: *Holy fuckshit, there's a whack job in here and my fly is down.*

There were six stalls beyond the urinal. Only one was occupied, and the shoes on the floor were polished wingtips—not standard issue tango attire, so I left it for last and checked the other commodes one by one, pushing the metal doors in slowly. Nothing behind door number one. Door number two: also empty. Door number three? The last occupant had neglected to flush, but he was long gone.

Wingtips turned out to be a tall English businessman, who gave me a very proper English sneer as he came out of the john. Either I was hallucinating or Turbanhead had vanished into thin, Lysol-scented air.

As I started to leave I discovered there was a third option: a janitor's closet behind the door. As I was testing the lock, Trace showed up with two plainclothes members of the airport security team. I couldn't understand their heavily accented English, but they understood mine well enough to call for someone with a key.

No, the security people don't have master keys at Bangkok International Airport. Then again, they don't at most airports. At least they knew how to find the janitor, who arrived in two minutes. Try that at LAX.

Guns drawn, they pulled the door open, revealing a thick stack of brooms, mops, and one very suspicious looking floor waxer.

"The roof tiles are missing," said Trace, pointing upward. "He got into the ceiling."

The security people got out their radios. I started climbing the walls.

Or rather, the stepladder leaning against the side of the closet. Poking my head through, I saw that the tiles hung on a network of straps and aluminum runners. Ordinarily, this wouldn't have been strong enough to support anyone, but a double row of steel cables had been added to the straps near the opening to the closet. Plywood had been laid over the runners to form a crude walkway.

One of the security people jabbered at me below, speaking English so heavily accented that I couldn't understand what he was saying. Finally, I realized he was trying to hand me a flashlight. I grabbed it, then pulled myself up into the ceiling. Girders, metal vents, and thick plastic pipes and metal tubes filled the eight-foot-high space, which stretched far beyond me. I felt like Dorothy at the edge of the Enchanted Forest in the *Wizard of Oz*.

There were only two plywood panels, but the steel cables continued well into the distance, a Yellow Brick Road to Tango City. The aluminum tracks they held up were about eight inches wide and were spaced roughly two feet apart. I followed them for about thirty feet, the aluminum sagging ever so slightly. Then suddenly the cables in front of me disappeared; it took a few moments for me to realize that the path turned here to my right. I followed, finding myself twisting and turning in a z-pattern before reaching another piece of plywood. A small backpack sat at the edge. I found a pair of night goggles inside and put them on. They were high-quality civilian jobs, close to the gen-3 devices our military uses. There were also six big magazines for a weapon that had become Saladin's calling card: the Minimi machine gun.

Trace and one of the Thai security people caught up with me as I inspected the pack. As I started out again, Trace started haranguing me, saying she ought to be the one to take the point. I guess Apaches never are comfortable unless they're in the lead. I did what I always do when a subordinate makes a dumb-ass suggestion—I ignored it.

The trail ended at a firewall made of plasterboard, intended to slow down the building's destruction in the case of a catastrophe. The board immediately in front of the reinforced ties was firmly anchored to whatever girders were behind it. The one to the left, however, was merely propped in place, and moved as soon as I put my hand against it.

"Why don't you lend me your pistol?" I said to the Thai officer.

Either he didn't understand or he pretended not to. Instead, he motioned for me to go ahead; he'd be right behind.

Thanks.

By now, the security people were moving to shut off access to the entire terminal. That was no small feat, given the large number of people who travel in and out of the airport every day. I wasn't there to watch, but I know generally what happened. The security gates were shut, planes were towed away from the building, and one by one the passengers for each flight were taken to different areas, including the tarmac, where they could be researched before being allowed to board. At the same time, specially trained assault troops—your basic SWAT team—began taking up positions around the terminal in preparation for an assault.

Let me stop here for a second and give the Thai military an unsolicited round of hoo-hah and general applause. The Thai army is not very large, but it's dedicated, and with the help of the U.S. and SEATO, the Southeast Asia Treaty Organization, they train regularly to deal with crisis. I'm not saying they could beat Navy SEALs in a fair fight, but they have the capacity to make a fair fight interesting.

Not that SEALs would ever fight fair.

"Stay behind the wall," I told Trace and the Thai security agent. "I'm going to drop the panel and see what happens."

I kicked the bottom of the panel and it flipped down. As the ceiling shook I rolled through the opening, half-expecting to fall through into the gate area below. That didn't happen, nor did the ceiling hum with machine-gun bullets.

I'd landed on a metal grille, which had probably been installed during the initial construction. The grille stretched along a set of girders at my right where the wall was anchored. Another firewall ran along my left about eight feet away; it was as if I were in a long hallway in the ceiling. It turned out to be a narrow passage between two different sections of the building.

My tango friend wasn't here, nor was it obvious where he had gone. I began moving along the grill-work—it looked like the metal decking on the side of a train bridge—deciding the most obvious path was the most likely one he had taken.

About thirty feet from where I'd come in, the decking stopped. The thick girders and strut work on the right continued, however, and I found that I could move along by holding onto the struts above and sticking my butt out like a fat woman doing a conga line.

What a glamorous business SpecWar is.

As I moved along the girder, I noticed a dim trace of yellow light filtering into the wires and thin metal ahead. The light came from a passage in another fire-wall dead ahead. This one was large enough to drive a truck through, and opened into a machinery space filled with ductwork.

"What do you see?" Trace asked behind me. She's practically a monkey, and had no trouble keeping up even in the dark.

"Not much. Where are our reinforcements?" I leaned around her and whispered to the Thai security man, asking him to find out where his comrades were. He whispered something back; for all I knew he could have been proposing marriage to Trace.

"Radio," I told him, miming the actions of using one. "Where are your troops?"

"I think he's saying they're on their way," said Trace.

"We don't want them ambushing us," I said.

Trace repeated that, more or less, a few times in very slow English to our Thai friend. After the third time, he started nodding his head vigorously. He said something into his radio, then looked at her and held his palm up. That seemed to be mean we were good to go, and so I did.

A spiderweb of ductwork, plastic pipes, and thick bands of wire extended about thirty feet beyond the opening. The area beyond that was relatively open. Light poured upward from three rectangular holes in the distance—spaces where ceiling tiles had been removed.

I was about fifteen feet from the nearest one when I caught a shadow moving at the far left. I froze, unsure whether it was my quarry or a member of the Thai airport security force. It disappeared to my left. As I moved forward to try to keep it in view, I spotted another knapsack and piece of plywood ten feet away to my right. I went to it, and below the knapsack found a Minimi machine gun, loaded and ready to fire. Someone had been planning one hell of a bon voyage party.

I took two magazines from the backpack and stuffed them in the front of my pants. There was another set of goggles in the ruck, so I handed it to Trace.

"There," I said, pointing to where I had seen the shadow. "You wait."

Three steps later, I felt the framework sag beneath my weight. Thinking I had made a wrong step, I leaned back, reaching for the last solid cable to get my bearings. As I did, a beam of light flared from the direction of the shadow.

"Down!" I yelled, and a second later a freight train plowed across the ceiling space.

It was either a train or a spray of Minimi machine-gun bullets, the sound compressed by the enclosed space.

I returned fire, but as I did, the ceiling began to give way, one or more of the cables severed by the other gunman's bullets. For a spit of a second I hung in midair, supported by curses and wishful thinking. But gravity is one mean mother, and in the next spit of a second I plunged through the roof of a newsstand, upending a rack of Clancy novels and tumbling into a section of romance novels. Two middle-aged Western women who'd been looking at the display blinked at me. I'm not sure if they thought I was some sort of book promotion or the answer to their dreams.

Maybe neither. They started to scream, then decided fainting was safer.

Back on my feet, I reloaded the machine gun, grabbed a nearby shelf and used it as a ladder, climbing up and poking the ceiling tiles off with the butt of the gun. I couldn't see very well; the glasses had been pushed half off my head and one of them had been damaged in the fall. A fresh spray of bullets gave me a rough idea of where my opponent was. I fired back, hoping to at least keep him occupied while Trace and the Thai security man with her retreated.

Up until now, the terminal had been relatively calm; my bet is that most of the people inside figured this was just some BS alert over misplaced luggage. The gunfire changed all that. People ran screaming and shouting in every conceivable direction. The sound from the gate hallway just outside the store was even louder than the gunfire, an eerie mix of pounding feet and high-pitched yelps. The stampede shook the floor, and my bookshelf ladder started to slide; I pushed myself up into the ceiling just as it began to fall.

The other gunman had stopped firing, probably to reload. I looked to my right, expecting to see Trace. Instead, a shadow crossed in front of a white blotch of light, a large gun in his hands.

Good guy or bad guy?

All I knew was, the shadow didn't have enough curves to be Trace. So I followed the SpecWarrior's rule of survival: Shoot 'em all and let God do the sorting.

Good decision. It turned out to be the bastard I'd followed into the ceiling in the first place. My first bullet caught him on the left side of his neck. My last hit the right side. The ones in between ripped through his throat like a Sawzall through an old two-by-four. His body slumped against one of the ceiling cables, holding him upright. His head flopped back, a few strands of skin and tissue keeping it from dropping completely off.

Beheading is too good for these bastards. If I'd been thinking, I would have shot only halfway through so he could writhe in pain for a bit before going to his version of hell. But I prefer to not dwell on what might have been.

"Dick!" Trace was right behind me, yelling in my ear.

"You all right?"

"Fuck you, I'm fine."

Well, excuse me for asking.

By the time we climbed down out of the ceiling, the Thai security people had secured the terminal, killing four other terrorists in the process. What exactly they were planning wasn't clear, though obviously it was something that required fairly heavy weaponry and had been in the works for quite a while. My bet is that they wanted to seize one of the gate areas and maybe blow it up with the help of a nearby fuel truck from the tarmac. The Thais don't like this theory, because it implies that there were more tangos there that day—you'd need at least a dozen, I think—which means that they missed a bunch.

I explained this to the head of airport security, who seemed about as interested in my reasoning as in catching a case of typhoid. He gave me the Thai version of a brush-off, staring at the floor and nodding "yes, yes, yes" when his body language said "no, no, no." Finally he looked at me, smiled, then told his aide in Thai to help me catch whatever flight I had come to catch.

Fine with me. I wasn't being paid to hang around. Or get shot at, for that matter.

Our flight had been boarding when the fun began. The aircraft had been backed away from the gate, then left there for more than two hours by the time we came out. The air crew was coping by spreading drinks around; the only people still annoyed by the time we came aboard were teetotalers.

The aide to the airport security chief made sure the air crew knew who we were, and the stewardesses treated us like royalty, insisting on giving us seats in first class even though the ever-frugal Trace had booked coach. Truth was, the 777 was only about half-full, so it wasn't exactly a sacrifice on the part of the airline, but it's the thought that counts.

About the time I settled in for my first Bombay Sapphire, the copilot came out and introduced himself. He said he was a big fan of the books, and wanted to get a picture with me when we landed, and even offered a tour of the cockpit. Before I could find a way to tactfully refuse—the word *no* came to mind—the pilot announced that they had just been cleared to proceed and the copilot retreated up front, promising a rain check for later in the flight.

Around about my third drink, the satellite phone came back in range of the satellite network, or whatever allows it to communicate. I checked back in with Rogue Manor, where Sean was now covering the fort. The news networks were just starting to report what had happened in Bangkok; I gave him a few details and told him to call over to our friends at Homeland Security, the DIA, and the rest of the alphabet to give them a heads-up. After that, I wanted him to make sure that Danny and Doc had gotten my earlier message to meet me in Rome; he should follow as soon as things were secure at home.

I left a message on Karen's machine: "I'm all right, no matter what you hear on the news." Then I pushed my seat back and took a quick nap.

Somewhere over the coast of Korea, I opened one eye and saw two bearded men standing up near the entrance to the cockpit, glancing around nervously. They were too ugly to be part of a dream.

They were also in the wrong spot to be waiting for the lavatory, which in that 777 was located on the left-hand side of the forward cabin.

Shit.

Calmly but with purpose, I stretched, twisting my

head around as if it were kinked and stiff from the seat. I couldn't see anyone else standing in the first-class cabin; most if not all of the rest of the passengers here were dozing. A curtain blocked my view of coach.

Maybe I was still dreaming, but neither of the ugly mugs morphed into J. Lo or a reasonable facsimile.

Trace mumbled something in the seat next to me, talking Apache in her sleep. I stretched my foot over and kicked her.

"Hey," I said.

"Fuck yourself," she grumbled. Trace is always at her best first thing in the morning.

I leaned my head over and tugged on her sleeve beneath her blanket, pretending to be looking for a little nookie with a fellow passenger. But the sweet nothings I whispered into her ear were anything but sweet:

"I think we have a problem here. There are two jokers up by the cockpit who look like they want to take flying lessons but aren't interested in landing. Check what's going on in coach. I'm going to make like I'm looking for the bathroom."

"Mmmph," answered Trace. "Fucking wild-goose chases." But she got up.

Both assholes burned holes into the back of Trace's head as she left the aisle. I'm not sure what I would have done if one had followed her; probably cold-cocked the son of a bitch and just dealt with whatever followed.

Trace got about two steps, then turned and came back to get her bag, as if she'd forgotten it. She leaned down and gave me a token peck on the cheek.

"I see what you're saying," she whispered. "Trouble follows you like a bad penny."

I watched her waltz her pretty butt toward the next cabin, then made a show of scratching my head and deciding what was good for the goose was good for the gander. I got up, looked after her as if I were calculating how long she'd be, then spun and walked to the front.

The lavatory on the left was empty. A stewardess stood near it in the galley area, a nervous look on her face—and a tall, thin fellow with a knit cap very close behind her.

"I'm sorry, sir," she told me. "This lavatory is out of order."

"Oh, that's okay, I wasn't coming to take a leak," I said. "The copilot offered me a tour and I thought maybe I'd take him up on it."

The stewardess and I locked eyes. She knew who I was but didn't know what to do.

"Perhaps you could call the copilot for me," I told her.

The man behind her stepped forward. "Is there a problem?" he said in very stilted English, as if he hadn't heard what we had been saying.

"Not that I know of." I smiled broadly. One of his hands was behind the stewardess's back, and the other was in his pocket. "Are you with the airline?"

"Yes, as a fact," said the man.

"A fact? Really?"

The cockpit door started to open. The man glanced in the direction of the two men with the beards, though he couldn't see them through the bulkhead.

I kind of wish he hadn't—it meant my fist struck

him on the side on the cheek bone rather than dead-on in the face.

The son of a bitch fell back against the galley, a plastic-sheathed razor-knife clattering to the floor. I leapt forward as the door to the cockpit opened, pushing past the crewman coming out and shouting to the pilot to alert the authorities that someone was trying to take over the plane. I spun back to slam the door home, figuring the best bet was to lock the cockpit.

As I did, though, I realized that the person I pushed past wasn't a crew member at all, but one of the hijackers. And he wasn't armed with a razor: he had a shiny Sig 9mm pistol in his hand, aimed squarely at little ol' me.

Part Three

Crashing In

In the long history of the world, only a few generations have been granted the role of defending freedom in its hour of maximum danger. I do not shrink from this responsibility—I welcome it.

—JOHN F. KENNEDY

12

There's nothing that pisses me off more than seeing a good handgun misused. Which by definition means any pistol pointed at me.

I slapped at the gun with my left forearm, pushing it away as he fired. The aircraft plunged to the left and I lost my balance. Instead of my fist hitting his jaw my whole body crashed against him, squeezing him against the side of the cabin. The Sig pistol flew upward, sailing out of his hand and caroming against the ceiling of the cockpit as the aircraft's nose hunkered downward. I managed to chop at the tango's jaw with my left arm two or three times before the plane pulled up abruptly, veering on its right wing and sending us tumbling back across the cabin. As the 777 lurched more or less level, the tango and I did a quick waltz to the floor. I landed my knee on his chest so hard his ribs cracked. Blood spewed from his mouth. I gave him two hard pops to the head with my right fist, then scooped up the pistol from the floor nearby and fired a shot point-blank into the bastard's skull.

Pulling myself up, I made sure the door to the

cockpit had locked. The pilot was hyperventilating at his controls, struggling with himself more than the plane. The copilot sat slumped in his seat, blood covering his shoulder, neck, and the lower portion of his head. A stewardess lay in the corner behind his seat. She, too, had been shot in the head and was dead.

Alerts and alarms were sounding. According to the instruments the cabin was losing pressure, and it appeared that one of the bullets had sliced through the skin. Only the monitoring system had been damaged, but we didn't know that at the time. There was a bullet hole directly behind the pilot's seat. Thinking I was stopping the plane from decompressing I pulled off my shirt and stuffed it in, the Dutch boy plugging the dike. The shirt draped down like a blue flag, the latest in cockpit decor.

"Are you all right?" I asked the pilot. He'd stopped hyperventilating and we were descending under steady control.

"OK. OK. Yes, OK. He pointed gun at my head." The pilot took his hands off the airplane's yoke to demonstrate.

"Both hands on the wheel," I told him. "I get the idea."

The pilot's face, normally light brown, was somewhere between red and purple. He looked Filipino, and his accented English was easy to understand.

"Have you called the controllers?" I asked.

"They may shoot us down."

"Tell them you're in control and that you want to land right away. Right away."

"Maybe they won't believe me."

"Let's hope they do. There are at least two in the back. We have to get down before they figure out a way to get in here."

Actually, I was more worried that the hijackers had found a way to get explosives aboard and would set them off.

"Where are we?" I asked.

"Heading for Japan. Over Japan Sea."

"Then alert the Japanese and ask where we can set down," I told him. "Get us on the ground right away. Do it, come on."

"They may not let us land."

"They'll let us land. They'll send us to a military airfield."

"Maybe not. Maybe they scramble fighters. Shoot us down. Take no chances."

"Relax. The hard part is over."

All right, so that was a big lie. But do you think telling him what a few ounces of C4 or a similar plastic explosive could do to an airplane at thirty thousand feet would have made him feel any better?

I bent over, undid the copilot's seatbelt, and lifted his lifeless body out of the seat. Then I slipped in behind the yoke, gathering my breath and checking the Sig. The small pistol had held only five bullets and was now empty.

I pulled out my sat phone and dialed Trace, but the call rang through to her voice mail. I picked up the headset and tried to figure out the aircraft's intercom system, which connected to the steward stations in the back. No one answered when I tried buzzing in the back, though it's possible that was because I didn't know what I was doing. I turned to ask the pilot, but he had his head pressed down toward the controls and his hand over his headset. I got up, and went to search the tango for more bullets.

A long, narrow plastic box was taped beneath his shirt, the sort of container cigar smokers like to use to carry a few *puros* when they're traveling. But this one didn't contain any of Havana's finest. Instead, there was a bomb, complete with timer and enough Semtex to obliterate the cockpit.

Not quite what I wanted to find.

I searched his pockets and found some folded papers, but no bullets or other weapons. Sitting back in the copilot's seat, I studied the papers. The pilot glanced over, then took the top sheet. It had settings for the airplane's navigation system. He couldn't tell by looking at the numbers where they would take us, but I had a pretty good idea—the second and third sheets had an aerial view of Kashiwazaki-Kariwa Nuclear Power Station in Japan.

Located in Niigata Prefecture about two hundred and twenty klicks northwest of Tokyo, Kashiwazaki-Kariwa is the largest nuclear plant in the world and a city unto itself. Even if the crash of an airplane there didn't cause a release of radiation, simply taking the units off line for a few days would cause a major catastrophe for Japan. The seven reactors there represent about thirteen percent of the country's nuclear reactors, which together supply something like a third of the country's electricity on any given day. Best case, suddenly shutting the plant would cause a cascade of blackouts through the country, frying circuits up and down the island. Forget about worst case.

The pilot poked me and pointed frantically at the other headset. I pulled it on in time to hear a hijacker hysterically demanding that we open the cockpit door or each passenger would be killed.

And to show they meant business, here was passenger one.

There was a muffled scream, then a gurgle, then more screams in the background, gasps, and two gunshots.

"Decide!" yelled the hijacker.

The pilot looked at me as if there was actually anything to think about. His hands were shaking violently.

"They want to blow up a nuclear power plant," I told him, showing him the picture. "If we let them in, everyone will die anyway."

As logical as that was, it didn't exactly calm the pilot. He began mumbling to himself.

We'd been gradually descending and were now at about eight thousand feet, where depressurization wasn't as critical a problem. (Not that it was a good thing.) But if the tangos in the cabin had at least one other gun, it was only a matter of time before they tried shooting off the lock to the cockpit door. The doors had been designed to take some abuse, and probably—only *probably*—would withstand a point-blank shot. Put a bomb the size of the one I had in my hand there, though, and it would be a different story.

I took out the sat phone, hoping to get Trace. But great minds think alike—I had just reached my finger for the quick dial when it buzzed.

"Dick, it's me."

"How many are there?"

"Four that I've seen. I'm in the back, almost at the galley."

"Weapons?"

"Two guns, both pistols. Knife things."

"The one in the cockpit had a bomb. It was in a plastic box used for cigars, long and thin. You see anything like that?"

"They have two backpacks. I can't tell what else."

"Where are they?"

"Four went to the front. There may be—"

The phone whistled and then clattered. I only figured out what had happened afterward: someone had been behind her in the galley, saw her talking, and snuck close enough to surprise her and bat her and the phone to the ground.

I pushed the phone closer to my ear. I heard Trace cursing, then yelling at someone.

"Take me, not the boy. Both of you. Come on. Me. Not him. Two," she added, which I assume was meant to tell me how many were there with her. Trace's voice got a little louder as she moved closer to the tangos, but it wasn't easy to hear.

"Let him go," she said. "You smoke cigars? Let me have one. The cigar case."

After that the phone screeched and went dead, probably smashed by one of the terrorists' heels.

"How long before we land?" I asked the pilot.

"F-f-fifteen."

"I hope you mean minutes, not hours."

The pilot nodded. But the truth was it might just

as well have been hours. We were history as soon as they set off the bomb.*

"Can you set the autopilot to keep us over the ocean?" I asked him. "Don't land. Just keep us over the water, in case anything happens."

All I got was a blank look.

"They have another bomb. I'm going to try and get rid of it, but I want to make sure that they don't get the nuke plant if I fail. OK?"

This time I knew he understood me, because his face shaded purple.

"When I yell go, I want you to jerk the airplane around. Twist, turn, whatever you can do. All right? Just go crazy."

"OK," he managed.

I got up. I armed the bomb I'd taken off the cabin hijacker, setting it for thirteen minutes. If I didn't get back before then, we'd all die. But at least the nuclear power plant would remain intact. I slipped the bomb into a pocket behind the copilot's seat, then had a sudden inspiration.

Or a brain fart, depending on your point of view. I grabbed the headset and told the pilot to switch on the intercom so I could be heard throughout the plane.

"Ready?" I asked, cupping my hand over the mike. "When you hear me shout, put the plane into as steep a dive as you can manage."

---

*Technically, it was possible that a bomb that size could have done only "minor" damage to the aircraft, killing a few people but leaving it intact enough to land. Their preparation convinced me they knew the best places to put it, though. I'm not stupid enough to advertise those spots.

He nodded.

"Good afternoon, ladies and gentlemen," I said in my best airline captain voice. "We've had a little difficulty aboard, a bit of turbulence. But we're going to take care of it—now!"

I undid the lock and pulled the door open. The pilot pushed forward on his controls, jerking the aircraft into a dive on its left wing. It wasn't quite as sharp as I'd hoped, but I wasn't in a position to complain—I was flying fist to face into one of the terrorists.

A hundred different things happened next, all in the space of ten seconds. The aircraft bucked back and forth sharply, descending, climbing, maybe even moving sideways. I dropped the tango I had hit and grabbed another next to him, getting a handful of knife as well as his wrist. In the meantime, passengers jumped from their seats and tackled two of the others. One of the terrorists began firing a gun as he went down. I leapt up, fell as the plane bucked sharply to the left, then grabbed the raghead with the gun. He pushed back from me and fired, once, twice, three times.

He could have fired twenty times for all the good it did him. His weapon was empty. I clocked him with a roundhouse so hard I thought I broke my hand.

In the back, Trace threw a hijacker who'd held a knife at her throat over her shoulder. His blade cut her in the process, ripping a jagged but shallow trench across the side of her neck and up the back of her head. She leapt forward, flying into a second terrorist, the one with the bomb. As they hit the ground, three male passengers jumped on top, punching and kicking, and Trace found herself in the middle of a scrum, clawing for the bomb. By the time she grabbed it and got out, both terrorists had been beaten to death.

Shame, that. Dying was too good for the bastards.

The boy who'd been taken hostage earlier had been cut badly. One of the stewardesses grabbed him, cradling him in her arms and hauling him back to the rear galley, where another crew member pulled down a first-aid kit. Trace, meanwhile, began sprinting up the aisle toward me.

As the plane leveled off, only one hijacker remained on his feet. He had a pistol in his hand, and stood about halfway down the first-class cabin, holding everyone else temporarily at bay.

"Give it up," I said.

I doubt he understood English. The other hijackers turned out to be from Indonesia and Thailand, but this one was an Arab, with a sunburned face and grizzly beard.

I'd tucked the pistol I'd taken from the cockpit into the back of my belt; it was empty but he didn't know that. I slipped my hand to it, then brought it up with as much dramatic flare as I could muster, holding it up but not pointing it at him.

"Drop your weapon," I said.

There were two passengers near him, standing at their seats. One was a middle-aged businessman type with a spare tire so big he looked like he'd wedged himself into the space. The other, though, looked like a football player. I was hoping that he would clock the bastard while I had his attention. His eyes darted back and forth in that direction, but he made no move to follow through.

The terrorist reached beneath his shirt, prying away the tape from another bomb.

"Drop the gun," I said.

He started to lower the weapon. My half-second of relief was followed by the realization that he was going to try to set the bomb off by shooting it. I threw myself forward, aiming to hit him—and realizing as I launched that I was too far, too late, and in general seriously fucked.

So fucked, in fact, that I not only heard the gun go off, but saw the muzzle flash.

How could that be when the barrel of the pistol was maybe six inches from the C4? Stable though it may be, the plastic explosive does not like to be jostled: and getting shot at close range definitely qualifies as jostling.

Simple, dear reader: It wasn't the tango's gun that went off, but the pistol in Trace's hand. She had found the weapon during the scrum in the back, and with her dead-eye aim airmailed our friend to paradise.

Thank God for that.

"Make sure there's no more bombs," I told Trace. "If any of the terrorists are still alive, we want them. Don't let anybody pound them, as tempting as it may be."

I spun around and sprinted toward the cockpit. My *soirée* had lasted not quite ten minutes. Which meant I had just under five minutes to defuse the bomb I'd set as doomsday insurance.

Plenty of time. Except that the door wouldn't open.

"OK, it's me," I yelled to the pilot. "It's Marcinko. It's over out here. We're OK. We have the plane."

I waited for a few seconds, trying to be patient—it might take the pilot a few seconds to undo his restraint and come and unlock the door.

Ten seconds? Twenty? Thirty?

Definitely not forty, and now it was fifty. And no sign of life from the cockpit. The plane just hummed along, heading straight and level toward Japan.

Check that: It nosed down and began twisting, the evasive maneuvers twice as crisp and desperate as the ones when I'd leapt out into the cabin.

Oh, shit.

13

There are only two possible responses to realizing that you've been suckered: One, you can stick your tail between your legs and hide under the fucking bed, whimpering and crying until the world goes away.

Two, you can go after the motherfucker with everything you have, even though you realize the odds are against you.

"Get me that surgical tape!" I yelled, starting to pry one of the bombs apart.

I didn't get the nickname "Demo Dick" by practicing restraint when handling explosives, but I had to fight my instincts now. This was definitely a situation where a little dab will do you.

I taped a small block to the lock and yelled at everyone to run to the back of the plane. I couldn't get the timer to take anything less than a minute. Cursing, I left it and started to retreat—then saw the tape unfurl from one side. The bomb fell in slow motion to the floor.

Mr. Murphy hadn't fucked with me in, oh, forty or fifty minutes, and now he couldn't resist stuffing it into my face. I took a half-step forward and then felt myself flying toward the cockpit door, the pilot having chosen that precise moment to renew his acrobatics.

Semtex may be stable for an explosive, but that doesn't mean you can play soccer with it. The plane lurched again and I was sure that the next sound I'd hear would be a loud thud, followed swiftly by the trumpets of angels. I flailed around the floor, the bomb a few inches away. As the plane shifted again, I dove on it, got it in my paws, then jumped back and slapped it against the door.

I *think* I creased the tape to make it stay, but all I really remember is launching myself in the opposite direction.

By the time it blew, I was at the middle galley. I fell or was pushed down by the blast—probably the first—then rebounded up, bolting for the cabin. The hatchway had a hole about the size of a watermelon, but it was still locked closed; I had to reach through and yank the damn thing open.

The pilot mumbled manically at the controls. I think he was probably praying to Allah, telling him to get those virgins lined up because he was thirty seconds from paradise. So much for the mystery of how the hijackers got their weapons aboard: The pilot had brought them in himself.

The bomb was in the flap where I'd left it. I yanked the timer off, disabling it. As I did, the pilot pushed the aircraft toward the green, brown, and gray patchwork of Japan's countryside. He was praying so loud and so fast it sounded as if he were singing a rap song.

Two hard punches to the side of the head failed to shut him up, much less get him to let go of the wheel.

I tried to grab hold of his neck, determined to pull his head off if I had to. The aircraft began to pull up sharply, and between my strength and the changed momentum, his neck snapped. Blood and vomit spit out over the controls.

I scrambled into the copilot's seat, trying to grab control of the plane. You'd probably love for me to tell you how I leveled the sucker off, took a sharp right, then flew the four or five hundred miles to Tokyo, setting the big jet down on the runway as lightly as a pro.

I'd love to tell you that, too. Problem is, what I know about flying a 777 would fit into the period at the end of this sentence.

Trace, a steward, and a Chinese kid who looked maybe fourteen pushed into the cockpit as I was trying and not really succeeding to level it off. The kid was a Taiwanese air force trainee—not a full-fledged pilot, but a hell of a lot more knowledgeable than I was. I gave up my seat chop-chop, and he leveled us off nearly as fast.

Meanwhile, the steward played with the radio. A ground controller screamed at us in Japanese and English to acknowledge. When we did, he told us that a pair of fighters was about thirty seconds away from blowing our wings off.

I respectfully requested that they not do that.

Our cadet managed to land us safely at Misawa Air Base in northern Japan. Misawa was chosen because it's huge—we had ten thousand feet to go squish on. The kid used all but the last three inches to stop us. But stop we did, and in one piece.

* * *

Two crew members and three passengers were killed by the hijackers, and three more were severely wounded. About three dozen other people were banged up with scrapes and bruises. One guy had a heart attack but survived. Besides the guy I had taken out in the cockpit, four of the terrorists were dead when we landed. Two others died within a few hours of landing.

The last goes on trial in two weeks. I can't be there, but maybe I'll get an invitation to watch his execution. Even better would be joining the firing squad.

After the many hells of Royal Thailander 1313, the remaining connections to Italy were mercifully boring. A few double Bombays helped smooth the way; an upgrade to first class, courtesy of a word from a *Kunika* supervisor, gave Trace and me room to stretch out. I arrived in Rome like many before me—ready to rip, ravage, and burn.

Doc and Danny were waiting by the gate when Trace and I cleared customs.

"Heard you had a fun time," said Doc. "You catch the news?"

"Are we in it?" asked Trace.

"Only as a footnote."

There had been two other hijacking attempts in the past twenty-four hours in Asia. And at New York City's John F. Kennedy Airport, security people grabbed teams of suspected terrorists just as they were going through the gates. Some of our friends at NATO had told Doc that an attempt in London had been scuttled, but the arrests were being kept quiet while the investigation proceeded.

"Saladin sent you another fax with a Web site, and this time he copied all the Arab news services," said Danny. "The war is coming."

"That's all he said?"

"That and the usual crap about how great God is. Be nice for once if they left God out of it," he added, handing me a printout of the pages. It was the usual terse diatribe, continuing over five pages in eight-point type.

"Pus Face called you around the time the hijackings started," added Doc. "He was frantic. Said he needed to talk to you. He's in Rome somewhere."

"Lucky him."

"Maybe he wants to thank you for saving Japan," said Trace. It was pretty obvious she was being sarcastic; everyone knew Pus Face had no idea where Japan was.

I thought about calling Pus Face—for about ten seconds. Even though personally he couldn't stand me, our earlier conversations had made it clear that he thought I knew what I was doing. He also wanted to make a splash big enough to earn himself another star. So *maybe*—emphasis heavily on *maybe*—he might help me do what needed to be done: Go directly to the pope and tell him what I suspected. I wanted St. Peter's shut down and searched immediately—by anyone other than Vatican security.

But after ten seconds I realized that as ambitious as he was, Pus Face was still a general, and when they'd pinned those stars on his coat they'd increased his risk aversion exponentially. Therefore I stuck with my original plan: heading to the American embassy to lay the case out to the ambassador. He seemed somewhat more reasonable, didn't hate my guts, and even *read books*, for Christsakes. So I figured he had to have at least a fourth grade education, twice Pus Face's.

As luck would have it, who did I meet in the hall of the U.S. embassy? Pus Face, who had penciled in his own tête-à-tête with the ambassador. Before I could say hello—or better yet, turn and walk in the other direction—he grabbed my arm and began running at the mouth about how the sharp work of Pus Men across the globe had stopped the so-called Saladin dead in his tracks.

I have to admit I was taken off guard. Not by his claim, but by his garlic breath. The scent was so strong he would have been barred from a battlefield under the Geneva Convention.

"You caught Saladin?" I said, stepping back and gasping for air.

"Caught him? No. But I put the alert out. I got the ball rolling."

"Well, good for you, General. Who is he, anyway?"

"Who's who?"

"Saladin. Who is he?"

"A bin Laden wannabe," said Pus Face.

"When is he going to strike next?"

"He's not. The raids today—it's over for him."

"You sure?"

The corner of Pus Face's mouth quivered. Doubt had managed to sneak into the vast empty void between his ears. Once there it echoed against the hard walls and grew so loud that even he couldn't pretend not to hear it.

"You tell me," he said. "You're the damn expert."

"Saladin is still alive."

"What? Where?"

"I thought you had him cornered."

"Don't be a wiseass, Marcinko."

"It's in my job description." All right, I was a little over the top. But he made it hard to resist.

"Tell me something I don't know."

"You know so little," I told him. "I wouldn't know where to begin."

Pus Face followed me into the ambassador's private office suite. He shined a smug mug at the ambassador, hoping to suggest that I was just a lunatic off the reservation. I just charged ahead, laying out my theory as briefly as I could, admitting that I didn't have concrete proof but arguing that this was a case where it was better to be safe than sorry. The basic calculus ran like this: Backass had staged the incident at St. Peter's so he could move enough explosives into the building to destroy it. He'd probably intended on using the stolen nuke—at that point I had only thin circumstantial evidence to link him to the operation at Sicily. But he would definitely have a backup plan. Or several.

"Our best bet here, Mr. Ambassador, is to go directly to the pope, lay out the situation, and ask him to shut down the cathedral. Then bring a neutral third party to search it and provide security until Easter Sunday: the Day of 'their' choosing, the holiest day on the Christian calendar."

"What sort of neutral party?"

"SEAL Team Six. Elements of the Ranger Regiment should be used. If it were up to me, no one would be allowed in or out of Vatican City until every brick in

the cathedral and surrounding buildings has been
X-rayed, tagged, and numbered."

The ambassador looked as if I'd punched him in
the gut. He was unable to speak for a moment—just
long enough for Pus Face to blurt, "That's the most
ridiculous thing I've ever heard. Dosdière as Saladin?
Give me a break."

"Which leg?"

I wasn't joking.

"Why would the Vatican hire a terrorist to head
their security force?" Pus Face continued. "It's ridiculous. He's not even Muslim."

"He is a Muslim, whether he practices or not. He
told me himself his father was from Africa. Check his
résumé. He has ancestors in both religions. It's possible that I'm wrong," I told the ambassador, turning to
him, "but this is where the logic takes us. 'The day of
their choosing' has to be Easter, because it's the most
symbolic day in the Christian faith."

"That was just a mistake in the way they wrote it,"
said Pus Face. "I've seen that Web page. It was some
sort of Freudian slip. They've already shot their wad,
Marcinko. We stopped them. We nailed them. You just
can't accept it. Of course not, because it means you're
out of a job."

Right. Like terrorism would cease with the arrests
of a few dozen or few hundred or few thousand slime
bags.

"If St. Peter's blows up, who's going to take responsibility?" I said. I figured this would get him to shut up;
in my experience career brass are a hell of a lot more
motivated by fear of being blamed for a catastrophe

than the hope of scoring a big win. But Pus Face had apparently already done the blame math.

"St. Peter's is not our problem," he said. "It's Dosdière."

"He *is* the problem."

"What if we lay out some of what you've told us," suggested the ambassador. "To Dosdière and his boss to see what he says. Not telling them we think he's behind it all," added the ambassador quickly. "But enough to persuade him to authorize an independent search. We could tell him we think his organization has been penetrated—which is true. We just don't say that we think it was penetrated from the top. His reaction may show where the truth is. And we'd have the cardinal he answers to make sure the threat was taken seriously."

I had thought of that myself, but I was afraid that it would be too easy for Backass to deflect. He might launch his own "investigation," effectively squashing it. He might ignore the warning, or he might push his timetable up. I didn't know the cardinal whom he answered to, or how he would react. We needed to isolate Backass from the security apparatus while the basilica was searched. The only way that was going to happen would be to lay out the whole situation—and not to a mid-level functionary, but to the man at the top.

"Going directly to the pope—it's a really big step, Dick," said the ambassador. "Really big. I'd have to get permission from Washington just to consider it."

"I think we should do more than just consider it. Today's Thursday—I think this is going down Sunday."

"All you have here, with due respect, is a set of gut feelings," continued the ambassador. "We don't have any evidence linking Saladin to the attempted theft in Sicily."

"Will you talk to Washington?"

"Will you get more evidence?"

"I'll try."

The ambassador nodded. "All right. So will I. But we're going to need more than a gut feel in the end."

"There's one gut call you better hope I'm right on," I said. "That he'll wait until Easter Sunday."

Evidence. Well, I wanted it too. Immediately after our meeting, I went off to use the embassy's secure communications center. Officially, I wanted to brief Homeland Insecurity on the situation in Asia. Unofficially, I wanted to light a fire under Shunt, the detective we'd hired to help trace Saladin's money route, and every member of the intelligence community I knew. Connect Saladin to the Sigonella incident, connect Backass to the faxes I got, find some evidence that tied the whole damn thing into a little bow for the powers-that-be—it was going to take a smoking gun on that order of magnitude to make believers out of Pus Face and his brethren. The problem is that undeniable proof doesn't just drop into an investigator's lap, even if he's busting his (or her) hump to get it. I cajoled, I roared, I kidded—they would do their best, and that was all I could ask.

I'd sent Trace, Doc, and Danny over to St. Peter's to look over the cathedral and see if they could find anything obviously out of place. By the time I was done at the embassy, they had each taken two or three full tours. We rendezvoused at a trattoria across the Tiber for an info dump and *vino rosso*.

"A lot of guys in dresses," sneered Trace. "God knows what they're hiding between their legs." Everyone laughed, but it wasn't a joke. There was no telling what sort of weapons the thick clerical robes might hide, as I'd already found out.

Backass had increased security measures at the church. Among other things, he moved the bomb and weapon scanners out into the piazza, added bomb-sniffing dogs, curtailed the number of tourists allowed inside at any one time, and installed roughly two hundred plainclothes security men and women in and around the cathedral. How many of those new security people might be ringers was anyone's guess.

"They could take the place over with a dozen people," said Danny. "Less, really. It'd be a real mess getting them out, because everywhere you look, everything you touch, it's worth a fortune. You have to think twice about tossing a grenade if you're going to blow up some priceless artwork."

"They did that already," I told him. "That's small potatoes. Saladin doesn't think big. He thinks *colossal*. He has to outdo bin Laden. That's why he wanted the nuke. Whatever he replaced it with will be just as big."

"Unless he completely called it off," said Doc. "Live to fight another day."

"Well, if he put a bomb in there, it would be big enough to wipe the building out. Bin Laden took down the World Trade Center, so he has to do at least that here," said Trace. "I mean—it should be obvious, right? We should be able to find it."

"That's what I'm thinking," I told her. "Did you?"

"Plenty of places were you could put little bombs," said Doc. "But to wire the whole place?"

"If he did that, we should see it," said Danny. "We have to poke around a little more than you can do on a public tour."

"It would be a big bomb," said Trace. "Huge."

"And obvious," I said. "Which is why we've missed it so far. We have to get back in there and look more carefully."

"No more tours, though," said Doc. "They've been suspended."

"I don't like tours anyway."

"There are so many security officers in there, though, they're tripping over each other," said Danny. "How do we get by them?"

"We don't." I smiled, and drained my wine.

Four hours later, two members of the Vatican security service came off duty. They hopped into a taxi a block from St. Peter's. Their driver was a typical Rome cab driver in nearly every respect: He muttered to himself, drove like a fucking madman, and considered red lights a challenge to his manhood.

The one thing that wasn't typical about him was the fact that he took the shortest possible route to their destination. This was because the driver—*Io*—was directed via a small ear set hidden below my raghead's turban. Doc was on the other side of the radio, using a map and a GPS device to tell me where to go.

Which just happened to be a club where a large group of security members hung out. (How lucky, right? Except this was my fifth trip of the night, and all the others had been to very dull apartment buildings.) The place was the Roman equivalent of a cop bar back in the States. During the day it was on the froufrou touristy side, serving weak drinks in frosted glasses. Around nine or ten o'clock the tourists went back to their hotels and a blue-collar crowd began drifting in. There were a lot of cops, ranging from military police or *carabinieri* to rent-a-cops.

One thing there wasn't a lot of was women, so when a golden-haired beauty in a low-slung miniskirt walked in, she pretty much had every eye in the place focused on her. Then again, Trace has that effect in most places.

Doc and I were watching from the far end of the bar. We'd been waiting for Trace to come in for about ten minutes. Two security people were sitting next to us, and both had Vatican IDs clipped on with the flimsiest alligator clips to their pants pockets. Italians like to claim that, since everyone in the country starts drinking in the womb, no one ever gets drunk. It's a myth, as anyone who's ever been to an Italian wedding can attest, but who were we to point that out? Neither man would have felt a train as it rumbled over their foreheads.

Doc was a bit more subtle than a train. He got up a little wobbly, muttering in Italian that he had to use the head, apologizing as he rebounded off our leering friends en route to the restroom. By the time he reached it, their IDs were in his pocket.

Trace sat at a table the size of an ashtray. Her skirt rode a little higher with each breath she took. Two waiters rushed over. She ordered the house specialty, an orange-red frothy thing called Rutto, which is Italian for burp. The place fell silent as the waiters raced each other back to the bar.

I got up and walked to a table at the other end of the bar, smiling at the two women who were there— both of whom had Vatican security tags on chains around their necks.

"*Ciao,*" I said to the women.

One gave me a stiff, stuck-up smile and put her nose into her wine glass. The other told me my face looked familiar though she knew I wasn't from the area.

"*È vero,*" I said. "It's true. I'm American. I've been here on an exchange studying security with the Italian state police and tonight's my last night. I have a plane in a few hours."

"American? Your Italian is very good," she said, pushing a curl back from her face. "Oh!" she said, realizing who I was.

"Sshhh," I told her, patting her hand. "I don't like a fuss."

Within a few minutes, Gina and her friend Maria were telling me that security had been greatly increased since my adventures. There was, however, a great deal of friction between some of the veterans and the newcomers; assignments had been shuffled and reshuffled, and the general chaos that accompanies any reorganization ruled. I grilled them gently, trying to find out as many details as I could without tipping my suspicions. I knew I couldn't trust anyone who worked for Backass at this point.

My aim was to get their ID, not get into their pants. Of course, it could be argued that the latter would inevitably lead to the former. But Mr. Murphy, watching the encounter with great interest, decided to intervene before I made the argument.

Actually, he decided to cough.

Doc had just returned to the bar when the man sitting next to him bent over and started coughing. My first thought was that it was Doc, running a diversion; I waited a beat or two before turning and looking to see what was going on. By then, the man was red in the face, clearly choking.

Doc sprang to his feet, put his fists into the guy's diaphragm, and began doing the Heimlich. The guy sputtered, then shot something out of his mouth. At the same time, someone on the other side of the bar got up, walked across the room, and bumped into Doc—grabbing his wallet from the back of his pants.

Or rather trying to. He got about two feet before Doc grabbed him by the back of the collar. The pickpocket was a thin toothpick of a guy, and Doc flung him to the floor as if he were a piece of sopresetta being laid on a hard roll.

The cougher darted toward Doc, fist loaded up for a sucker shot to the back of the head. He missed his intended target, however—I arrived in time to throw him off course, sticking my foot out and pushing his rear to add momentum as he flew by. He rocketed into one of the large windows at the front of the room, tumbling into the street with a tremendous clatter, shattering the thin plate of frosted glass.

If I had it to do over again, I would have adjusted my aim and sent him into the nearby tables or maybe the bar. Not because of the damage, but because I had inadvertently helped the sleazeball escape. He rolled onto to his feet and ran down the sidewalk to a small

Vespa scooter nearby. The pickpocket squirmed from Doc's grasp and squirted out the door after him.

Had to be the world's dumbest thieves, right, picking a cop bar to run their routine?

You'd think that. Almost certainly it would have been a suicidal move in the U.S. or any other civilized nation. But Italy is a world unto itself, and rather than hop up and help us, the cops in the bar began arguing about who was entitled to make the arrest.

The owner, meanwhile, had more immediate concerns than justice. He jumped up and down in front of Doc with his palm out, demanding he pay for the broken window. Unfortunately, the man didn't understand English, and was so excited that Doc couldn't understand his Italian. So I stepped in to translate, using sign language: I threw him out the other window.

Doc and I left immediately. Trace followed a few seconds later, having clipped two more IDs in the chaos.

I learned back in my Red Cell days that it's generally not necessary to doctor photo IDs. Ninety percent of the security people you'll encounter won't even bother checking the postage stamp–sized face on the card. Holding your thumb over the photo takes care of the other ten percent.

We sketched out a plan for a sneak and peek inside the basilica, making refinements based on what the two ladies had told me and what Doc had overheard from the men at the bar. The toughest part of the job was meeting the grooming standards and finding the right shade of blazer to wear. God knows you wouldn't want a security person in sky blue when cerulean went better with the drapes.

Despite all the feelers I'd put out earlier in the day, nothing firm came back. Shunt, though, came back with an interesting observation after analyzing the communications system used by some of the different terrorist groups we thought were associated with Saladin, including our Afghan friend Ali Goatfuck and the Thai crazies. They relied on fake email addresses to send coded* messages the intel people believed were related to funding transactions. While the intelligence professionals concentrated on figuring out what the codes meant, Shunt looked at the addresses themselves. Some were set up through public services that didn't require much in the way of identification, and others in companies and organizations that had been hacked into. According to Shunt, in most cases this wasn't "real" hacking; the accounts were simply stolen and used before the system operators caught on, usually for about a week or so. Most corporate email systems used very simple security procedures, and even those with sophisticated firewalls could often be breached without detection or fancy computer work. (An obvious example that won't give away the family jewels: Many notebook

---

*Coded as opposed to encrypted. The latter involve (usually) complex mathematical formulas that translate plain text into what looks like hieroglyphics. These are great—but like any mathematical problem, can be "solved" given enough time and computational power. A code relies on a prearranged meaning, and if used properly can be impossible to break by math alone. If you and I agree that the word *Easter* in an email will signal an attack, only you or I can figure that out.

computers used by corporate types have a security protocol that uses a special key or encryption code to communicate with the office network. The encryption prevents people from driving up and tapping into the network with a "foreign" computer. But since the stolen notebook already has the key aboard, it gets right on.)

Someone at the NSA (No Such Agency, of course) had tracked down the physical locations of some of the systems used. His reasoning was that, even though you could break into a computer from anywhere, you'd probably want to know a little something about the organization that used it first. Besides, it was possible that employees or others there were somehow involved. The NSA analyst found computers in most of Europe and Asia, Morocco and Egypt. He couldn't see a pattern, and he gave up after finding and cataloging the physical location of fifty systems. But looking at the list, Shunt realized that twenty were associated in some way with the Catholic Church. He also believed that the others were taking advantage of a hole in the programming for VPN firewalls in the same way.

When he started to get into the technical aspects, I brought him back to target.

"Are the Catholic Church systems especially vulnerable?"

"No way, Dude. The thing about this system, like, is that it doesn't give itself away if you're on the outside. So like, I'm dialing in, right? I can't figure out that they're using the set of appliances and software that's vulnerable."

"You can't guess?"

"Uh, technical answer, or short answer?"

"Short."

I could hear the disappointment in his voice. "You could guess. But, like, if you knew ahead of time, you wouldn't worry about, like, a white hat inside trying to trap you. See, because you could be traced when you come back to pick up the email. Like, you could get by that, right? But uh, it could be a pain in the ass like, make you work a bit. Most people are like, you know, lazy. Like why work extra when you could be playing Doom, you know?"

Shunt continued with some qualifiers, listing the arguments against a connection with Backass. But then he gave a strong argument in its favor: The Vatican computer systems had been overhauled a few months after the security chief took over the job.

Admittedly, none of this tied Backass into the terrorist network directly, but it was one more promising link. I told Shunt to check Backass's résumé and see if any other company he'd worked for before coming to the Vatican had been used.

"On it, Dude. And like, should I check the systems to see if there's like, anything else incriminating, like?"

"Is the pope Catholic?"

"Uh?" Shunt thought about it. "Is that like, a trick question?"

Program note for pagans: Good Friday is the day that the Romans took Jesus up the hill and draped him across the cross. It's a huge day at St. Peter's and at most Catholic churches, where the event is remembered with a number of solemn services. The Vatican had curtailed these because of security concerns, canceling most. Still, a good-sized crowd filled the chapels at the side of the church, praying and celebrating mass as preparations for Easter continued in the rest of the church.

Large platforms topped by decks of seats filled the center of the basilica. These looked more like bleachers than pews, and would be filled by VIPs (mostly high-ranking clergy) at the special Easter midnight mass Saturday night. Security guards formed a ring around the bleachers, standing every five feet or so, arms folded, tight-lipped, and bored. Another ring of guards, these spaced every ten or twelve feet, stood around the sides of the cathedral, never blocking the views of the side altars but not exactly unobtrusive either. It was as good a psychological show as I'd seen in a while, but that was all it was—a show. Security had already been broken by three ersatz guards, who mingled with the other groups of floaters in the building, ogling tourists and extending their frowns into every conceivable corner.

Those three were Trace, Doc, and Danny.

Where was I, you ask?

Don't ask me, ask the convivial Paulist priest, who had credentials from the Vatican telephone service and was prowling, or rather inspecting, the back areas of the cathedral to make sure that cell phones would be automatically disconnected. Like many of his brethren, the father had found his true vocation after working in the world, and brought his skills in telecommunications to the service of the Lord. His English had the accent of America, where he had spent his youth; his

Italian tended to be selective, depending on the circumstances. The good father could explain this with the steady gaze and quiet air that only faith and a loaded handgun can bring to a man.

The cassock chafed a bit, but that's a personal problem.

The most obvious place for a bomb would be under the grandstand pews. Velvet draperies hung down at the sides and back, so if you stuck something underneath, it could just sit there undetected until curtain time. But a team of security people were checking this out often enough for Danny and Doc to join in. Using their eyes as well as a pair of "sniffers" that could detect the molecules used in explosives, they'd come up empty. So had checks in the slightly less obvious hiding places, like confessionals and back rooms. It was my job to look in places that would be even less obvious.

The gear I had in my hand looked like a portable radio set and came complete with a pair of headphones. It was useless for detecting cell phone signals, but it was just the thing to check interior cavities where a bomb might be hidden. The people at Law Enforcement Technologies say it's just a sophisticated version of the stud finders professional carpenters use in older homes so they can do maximum damage when hanging a picture. Sensitive enough to detect the difference between a solid marble pillar and one filled with plastic explosive, it couldn't actually identify the explosive. For that, I'd have to use the sophisticated "sniffer" I had strapped beneath my cloak, which might not work if the bomb had been sealed to prevent detection. But first things first.

I searched the central area of the church, walking along the long aisle created by the massive pillars. A pair of large bombs here would kill the most people and have a good chance of bringing the building down. The stone piers would make it possible to set up a fairly large bomb panel in a rectangular shape. Replacing the large panels—they're bigger than a man—would not be easy, but could have been done under the cover of repairing the damage made by the machine-gun bullets.

The pillars were solid. A few hours of inspection didn't turn up anything in the walls either, or the altars, or anywhere else for that matter.

Obviously, I was missing something. I decided to go back to square one and turned the unit off, trying to look at the interior of the church the way Saladin might. How would he blow it up?

If Backass was Saladin, he'd be looking at it from about five-eight. So I squatted and tilted my head to the side slightly, turning to the right. At which point I found myself staring eye to eye with Backass himself.

I doubt most people would have recognized me dressed as a priest. Anyone who knows me well would insist the robes would disintegrate as soon as they touched the flesh. Backass, unfortunately, didn't know me that well. He scowled, then stepped forward, two gorilla-sized bodyguards tripping over their long simian arms to keep up.

"Just the man I was looking for," I said, raising myself to my full height.

"Why are you dressed in priest's robes?"

"I've been feeling a little spiritual. What did you bring in here after the attack three weeks ago?"

"We've increased security, as you can see. Though obviously we haven't done as good a job as we should." He turned around, playing the concerned security chief. "How many of your people have infiltrated our ranks? I owe you a debt of thanks."

Backass pointed at one of his supervisors. Before he could begin to berate him, I grabbed Backass's shoulder and spun him around. "Are you out to assassinate the pope? Or do you just want to destroy the building and kill a few thousand priests and nuns?"

Something flickered across Backass's face. But then it was gone.

"Take Mr. Demo Dick and his people out of the cathedral and off Vatican property," he said. "Be careful not to stand too close. There's a good chance God will strike him with a thunderbolt if He sees him on sacred ground."

"You were supposed to gather evidence, not cause a major diplomatic incident with the Catholic Church!" yelled Pus Face an hour later at the embassy. The American ambassadors to Italy and the Vatican stood uncomfortably a few feet away. The ambassador to the Vatican, a short man of about eighty, looked so pale he looked as if he'd fade into the air any moment.

"You went too far, Marcinko," continued Pus Face. "Too far."

"No, I didn't go far enough."

Pus Face was so mad, his hair vibrated with anger. Unlike Danny, Doc, and myself, Trace had been apprehended by members of the Swiss Guard. Though not under Backass's jurisdiction, the captain of the Swiss Guard complied with the directive that she be kicked out of Vatican City and added his own, demanding to know who her commander was before letting her go. Pus Face had subsequently been called by every available official in the Holy See, who promised that *his* superiors would hear of the sacrilege his "deputy" had committed. Apparently one or two had succeeded in locating someone at the Pentagon—probably a janitor—and Pus Face had already received two emails directing him to explain himself.

"I think perhaps I should take the lead on this," said White, the ambassador to Italy. "Maybe Dick and I should discuss this alone."

The other ambassador didn't need any more of a hint; he sprinted out of the room and down the hall. Pus Face's eyes whirled as he did the internal calculus. On the one hand, he wanted to strangle me; on the other hand, pissing off the ambassador would only remove any possibility of having him bail him out. He finally clamped his teeth together and began grinding them furiously as he walked away.

"You wouldn't believe the phone calls I've had," said White when the others were gone. He went to the credenza at the side of the room, opening it to reveal a bar. "I don't think there's a Catholic in the country who hasn't complained." He smiled and added, "You're used to this, aren't you?"

"It can happen."

"I'm not used to it. This isn't exactly a high-pressure job under normal circumstances. Although the fact that I raised three girls has given me some

perspective." He pulled over one of the leather-
bound chairs and sat down. "Is Dosdière definitely
Saladin?"

"I'd like to say definitely, but I can't." I updated
him on Shunt's theory.

"Still not much, huh?"

"No, sir. But I wouldn't go to mass at midnight if I
were you."

"I'll back you on this, Dick. I already have. But
there's only so much we can do. The Vatican claims
it's taking precautions, and of course Dosdière is out-
raged. Did you call him Saladin?"

"No, as a matter of fact I didn't. It was probably
obvious that I suspect him."

"He wants you fired."

"Good thing I don't work for you."

"Good thing all around." The ambassador smiled.
"At least they've called a security alert. They'll search
the church inch by inch."

"They have already. Several times."

"I have to say, I hope you're wrong."

"I wouldn't mind being wrong. I hope I am."

By the time I got out of the embassy, it was after
eight. I was supposed to rendezvous with the rest of
my team near Fontana di Trevi, Quirinale—Trevi
Fountain—in a tourist quarter dominated by the huge
statue of partying Roman gods. Trace and Danny were
standing at a souvenir shop, trying to decide whether
to buy a pair of coffee mugs with the Colosseum on
them, or go with the set of the Forum. Doc was engaged in a discussion on cameras with two English
tourists nearby. I passed by them and walked down
two blocks to a small café. The gang filtered in a short

while later, having circled around to make sure no one was followed.

"Well, you were a bad boy, weren't you?" said Trace, pulling out her chair. "Did Pus Face spank you?"

"I've been excommunicated."

"I got a hit on the sniffer under the dome," said Doc. "It was just momentary. I was trying to adjust the sensitivity when the supervisor came up. I palmed my security badge and played tourist. Then they sounded the alert and cleared the place, and I got nabbed, along with Danny."

I pulled out a tourist schematic of the basilica and had Doc show us where he'd gotten the alert. It was about halfway between 46 and 42—the canopy to the Papal Altar (46) and St. Peter's Chair (42), the Scud missile at the back of the church.

"I didn't get a hit there," said Trace. "You sure?"

"I don't know. It wasn't a strong hit. It might even have come off of someone's clothes." Doc may not be a technophobe but he's close, and if anyone would have had problems with the equipment it would be him. And even if he had been operating it under perfect conditions, a transitory alert is not exactly a smoking gun.

This probably isn't a good place to go into detail about portable (or standing, for that matter) explosive detectors. The truth is that even the best of the units—and Law Enforcement Technologies' stuff *is* among the best, along with devices made by Global Security Solutions and a few other very specialized, very advanced companies—can give false positives. In general, they're best used in relatively closed spaces or at very close range, checking a car or a piece of luggage, for example. We were pushing our unit to the very edge of its capability, if not beyond.

Still . . .

"The altar right under the dome is cordoned off," said Danny. "How close were you?"

"At the velvet rope."

"Those four pillars, the pieces that hold the canopy over the altar—they'd be perfect spots to put a bomb," said Trace.

"If you had enough explosive, you could take out the pope—and blow off the dome," added Doc. "A good enough explosion there, everything above comes tumbling down."

"I think we should take this to the ambassador," said Danny. "Demand a sweep."

"No. Backass will just do it himself," said Trace. "And claim it was fine."

"We could go on Italian TV and demand that the place be inspected," said Danny. "Put a little pressure on them through the media."

"That's a good idea—unless we're wrong," I said. "Then we've blown our only shot. We have to find the bomb ourselves."

"How are we getting in?" said Danny. "They have all our photos except for Trace's. They're watching the streets, the square, every alley—the security people all have photos, and video cameras, even in the sewers."

"We'll just find an easier way to drop in," I told him. "No big deal."

It was a little more involved than I thought it would be. Pus Face had sent out a series of directives to the effect that I was a raving lunatic, not to be trusted. This increased the degree of difficulty as I lined up the resources I needed, making people who wanted to help me have to go through a few more hoops. By the time we got everything together, it was nearly nightfall Saturday, only a few hours before the VIPs would begin filtering in for midnight mass. I like to work at night, but I can do without the tight deadlines.

Among the many questions we weren't able to answer at the time was how Backass intended on getting out of Vatican City, either before or after the attack. The original Saladin wasn't a suicide bomber and Backass didn't strike me as one either. We couldn't figure out what the escape plan was, but if it involved either of the Holy See's 737s, Backass was shit out of luck. Several key components in both aircraft were removed Saturday afternoon. It's amazing how much access coveralls and a few smudges of grease on your face can provide.

There are two types of high-altitude jumps, and each has its own special pleasures. High-altitude, high-opening jumps—HAHO for short—are a little like parasailing adventures. You jump out of an aircraft, deploy your chute, and basically turn yourself into a glider. Depending on the circumstances, you may fly forty miles to your destination. I wouldn't necessarily term it leisurely—for one thing, if the mission calls for a HAHO jump, there's a *real* good chance some of the folk down there have guns—but the pace is steady and as predictable as this sort of work can get, assuming the chute opens when it's supposed to.

The alternative is a high-altitude, low-opening (HALO) jump. The beginning and end of this jump are the same as in a HAHO—you get off the plane, you land on the ground. In between though, you're not pretending to be a glider. You're a rock.

Or two rocks in this case: Trace went out with me, falling from the back of a specially rigged MC-130 made available with Frankie's help and completely and totally without the authorization of Pus Face, Kohut, Crapinpants, or any of the other names that may or may not have appeared in the paperwork. Gravity tugged us to the tune of 180 miles an hour.* We were aimed at a sparkle of light smaller than the period at the end of this sentence. That was Rome—St. Peter's was about the size of one of the molecules inside the period.

Yeah, I know it looks like fun—and it is. But don't let anyone tell you that a night jump into an urban area from the stratosphere is *easy*. It ain't. On the other hand, waiting to deploy until we were about five hundred feet off terra firma made it impossible for the two anti-aircraft batteries the Italians had moved in to spot us.

I got the audible tone in my headset and deployed. In the space between pulling the ring and feeling the ball-crunching tug that told me I'd deployed, I consoled myself with the realization that I was exactly on

---

*The copy editor wants to see my math on terminal velocity, contending I could have been doing "only" 150 or so. I told him he can do the math himself. Not only will I supply the calculator and parachute, I'll kick him out of the airplane for free. [The copy editor graciously yields to superior knowledge and/or firepower.—Copy Editor]

beam for the spire at the top of the basilica dome. If the chute didn't deploy, I'd end up as Dick on a stick.

It did deploy, with a hefty pull. It's not always an advantage to have big balls, but it's better than the alternative, all around.

I took my mind off my pain by making sure Trace's chute had opened, then got serious about landing. St. Peter's loomed a hundred feet away. I tipped the canopy to straighten my aim, riding down almost precisely on target. I opened my arms and hooked onto the funnel-like mast at the very top of the cupola: bull's-eye.

Trace came in a few feet below and to the right, grabbing onto the upper crown of the cupola. We climbed down on opposite sides to the top of the large pillars that form the crown base. This was our most vulnerable thirty seconds—we had to stow our chutes quickly without losing them or falling off the cathedral. We were visible from the roofs of most of the nearby buildings, and the only thing in our favor was the utter audacity of what we were doing.

Which was why, frankly, I figured Mr. Murphy would show up. He didn't, though. I got my chute stowed easily, tucking it between the railings, then secured a rope to the rail and another forty feet to a second railing, this one at the base of the pillars themselves.

If you've never seen the cathedral and its dome, picture a large beach ball with a toilet paper tube on top of it. The beach ball sits in the middle of a hat box, which is perched on a giant footlocker. We were at the base of the toilet paper tube. A narrow observation deck rings the cupola, with pillars on the outside and windows. Inside, a set of stairs with more than three hundred steps leads through the narrow cavity down to the base of the dome.

When we got squared away, we scouted the cathedral roof below. Sharpshooters had been posed at the lip of the roof at the front of the building, where they could train their high-powered rifles on the piazza. But otherwise there were no guards at all in sight. Everyone was watching the doors and nearby streets.

A jammer had been installed inside the cathedral to block anyone from using a radio or cell phone to set off a bomb. The system rendered conventional radios useless, so Trace and I had packed a line-of-sight laser unit to communicate with Doc and Danny, who were standing by in the MC-130 as backups in case we landed in the Coliseum by mistake. Hitting the plane with the laser would have been pretty difficult, so we set up a receiver unit on the roof of a building to the north. From there, the signal was transmitted via a conventional microwave to the aircraft. The sending unit, which looked a bit like a futuristic, sawed-off ray gun, had to be sighted into the general area of the receiver, and then guided with the help of a small set of indicator buttons until the beam "locked" with the receiver device. It was a bit awkward to use, and it took me several tries before I got a lock tone and was able to give Doc the good word. He barked "good" and signed off. It would take at least an hour for him and Danny to get down and get close enough to play cavalry if something went wrong.

If we'd been tourists, we could have just opened the door and let ourselves in. But Trace's traipse through the church on Friday had revealed new alarms and a video security system on all of the doors, including those on the dome and inside the cupola. Besides fixing the window I'd fallen through, they'd also installed alarms on it and all of the others. They'd even put alarms on the smaller eyebrow windows that opened into the dome interior. While at this hour it was likely that an alert would be disregarded as a malfunction, we couldn't take the chance.

There was one set of windows that had no alarms: the windows at the base of the cupola. This made sense, since the doors leading to the cupola were locked and alarmed; even if you went through the window, you'd be stuck.

Unless, you went straight down three hundred feet to the balcony at the base of the dome.

With help from my glass cutter—the diamond-tipped kind, not my fist—I removed the panels and then cut out enough of the frame to slip through. Down below, a scattering of priests, brothers, and nuns were getting the interior of the church ready for the midnight mass. They were supposed to be done and out of the building at exactly 10 p.m. At that point, St. Peter's would be swept by security forces one last time, with the doors opening for the mass at 11 p.m.

My watch read 9:08.

"Still want to go first, Spider-man?" asked Trace, getting our ropes ready. The dome is about three hundred feet high; we had 120 meters of 11mm rope with us*—just enough for me to kill myself with.

"Just make sure it doesn't tangle," I told her.

---

*Don't try this at home.

"It's the bar I'm worried about." She was referring to a long, flat piece of steel that fit outside the window and anchored the rope in place.

"That'll hold as long as the cupola does," I told her.

"Exactly."

If it didn't hold, I'd plop straight down into the bronze altar canopy, ending up a holy hood ornament. Which I'm sure would have fulfilled the prophecies of some of the nuns I'd had back at St. Ladislaus Hungarian Catholic School.

I made like a spider sneaking up on Miss Muffett, slipping through the window and lowering myself into the painted heaven above the altar. I had a rappelling harness on, and the process was a hell of a lot easier than it sounds.

For the first ten feet. Then I slipped down a little faster than I thought I would. No biggie really, except that the shift in my momentum started me swinging on the line.

Swinging was fine; I had to get to the side of the dome anyway. What I didn't like was spinning. And I started spinning so much I could have been a fucking ballerina. At the same time, I was twirling across the damn dome, a pendulum gone crazy. Finally I slammed face-first into one of the prophets in the ceiling.

He didn't seem to mind, or at least he didn't hold it against me. He stopped me from spinning, though not from swinging, sending me back out into space. Now I was like a stinking yo-yo, though headed in only one direction—down. The windows loomed closer and closer, and on one swing I thought I would put my left foot right through the one I had broken a few weeks before. I missed, however, and managed to get my foot onto the railing on my next pass. Not pretty, but I made it in one piece and without setting off any of the alarms.

Trace, of course, came down perfectly a minute later. Sometimes that woman is so damn good all I want to do is smack her.

We slipped into the hallway out of sight, pulled off our jumpsuits, and donned more appropriate garb—a monk's robes for me, and a white nun's habit for Trace. I shaved off my beard for the mission—the sacrifices you make for this job. I hadn't seen my face in almost twenty years, and I looked about as ugly as a breeding cow's pussy. I'd also had my hair cut monk-style, with a tonsure at the back. (It's a bald spot to make it easier for God to aim his thunderbolt if you mess up.) But there was one consolation: After all this raping and scraping, I wouldn't have to do any more novenas to get my ticket through the pearly gates. St. Peter wouldn't recognize me.

I pulled out the handheld explosives detector and turned it on; it took roughly a minute to warm up and get ready. The alert was piped through an earbud; I arranged the cowl to make the wire less conspicuous. Trace's habit was one of the old-fashioned kinds and covered her head, making her earpiece easy to conceal.

Backass's people had set up an impenetrable perimeter around the cathedral, which meant that once you penetrated it you were home free. But just to keep the people on the perimeter from getting bored, I had arranged a small diversion. As Trace and I made our way down the staircase from the dome, a taxi raced up Via Della Conciliazione toward Piazza San Pietro in front of the basilica. The driver, though certainly as crazy as any native Italian (which says a lot), was in fact Sean Mako, who'd stepped off a plane a few hours before at Leonardo da Vinci airport. Hailing a taxi, he had struck a deal with the driver, who agreed to show Sean the city for "only" two thousand Euros and as much *vino* as he could drink. This proved to be only a glass and a half after Sean slipped a little GHB into his first Chianti. (GHB is gamma hydroxybutyric acid, better known as the "date-rape drug." Not FDA approved.)

Sean left the driver in the bar where they had stopped and continued the tour in do-it-yourself mode. At precisely 9:15, he raced down the broad avenue in front of the basilica, dodged two roadblocks, and veered across the circle. He then cut back to the right, swung completely around the obelisk at the center of the square and managed to get up one of the long, shallow-rise steps before his wheels and caltrop-shredded tires finally gave out.

Sean had picked up a passenger along the way—supposedly for authenticity, though personally I think he was trying to make a little money on the side. The passenger got out calmly and began walking away, ignoring the forty or fifty armed guards who rushed them. Sean claims that at this point he began singing "O Sole Mio" at the wheel. I take that with a grain of salt, though I believe him when he says the Vatican drunk tank is a cheap place to spend the night.

As more than a hundred law enforcement officials completed the arrest, Trace and I reached the hallway behind the Altar of St. Leo the Great on the main floor of the church.

"You look lovely in white, Sister," I told her.

"Up yours, Brother," she said, grabbing a bouquet of flowers from a box near the archway and walking into the church.

I gave her a few seconds, then followed, head bent and hands folded, walking toward the center of the church. If I looked like I was praying, it wasn't an act—at this point I figured that if I didn't find the bomb, I'd be blown up.

The area around the Pope's Altar and the huge bronze canopy over it had been cordoned off with thick velvet ropes, but there were no security guards to stop anyone from getting past. In fact, the only people in this part of the church were two brothers in black robes arranging microphones at an ornate kneeler at the center aisle. They were uttering bits of Latin prayers to test the devices.

I walked to the rear of the Pope's Altar, genuflected, then unhooked the velvet rope so I could pass. The altar was on a platform that would make a perfect hiding place for a bomb; packed with enough explosives the force would easily lift the roof above. I knelt as if praying, then slipped the probe of the sniffer out, moving my hand steadily across the step.

No *bing*.

I made my way around the platform, from right to left pretending I'd been assigned to smooth the rug so His Holiness wouldn't trip. If there were stray molecules of explosive, the sensor wasn't finding them. I moved up and checked the altar itself, arranging the candles as if I'd noticed one out of alignment. The ear-phone remained silent.

I started around to the front of the platform, be-tween the altar and the Tomb of St. Peter. As I did, one of the priests asked what I was doing.

I'd been so intent on using the sniffer that I had lost track of who was around me. The priest stood at the railing that surrounds the tomb. Bowing my head in his direction without answering, I genuflected—when in doubt, kneel, as the nuns used to say.

"Brother, what are you doing?" demanded the priest. He was speaking Italian.

"I'm looking for bombs," I told him, lowering my head slightly and pulling my sleeve up to show him the device. "This tool looks for traces of certain mole-cules in the air."

As I looked up, the priest's eyes seemed to snap into mine and hold them. "You're not a priest, are you?" he said in Italian.

"No, I'm a security expert from the U.S. The robes are meant to make me less conspicuous."

Now the priest's stare made me feel as if I were in the confessional at St. Ladislaus, having to confess—well, never mind what I had to confess. I would have felt more comfortable staring down the barrel of a ma-chine gun than holding the gaze of the white-haired shepherd of God. Finally, he nodded solemnly.

"Do your best, my son," he told me.

If he said something else, it was drowned out by the distinct buzz from the unit as I reached the front of the altar, the probe pointing over St. Peter's Tomb.

* * *

Time out for a second if you haven't seen the inside of the basilica. St. Peter's Tomb is a large semicircular area in front of the Pope's Altar, one level down and set off by a railing. (Technically, it's called "*Il Confessio,*" a term for a crypt that has linked passages.) It looks more like an elaborate chapel than a tomb, and includes the niche where the saint's bones are preserved.

St. Peter's Tomb sits like the tip of the iceberg at the peak of a large underground necropolis or burial ground that the basilica and its predecessor were built over. The grottoes or tombs of the popes flank St. Peter's. Around and below them are the remains of the Roman graveyard that St. Peter was interred in. Mausoleums and passages through the city of the dead extend beneath the basilica. The grottoes and the necropolis—called *Scavi,* Italian for excavations—lay beneath the floor beyond the tomb and are ordinarily reached through small stairways in the pillars beneath the dome.

A temporary platform had been placed across part of the Tomb near the altar to make it easier to celebrate mass. This was where I was standing when I got the alert.

The sniffer had found an extremely minute trace of PETN—an important ingredient in Semtex and similar plastic explosives. But it was a fleeting hit. I reset the device and failed to get another alert, even when I selected specifically for PETN.

Two false positives in the same area?

An area not accessible to the public?

I squatted down and slowly wanded the temporary platform but got nothing. Then I went across the platform to the railing, leaning over the side. A fence-like grille had been installed around the area below the temporary platform, blocking off the metal doors at the sides. As I put one foot over the railing, trying to find a space between the ring of candles to get over, a voice behind me said, "No, brother."

I turned slowly. The priest I'd spoken to a few moments before stood a few feet away, frozen. Next to me was the other cleric who'd been with him, holding a 9mm Ruger.

14

"Very slowly," said the padre with the pistol, "move back from there."

"Here?" I said loudly. I held my hands out at my side and stepped back.

"That way," he said, pointing toward the left side of the nave.

"Why?"

He answered by raising the pistol. I took a slow step backward. Trace was somewhere nearby, and I hoped that if I moved slowly enough she would hear what was going on and ambush him. I took another step, and then tripped on one of the rugs.

I honestly lost my footing, but if the pretend priest had been close enough I would have bowled him over. He'd remained several feet away, lowering his pistol with a slight grin as he sighted down the barrel.

The grin was knocked off his face by a roundhouse to the side of the head by the priest who had stopped me earlier. The gun fired as he fell, the bullet ricocheting off the floor a few feet from my chest.

"Run, my son!" said the good priest. "Get help!"

And then he dove on the other man. The pistol

flew across the floor. I scooped it up as two monks—or I should say, two men dressed as monks—ran from the back of the church, pulling Rugers from beneath their robes.

I dropped the first with one shot. The second man slid off to the right, out of my line of fire—but right into Trace's; she took him down with her Kimber Compact.

"Get upstairs and get to the radio!" I yelled to her. "The bomb is in the crypt somewhere!"

"Are you sure?"

"Go! And don't take the elevator—they may cut the power."

The good priest had pinned the bad priest by his arms and was kneeling over him on the floor. I administered a dose of anesthetic—a quick kick to the bad priest's skull—then gave the Ruger to the other man. "There's a bomb below! Don't let the pope into the building!"

"By God, I won't."

I bolted over the railing, sliding down the steps. It took all of two seconds for me to realize there was no way I was getting into the crypt area from here. But the sniffer got strong hits from both sides of the tomb area; I'd been walking back and forth over the explosives.

I jumped back over the railing and headed in the direction of the entrance Karen had used during our earlier visit, now hidden behind a row of pew grandstands. Somebody shouted as I ran. Gunshots followed. I slid down in front of the entrance—which, of course, was locked. Luckily, it was only the standard brass lock, easily picked. I reached beneath my monk's cloak and took out my lock picks. I could hear the security people running up the center of the church as I found the right one and fit it into the lock.

Only to lose my grip and have it drop to the floor, whereupon Mr. Murphy gave it good kick under the locked gate.

So where was Trace while Murphy and I were dancing on the main floor?

I *thought* she was upstairs somewhere, retracing her steps to the balcony and the rope or maybe out on the roof, where she could climb up to the dome and then the cupola from the outside. But she wasn't.

As she headed toward the staircase, she found a group of nuns—real ones—lying on the floor in one of the side chapels. Trace got them up to their feet, thinking to herd them to safety. A wave of security officials appeared just as they began to move; Trace ducked to the right and the sisters went with her, following her into a side chapel and then behind an altar into a short hallway and an empty room, which turned out to be a dead end.

The good priest must have seen me drop the pick, because he began yelling to the security people to attract their attention. Meanwhile, I fitted a slightly smaller one into the lock. No more tootsie fingers this time: I clicked open the lock and grabbed at the metal bars of the door. A few yards away the security people reached the priest, hauling him to his feet as I closed the door behind me, locking it.

"Marcinko!" yelled someone as I slammed the door shut. "It's Marcinko!"

I rushed down the steps, my way lit by a dull yellow emergency bulb at the top of the passage. I twisted with the staircase, turned right and then left, then hopped down a short flight of steps that took me below the level of the papal crypts to the more ancient necropolis. By now I was completely in the dark; I pulled out my LED pinlight and pushed ahead into a narrow passage. After three or four steps, I found my way barred by a security gate, which had been installed very recently; shavings from a masonry drill used to put in the anchors lay on the floor. I picked the lock, slipped past, then pushed it closed quietly as I heard guards coming down behind me.

The walls of the hallway looked like the sides of a Roman street, with the mausoleums to the left and right. There were crypts and huge masonry walls as well, a collection of graves and parts of the first St. Peter's Basilica intermingling. I went down the narrow hallway in what I thought was the direction of St. Peter's Tomb. The sound of the guards grew louder; they were at the gate I had just come through. I found an opening between two Roman sarcophagi in the wall and tucked into it, thinking it was a shallow niche I could stage an ambush from. But as I pushed in, I saw a passage behind the shadows on my right. The narrow metal door swung open easily. I went through pistol first, stooping to fit into the hallway.

A spiderweb so thick it felt like a hand reached out to grab my face and shoulders. I fell back against the wall in the dark, listening to see if the guards were close. They sounded as if they were pounding on the security gate, so I pulled out my light to see where I was. I half expected to find the room piled with bones.

But instead I found myself in what looked like a large, bricked room. There were dust-covered indentations in the walls, each numbered with Roman numerals. At the right of the room, a doorway about five feet high and maybe two feet across opened into another hallway. I squeezed through, half walking, half stooping like the hunchback of Notre Dame.

The passage stopped at another hallway. I had the choice of left or right. As I examined it for some hint on what the right direction might be, I saw a thin black wire against the wall ahead of me.

I turned to the right and followed the hall and the wire for about thirty feet before realizing I was moving upward. If the wire was attached to the bomb—a big guess, granted, but how many Romans ran speaker wire into their sarcophagi?—the bomb logically would be the other way. Retracing my steps, I reached the original passage, where I heard the muffled sounds of the security people who were pursuing me. I kept going, softening my breath not only to make as little sound as possible but also to hear better. The darkness had a hollow hum to it, the sort of sound that you hear in your head when you wake up in a Cambodian hotel at 3 a.m. with the AC going full blast, though it pumps nothing but hot air. The hush seemed to grow louder as I went; it was the echo of machinery from somewhere above, deadening sound throughout the underground passages.

After about twenty feet, the passage widened enough so that my arms no longer scraped the sides. I still had to stoop, though not quite as steeply. Caged lights were hung along the top of the ceiling, running in a metal strip but not turned on; if there was a switch anywhere nearby, I didn't see it and wouldn't have turned it on if I did.

A draft let me know there was another passage ahead, and sure enough, twenty or so paces after the intersection I came to it. It had been gated off not only with a security fence but thick wire-mesh fencing. It had been bolted on angled pieces of iron, so there was no way to loosen it from my side.

As I examined the gate, my flashlight beam caught dark-colored bottles about the size of water coolers stacked high to the ceiling, interspaced with thick black pads. Large boxes ringed what I could see of the room, and the bottles filled the rest of the space.

I'd found the bomb.*

I knelt down and picked up the wire. I could cut it easily, with my teeth if I had to, but it was likely that whoever had rigged the bomb had taken that into account. Cutting the wires might set it off rather than rendering it inert.

I had maybe an hour to decide which it would do. In the meantime, I either had to find the detonator, or get inside the room and figure out how it worked.

As I rose, something cold smashed my shoulder, pushing me into the fence.

---

*The bottles held liquid explosives similar to rocket fuel. The boxes contained a plastic explosive made mostly from PETN, which will ignite them and produce a pretty good explosion on their own. The pads were more plastic explosives. There was also a network of blasting caps to get everything rolling, though I couldn't see it from here. In layman's terms, this is one big fucking ka-boom we're looking at here. Not as good as a nuke, but still pretty big.

It wasn't the hand of God, or a devil's claw. It was the business end of a Minimi machine gun.

"He has a pistol in his front belt, and there'll be at least one more, probably two. Shoot him if he resists."

"Now why the fuck would I do that?" I growled as light flooded into my face.

"Because you think you'll escape eventually."

"I don't think, I know."

Backass laughed. Two plainclothes Vatican security agents—Backass plants—were standing about six feet from me, holding machine guns with high-powered lights where scopes would normally be mounted. The lights were bright enough to blind me.

"You haven't changed, Marcinko. Still the arrogant American he-man, a walking, talking Superman."

I'd have thanked him for the compliment, but I was too busy rebounding from the sharp poke to the side of the head another of his henchmen had delivered. I started to grab for him, but he'd jumped back out of reach.

"It's not a problem for us to kill you here," said Backass. "Take his gun."

I pulled my pistol out and slid it along the floor. Then I rolled up my right and left pants legs and took out the Glocks I had strapped there.

"I could have killed you a dozen times," said Backass. "You've been lucky. You've always been lucky. You complain about not having luck, about Mr. Murphy, but you're the luckiest son of a bitch I know. You were lucky in China, in Thailand, in Las Vegas."*

*See *Rogue Warrior: Vengeance.*

"What about Las Vegas?"

"I gave them the money, Dick. It's always been me."

"You were too much of a wimp to take a shot at me yourself."

Backass laughed. He'd started moving up the corridor. The minions around me prodded me to follow. We walked up past the point where I had entered the corridor, continuing up the sloped hall for about ten feet before turning left into a hallway so narrow my shoulders touched both sides. This led to an even narrower staircase. The steps seemed to be bricks and were so shallow only about half of my foot fit on the treads. I was in the middle of the pack; if I played bowling for tangos, the best I could do would be to tumble two-thirds of them, leaving Backass to fry us at the bottom with his Minimi.

Five or six times we reached landings no bigger than the chair you're sitting on, reversing direction to continue upward. Then we came to a corridor similar to the one we'd started in, turned left and found another set of staircases. A string of thin, rectangular LED units illuminated the treads. There was enough light for me to see the thin wire that came up along the staircase—the detonator wire.

We reached another corridor, this one a succession of zigzags, before finding yet another staircase. Here the walls were farther apart, though I had to lean forward slightly, my head just brushing the ceiling rafters. The steps curved—we'd reached the dome and were moving up toward the cupola. I hoped Trace would be waiting at the top, MP5 ready.

"So you hate my guts, huh?" I said. "How'd I

manage to make such an impression? I don't even know you."

"There are many of us, Marcinko, an army of people you have fucked. Some are Muslim. Some are Asian. Some are American. A number even were part of your navy. We're members of a very large club—people screwed by Dick."

"I don't screw people. I treat everyone equally—"

"Like shit."

"Well, at least you read the books."

I stopped, putting my hand on the wall and pushing a forlorn breath out of my lungs. Any EMT within listening distance would have called a stretcher.

"You're getting old, Demo Dick. A has-been. I'm doing you a favor," snorted Backass from above.

"How's that?"

"There's nothing more pathetic than a broken-down old sailor. Look at yourself. You can't even walk up a flight of stairs. You're a wreck."

I wheezed louder.

"When you saw me in Cairo I was a boy," he said. "But you let your man shoot me even so."

"When was that?"

"When you kidnapped my father."

Of all the things I've ever done—and there have been many—I've only kidnapped one person in Egypt.

"Azziz was your father?"

"How did it feel to shoot a child, Marcinko? Did it make you feel good? But I didn't die."

The incident he was referring to had gone down when I was on Uncle Sugar's black payroll with Green

Team, a successor to Red Cell. We'd been sent into the Cairo slums to apprehend Mahmoud Azziz abu Yasin from his flop there and take him to a place more likely to induce candid discussion. Azziz was a scumbag of the highest sort, a terrorist before it was fashionable to be a terrorist, a truly sick psycho who'd organized several plots against Westerners.

A boy—his age was somewhere between twelve and sixteen—had popped out of the hallway just before we hit Azziz's pad. Nasty Nicky Grundle popped the kid with a silenced MP5 before he could give us away. We thought at the time that he was one of the bodyguards, but I have to admit he didn't show a gun. It was certainly possible that he was an innocent bystander in the wrong place at the wrong time.

Not pretty, but war's like that. Ask any of the sixty-five people in New York, Chicago, Houston, or D.C. Azziz killed before we bundled his ass off to face justice.

"I wasn't the one who shot you."

"You do remember. Good. Allah was with me that morning," Backass continued. "In many ways. Only one of your man's bullets hit—and that in my shoulder. I still have the slug."

"I'll have to tell Nick he should take some target practice."

"I was taken to live with my mother's uncle, adopted—and trained to fulfill my fate. The crusader side of my family believed I was with them, but I have worked since that day to achieve my vision."

He rattled on, spewing the usual self-delusional bullshit about being anointed as the savior of his religion and his people. You'd think an egocentric maniac would at least make an *effort* to be original; just once I'd like to hear one of the chosen say, "I don't know if I'm *really* God's choice, but fuck it; I'm going for it anyway."

To fill in the backstory: Backass was hustled off to one of his European aunties to recuperate. For his protection, he was given the identity of a cousin who had died two years before of typhoid. The rest of his background—the connection with European aristocrats, etc.—that the security agencies relied on when they checked him out came from this part of his family. He'd led a double life from that morning in Cairo.

If not sooner.

I let him gloat for a while, making sure he had the conceit juices flowing.

"So, is this your funeral pyre, or do you have an escape plan?" I asked.

He just laughed.

"How are you going to blow us up? I take it I saw rocket fuel down there. As I understand it, that stuff won't ignite on its own."

"Still full of yourself, huh, Dickie?"

"Well if you're so much in control, how are you going to do it?"

Backass simply turned and continued walking up the steps.

The breeze in the passageway had gradually picked up, and the air became chilly and damp as we went. I started to pick up the pace, closing the distance between myself and Backass. But I'd played the tired old fuck a bit too hard; a turn of the staircase later and he was already outside. One of the two guards above me jogged toward the exit. I waited until only one was left in front of me, and then sprang, grabbing his leg and pulling him down, rolling to the side and firing my pistol with my left hand into the assholes behind me.

Yes, I'd given up my hideaway Glocks. But a monk's habit is big enough to conceal many things, including a seven-shot PPK .380.

The little gun sounded like a runaway subway train. Because the staircase was so steep, the guards behind me couldn't elevate their weapons properly, or at least not quickly enough to avoid getting shot. I didn't have that problem.

The machine gun the tango had been carrying clattered by me on the staircase. I took a swipe at it, but the law of gravity has more pull than the law of necessity, and I missed. As I ducked down after it, guards from somewhere below began firing. A shower of stone splinters and lead filled the landing. I grabbed for the machine gun and pulled it up to fire just as they turned the corner. About mid-blast, my face seemed to catch fire and I fired blindly, working the gun back and forth. I lost my balance and tumbled down, six or seven steps. By the time I landed, all of the other gunfire had stopped.

I had to use my thumb to open my eyes. Blood covered my hand when I finally managed to see. I'd been hit in the face, chest, and neck—I could feel the pain—but since I was still breathing, I figured it had been by stone shrapnel from the centuries-old wall. There were four bodies near me on the landing, and another two on the steps behind the bend. One of the men had a Model 12S Beretta with a fresh magazine taped to the spent box; I grabbed it, loaded, and started trudging up toward the door. A helicopter began pounding the air in the distance.

The cavalry, I hoped.

Burp gun in hand, I burst through the open door into the night, pirouetting around the jam onto the walkway at the base of the dome. The helo had dropped into a hover on the other side of the dome, over the Left Transept.

It was a civilian helicopter, not an Italian military chopper. Backass's escape plan.

As I started to cross the roof, a fusillade of bullets erupted from the columns at the base of the dome. All I could do was duck.

So where the hell was Trace Dahlgren's pretty little butt, anyway? Why wasn't she waiting there to save mine, as she had so many times before? To find out we have to backtrack to the small room where she had found herself with the nuns as the security forces closed in.

Backass hadn't replaced all of the Vatican security team, but Trace was in neither a position or a mood to start trusting any of them. And she knew they would feel more or less the same about her. The nuns, on the other hand, did trust her, and the feeling was mutual. As soon as they saw they were cut off, one of the sisters—the oldest and frailest, by Trace's description—pushed Trace to the back of the pack and then walked to the door. In a voice barely above a whisper, she told the first security people to arrive that the *terroriste* had gone through the door behind them, which led downstairs.

"St. Peter, preserve us," she cried in Italian, falling

to her knees, supplicating St. Peter to save his church. The rest of the nuns, Trace included, dropped as well.

How much was an act and how much genuine prayer is hard to say. But it surely saved Trace's life. The first two guards—Backass plants, as it turned out—hesitated just long enough for four or five others to come up behind. The old nun rose and hobbled forward, urging them to do God's work and rid the church of the terrible devils who had disappeared down the nearby staircase.

"*Si! Si!*" yelled the men, and together they ran off in the wrong direction, as most of us do when we're chasing the devil.

Trace kissed each of the women, imploring them to warn the pope not to come to the church.

"Where are you going, sister?" asked the oldest nun.

"I need to get to the roof."

"The elevator and stairs will be guarded by now." The nun took her by the hand and led her through the chapel to a side door that would take her to a set of stairs rarely used; when she reached the fifth landing, she could turn left and find the passage to the dome if she wished, or go the other way and get out onto the roof.

"God is with you," said the nun in Italian. "But just in case, have your pistol ready."

Trace leapt up the stairs. When she reached the landing the nun had told her about, she started for the dome. But she heard someone ahead, and so turned and went out onto the roof. She made her way across to the other side of the dome, climbing to the large windows. Even without people shooting at her, climbing up the outside of the dome wouldn't have been all

that easy, so she decided to go inside and use the rope
we had taken from the cupola. She figured there was
no sense worrying about alarms now and broke the
glass on the nearest window. She climbed down to the
base of the windows, then hung over and jumped
down to the balcony. Unfortunately, the jump was a
bit higher than she thought, and she hit the floor so
hard she keeled to the side, sending her pistol flying
from her hand.

Inconvenient, given that two security people were
just coming through the door twenty yards away.

Fortunately, about the last thing either man expected was a flying nun careening through a window
into the dome. Trace jumped to her feet and grabbed
the rope we had left tied to the safety fence around
the railing. One of the men took aim, but the other
shouted at him not to fire; Trace didn't stop to ask
whether he was worried about hitting her or the frescoes nearby. She swung out over the space and shim-
mied up the line like a rat climbing from the hold of a
sinking freighter as the water closed in. She pulled
herself through the window of the cupola, then sliced
the rope with her Emerson knife so the men couldn't
follow.

Trace got out the laser communications gear and
set up to transmit. She couldn't get a connection right
away—and then still couldn't. She figured it was just
Murph screwing with her head, until she realized that
something was in her way: an approaching helicopter.

She waited as the chopper came in. Somewhere
around here I made my play inside, though she didn't
hear it because of the noise from the rotors. Finally she
was able to make the connection and, without waiting

for a confirmation from Doc or Danny, began broad-
casting the fact that there was a bomb in the cellar of
the basilica.

Which brings us to the point where I was mistaken
for a rabbit in a shooting gallery, more or less.

My eyes were puffy from the stone and plaster
splinters and caked half-closed with blood. If I could
have seen any better, I probably would have been
more careful. I might have stayed down, or at least
thought about finding a different way to the other side.
But everything beyond five feet was a blur, and maybe
because of that I thought there were only one or two
people firing at me. So when the bullets stopped
sparkling, I emptied the Beretta at the shadows.

When I reached the bodies, I found not one or two
but five. I hunted through them for a fresh magazine
that would fit the gun, finally finding one.

"Don't bother, Dick!"

The shout was punctuated by a rifle butt to my
neck. The gun and magazine flew from my hand and
careened across the roof. I followed it, sprawling
against the tiles.

"Too late, Dickie!" yelled Backass. He held up a
large metal box. Then he laughed, and threw it down.
"Too late!"

He sprayed his Minimi around me as I scrambled
away. I scrambled around what looked like an oversized telephone booth a few yards from the dome. I
reached beneath my monk's outfit and took my last
pistol, another PPK. By the time I went to return fire,
though, Backass had run back toward the chopper.

I stumbled after him. The helicopter's two floodlights played on the roof, framing him for me. As he grabbed at the door, I fired.

Between my blurry eyes and the bad angle, my first two shots missed high. I could hear a crusty old master chief's voice loud and clear in my head: "Excuses are for whiners, you no-good shit-for-brain asshole idiot. Keep at it until you plug the SOB, and then plug him some more."

So I did. All of the subsequent subsonic rounds, personally handcrafted by Doc Tremblay, struck Back-ass square in the back.

All the bastard did was throw down his gun and jump into the chopper. The son of a bitch had a bullet-proof vest on under his clothes.

I cursed, then whipped the gun at the helicopter as it started to back away.

Trace had watched the whole thing from above. Figuring that her backup pistol wasn't going to be taking a helicopter down, she dug into the backpack we'd left with the com gear looking for something to take the helicopter down with. All she found was the miniflare set.

When the helo started to rise, she waited until the hatch at the rear was open and level with her and fired. The flare tailed left a few yards—right into the cockpit. Trace saw a little flicker of flame, but from her perspective it looked as if the flare had bounced against the Plexiglas and been extinguished.

I could tell right away that it had gone through the window. The helicopter tilted on its axis as it moved away, bending over as if it were a drunk. Then its tail whipped around and it began to climb, seesawing in a three-dimensional weave across the sky. Finally it pitched forward and plummeted downward, bursting into flame just before it hit the ground.

The glow of that fire warmed me from two or three miles away.

The reality set in—we were standing directly above a pile of explosives big enough to send us to the moon and dig a hole to China. And the timer had already been set.

15

The box Backass had had in his hand consisted of two toggles, neither of which was marked. Presumably it had set off a timer, though he hadn't thought to include operating instructions with the unit. Switching the buttons the other way was just as likely to blow the bomb up immediately as shut it down.

But what the fuck.

I popped them. Nothing happened. I ripped the wires out of the box. Nothing happened again.

End of problem? Or the calm before the storm?

I started racing toward one of the doors back into the church. A pair of Vatican security people popped out when I was about ten feet from it.

"There's a bomb downstairs, in the area near St. Peter's Tomb," I yelled. By the time they reacted I was by them. A second set of guards met me just inside, but they too let me pass, either because they understood the warning I was yelling or I just seemed like too much of a madman to stop.

Vatican security people were flooding into the cathedral, augmented by Italian soldiers, *carabinieri*, and members of Digos,* the counterterror unit of the Ministry of the Interior. As I ran out into the nave, a pair of riot police grabbed me, but were warned off by a familiar bark.

"Yo! He's with us," said Danny. It doesn't matter what language they're speaking; police officers understand each other, and the *carabinieri* let me go. Danny and Doc were flanked by two members of ROS, the *carabinieri* SpecOp unit.

"The bomb is below St. Peter's Tomb, in the area they closed off to tourists after the other incident," I yelled as I ran toward the entrance to the crypts. By the time I got up near the altar area, security people were already working to undo the fencing that had been installed to prevent anyone from using the underground entrance in St. Peter's Tomb.

"I hope that's not your blood," said Doc, huffing as he caught up to me.

I pulled out the box Backass had used and shoved it into his hands. "What do you make of this? How's the bomb wired?"

"You're changing the subject."

"Worry about me later. Why hasn't the bomb exploded?"

Doc pulled out a knife and pried the box open. It clearly wasn't a detonator—we'd all be dead by now. "It may have started a timer, or locked out some sort of system to stop the bomb. My guess is that it's somehow rigged so that once the toggles were thrown, it couldn't be stopped. It also might be a blind."

---

*Digos is an acronym for *Divisione Investigazioni Generali e Operazioni Speciali*, but Italians don't capitalize the letters.

"There's definitely a bomb downstairs."

Doc nodded, but I saw his point. Backass had all but given me the unit. He knew I'd trace the wire down and try to disarm the bomb.

His way, maybe, of guaranteeing I'd be inside when it blew.

With the help of a pair of bolt cutters, the gate was removed and the security people surged downstairs. Doc, Danny, and I joined the flow. Within a few seconds, we all reached another gate. As a *carabinieri* struggled with the bolt cutter, one of the Digos supervisors suggested bringing a blowtorch down. That would have gotten us past the gate all right—right up to the big pearly one.

Where we might be headed at any moment anyway.

I twisted my fingers into the wire and with the help of one of the security people snapped the gate off its restraints after about two-thirds had been cut away. As we made our way down to the rooms that had been filled with explosives, a second group of security and ROS bomb people broke through the gates on the other side. Within seconds, they began dismantling the major components of the bomb, using a fire-brigade approach to carry out the large bottles of explosives through the winding corridors.

Which, frankly, was probably more dangerous than using a blowtorch on the gates.

"The wire snakes through over there," said one of the bomb people as we examined the bomb from our side of the chamber.

"Then whatever's going to detonate it is in the other direction," I said, pointing to the right side of the room. "Let's look."

The others didn't completely believe me—and all right, yes, it *was* a guess—but we had enough people to clear components from both sides. Rather than completely clearing the space on my side, I had just the top layer removed, enough so I could squeeze in.

"The wire—it ends! It's not connected!" yelled someone in Italian on the other end of the chamber.

The others started murmuring words like "fake" in Italian. I kept crawling. About two-thirds of the way into the large chamber, along a foundation wall dating to the first basilica, I saw a large black suitcase tucked between a trio of bottles.

"Doc!" I yelled. Then I scrunched around so I could lift one of the bottles out.

That was all I said, but Doc knew what I meant. He stopped the rest of the chain gang and reorganized the men, so that when I managed to pull the bottle up over my body and squeeze it over my legs, someone was there to grab it.

And drop it.

Into Trace Dahlgren's arms, who walked up to the pile of bottles at just that moment. She fell back, tottering under the weight and not quite realizing what she had. But before her lovely butt could hit the ground it was caught by two of the luckiest ROS agents in the world.

You can call Trace's timely arrival a miracle, if you want. Or you can be like her, and bitch and moan that the idiot security people had detained her for the past ten minutes, or she would have been there ten minutes earlier.

* * *

I pulled the suitcase out and slid it back to Doc, then scrambled as gingerly as I could to get out. Doc began heading upstairs to the main floor of the church, but the fire brigade of bomb components blocked his way.

"This way," I yelled to him, pointing down the corridor. "Down here."

"There's no exit," said one of the Vatican people.

"There will be soon if we don't disable the bomb," I said.

The corridor opened into a large room that had once been part of a mausoleum of a well-to-do second-century Roman family. Constantine had had it filled with rubble when he built the first St. Peter's. Now the Roman ghosts watched us as Doc examined the bag.

"I think it's booby-trapped," he said. He had managed to pry the side near the latch open just enough to reveal a wire.

"Maybe we can cut open the side."

"Maybe it'll explode before we do. I'd bet there's something along the lines of Semtex packed around the exterior."

"Better off taking it outside," said Danny, who with Trace had just caught up to us.

I bent down. Doc wedged the knife into the side a little more, twisting gently. I could see a liquid crystal watch face, but the digits were blocked by the wires and the knife blade.

"Definitely a timer," I told them.

Doc gave the suitcase a pensive stare. Bomb-disposal teams have fancy X-ray machines and robot disablers; I've got Doc. He pried the lid up every so slightly, then a little more, then a little more.

"I remember a bomb like this I saw once in Egypt,"

he said. "They had it wired so that if you snapped open the latch, it would blow. But they had a way of disabling that. Pretty damn clever, actually. Too clever, I thought. The only reason you'd want *another* wire like that, would be if you thought you were going to screw up. And who the hell plans to screw up?"

"Would you get to the fucking point?" blurted Trace.

I put my hand on her shoulder.

"I am getting to the point," said Doc. "But then I realized that it wasn't just in case you screwed up—it was to confuse someone who was trying to defeat the bomb. Because you would look at two wires, right, and you wouldn't know which one was which. We need some wires with clips to extend the circuit so we can clip it."

Danny went in search of the bomb squad people to get what Doc needed. Trace took out her flashlight and we went back to examining the suitcase.

There were two wires, just as Doc had predicted. He used Trace's knife to slip them out, pushing gingerly. They were twisted together, and there was less than two inches of play.

"One of these sides must come off," he said.

"Let's try to get a look at the timer," I said. "Trace, my eyes are for shit."

"About time you realized you need glasses," she said, squatting down.

"Fuck you, too."

"Thirty seconds."

Doc and I looked at each other. Before either one of us could say anything, Trace added, "Twenty-eight seconds."

"We have to take a chance that one of these wires will turn off the latch wiring," said Doc. "And then we have to disable the timer."

"Which one?"

"Fifty-fifty."

"You don't know?"

Doc put his knife blade between the wires and took a breath. His fingers twitched, but he didn't cut either one. He turned his head toward me and opened his mouth to say something. But he couldn't force anything out.

"Which one?" I said.

Doc shook his head.

"Doc?"

"I—I don't know if I can guess."

"I'll make the call," I said, grabbing his hand. "See you two in heaven. Or the other place."

16

Sure is hot down here where I'm writing this.

But not *that* hot. Virginia gets its heat spells every now and again.

I got the right wire. Once the suitcase was open, Doc's trembling fingers had an easy time disabling the guts of the bomb. We figured out later that the timer must have been set when the bomb was originally planted. It had been set to go off before the mass, at about the time His Holiness the pope was originally scheduled to enter the basilica.

As a matter of fact, the pope had chosen that moment to enter the church and was upstairs almost directly above me when I chose which wire to cut. Informed of the situation, the pontiff had insisted on going to the church over the strongest possible objections of his aides and the security people. God, he said, called him there.

So maybe it wasn't luck at all that I picked the right wire. Mass began even as the security people continued hauling the bomb materials away. The faithful flooded into the square and then the church, over-whelming the security forces. Miraculously, no one was hurt. Afterward, people spoke of the mass as a once-in-a-lifetime and even once-in-a-century event. The media called it the most wondrous service since the basilica had been opened.

I missed it myself. I'd been spending so much time in church lately I figured God wouldn't mind if I took the day off.

They found five charred bodies in the wrecked helicopter. One of them is believed to be Backass's—but since they didn't have dental or DNA records for him, no one is one hundred percent sure. I like to think of him as a crispy critter right now, though knowing Backass, this may be another one of his convoluted plots. In any event, I haven't gotten any faxes signed "Saladin" since the helicopter went down.

As we'd figured out earlier, BetaGo was a legiti-mate company that had been infiltrated by Backass and his associates. He had already spent consider-able time cleaning up his tracks before I was "hired," but investigators believe they have a few more promising leads on terrorist groups and fronts that they hadn't know about. The terror network in Thai-land was broken up following the raids and the at-tack on the airport and airplane; how long before a new one forms is anyone's guess.

My guess is thirty seconds.

As for the second coming of the blackshirts—for the moment, it remained too far-fetched for me to put much stock in. The Grand European Conspiracy—"Power Broker" and the continuing machinations of P2—well, I won't say I didn't believe them exactly, but after my fun and games in the pope's backyard I wasn't in much of a mood to go probing around in search of more problems in the shadows. Bishop Marcinkus, the plot to repurify Europe—it seemed too far-fetched to be anything but the paranoid ramblings of an ex-CIA informer down on his luck. The fact that Backass had endorsed the story didn't exactly lend it any credibility.

I later found out that P2 wasn't a figment of Backass's imagination, nor was it a diversion. But I'm not telling that story right now. Maybe I never will . . .

My face may have looked like shit, but the cuts that had caused all the blood to pour out weren't life-threatening. I have so many scars on my body already that three or four more weren't even noticeable. I'd broken one of my ribs somewhere—maybe even back in Thailand—and twisted the hell out of my right knee, but none of my injuries were serious enough to require more than the attention of Dr. Bombay.

The Vatican kindly offered one of its aircraft to take me and the rest of my people home. I accepted, and just to show my gratitude, replaced the gear we'd removed from the airplanes.

Eighteen and a half hours after defusing the bomb in the dank catacombs beneath St. Peter's, I arrived back at Rogue Manor. I headed straight to bed. Thirty-six hours later, I woke to find Karen hovering over me. Either I was already in heaven or I ought to send my well-earned pass to the pearly gates back to St. Peter and earn it again some other time.

Karen had come to take personal charge of the next stage of my convalescence. Which duly began with a light kiss and a prescription that even a Rogue blushes to mention. . . .

Index

Pulse-pounding excitement from Pocket Books!

Prayers for the Assassin
Robert Ferrigno
"I pledge allegiance to the flag…of the Islamic Republic of America…."

Seven Deadly Wonders
Matthew Reilly
A lost ancient relic. A flight for ultimate power. The hunt is on—and only the winner survives.

Deception Plan
Patrick A. Davis
Probing the wreckage of a U-2 spy plane, a military investigator uncovers the shocking truth—about his own past.

The Wall
Jeff Long
A half-mile up the sunlit walls of Yosemite, a rope breaks, a young woman plunges to her death…and the rescue from hell begins.

The Triangle Conspiracy
David Kent
Faith Kelly's latest case leads her into a web of lies, conspiracy…and murder.